SYDNEY MANN

The Dark Wood

Rose,

Even the smallest flame
can drive back the darkness.
Let your light shine!

~Syd

Contents

Acknowledgement	v
The Harvest Moon	1
The Shadow Guard	9
The Luna Market	21
An Unexpected Proposal	26
A Friendly Warning	35
A Dubious Threat	40
The Fallen Star	56
The Northern Lights	66
An Impossible Truth	74
The Questionable Quest	83
The Shade Attack	89
The Unlikely Accomplice	96
The Secret Passage	106
The Wrong Invitation	113
The Historian's Request	118
The Hidden Agenda	124
The Winter Solstice	131
The Unwelcomed Guests	141
An Awful Confession	147
A Dangerous Resolution	152
A History Lesson	159
The Birth of Hope	165
The Winning Sport	175
A Dismal Distraction	182
The Hollow Ambush	188
The Friendly Enemy	196

The Result of Revenge   201
A Light in the Dark   208
The Unwilling Patient   214
The Peace Offer   220
The Truth Revealed   225
A Fateful Blow   231
A Frantic Flight   237
The Smallest Spark   241
A Chance Discovery   247
The Prison & Inquisition   254
The Forsaken Found   264
A Traitorous Heart   270
A Grave Mistake   277
A Fool's Hope   286
The Promise of Pain   291
The Reluctant Reunion   298
The End of Forever   303
A Fate Divided   311
Epilogue   318
Afterword   328

Acknowledgement

To my husband, who understands what it means to sacrifice. Thank you for your enduring patience and support while I stumbled on this path for years and years. You didn't always understand, but you stood behind me regardless. And to my son, whose love of reading reminded me of the joy of getting lost in books. You are one of the reasons why I decided to pursue this dream I had put on hold. But make no mistake, you and your father are my greatest dreams come true.

1

The Harvest Moon

From her lofty perch in the towering sugar pine, Stella could easily see over the double walls of Caligo to where its citizens were lighting large, white lanterns. A warm glow began to fill the city square, softly at first, then brighter and brighter. Before long, the cobblestone square shone with a radiance that nearly made her eyes water. Then, at the resounding chime of a gong, the lanterns were released. Stella watched in wonder as thousands of ethereal lights drifted up into the black velvet sky, floating higher and higher, until they mingled with the multitude of stars that sparkled overhead. The sight was beautiful and breathtaking, lifting her spirits before they plummeted back down.

The people of Darkwood had celebrated the Harvest Moon in a far more humble and solemn manner. Earlier that night, she had joined the rest of the forest dwellers to float paper boats bearing tiny candles down the gentle waters of the Algus River. A remembrance of those who had been killed in the past year.

When the last of the lanterns vanished from sight, music replaced the reverent silence as the people of Caligo began to drink and dance. Hidden in the shadows, Stella observed the jewels that flashed from the women's necks and wrists, while flickering torch lights gleamed off of the gold and crystal goblets they held in their delicate hands.

It was time to go, before her anger was roused. There was no good in watching the privileged citizens of Caligo make merry. They had no idea what those outside the city walls suffered. Or perhaps they didn't care.

Stella began to stretch for the branch below her but immediately froze, every muscle going as rigid as a corpse at the sudden sight that caught her eye. The man was tall and powerfully-built. With raven hair, fair skin, and broad shoulders, he cut a striking figure among the citizens of Caligo over whom he stood by at least a good half foot.

He ruled from an even greater distance—a vast, insurmountable gulf. It was Draven, Noctum's immortal king. Even from afar, the man inspired a deep-seated awe and fear. A natural reaction to one who had not only lived for millennia, but did so with ruthlessness and invincibility.

The king was more god than man.

Watching him now, Stella had to suppress a shudder. Elegant yet dangerous, Draven reminded her of the panthers that stalked the forest. Prowling through the crowd, he stopped before a beautiful young woman who stared up at him helplessly—vulnerable prey caught in the hypnotic gaze of a deadly predator. Draven reached out to stroke the woman's face, paying no heed to the man at her side. He could have been her husband, it didn't matter. Draven was king, and in Noctum everything belonged to the one who ruled the realm. Troubled by what she witnessed, Stella continued her descent to avoid the disturbing sight, unwilling to watch what unfolded. It wouldn't end well. It never did.

The moon's bloated yellow face guided her through the woods with its sallow light. The incessant keening of insects filled the air as she trod along, less soothing than the summer chorus of frogs and crickets, but preferable to the heavy silence of winter. Or of danger. She listened intently, her ears alert to any discordant noise or lack thereof. After nearly eighteen summers in Darkwood, she had learned the necessity of caution. Which was why a sword swung at her side, while a dagger hung at the other, both ready to be wielded in an instant.

Monsters and wild creatures weren't the only things that killed in the forest. A murderous thief had stolen her da's life, along with the pelts he had labored to collect. Her ma had died less than a year later, grief and heartbreak eroding her will to live. It was Stella's brother, Erik, who had found her frozen body in the middle of a snowstorm. That was five winters ago and Stella had been living with her brother—and then later his wife, Marta—ever since.

A sliver of light appeared up ahead, penetrating the tangle of branches that concealed the cottage just beyond. *Nearly there*, she thought, allowing herself to relax. A moment later, the sound of wailing pierced her ears. She reached for her dagger. *Marta!* After a moment of hesitation, she broke into a sprint, rushing headlong through the trees. As she ran, several terrifying scenarios played out in her panicked mind. An intruder—someone had broken into the cottage. A Shade—please not that! Or maybe it was the baby? Marta had already suffered the loss of her womb once before. Stella braced herself for any of these possibilities, desperately wishing Erik hadn't gone on patrol.

Reaching the small clearing, Stella skidded to a halt when she beheld the scene before her. Though their features were obscured, she easily recognized the silhouettes of the three people in front of the open cottage door. Garrett was there, along with Jenna, and between them they supported Marta, who sagged as she clutched at her rounded belly. The sight wrenched her, but even more disturbing was the sound that poured out of her mouth. It was the desperate wail of someone whose heart was breaking—which could only mean one of two things.

The baby or…

Stella turned to Garrett, Erik's closest friend and his brother-in-arms. They never patrolled without the other, yet Garrett was here while her brother was not. Cold dread slithered down her spine, but she shook her head in adamant denial.

No, it couldn't be.

It was Jenna who noticed her. Jenna whose tear-streaked face confirmed what she refused to consider. "I'm sorry, Stella," she choked out, her voice managing to carry over Marta's wails.

Stella's hands began to tremble and her dagger fell. When an arm encircled her, she turned to her friend. "Erik?" she whispered hoarsely, praying she was wrong.

But Jenna nodded as tears streamed down her face. "It was a Shade."

A Shade. Those pale creatures of nightmare. Darkwood's greatest threat. The very reason Erik Varden had joined the Shadow Guard. She supposed it was fitting he'd died fighting one. But not this soon. Not when he had finally found a woman to love, a woman who would be giving birth to his child. It wasn't fair. *Poor Marta!* Her weeping had subsided, but Stella saw it was only because Garrett had brought her into the cottage. Gently, Jenna began to lead her inside as well, and she had no strength or reason to resist.

Stella watched, dazed, as Garrett emerged from the bedroom and closed the door. Behind it, she could still hear Marta's mournful sobbing. It twisted something deep inside her. She should go to her, try to offer some comfort, but she was still trying to grasp the shocking truth that had just been thrust upon her. *Her brother was dead!* It didn't feel real. Erik was strong and courageous, larger than life. How could he be dead?

"I'm so sorry, Stella."

Stella blinked, bringing her vacant gaze back to focus. She saw that Garrett was sitting in the chair across from her. For the first time, she noticed the scratches he bore. The ones on his face were shallow and had just missed his left eye, but the gouges on his right arm and chest were deep enough to rend through the thick boarskin armor. Armor she herself had fashioned.

Stella stared at the blood that seeped from his chest. Had he come straight from her brother's side? Erik had sometimes returned home with injuries, but none had looked like these. Then again, he had never encountered a Shade directly. Not until now. "Are those from its...claws?"

Garrett nodded somberly. "It was a swift and vicious attack. The Shade came out of nowhere."

She squeezed her eyes shut, willing herself not to imagine the scene. "Tell me what happened," she urged, her voice breaking as she settled her gaze on Garrett's bleak face.

"We were patrolling Heath Ridge. At around the ninth hour, Erik signaled that he heard a noise. A second later, a Shade launched itself from a nearby ravine. It went straight for me before I had a chance to draw my sword. Had your brother not already drawn his own, I would have—" Garrett faltered, his throat convulsing, and the guilt in his eyes pierced her to the soul. "He saved me, Stella. And because he intervened, he bore the Shade's full wrath."

Jenna gripped her arm as hot tears began to stream down Stella's face. Silence fell, heavy with grief and regret. It was some time before she could find her voice again. "It didn't...it didn't drain him, did it?"

Garrett shook his head. "Damian arrived before it could and slayed it." There was a note of admiration in his voice.

"Damian?"

"A new guard." Garrett winced, reaching for his chest, but stopped short of touching his wounds. "Not new to the Guard, but new to Darkwood. He moved here from Umbria a few nights ago."

Stella rose and went to retrieve her pitcher, her movements stiff, almost mechanical. Pouring water into a bowl, she then reached for a clean rag and brought both to where Garrett sat. "Where is my brother's body?"

Jenna wordlessly took the bowl and cloth from her.

"At the barracks," Garrett replied. "We'll hold it there until the funeral."

"Can I see him?" she asked, watching as Jenna cleaned her husband's wounds.

"I don't recommend it," Garrett said sadly. "As I said…it was a vicious attack."

Stella was suddenly struck with the reality of her loss—its finality. Swift and brutal, it stole her breath and pierced her heart. Overcome by the intensity of her pain, she dropped her head into her hands as violent sobs wracked her. First her da and her ma, and now her only brother. Arms surrounded her, holding her tight. Stella was grateful, for she truly felt as if she would fall apart.

What happened next seemed to pass in a fog. Stella recalled Jenna laying her down on the couch. She remembered voices conversing in low tones as she fought to keep her eyelids apart. She must have drifted off to sleep sometime afterwards, because the next thing she knew, she was opening her eyes to darkness and silence. The rough burlap of the couch was damp beneath her cheek, and her body ached from her uncomfortable position. But someone, Jenna most likely, had thoughtfully draped a blanket over her. She longed for her bed, but the effort to reach it seemed too great. So she closed her eyes and willed for slumber to return. In sleep she could forget. And perhaps when she woke up, she would find that everything that had passed was all just a horrible dream.

* * *

The night was bitter and chill. Shivering, though not entirely from the cold, Stella watched as the hungry flames consumed her brother. The last rites had been given, the ceremony completed, but a large number of mourners still remained. A majority of them were heavily armed, the hilts of their swords and daggers glinting in the orange firelight. Fellow members of the Shadow Guard to which Erik had devoted his life. A number of them had spoken, extolling his bravery and skill, his honor and integrity. It gave her a measure of comfort to know that he had been respected by his brothers-in-arms. Small comfort in light of his loss, but comfort nonetheless.

One of the logs upon the pyre shifted and snapped. She watched as sparks flew upwards, reminding her of the sky lanterns from the Harvest Moon Festival. Had it only been three nights ago? As her brother's body disintegrated, she followed the trail of sparks, imagining they carried his soul to heaven, piece by piece.

She returned her gaze to the pyre, which burned alongside the Algus River. In times past, a boat would have borne her brother's flaming body as it drifted downriver. But that practice had been banned centuries ago. Too many people died in Darkwood, and no one wanted to pollute the water.

One by one, the soldiers of the Shadow Guard began to disperse, until only Marta and Stella remained. Though her sister-in-law stood by her side, they were separate in their grief. Marta had lost a husband and the father to her child, while Erik had been the last and only remaining member of her family. Though her pain didn't compare to one who had lost her heart, Stella felt adrift and utterly alone.

The fire continued to burn, and as she watched it, concerns for the future infiltrated her haze of sorrow. What would happen to Marta and the child she carried? What would happen to *her*? Stella made decent coin with her leatherwork, but would it be enough to provide for two women and a baby? Living in Darkwood was hard, it was much harder with no man to protect and provide.

Before her, the flames suddenly leapt apart, revealing something that glinted in the darkness between. Squinting her eyes, Stella could just make out the tall form of a man standing on the opposite side of the pyre. He hovered in the shadows, all silence and stillness. Were it not for the gleam in his onyx eyes and the sheen on the hilts of his blades, she might not have noticed him. But now that she did, he held her gaze, if only because he seemed to be staring at her with startling intensity.

Who was he, she wondered, trying to make out his shadowed features. But he stood too far from the flames. Then a rogue wind blew, fanning the fire. For a moment, she caught a glimpse of black hair and piercing eyes, before the agitated flames concealed him entirely. By the time the flames settled down again, the mysterious man was gone.

But Stella didn't move, not until all that remained of her brother were dust and memories.

2

The Shadow Guard

*O*ne month later.

The market lights beckoned in the distance. Stella could see them peeking out from between the tightly woven branches of the oaks and alders up ahead. Soon, the aroma of herbs and roasted meat drifted through the cool air, followed by the chatter of numerous voices. Following her senses, she made her way toward the inviting sights, sounds and smells until she reached the crumbling walls of an old ruin. Likely a grand estate from a time long past, it now served as the site of Darkwood's lively marketplace. Stalls lined its lichen-covered stone walls and more were scattered throughout its center, floating like islands in the stream of forest dwellers looking to barter or purchase.

Stella paused at the wide arched opening. This would be her first time back to the market since Erik died. Despite his duties to the Shadow Guard, he had always accompanied her. There was no one to protect her now, except herself.

With a sigh of resignation, she shifted the heavy sack that had begun to slide off her shoulder and stepped inside, immediately immersing herself in the writhing throng. Her stall was at the far end of the marketplace, so she began to weave her way past jostling elbows and swirling skirts to reach it. She had just passed the stands selling food and drink when she suddenly halted.

The man stood maybe thirty feet away. Heavily armed, as befitting a Shadow Guard, he was leaning against one of the posts of the pergola that sheltered several trestle tables nearby. She spied a sword at his left hip and several daggers strapped to his leather-clad form. But it was his dark eyes and equally dark head of wavy hair that snagged her attention. She'd caught only the briefest glimpse of both once before, but there was no mistaking who they belonged to. It was the man from the funeral, only this time his gaze was fixed on the pretty woman latched to his side.

The woman, Ana, was well-known to Stella. Though perhaps she was better known to the men of Darkwood, among whom she bestowed her favors so generously. Slightly older than herself though certainly more experienced, Ana was accustomed to entrancing the members of the opposite sex. In this instance, however, it looked as if the tables had been turned. And no wonder. Freed from the shadows that had obscured his features, it was easy to see that the man from the funeral was strikingly handsome.

Stella frowned as she thought of how he'd been staring at her over the fire. At the time, she had wondered at the reason. It was disappointing to discover he was merely drawn to a comely face. As if sensing her gaze, the man's head snapped up and he began to search the crowd. Startled, she turned aside before he could spot her and continued on her way.

At her stall, she unlocked the cabinet beneath the counter and grabbed her lanterns. Lighting them, she then hung the lanterns from the eaves and began to pull out the items from her sack. It didn't take long to arrange her leather goods on the tilted stand in the center of the stall. From belts to gloves, scabbards to gauntlets, all were clearly displayed but out of reach. She'd labored too hard on each to lose a single item to theft, and there were many light fingers in the crowd.

"Been gone for some time," Ned called out from the stall to her right, where he sold metalware, from gardening tools to pots and pans. "Grieg was angling to take your stall. Good thing you came back when you did."

"This stall is bought and paid for," Stella said with a deep frown. "He has no right to try and take it."

"Nevertheless, he was haranguing old Joss, saying he was losing profit by leaving the stall unoccupied for so long."

It was a good thing Joss, who managed the marketplace, had been a friend of Erik's. He'd attended the funeral and understood the reason for her prolonged absence. Unlike Ned who hailed from Blackbriar and only knew Erik by name and face. "Well, I'm back now," Stella said somewhat lamely.

"And glad I am for it," another voice remarked.

Stella turned to see that it was Ezra, the older man who usually occupied the stall to her left. His son, Isaac, remained behind the counter, watching her with interest.

"Been needing a new pair of gloves and the one I bought from Lars is already falling apart at the seams," Ezra grumbled. "Those look to be my size," he said, pointing to a pair that hung on the stand.

Though he groused at the cost, Ezra paid it in full. Known for her craftsmanship, Stella's goods were much esteemed and highly sought after. It wasn't long before a steady stream of customers began to swing by. Because of the items she usually offered, most of her customers were men. So Stella was used to the flirting that accompanied their haggling, nor was she a stranger to unwelcome advances. But as feared, several men seeking more than leather goods sought to press their suit. And with her brother no longer there to discourage them, they were bolder and more persistent in their attempts. By the time Stella sold her last item, she was drained from the effort of fending them off. Otherwise, she couldn't complain. Her sack was empty, but her purse was full. It was time to go home.

The market had begun to wind down, allowing Stella to slide past the remaining vendors and shoppers with ease. Now that the crowd had thinned and most of the stalls were vacant, it was easier to see the jagged walls of the surrounding ruin. Constructed of hewn gray stone, it stood no higher than six feet in most places, ten at its highest. Lights were usually interspersed every few feet or so, but many had been extinguished by the vendors who had already departed. Only those that remained kept their stalls lit. By the time the last vendor left for home, the ruin would lie in complete darkness.

Out on the main lane, Stella trailed behind a trio of old women who talked of trifling matters. Several other forest dwellers followed behind her, having also completed their business at the market. Though some of their faces were familiar, none were those she would consider friends. Still, friends or not, she was glad for their company and the sense of safety it provided.

Hundreds of people lived in Darkwood, spread out among the hundreds of leagues of forest. Most lived in cottages like herself, but a number chose to build their homes in the branches high above. One by one, or in small groups, they began to veer off toward their respective homes. Eventually, even Stella left the main path to venture onto the narrow lane that led to her cottage.

Up above, the moon shone full and bright, highlighting the forest in silvery white. Like most people of Noctum, Stella was accustomed to functioning in the dark, even on the blackest new moon nights. But when the moon was full, she hungrily devoured everything in sight. Especially on crisp, cloudless nights where everything appeared as clear as pure ice. Tonight, she could see the individual leaves of the trees, observe the owls perched on the branches overhead, even glimpsed the occasional rabbit before it darted behind a bush or down a hole.

She was glad for moonlit nights when she didn't have to stumble like the sightless.

When the forest appeared serene.

When she could swiftly spot trouble.

Stella whipped out her sword the moment she noticed the shadows shifting in the trees ahead of her. They soon slunk out to surround her, taking on the forms of three unfamiliar men.

"Well, aren't you a pretty thing," one of the men crooned. He was short and wiry, with a lean face set in a hideous leer.

"Looks like our lucky night," the stout one said, gazing at her lewdly with his beady eyes. "I guess we get to have some fun after all, ay boys?"

The third one merely grinned as he slowly, ominously drew out his sword.

Fear slithered down her spine and crawled over her skin, raising the hairs on her arms and neck. Hadn't Erik always warned her of this very thing? He had admonished her time and again not to wander the woods alone. But she was loath to give up her independence, which was why he had insisted she learn how to defend herself. And defend herself she would. Though could she possibly stand against three men?

"Come on now," the stout one said. "You don't want Kirk here to hurt you, do you? If you play nice, we may let you go when we're done."

"I have friends in the Shadow Guard," Stella warned, finding her voice. "If you so much as touch me, they'll come after you and won't give up until they track each of you down."

The third one finally spoke, his voice low and raspy, reminding her of a serpent. "Then I guess we can't leave you alive after all." His blade glinted in the moonlight as he swung it toward her.

Stella blocked it before kicking him in the groin. He doubled over just as the other two charged, swords drawn. A wide swing had the short one falling back, though the stout one met her blade with his own. Her arm vibrated from the jarring impact, but she ignored the pain and quickly swung again. The move was sloppy but it drove the stout man back, allowing her to reach for her dagger. She hurled it at the short one who had suddenly lunged. It sunk into his gullet, but she barely had time to register it. While the stout man gazed at his friend in dismay, she struck his sword aside, seeking to drive her

13

blade into his soft belly. But he blocked her thrust with a violent blow that nearly tore the sword from her hand. She gripped her hilt tighter, her gut churning. He might be stronger, but she was quick.

From the corner of her eye, she saw the third man rise as he recovered. *Should she run?* Maybe, but better to deal with one assailant rather than two. Grabbing her sword with both hands, she dropped to a low crouch and spun, her blade slicing across the man's chunky calves. He dropped like a felled tree, screaming. Just one more left. Turning to face the last man, she saw a malevolent look in his eyes that promised no mercy. But no sooner had the man charged that he jerked to a stop, his eyes widening as if in shock. A second later, a silver blade tore through his chest. She watched, stunned, as the man fell to his knees before tumbling face-first to the ground. Only then did she notice that a fourth man had entered the fray.

He was staring down at the man he had felled with cool contempt, sliding his blade from his body. Then he looked up to meet her startled gaze. "Are you alright?" It was the man from the funeral, the unknown Shadow Guard. Though his voice was calm, his dark eyes were anything but.

"Where did you come from?" she asked, trying to make sense of his sudden appearance.

"You're fortunate I happened to be nearby."

"Am I?" She glanced down at the two groaning men she had incapacitated on her own. The short one had managed to remove her dagger from his gut, but he was bleeding out.

"My legs!" the stout one cried, tears of pain streaming from his eyes. "If you've crippled me, I swear I will kill you!"

Ignoring him, Stella circled around his writhing form to grab her dagger from beside his dying friend. She saw her rescuer kick at the stout man's legs, causing him to shriek in agony. "What did you say?" The stout man glared up at him in defiance but wisely said nothing. "Your one friend is already dead and the other soon will be," the Shadow Guard drawled. "Would you like to join them?"

The stout man shook his head.

"Then know this," he warned, his voice soft but threatening. "If you ever come near her again, I will track you down and kill you myself." Then he drew the tip of his sword, still dripping blood, to the man's thick neck. "Understand?"

This time the stout man nodded vigorously, his jowls jiggling.

Making a sound of disgust, the guard turned away to wipe his blade on the trousers of the man he had just skewered. Stella's blade was soiled as well, but she opted to brush it on the leaves of a nearby bush instead.

Returning his sword to his scabbard, the guard turned to her and said, "Come, I'll walk you home."

Stella studied him warily. "I don't even know who you are."

"But I know you, Stella," he drawled. "You're Erik Varden's sister."

"I saw you at my brother's funeral," she acknowledged. "And I know that you're a member of the Shadow Guard, but I don't know *you*."

He gave her an assessing gaze, and she wished she could read the thoughts hidden behind those ebony eyes of his. "My name is Damian Dagnatari."

Stella's eyes widened. "The one who killed the Shade that…" She didn't finish, couldn't finish. Her brother was dead, but it still pained her to think of how he'd been killed.

Damian nodded, his eyes never leaving her face. "I'm sorry about what happened."

Stella studied the man before her. Dark where Erik had been fair, lean where her brother had been broad. He was also taller, his muscles less bulky though more defined. But the biggest difference wasn't physical, and it was something more sensed than seen. Erik had always made her feel safe and secure, whereas Damian exuded an aura of danger. It was something in his dark eyes. Or perhaps it was the fact that he had chosen to stab a man through with a sword when he could have easily just injured him.

"Come, I'll walk you home," he repeated, striding ahead without waiting for her. His movements were smooth, almost fluid, his presence commanding.

Stella hesitated. The man had come to her aid. She supposed she should be safe enough in his company. Setting aside her misgivings, she followed after him. When the scent of leather and spice tickled her nose, she saw that he had slowed in order for her to catch up. Standing at his side, she became conscious of just how tall he was. Her head reached no higher than his chin.

"You should know that the Shade was already at death's door when I dispatched it. Your brother dealt the crippling blow. I merely finished the creature off."

She looked at Damian in surprise. Garrett hadn't mentioned that, but perhaps he'd been in no state to. Eaten away by guilt, it was clear that Erik's sacrifice on his behalf had been foremost on his mind.

"I'm glad it's dead," she said. *If only her brother were still alive.*

"You of all people should know how dangerous these woods are, so why do you travel alone?"

"I don't have much of a choice," she replied. "And as you saw, I can handle myself."

"Granted, you have some skill with a sword, but that's no reason to throw yourself in danger."

"I was merely heading home. How is that throwing myself in danger?" she asked defensively.

"No woman should travel alone," Damian insisted. "It's foolish."

Stella stiffened, but willed herself not to react. "As I said, I have no choice. If that makes me a fool, then so be it. Perhaps you should leave if you'd prefer not to associate with someone so foolish," she countered, pulling ahead.

A strong hand gripped her upper arm, preventing her from taking another step. "But you're a beautiful fool. And I would associate with you if only to keep you from killing yourself."

Stella shot him a withering glare then yanked her arm free. "Don't insult me and don't touch me again!"

"That wasn't meant as an insult," Damian replied without apology, matching her hurried pace. "As for the latter, I can't make any promises. You're far too alluring."

Stella was infuriated by his gall. Did he think she could be disarmed by his arrogance? Perhaps he was accustomed to swaying other women in such a manner, but she had never been susceptible to flirtation or flattery. She rounded on him. "Look, I appreciate you coming to my aid, as unnecessary as it was. Neither do I require your escort home. So please go, you've done enough as it is."

But Damian made no immediate move to leave. "As I said, I never meant to offend you."

"I doubt that somehow."

"But I *will* see you home, whether you want me to or not."

Stella stared at him in disbelief, but saw in his resolute expression that he meant what he said. "You're under no obligation," she insisted, still unwilling to yield.

"This I know."

Stella grit her teeth. "You have no right."

"To see to your safety?" A hint of amusement shone in his dark eyes. "My duties as a Shadow Guard say otherwise."

Exasperated, Stella turned without another word and continued homeward. When Damian came alongside her, she did her best to ignore him. But his leather and spice scent enveloped her, making it almost impossible to. Soon enough, her gaze strayed from the path. At a glance, she noted his confident ease, his smooth stride, and the way his dark eyes glinted in the moonlight. She sighed inwardly. The man was dangerous in more ways than one.

As the silence deepened, Stella became aware of a growing tension, one that seemed to radiate from Damian alone. It became so pronounced it was almost palpable. A living, breathing thing that had her thinking of a restless animal—caged and eager to be released. Not the most comforting thought since she was all alone with him.

The question was, what was putting him on edge?

She shot a nervous glance his way.

"I make you uneasy," Damian observed, startling her. He hadn't looked once in her direction.

"What makes you say that?" she countered, wondering what had given her away.

"It's in your body language," he replied, which immediately caused her to stiffen. He let out a low chuckle at her reaction. "And now I've made you even more uncomfortable."

Flustered, Stella halted in her tracks, feeling like a rabbit caught in a snare. "Did it ever occur to you that I don't like the idea of you knowing where I live?"

"It's too late for that," he replied. "I already know where you live."

"What? How?" she demanded, trepidation curling in her belly.

"Your brother had me over, almost a year ago. You weren't there at the time. Nor did he mention having a sister." The last part was added with a noticeable frown.

Her fear dissipated, though her wariness remained. "Then how did you know I lived with him? That I'm staying at his cottage now?"

"I've learned quite a bit since moving to Darkwood."

Stella studied him, wondering what else he knew. Especially about her. The members of the Shadow Guard tended to be a closed-mouthed lot, yet who else would he get his information from? Ana perhaps? The thought made her frown. "Why did Erik have you over?"

"Shadow Guard matters."

Stella huffed in irritation. The Shadow Guard operated on stealth and secrecy, so she knew she would get no further, even if she were to press. Erik had kept many things from both her and Marta. Just as Garrett often kept Jenna in the dark. Not that it made the knowledge any easier to accept.

She continued moving again. "Is it true you moved here from Umbria?" she asked, changing tack.

"It is."

"Why?" she pressed, when he made no effort to elaborate.

"There were matters I needed to attend to here."

"What kind of matters?"

"Private matters."

Stella grit her teeth, and renewed her efforts to ignore him. Perhaps he was just being discreet or perhaps he had something to hide. If the latter, then she had even more reason to be on guard. After all, if Erik had chosen not to tell Damian about her he must have had good cause. Besides, she could see for herself that the man was clearly trouble, what with his devilishly good looks, dangerous aura and wandering eyes. She was better off keeping some distance between them.

Just then, she spotted her cottage glowing softly in the moonlight. As usual, the sight of it filled her with both sadness and relief. A strange combination, she knew. Though at the moment, the relief was the greater. Hurrying toward it, she unlocked the front door with trembling hands, glad they were hidden from view. The attack had affected her more than she cared to admit, though Damian didn't need to know that.

"Do you live here alone?" Stella jumped, surprised to find him at her back. She hadn't heard him approach.

"I do," she replied, staring at the door, not wanting him to see that the admission bothered her. It still stung that Marta had moved in with her ma and da, though she understood her reasons.

"That's not very safe," Damian censured.

"As I said before, I don't have much of a choice." Though if she married one of her suitors, she could make her abode in the Hollow. It was thick with homes, both in the trees and on the ground, and their proximity to one another lent a certain amount of security and protection. Most of the people of Darkwood lived in the Hollow. She wondered if Damian lived there as well.

"How far is your nearest neighbor?" Damian asked.

"Maybe half a league," she replied, frowning when she realized how close he stood to her.

"Too far for anyone to come to your immediate aid should you need it," he noted with disapproval.

Stella shrugged. "Then pray I'll never need it," she replied, slipping through the door.

But before she could shut it behind her, Damian stopped it with his hand. "Try and stay out of trouble, Stella."

She forced herself to meet his gaze, studiously ignoring the leap of her heart when she saw the interest in his eyes. He was making no effort to hide it, which irked her when she remembered him with Ana. "Oh, I intend to," she replied, gazing at him pointedly, before finally shutting the door in his face.

3

The Luna Market

Stella studied the dark brown armor Garrett wore with a critical eye. Issued by the Shadow Guard, the uniform was functional and well-made. But the fit, while not exactly poor, was far from ideal. In Garrett's case, the section around his waist seemed snug, while his vambraces were loose. It couldn't be comfortable.

"Yes, of course, I'll make you a new set." It was fortunate she still had the boarskin leather Erik had given her months ago. "Why didn't you ask sooner?"

"I thought I could work with this," Garrett replied, shaking his left vambrace with a sigh. "And I tried to for as long as I could."

She wanted to tell him he shouldn't have. Erik had complained often enough that ill-fitting armor compromised his performance. Yet most in the Shadow Guard had no choice but to make do with the armor they were given. It was only because of her skill with leather that Garrett and Erik had enjoyed the privilege of custom armor, making them an object of envy among their fellow guards. "I'll just have to take your measurements. Unless you kept your old armor and want me to use that as a model."

"I did keep it," he replied, his countenance briefly clouding. She wondered if he was thinking about the last time he'd worn it. "When should I bring it by?"

"What about tonight?" she suggested on a whim. Though she saw him often enough, it was only because he and Jenna made it a point to come by to check on her. It was time she repaid their kindness. "You and Jenna can join me for dinner."

Garrett ran a hand over his brown beard, thinking. "That might just work."

Stella nodded. "Alright then. I'll see you tonight."

"Thank you, Stella. I apologize for stopping by unexpectedly."

"You always stop by unexpectedly," she said lightly.

He smiled, but it failed to reach his gray eyes. Since the attack, the spark that usually lit them had yet to return. She wondered if it ever would. "True enough. And now I must apologize for having to leave abruptly."

She was accustomed to that as well. Not that she minded in this case. There was someplace she wanted to go, and the sooner Garrett left, the sooner she could head there. "I take no offense," she assured him.

He nodded his thanks. "Be safe, Stella." Then with an absent wave, his brisk strides took him away from her door. In moments, he had crossed the clearing and was disappearing into the woods to the west.

* * *

Three times a month, when the moon was at its brightest, the barren expanse that separated Darkwood from Caligo was transformed into what was known as the Luna Market. It was on this occasion, and this occasion alone, that the citizens of the city deigned to mingle with those from the forest. Stella found it ironic that a field which had been drenched in the blood of both should now be the site of a popular market.

She surveyed the colorful lights and bustling activity under the silver glow of a full moon. Scarlet pennants waved from the tops of dozens upon dozens of stalls, each bearing a black hawk. Draven's crest. And strung from stall to stall, strands of red, yellow, blue, green and orange lanterns lent the market a festive air.

Pulling her hood up, Stella slipped into the sea of shoppers, quickly blending into the crowd. Financed by the king himself, the Luna Market was far larger and much more impressive than Darkwood's weekly ones—as much a place of spectacle as an occasion for business. It was no wonder the market was popular among all, despite the risks in attending. Even Stella found it hard to resist its draw.

Though ever vigilant, she wandered the maze of stalls without aim, indiscriminately taking everything in. Around her, leathers, furs and coarse cottons mixed with velvets, satins and embroidered silks. Cloying perfume clashed with the odor of unwashed bodies, and cultured conversation blended with rough speech. The market was a feast for the senses, a temporary escape from long nights of quietness and solitude. But beneath the eager chatter, below the veneer of carefree frivolity, ran a current of unease.

The citizens of Caligo were afraid—and it wasn't the forest dwellers they necessarily feared. For all their wealth and privilege, Stella suspected that those from the city were little better than prisoners, trapped in a gilded cage. It took but a careful observer to see past their feigned carelessness and forced cheer. As if to prove her suspicions, a woman in a red velvet gown let out a trill of shrill laughter, causing Stella to cringe. Overly-bright, the laughter bordered on hysteria, making a mockery of the dread in the woman's eyes. Clearly, all was not well in Caligo.

Stella thought back to the young woman Draven had set his sights upon at the Harvest Moon Festival. She wasn't the first, nor would she be the last of his victims. Which was why her da and Erik had urged her to stay far away from the Luna Market.

Reaching up to pull her hood forward, Stella's gaze was caught by a movement to her right. It was the black armor she immediately noticed, which was why she first assumed it was one of the king's soldiers, the Nighthawks. Their presence was pervasive, you couldn't turn around without spotting one of their black-clad forms. But this Nighthawk wore no intimidating helmet of black steel to hide his face, and Stella nearly gasped aloud when she recognized it.

Draven! And he was alone, without guard or escort. Not that Draven—invincible, immortal king—required protection. She need only consider the ground she stood upon to tremble in fear. Stella herself had seen the king rip out a man's heart where a merchant was currently selling delicate baubles. And where several young women twirled about in a graceful dance, he had slain two forest dwellers, ripping them limb from limb.

Unchallenged and unimpeded, the king walked through the crowd, which parted for him like wind through wheat. For a moment, Stella froze, paralyzed by fear. Then, with her heart galloping like a spooked horse, she promptly altered her course, doing her best to hurry away without drawing notice. Only when she reached the safety of the woods did she allow herself to breathe a deep sigh of relief.

When her trembling ceased, she headed for her favorite sugar pine and began to ascend. Her cloak and heavy skirts were a hindrance, but she had climbed the tree so often it was now second nature. Settling onto her usual branch, she gazed out over the market. The bird's-eye view allowed her to easily track the king's movements. Despite the crowd, he was hard to miss with his unusual height. She watched as he weaved through the market, much as she had earlier, only it was clear that he did so with intent. He scanned the crowd, his gaze sliding over the women of Caligo, but pausing on every female forest dweller.

It chilled her to her very bones.

Stella held her breath as woman after woman was subjected to Draven's scrutiny. Then a hooded figure crossed the king's path. When he reached out to yank down the hood, Stella gasped. Fortunately, the woman underneath turned out to be an old hag. But it could have easily been her. Still considering her fortune, she spotted a young girl, no more than sixteen summers in age, heading in the king's direction. She was lovely and delicate. Worse, she had a look of sweet innocence to her, innocence that would be obliterated if she continued on her path. Fear for the girl had Stella's heart banging against her chest. She was smiling at her mother, utterly unaware of the danger that lay in her path. *Turn aside! Quick, before he sees you!* But it was too late. Draven spied the girl from a distance and like a wolf on the hunt, he pounced. Those who stood nearby looked on, somber and helpless. Stella reached for her dagger and clutched it in a white-knuckled grip. But, in the end, all she could do was watch, sickened, as the king pulled the terrified girl away from her sobbing mother.

4

An Unexpected Proposal

S tella stared long into the abyss, her toes lined at the very edge of the steep cliff. Even on full moon nights, there was no seeing to the very bottom—though a tossed rock was enough to prove the drop was very far indeed. Some believed the Shade resided in those unseen depths, which was why so few ventured to the area. There was also the fact that many had fallen to their deaths by unwittingly straying too close to the edge. She lifted her gaze. Across the vast expanse, she could see the faint outline of the Altous Mountains. A number of brave souls had dared to descend the cliff in the hopes of scaling the mountain. So far none had succeeded. At least, none that anyone knew, for no one had ever returned from an attempt.

Stella no longer wondered what lay on the other side of the mountains. Curiosity was a luxury when you were just trying to make it from one night to the next. Her family was gone, and hope had soon followed. Without either, it was hard to go on knowing she would have to face the bleakness of Noctum alone. With no promise of justice, no freedom from fear, and little expectation of either peace or happiness, it was a life hardly worth living. But here, at the edge of the cliff, it could all come to an end in an instant.

It was tempting…so tempting. The only thing that held her back were the promises she had made. To Marta, who had asked her to be present for the birth of Erik's child. To Jenna, who had pleaded with her not to lose heart. To Elias, who had begged her to wait for his return. And to Garrett, who she still owed a set of armor to.

The last thought brought her up short. She had promised Garrett and Jenna dinner in just a few hours! Stella let out a hoarse laugh at the thought of being saved from her morbid musings by something as mundane as the need to cook. But in truth, these were the very things that carried her through the hours. One foot before the other. One breath and then another. If she focused on the minutiae instead of the weeks, months, years that stretched before her, it was easier to get by. Glancing downward, she took one last look at the dark abyss, then turned around as she chose to face another night.

* * *

Stella assessed the food on the table with satisfaction. The roasted ham, steamed carrots, creamed potatoes, and rye bread smelled delicious, though she doubted she'd be able to eat a single bite. The incident at the market still haunted her, robbing her of her appetite. When loud rapping sounded at the door, she took a deep breath and schooled her features. Garrett and Jenna were here, and they worried for her enough as it was.

Pulling the door open, her eyes first fell upon Garrett carrying his ruined armor. But it wasn't Jenna who stood at his side. Instead, it was Damian.

There was no hiding her shock...or displeasure.

"Jenna is sorry she couldn't make it," Garrett apologized, noting her expression. "Her mother fell ill and she had to tend to her."

"So you brought a fellow Shadow Guard instead," Stella remarked, using the blandest tone she could manage.

A look of confusion crossed Garrett's face. "Damian insisted on checking in on you. He told me about the attack."

"I see," she said, irritated. She had hoped the matter would be kept between them.

"I can't believe you didn't tell me about it," Garrett rebuked. "That's not something you should keep to yourself."

"It hardly matters now, does it?" she replied, shooting Damian a cutting look.

"Not in this case, no." Garrett shook his head, whether in exasperation or disapproval she couldn't say. Likely both. "I would argue with you about it more, but we just got off patrol and I'm starving. And whatever you have in there smells good."

Stella stifled the urge to smile. "Come in," she relented, opening the door wider. Garrett hurried in eagerly, but she turned her face as Damian slipped past, refusing to acknowledge his presence. When the two men stood inside the cottage, their large frames immediately crowded the small space.

"That smells so good," Garrett repeated, his eyes on the food as he laid his armor down on her work table then removed his sword belt. "Thank you for offering dinner. With her mother ill, Jenna didn't have time to cook so I would've had to make do with jerky and day old bread."

"Then I'm glad to spare you from a cold meal," she replied, watching surreptitiously as Damian scanned the cozy cottage while removing his own sword belt. She turned back to Garrett, recalling what he'd said earlier. "Did you two patrol together?"

A look of guilt passed over his face. "Damian had been patrolling without a partner since he moved here, and so…" Erik had been replaced.

"You're partners now?" she supplied.

Garrett nodded, unable to meet her gaze.

"That's good," Stella said, swallowing the lump that had formed in her throat. "You shouldn't be patrolling on your own. No one should."

Damian raised his brow at that.

Pretending not to notice, she gestured toward the table. "The food is ready. Go ahead and have a seat."

Accustomed to dining at her table, Garrett grabbed the nearest wooden chair, which creaked beneath his weight. Damian hesitated, however. "Aren't you going to join us?"

Garrett looked at her expectantly, his brow furrowed. She hadn't planned on eating, especially now that Damian had joined them. With a silent sigh, she took the seat left of Garrett while Damian chose the chair across from her. She hoped it would be a quick meal.

While Garrett cut into the ham, Stella offered some bread to Damian. As the host, it was the polite thing to do, though she avoided looking at him while doing so. Once their plates were filled, the men immediately began to eat, practically shoveling the food into their mouths. She watched, mildly amused, as she picked at her plate. She supposed she should be flattered they found her food so palatable, but she was still unsettled by the fact that Damian was in her house, sitting at her table, eating her food.

"Aren't you hungry?" Garrett asked, as he helped himself to a fifth slice of ham. "Your food is delicious. Why aren't you eating any of it?"

"Maybe because I sprinkled it with poison," Stella replied, straight-faced.

She heard rather than saw Damian drop his fork, but Garrett merely chuckled. He was used to her odd humor, though it was the first time she'd jested in any way since Erik died.

Clearing her throat, Stella took a bite of ham. She still wasn't hungry, but perhaps eating would help keep the tears at bay. For a time, all that could be heard were the sounds of chewing and the scrape of forks against plates.

"Your skill with leather is most impressive," Damian remarked, breaking the strained silence.

Stella looked up, immediately wary.

"I had heard your leathercraft was exceptional, but it wasn't until I saw Garrett's armor that I realized just how good you are."

It wasn't just Garrett's armor he had seen. Erik, too, had been wearing his armor when he was killed.

When Stella made no reply, Damian continued, undeterred. "Garrett says you're making him another set. I was hoping I could persuade you to make one for me as well."

Stella suppressed a sigh. Fashioning armor was a laborious process, one she'd reserved solely for her brother and his best friend, who also happened to be her best friend's husband.

"I'm willing to offer generous compensation in return," Damian added, rightly reading her reluctance.

"I told him you didn't make armor for just anyone," Garrett said, with a shrug of his shoulders.

It was true. But Damian's offer piqued her interest. Just how generous was he willing to be? Even with her goods fetching top coin, the threat of poverty always hovered in the near distance. As it was, there was little left of her proceeds from the market after purchasing some necessary supplies. Hence, Damian's offer was not something she could easily dismiss. "Exactly what do you mean by generous?" she asked him.

Damian shot a quick glance at Garrett. "I think it best I disclose that in private."

Stella arched her brow.

"Is that really necessary?" Garrett asked with a frown.

"It is," Damian replied firmly. "The matter is between Stella and I."

Garrett's frown deepened and he stared at Damian long and hard before turning to look at Stella. "Are you alright with this? If not, just say so."

Stella was grateful for Garrett's protective concern, but she was curious to see what Damian laid on the table. "I think it should be fine. He would be a fool to risk losing you as a partner. Worse, he risks losing a body part if he tries anything with me."

Damian laughed in amusement, not at all impressed by her bravado. "Warning noted."

"Then whatever he offers, demand double," Garrett added, relaxing once more.

"Who taught you how to craft leather?" Damian asked, leaning back in his seat. It looked as if both men were finally done eating, though Garrett was eyeing what was left of the ham as if debating whether or not to indulge in more. "Was it your father?"

"No, it was my mother who taught me. My father was a hunter and made his coin in pelts, but he also supplied us with the skins we needed."

"That must have worked out well," Damian remarked.

"It did," she agreed, as an image of her ma and da drifted forward from a carefully guarded corner of her mind. In it, they were sitting at this same table, working side by side. It was nothing remarkable, but they had been happy, together and alive.

"Who supplies your skins now?" Damian asked, pulling her from her thoughts.

"I do," Garrett supplied. "As much as I'm able to, that is."

"It's thanks to Garrett that you get to enjoy this fine ham," Stella remarked, though guilt gnawed at her. Not only was hunting time-consuming, it was difficult and dangerous. She had tried it on a few occasions, and had met with failure each time. Though she was skilled with a bow, she lacked the patience and fortitude that hunting required. How did anyone manage to sit unmoving in the cold for so many hours, or go stalking through the forest for as long? On her last attempt, she had narrowly escaped being mauled by a jaguar after being so focused on the deer she was tracking. The incident had left her shaken and she hadn't tried again since. But it was one thing having her da and Erik hunting for her, quite another to have someone unrelated take on the task.

Marta's last piece of advice before she left echoed in her ears. *You need to marry and soon.* She shut her eyes at the unwelcome suggestion.

Erik had been overly-indulgent, allowing her to rely on his support to evade marriage. But she no longer had the luxury of waiting for the right man. She needed a husband if she intended to survive. The question was, could she commit herself to someone she didn't love? What kind of life would that be? Once again, Stella felt as if she were standing at a precipice, only this time she had no choice but to leap.

Her eyes flew open and immediately locked with Damian's. Dismay shot through her when she saw that he had been watching her, catching her unguarded moment of turmoil. His dark eyes seemed to see too much and that frightened her. She yanked her gaze away, turning to Garrett. "Please take some food back to Jenna." A polite way of hinting she was ready for them to leave.

But Garrett shook his head. "I'm certain she ate at her ma and da's." His way of ensuring she had enough food for the next night. He rose from his seat nevertheless, taking the hint. "Thank you again for the delicious dinner. We've imposed on you long enough."

Rising, she watched as both men strapped on their weapons. Damian was a good two inches taller than Garrett, and his dark brown leathers showed off his lean, muscular build to advantage. She could see no reason why he required custom armor when his standard one appeared to fit just fine.

"Goodbye, Stella," Garrett said, pausing just outside her door. "Be sure to lock up behind you."

She never forgot to lock the door, though it wasn't much of a deterrent to most of the threats that hid in the forest. Giving Garrett a brief hug, she said, "Tell Jenna she owes me a visit."

Garrett nodded and began to leave, but paused when he noticed Damian lingering.

"I need to discuss my offer with Stella," he remarked, by way of reminder.

When Garrett glanced at her, she nodded in reassurance. Still, he gave Damian another long, hard look—one full of warning—before striding out of the clearing.

The effect of his absence was immediate. Alone with Damian, Stella was suddenly flooded with nervousness. Without Garrett's presence to act as a buffer, Damian somehow seemed more potent, more intimidating, even though all he did was gaze at her

"So...your offer?" she prompted, eager to get the conversation over with.

Damian leaned against the doorframe, crossing his arms. A move that suggested that, unlike her, he was in no rush at all. "I was prepared to offer you compensation by coin, but I think I can offer something of even greater value."

"Oh?" she asked dubiously. She could think of nothing more valuable than money. "What might that be?"

"I could hunt for you instead. Provide you with the skins you need, so that Garrett won't have to."

Stella was right. The man was far too observant. He had seen her guilt and was now using it to bargain with her. A smart move, and very effective. "For how long?"

"Three times a week for two months."

It was a generous offer, almost too generous. There was also the fact that the arrangement would bring them into frequent contact with one another, something she was leery of. But when she considered all that she had to gain, she could hardly turn it down. The service he offered exceeded what she would have expected to receive monetarily. Just as important, she would no longer have to impose on Garrett. "I accept."

Damian appeared surprised by her ready agreement, though there was a look of triumph in his eyes. *Had she been too hasty?*

"I know it will take some time to complete Garrett's armor," he said. "But I see no reason why I shouldn't start immediately. Consider it advanced payment."

"Are you certain?" she asked, furrowing her brow.

"I'd rather hunt now than when winter arrives."

Stella thought about that, and considered delaying his payment.

But if he supplied her with enough skins now, perhaps she could earn enough coin not to have to hunt in the winter. "Fine," she agreed, nodding.

Damian straightened, though the movement was unhurried, almost reluctant. "Good. Then I'll begin tomorrow night."

5

A Friendly Warning

"How's your ma?" Stella asked, placing two steaming mugs of tea on the table.

Jenna wrapped her thin hands around the one before her, seeking its warmth. "Better, though her cough persists." Taking a tentative sip, she placed the mug back on the tabletop. "But that's not what I came here to discuss."

"I thought you came because you missed dinner the other night," Stella said, sitting down across from her friend. "And because I asked."

"Partly. I came to discuss my replacement at said dinner," Jenna replied, pushing back a wayward auburn lock.

"Oh?"

Jenna shot her a worried look. "Is it true you're going to make armor for Damian Dagnatari?"

Ahh, so there it was. Of course, Garrett wouldn't keep such a thing to himself. "He made me an offer I couldn't refuse."

"And what offer was that?" her friend asked, curious.

Stella paused to consider before answering. Damian had insisted on making his offer in private, but Garrett was bound to find out anyway. "Suffice it to say that your husband no longer has to hunt for me."

"He offered a trade of services?" Jenna asked in surprise.

Stella nodded. "He's agreed to do my hunting, three times a week for two months."

Jenna's hazel eyes widened. "That's *very* generous. Suspiciously so, don't you think?"

"I don't know what to think." Not necessarily true. She suspected Damian hoped to add her to his list of conquests, though she refused to voice that to her friend. "I barely know the man," Stella said. "Does Garrett? After all, he and Damian are partners now."

A flicker of dismay flitted over Jenna's face. "He knows enough," was her vague reply.

"Meaning?" Stella prompted.

"Let's just say that Damian's reputation precedes him."

"Don't be coy," Stella chided. "Tell me what you know."

Jenna sighed. "I don't mean to be coy. It's just…I'm not certain how much I'm allowed to say. But I will tell you this. The man is dangerous."

It was just as Stella suspected, but she needed to know more. She needed details. "Dangerous how?"

"For one thing, he's one of the most lethal warriors in the Shadow Guard."

"He did kill a Shade," Stella acknowledged, a feat not easily accomplished. With their unnatural strength and speed, it usually took more than one guard to take down a single Shade. It was a wonder that Erik had nearly succeeded in his attempt. Pride mingled with sorrow, as it always did when she thought of her brother.

"And it's not the first time he's done so."

"Truly?" Stella marveled.

Jenna nodded. "They say he's killed over a dozen Shades, most of them on his own."

Stella stared at her friend in disbelief. "Surely the men exaggerate!"

"Perhaps," Jenna said with a shrug. "Even Garrett seemed dubious when he told me. He says he has a hard time believing half the rumors he's heard about Damian. But there is one thing Garrett knows to be true, because he heard it from the commandant himself. Apparently, Damian had been offered the position of commandant several times. But each time, he refused, preferring to fight rather than lead."

Promoted to commandant? Damian couldn't be much older than Garrett. Or even Erik, who had achieved the rank of captain sooner than most his age. "He does strike me as more of a fighter than a leader."

"Apparently he's quite the lover as well," Jenna added with an embarrassed look.

An image of Ana clinging to Damian darted through her head. "And is that truth or rumor?" Stella asked, already guessing the answer.

"Truth. He's said to have left a trail of broken hearts in Umbria and is already making headway here in Darkwood."

Though Stella was far from surprised, she found little satisfaction in being right. "With looks like his, I suppose it's to be expected."

Jenna twisted the mug in her hands. "So you'll be careful, won't you?"

"With Damian?" Stella huffed. "Of course. You know I can't abide such men."

"I know, but you're making his armor and he'll be hunting for you, which means you'll be spending quite a bit of time in his company. Much of it alone."

Jenna was right. Unfortunately, there wasn't much she could do about that. Even if her friend accompanied her on occasion, it was unrealistic to expect her to be available every time Damian came by.

"Not to mention the fact that he *is* incredibly attractive," Jenna added.

"Attractive, but far from irresistible," Stella firmly replied. "Besides, I saw him with Ana Septiva. I wouldn't touch any man who's been with her." Which was why she had turned down so many of her suitors.

Jenna curled her lip in disgust. "And I saw him with Nettie Loula *and* Carlina Mattoc."

"At the same time?"

Jenna nodded.

"Then you needn't worry," Stella assured her. No, she was in no danger with Damian. Not her affections, at least. "Would you like more tea?" she asked, eager to change the subject. Talking about the dark Shadow Guard was tempting her to reconsider their agreement.

"No, I'm fine," Jenna replied. "How is Marta faring, by the way?"

"As well as can be expected. She's eating, at least. And the baby is growing."

"But?" Jenna asked. Somehow she always knew when Stella was holding back.

"She rarely leaves her room…or her bed. But even so I don't think she's sleeping enough."

"Oh," Jenna replied softly, looking troubled.

"What is it?" Stella gently pressed.

"Garrett doesn't sleep much either. Not since…well, not since the attack."

Stella felt her heart lurch, thinking of all the people still affected by her brother's death. "I didn't know that."

"He has nightmares about what happened," Jenna admitted solemnly.

"About the Shade?" Stella said, her voice a weak whisper.

Jenna dropped her eyes. "Mostly about not being able to save Erik."

"There was nothing he could have done," Stella was quick to assure her. "It's not his fault."

"You'll never be able to convince him of that," Jenna sighed. "He blames himself for not drawing his sword sooner, for not being prepared. He even thought about leaving the Shadow Guard."

Stella gazed at her friend in dismay. "He's not going to, is he?"

"I urged him not to, but I'm certain it was Damian who convinced him to stay."

The admission surprised her. "Then perhaps he'll make a good partner for Garrett after all." She was just glad that he wouldn't be throwing away five years of training. Being a Shadow Guard was dangerous, but there was no position more respected...or necessary.

"I suppose he might," Jenna replied thoughtfully.

They talked a while longer about various matters, during which Stella debated whether or not to mention what she'd witnessed at the Luna Market. In the end, she decided not to say anything, knowing Jenna would berate her for attending the market to begin with. Besides, there was nothing to be gained from the telling. It wasn't as if anything could be done about what she saw. They were helpless to save the girl, nor could they prevent such a thing from happening again. There would be more victims, there always were.

6

A Dubious Threat

T he creature watched her with alarming intensity. Black as night with eerie amber eyes, it tracked her every move, noting every tic and twitch as if waiting for a reason to attack. Tearing her nervous gaze away, Stella turned to its master. "I didn't know you had a hound."

"Dartan always hunts with me," Damian declared, reaching down to rub the dog's large, furry head. He didn't have to reach far. "He's an exceptional tracker."

Stella looked up from the dog to study the glassy-eyed doe on his shoulder. Damian had caught her off guard, striding into the clearing with both the deer and the dog in tow. She hadn't expected him until later, which was why she'd been in her garden weeding instead of waiting for him indoors as planned. Out in the open, she felt vulnerable, exposed. All the more so with the sinister hound at his side. She wanted to flee to the safety of her cottage, but feared the dog would give chase.

"Does my dog frighten you?" Damian asked, sounding amused.

Stella allowed herself a brief glance, just enough to observe the smirk on his handsome face. "He's an ugly brute," she said, wishing she could be talking about the master. "It's a good thing he can track."

"You have him to thank for this catch. But if it's an attractive face

40

you're interested in, just keep your eyes on me."

"Conceit is hardly attractive," she retorted.

But Damian only grinned, unfazed by her remark. "True, but my face is, as is yours."

Stella struggled but failed to come up with any sort of reply, so she just pinned him with a look of scorn.

"I'll go ahead and skin this for you," Damian said, clearly amused by her reaction.

After hanging the deer from a nearby tree, Damian proceeded to remove his shirt. Flustered, Stella quickly averted her gaze and grabbed her spade from the ground before heading to her cottage. As soon as she opened the door, Dartan hurtled past, brushing against her to settle down by the hearth. She gaped indignantly. *Arrogant dog! So like his master.*

When it became clear the dog intended to stay, Stella sighed and grabbed Garrett's armor. She left the door open, hoping the dog would get bored and leave. Then she began to work on the leather in earnest, determined to keep both her hands and her mind occupied. She soon lost herself to her task, and over an hour passed as she focused on the careful stitching required to keep the layers of leather secure. But even in concentration, her traitorous thoughts kept dredging up the brief glimpse she'd caught of Damian's chiseled chest. Finally fed up with herself, she growled in frustration. An answering growl came from the direction of the hearth.

"What are you growling at?" Stella demanded.

Dartan barked.

"Don't you bark at me you mangy wretch."

"Why do you insult my dog? After all his hard work on your behalf, the least you could do is show him some gratitude."

Stella turned to see Damian standing at her open door, his chest still bare and now slick with sweat. He was also flecked with blood. "I let him stay, didn't I?" she retorted, turning away before he could notice her heated face.

In lieu of answering, she heard him stride toward her. "You're further along than I thought you would be," Damian said, gazing at her work.

Stella lifted the breastplate to inspect it, glad for something else to focus on. She had sewn three overlapping layers of leather down the center, but still had three more layers to add to the chest area. After that, she needed to reinforce the stitching with some rivets. Once the breastplate was done, she would have to attach it to the backplate. The pauldrons would follow. And there were still the tassets, gauntlets and vambraces to work on. Her work on Garrett's armor was far from complete. "It's a start," she said with a weary sigh. Her back ached and her fingers were needlesore. "Was there something you needed?" she asked, biting back her impatience as he continued to hover over her.

"Yes," he replied. "Could you spare a rag?"

Stella rose without a word and went to retrieve one from the sideboard. She approached cautiously, careful to keep her eyes above his neck as she handed him the cloth.

"Thank you," he said, taking it.

She ignored the brush of his hand against her own. "You should wash up. You have blood all over you and you smell awful," she declared, anxious to remove him from her presence.

Damian chuckled as he left to do just that. She realized her suggestion had been unnecessary, for it was what he'd intended all along. When Dartan darted outside to join his master by the pump, she quickly shut the door after the pair, exhaling in relief.

Why did the man have to be so physically appealing? It was a good thing she was aware of his shortcomings. Were it not for his philandering ways, she could easily find herself mooning over him.

Damian soon returned, and Stella was glad to see he had donned his shirt. "I'll be back two nights from now," he told her, as he handed over several cuts of venison. "The skin is hanging out to dry."

"Thank you," she said primly, taking his offer. "And good night."

She promptly shut the door before he could reply, smothering the twinge of guilt that shot through her. Theirs was purely a business arrangement, nothing more, she reminded herself.

* * *

The Tangleroot Tavern was as crowded and lively as always. Stella generally avoided the popular establishment, but tonight she had good reason for paying a visit. Ignoring the whistles and appreciative looks directed her way, she slowly scanned the smoky interior, searching. But instead of finding the person she was looking for, her eyes landed on Damian. He was already staring at her, but when she saw his companion, she briefly lifted a brow before letting her gaze move on. He was with Ana again, which helped to justify her actions from the other night. She had been right to keep him at a distance. So then why did she feel a sense of disappointment?

Foolishness, she chided herself.

At the sight of a flaming mop of red hair, Stella banished all thoughts of unworthy, dark-eyed scoundrels as she began to cross the room. A soft smile curled her lips when the young man at the other end spotted her and began to make his way over. They met each other halfway.

"Elias," she greeted softly, wrapping her arms around him. But she laughed in surprise when he spun her around in a tight circle despite the crowd surrounding them. No one complained. The tavern owner's son was well-liked. He'd also been sorely missed after a year's absence. Dizzy with happiness, Stella looked up into his thin, angular face once he put her down. "You don't know how good it is to see you."

"I've missed you too, Stel," he said, throwing an arm around her shoulders as he led her to a back table. His bright smile dimmed as they sat. "I'm sorry about Erik. And I'm sorry I couldn't be here for the funeral."

Stella briefly closed her eyes. "I know." It would have taken him three weeks to travel from Nyxus to Darkwood. Too long to have made it to the funeral in time. "And it's alright. Jenna has often been at my side, along with Garrett. I'm just glad you're here now." She studied him earnestly. Then lowering her voice, she asked, "Are you done? Are you back for good?"

Elias glanced around the dim, noisy tavern. It was packed with people, but the loud laughter and boisterous conversations allowed them to speak in confidence, giving them a measure of privacy even in the midst of so many people. "Yes, my apprenticeship is officially complete," he whispered back. "You are now looking at the newest historian."

"Congratulations, Eli. When do you finally get to see where you'll be working?"

Stella was alluding to the Repository, the place where all of Darkwood's important records were stored for safekeeping. It was a highly guarded secret, one she knew about only because she had overheard her brother and Garrett talking about it one night. In their discussion, she had learned that a new historian was being sought for the Repository, since the current historian would be taking the place of the aging librarian. She had listened as they determined who would be escorting the new apprentice to Nyxus to be trained. Several weeks later, Elias was heading off to Nyxus with Garrett. That was when she knew her friend had been chosen. The apprenticeship took three years. Stella informed Elias she knew about the Repository after his first year, and he'd nearly had a fit. She still had no idea where the Repository was located, but she was aware that only a select few even knew it existed. Herself included.

"Stella." There was a note of warning in Elias's voice. "You know I can't tell you where the Repository is."

"I didn't ask where it was, did I?" she returned innocently.

"No, but I know you're dying to find out."

Stella sighed, unable to deny the truth. So much of Noctum's history had been lost, destroyed by Draven in his attempt to keep them in ignorance. Knowledge was power, and it was easier to rule a people who were kept in the dark. No books existed outside of the city walls. No parchment either. And it was against the law to know one's letters, which was why parents were forced to teach them to their children in secret, scratching letters and words in the dirt. What Stella knew of Noctum's history had been passed on orally, stories told in hushed voices behind closed doors. And what she knew was this: Noctum consisted of thirteen cities, each ruled by a royal, including Draven who ruled the capital of Caligo. This he had done for at least three thousand years. As for the people the royals ruled, they were divided into two groups—the wealthier city dwellers and the less fortunate forest dwellers. Though neither were immune to Draven's cruel whims.

What Stella knew was disheartening, but what kept her up at night were the things she didn't know. What sort of knowledge was hidden in the Repository? What secrets had been kept from the general populace? She hated being ignorant, but she knew that the information was carefully guarded because they couldn't risk Draven finding out about it. That alone told her that the information was valuable enough to hide. And soon Elias would have access to that information!

Envy curled through her, souring her belly. She was just as intelligent, just as adept as Elias. Though granted she didn't possess his unique ability. She sighed. There was little hope Elias could be persuaded to share what he learned, not when the penalty was punishment and the loss of his position.

"I don't expect you to tell me, but can you blame me for being curious?"

"I suppose not," Elias relented, his gaze narrowing slightly as he gazed at something over her shoulder. "Who is that man with Ana?"

Stella resisted the urge to turn around. "His name is Damian

Dagnatari. I'm surprised you haven't heard of him. He's your brother-in-law's new partner."

Elias's hazel eyes, reminiscent of his sister's, widened at that. "Is that right? Garrett didn't tell me. Then again, Jenna didn't give him much of a chance." He glanced once more over her shoulder before meeting her gaze. "Is there any reason why Garrett's new partner keeps glaring at me?"

"Is he?" Stella asked, tensing involuntarily.

Elias nodded. "It could be he has a thing against redheads, but that wouldn't be fair, would it? Perhaps you could enlighten me?"

Stella shook her head, perplexed. "He's new to Darkwood. Perhaps he doesn't realize that everyone is supposed to love Elias Parnassa."

Elias smirked at that. "He'll learn soon enough. Besides, I think it has less to do with me than it has to do with you. Is there something I should know?"

"It's nothing really. He and I have a business arrangement, nothing more. In exchange for making him armor, he's agreed to hunt for me so Garrett won't have to."

Elias lifted a brow. "That doesn't explain the glaring."

"I don't see why he should be upset. He seemed fine last night."

"You were with him last night?" Elias questioned, looking intrigued.

Stella felt her face flush. "He came over to bring his catch, nothing more."

Elias leaned in closer, a hint of mischief in his eyes. "Are you certain that was all? The fact that you keep saying 'nothing more' leads me to believe there *is* more."

"Of course, I'm certain!" she replied, with far too much vehemence.

"Hmmm." Elias looked dubious. "My guess is he's interested in you."

Stella scoffed. "He's with Ana, how interested could he be?"

"Clearly, you don't understand men at all."

"What is there to understand?" she challenged. "That it's perfectly alright to be with one woman even if you're supposedly interested in another? Is that what you think?"

"Of course not," Elias said, shaking his head. "You know I would never do such a thing." It was true. Elias was nothing like Damian. Her friend had been infatuated with the same girl—woman now—for years. "In all seriousness, Stella. He looks ready to tear my head off just for talking to you."

Stella shook her head in adamant denial. "He's a philanderer. If he has any interest in me, it's just the thrill of the chase he seeks. Probably because every other woman falls for him so easily."

"He's in for a challenge with you, isn't he?" Elias said, smirking.

Stella huffed. "He's in for certain failure."

"Oh this will be fun to watch," Elias remarked, before something else snagged his attention. "Brace yourself. We have another hopeless admirer approaching."

Before she could ask who he was talking about, Anson Mellac was at their table. "Elias. Stella." His gaze lingered on her face before briefly dropping to her chest. "I see you're back, Elias," the brawny carpenter drawled. "How long will you be in Darkwood this time before you're off on another one of your mysterious trips?"

"Taking care of an ailing relative is hardly mysterious," Elias replied casually. "I hear you recently finished building your new house. Congratulations!" Stella admired the ease with which her friend deflected and redirected the conversation.

"Thank you. I'm glad to finally have it done." Anson went on in detail about the unexpected problems that had arisen during construction and the genius with which he solved them. Then he turned to Stella and said, "All it needs now is a woman's touch."

"I'm certain any one of your four sisters would be happy to help you there," Elias suggested, earning him Stella's gratitude.

"There's only one woman whose touch I'm interested in," Anson said, staring at her in a way there was no mistaking. It was also clear he meant something other than a woman's domestic influence.

"Speaking of new homes," Elias jumped in, before Stella could be tempted to set Anson down. "I'll be moving out of my ma and da's soon, getting a place of my own."

"You are?" Stella asked in surprise. "Where?"

"A nest in the Hollow."

A nest was what they called a house built in the trees. Stella wondered which one Elias intended to occupy. Several currently sat vacant, the former inhabitants dead for one reason or another. The most recent, Sven, had been killed by a pack of wolves.

"A nest?" Anson sneered. "Those are little more than shacks."

Elias shrugged. "It may be small, but I'll have it all to myself."

Stella smiled in sympathy. She knew all too well how overbearing Jenna and Elias's ma could be, which was why Jenna had been so relieved to marry Garrett. It was too bad Elias couldn't move into the cottage with her. She had the room to spare and then she wouldn't have to be alone. She kept the thought to herself, however. It was hardly appropriate to live with a man who was not her husband or a family member. "It's what you've always wanted."

Elias nodded in agreement. "Though ma is hardly pleased."

Very little pleased Maria Parnassa, but Stella refrained from saying so. Especially in front of Anson Mellac, who she now eyed with irritation. She had hoped to have more time alone with Elias, but Anson seemed intent on lingering.

"Speaking of your ma," the interloper began, gazing at the entrance to the tavern.

"Oh no," Elias muttered as Stella turned to see his mother heading toward them. He jumped up to intercept her, and she knew that that was the end of their visit. Disappointed, she rose to her feet and made her way past mother and son. "Good eve, Mistress Parnassa. Goodbye, Elias. It's good to have you back." Then she exited the tavern.

Outside, the night was cool and perfectly still, a contrast to the heat and noise she had just escaped from. The tavern stood at the edge of the Hollow, so here and there she spotted lights glowing from homes both on the ground and hidden in the trees. Her own cottage sat two leagues away. With a sigh, she turned her back on the lights to delve into the darkness where her home awaited. But before she could take a single step, a large hand clamped around her upper arm.

"A word if you please, Stella."

Stella turned with reluctance. "What is it, Anson?" she asked, firmly pulling her arm from his grasp.

"I need to know why you refuse to marry. I know you've turned down every man who's asked, but why turn *me* down? I have the most to offer and could provide for your every need, so why say no?"

Her dismay turned to annoyance. How many times did she have to refuse him before he'd give up. Perhaps the time for diplomacy was over. He clearly couldn't accept a polite no for an answer. "Because you got Ellie Loula with child and left her to deal with it on her own. Why won't you marry *her*? It would be the right thing to do."

Anson's face reddened with embarrassment and anger. "Ellie lifts her skirts for any man who looks her way. Just because it was my seed that took doesn't mean I should be saddled with the lightskirt."

"And I won't be saddled to a man who dallies without discretion and shirks his responsibilities," Stella said with contempt, turning away from him.

Anson grabbed her in a bruising grip and yanked her around to face him. Fury transformed his reddened face. "Who do you think you are, Stella? You think no one is good enough for you just because of your pretty face? But you don't have many options, do you, now that you're by yourself? Anything could happen to you out there in that lonely cottage of yours."

Stella gazed at him in alarm. He never would have dared to threaten her were Erik still alive. But therein lay the problem. Her brother was dead, which meant it was up to her to figure out how to handle Anson. "What exactly are you trying to say?"

Anson gave a nonchalant shrug, but his eyes remained flinty. "Do you think anyone would hear you scream? Do you think they could rescue you in time?"

Just then, the door of the tavern flew open and Damian exited with Ana. Stella's eyes darted to the couple before she could hide the fear in them.

"Stella, is everything alright?" Damian asked, his gaze darkening as they slid over to Anson.

"She's fine," Anson replied stiffly. "We were just talking. Now run along and mind your own business." He eyed Ana with a lascivious half-smile. "I'm sure the girl is eager to get you alone, aren't you Ana?"

"Why don't you mind *your* own business, Anson?" Ana retorted, as she tried to tug Damian forward. Tried, but failed.

"I'll hear it from Stella herself," Damian said, turning away from Anson in clear dismissal.

Damian stared at her, waiting for an answer. Both Anson and Ana glared, the first in warning and the second in jealousy. It was an uncomfortable scenario, to say the least, and Stella had no patience for it. "I'm not alright," she admitted, boldly meeting Anson's gaze. "Because I don't like being threatened."

Damian removed Ana's hand from his arm, paying no heed to her angry pout. Turning to Anson, he said in a low voice. "You threatened her. Why?"

Anson took stock of Damian's array of weapons before glancing at the tavern, seeming to find assurance in the knowledge that they were in a public place. "I did no such thing," he said in a calm reply. "I merely said it was unsafe for her to live alone in such a remote cottage, which is the truth."

"You also said no one would be able to hear me scream," Stella added.

"Also the truth," Anson said smoothly.

"Or rescue me in time," she added.

"And what would induce you to say such things to her?" Damian asked, his voice soft yet dangerous.

50

"I was merely expressing my concern for her safety."

Anson's reply sounded convincing enough. And Damian himself had expressed much the same thing. Though she was unable to refute Anson's words or prove his true intent, she was unwilling to let him get away with harassing her. "If you're so concerned with my safety, stay away from me, Anson. I mean it." With that, she spun on her heel and hurried off, hoping that Damian and Ana's presence would prevent Anson from following.

She was wrong.

When she heard footsteps dogging her, Stella whirled around, intending to tell Anson off. But it was Damian she came face to face with. Startled, she paused before asking, "Why are you following me?"

"To make sure you get home safely."

Stella glanced behind him. Through the trees, she could clearly see the tavern, its windows leaking yellow light into the darkness. What she couldn't see were either Ana or Anson. She could only assume they had gone back inside.

"There's no need," Stella replied as she continued on her way. "So long as Anson doesn't follow, I'll manage."

Damian didn't bother to respond, but pulled up beside her in a few long strides. Vexed, she turned to him and spat, "Leave me be, Damian. If you don't hurry back to Ana, she might very well take up with someone else."

"That's fine by me," he drawled. "Besides, deep down inside I know you'd rather I be with you instead."

"Oh, yes," she returned archly. "Because I want nothing more than to enjoy your fickle attentions. You're no better than Anson, you know, thinking you can throw your weight around and refusing to take no for an answer."

The next thing Stella knew, she was facing Damian, his hands gripping her shoulders as he glared down at her. "You dare compare me to that oaf?" he growled. "When have I ever threatened you? And what have I ever done to earn your distrust?"

She pulled away from him with a violent jerk, tired of being manhandled. "Nothing," she admitted grudgingly. "Yet."

Wishing he would just leave and hoping she'd angered him enough to do so, Stella hurried off. But Damian was not to be shaken. He stalked beside her, seething in silence. She took note of his rigid jaw and clenched fists. "What are you so upset about?" she retorted, hoping it hid her mild alarm. "You're not the one being followed against her will."

Damian turned to her, his gaze fiery. "Are you always so aggravating?"

"Are you always such an ass?"

He stopped in his tracks, a look of indignation on his face. She might've laughed if he wasn't already so affronted. "Did you just call me an ass?"

Stella knew she should probably back down to defuse the situation, but was overcome by a perverse desire to push him further instead. "Surely I'm not the first person to ever call you that."

Damian crossed his arms, causing them to flex and bulge. "No one has ever called me that," he declared.

"Not to your face perhaps." Feeling a smug sense of satisfaction, she spun away. Clearly, Damian hadn't been set down often enough. It was a good thing she was willing to offer the service.

"And what makes me such an ass?" he demanded, as he kept apace with her brisk steps.

"The fact that you never listen to me and refuse to respect my wishes!"

"Only when it comes to ensuring your safety, which you seem to have a reckless disregard for."

"And you seem to have too much regard for it. If you're trying to make me feel obligated to you, it won't work."

A vise-like grip immediately stopped her. "And what sort of obligation are you alluding to, Stella?" Damian asked, anger in his low voice.

She yanked at her arm, but he refused to release it. "Let me go!"

"Not until you answer my question."

Stella suddenly found it difficult to breathe as Damian's warm breath caressed her face, his dark eyes boring into her own. Why did he have to stand so close? "I'm not like Ana or any of the other women you're used to. I'm not easy."

If possible, Damian's eyes seemed to darken even more. He stared at her for a long moment—what felt like an eternity but couldn't be more than a few seconds—then he let her go. "No, you're not. Though my regard for your safety has nothing to do with obligating you to myself. After all, as you seem to be well aware of, there are plenty of women who are more than happy to oblige me."

Stella stared at him with a mixture of indignation and contempt. "Then, please, by all means, attend to any of those other women. At least *they* want you around."

"There'll be plenty of time for that later, after I ensure your safe return home," Damian said smoothly.

Stella stormed off, fuming. The man was so arrogant, so conceited, so…infuriating! Though to be honest, she was just as furious with herself. Because for one moment, when Damian had pulled her close, she had actually wondered what it would be like to kiss him. Disgusted by her traitorous desires, the sound of her tormentor following from behind did little to improve her foul mood.

"You know what?" she spat. "I was wrong. You're not an ass. You're a pig—a selfish, disgusting pig."

"That's not very kind, Stella," he said, a note of warning in his voice.

"I wasn't trying to be."

A flash of anger darkened his face before cooling into thoughtful consideration. "Could it be that the reason you're so mad is because you're jealous?"

"What is there for me to be jealous of? I don't envy any of those women."

"Perhaps it's not them you envy, but the attention I give them."

"Don't flatter yourself," she snapped. "I asked you to leave, remember? You're the one who refuses to go."

"This mean, petty side of you is not very attractive," he said flatly.

"Good, if you don't like it then leave."

"I already told you I wouldn't, so I suggest you save your breath."

Oh, she would save her breath alright! Jealous indeed! How dare he even suggest such a thing? Just more evidence of his arrogance. He couldn't seem to fathom anyone despising him much less resisting him, so jealousy was the only possible explanation.

"Is Anson one of the men you turned down for marriage?"

"What do you know about that?" she asked, forgetting her vow to keep silent.

"I know what Garrett told me," he replied matter-of-factly. "I know that you've refused at least three offers for your hand."

Stella scowled and fixed her gaze forward. Why were he and Garrett discussing her suitors? Though it was more than three she'd rejected.

"Did none of them suit you?" he asked. But she refused to answer. "Stella?"

In the silence that followed, she could hear the hoot of a distant owl.

"So you're not speaking to me now?"

More silence.

"That's not what I meant by saving your breath."

Still, she remained mute.

"You're acting like a petulant child," he said impatiently.

Stella felt a surge of triumph. Finally, she was getting under his skin the way he did hers. The silence stretched, growing frostier with each passing second. It made the trek uncomfortable, but she was determined to hold her tongue until the very end.

There was an unfortunate consequence to the lack of conversation, however. It directed her attention elsewhere. Without meaning to, she found herself becoming aware of Damian's quiet but sleek movements—the smooth glide of his limbs, the ripple of muscle beneath his taut skin. To her frustration, the more she tried not to think about these things, the more she noticed them.

When at last they reached her cottage, Stella practically flew to the door. "Thank you for ensuring my safe return home," she said curtly yet politely. "I hope you enjoy the rest of your night."

Damian was taken aback by her last remark and seemed uncertain how to respond. But then a salacious smirk twisted his lips. "Oh, I will," he assured her, before sauntering back the way they had come.

Whatever advantage Stella had thought to gain dissipated as she watched him leave, likely to pick back up where he'd left off with Ana. She wanted nothing to do with the man, she reminded herself, and determined to put him far from her thoughts. That is, until she had to see him again the following night. Sighing, Stella stepped inside the cottage and wondered why it was that the space felt emptier than usual.

7

The Fallen Star

Stella stirred, roused from a fitful slumber. It took several slow blinks to realize what it was that had awoken her. Wind shook the windows and whistled through the cracks as she turned to lie on her back. Bleary-eyed, she rose from her bed to light a candle and don her robe. When she ventured to unlatch the front door, it flew from her hand with a loud slam, blowing out the taper she cradled in the other. Undaunted, she set down the candle and stepped outside to find that the forest had come alive.

All around the clearing, the trees swayed like dancers in a trance. Her hair whipped about her face and her skin pebbled as she watched the undulating trees toss its branches and rattle its leaves. The weather was restless, like her own troubled spirit. It seemed to beckon to her, calling her to abandon the cares that weighed her down. Closing her eyes, she breathed deep of the sharp, cleansing air and imagined it blowing away her grief, removing her worries and fears.

When she opened her eyes, she saw tattered clouds flying across the face of a quarter moon—as ephemeral and elusive as the hopes she harbored in her heart. Stella watched the clouds until she began to shiver, then she turned to go back inside. As she did, a bright light suddenly lit the dark sky. She snapped her head around, staring in

THE FALLEN STAR

amazement as a ball of fire shot over the forest like a shooting star. She watched until it vanished from view, disappearing into the very heart of Darkwood.

* * *

The path was narrow and rocky. Though hidden from sight, Stella traveled it in silence and stealth. She had almost missed the path altogether. Not only was it difficult to detect, it was distant and challenging to reach, which was why she had traveled it only four times since her discovery of it over a year ago. This time would make it her fifth, if she didn't twist her ankle or fall into a thornbush first. The ground was thickly covered with spiky bushes and poisonous plants, which was why almost no one ventured into the area. It was purely by chance that Stella had first stumbled upon the spot she so zealously guarded. It was a treacherous trek, but the destination was well-worth the attempt.

When the scent of moss and clover tickled her nose, she knew that she was close. Soon, the murmur of water reached her ears as leafy ferns brushed against her skirt and hard ground gave way to springy peat. It wasn't long before she was standing at the edge of a small, dark pool where she paused to take in the wondrous scene. The last time she'd come, the grotto had been bathed in moonlight. Tonight there was a new moon, and if possible, the grotto was even lovelier than ever. The pearl blossoms that dotted the surrounding stone walls glowed more brightly in the deeper darkness, as did the water lilies that floated on the pool's surface. When a sudden breeze blew, it stirred the blossoms and created a flurry of luminous petals that swirled in the air before drifting down to the dark water.

Stella soaked in the sight, reveling in the profound beauty. And then she began to undress. When she slid into the pool, she sighed in pleasure at the feel of the cool liquid upon her skin. It was the closest she came to feeling peace and contentment. This was her refuge, her own private sanctuary, a place to think and dream and escape. She swam, using long, lazy strokes. Unlike the calm of the pool, her inner thoughts were troubled and turbulent.

No one else had seen the fireball shooting across the sky two weeks ago. At first, Stella had been astounded. How was it possible that she alone had witnessed the unusual phenomenon? But after questioning every person she dared and receiving the same negative answer, she began to wonder if she had seen it at all. Perhaps it had just been a part of an elaborate dream. The wind *hadn't* really awoken her and she *hadn't* really seen that ball of fire. After all, wouldn't the forest have been set ablaze? Still, despite evidence to the contrary, she couldn't shake the conviction that what she had seen was real. The night had been so vivid and clear in her memory. She could still hear the howl of the wind and feel its sting upon her face.

She had been so convinced about the fireball she'd even asked Damian about it. His reaction had been no different than the others—a mixture of bewilderment, doubt and concern. She was annoyed with herself for confiding in him, but he had been there and he had been available. Too available. As often as she saw him, it was proving near impossible to keep him at arm's length. Sometimes literally, when he managed to encroach on her personal space.

Much as it irked her, she had to admit that she was not entirely immune to the man. And though she more or less succeeded in resisting him, there was no denying his appeal. The man was physically attractive in every way, from his face to his physique. It really wasn't fair. Her best defense against him—her only defense really—was to remember what manner of man he was, to picture him with Ana or some other lightskirt. Fortunately, the exercise always proved effective.

Besides, her hands were full enough with the other men vying for her affections. Two of her more persistent suitors had even gotten into a brawl over her at the marketplace. It had been embarrassing, but she reminded herself that it could be worse. At least Anson hadn't bothered her again. In fact, he had kept a wide berth. But her suitors—whether welcomed or not—were a reminder that she *did* need a husband. And sooner rather than later.

Stella was grateful for her friends, the only bright spots in her otherwise dismal existence. Elias, in particular, had given her a reason to smile again since his return. He'd come by to visit on several occasions, helping Garrett with such tasks as chopping wood and practicing combat with her. He'd even promised to help Garrett take over the hunting once Damian was done. Lately, she had begun to wonder what it would be like to have Elias for a husband. She had never been attracted to him in that way, but perhaps she could be content with him, unlike the others. But even if she could settle for mere contentment, there was no getting around the fact that he was in love with someone else.

With a sigh, Stella turned to float on her back. The stars were brilliant and countless in the vast evening sky, so close it felt like she could reach out and pluck them. An illusion, she knew. They were as distant and unreachable as any hope for happiness. When one of them began to fall, she thought once more of what she had witnessed two weeks ago...or thought she'd witnessed. Stella furrowed her brow in frustration. Never before had she doubted herself so completely.

Just then a sound reached her ears, causing her to startle. Stella immediately submerged her body, her heart tripping within her chest as her eyes darted along the pool's edge. Something had rustled near the shore. When, after a time, no other sound or movement was detected, she convinced herself it was probably just a small creature, a rabbit or squirrel or the like. But just to be safe, she swam to where her dagger lay within reach. Grabbing it, she began to throw her clothes on in haste, wondering if the feeling of being watched was simply a product of paranoia.

Once she was fully dressed, Stella felt more at ease. Her clothes stuck uncomfortably to her wet skin, but at least she was no longer exposed. If only she could shake the sense of having eyes upon her.

"Please, I won't hurt you."

Stella's heart flew to her throat at the strange, unexpected voice. She spun, ready to attack, as she faced the man that had suddenly appeared behind her. Though it was dark, she could see enough of him to make out his tall form standing maybe six feet away. Much too close for comfort. Worse, he was armed, for she could see a sword hanging from his side. Were the pool not directly behind her, she would've backed away. "Who are you?" she demanded, her voice hoarse with fear.

"My name is Luc."

Stella was thrown off by the unusual inflection of his voice. Neither the accent or the name were familiar to her, but it was the first that bothered her more. The accent was subtle, distinct, and odd enough to be intriguing. "What do you want?"

"I...I was hoping you could help me."

Stella had been gripping the dagger so tight her fingers began to tingle. She loosened them, but kept the blade pointed at the stranger. "Help you with what?"

"I've been wandering these woods for...I don't know how long. Days, maybe weeks? But I could use some food and shelter. Some medicine, too, if you have any?"

Days? What was that? "You're hurt?" she asked aloud.

He reached for his arm and Stella jerked her dagger at the motion. "I climbed a tree to escape some wolves. Unfortunately, there was a wildcat already in it. I'm afraid my arm might be infected, though I haven't been able to see it to know for certain."

Stella stared at him warily, wondering if he spoke the truth. "Where are you from?"

"Aurelia."

"Never heard of it." Just as she'd never heard anyone speak like him. Her unease grew. Everyone knew that Noctum had only thirteen cities, each ruled by a royal. Was it possible there was another she hadn't heard of? One that had been hidden from her and the rest of Noctum's citizens? She wouldn't put it past Draven to keep secrets. "How long have you been here?"

"Here in Callipia?"

Callipia? The man was clearly lost. "You're in Noctum," she corrected. "But what I meant was, how long have you been *here* in the grotto?"

Luc hesitated before answering. "I've been here the entire time."

"You were watching me!" Stella took a threatening step forward, her dagger ready to gut.

"I was here for the water. Then I fell asleep," he rushed to explain. "When I woke up, you had suddenly appeared. I swear!"

"How much did you see?" she demanded, despite her intense mortification.

"Not nearly enough," he mumbled.

"What?" Surely she hadn't heard right.

"I didn't see much," he said louder. "Just your general shape, none of the more interesting details. Don't worry, your modesty has been preserved."

Stella exhaled in relief, though she wavered between indignation and reluctant amusement at what he'd referred to as her 'more interesting details'.

"Now will you help me?" he pressed.

"Help you with what?"

"My arm, my stomach," he said, exasperated. "Have you not been listening?"

"Listening to what?" she asked, distracted by his accent.

Stella heard him let out a heavy huff. "I'm going to die out here," he muttered under his breath.

Stella found herself smiling. Though the man was a complete stranger, she could sense no real threat from him. He was so disarming, even charming in his manner. All the more reason to remain wary, she sternly reminded herself.

"You wouldn't just leave me here to die, would you?" Luc asked, with exaggerated pitifulness.

"I see that you're armed," she pointed out, using a firm tone to convey she would not be easily swayed or duped.

Luc nodded in the darkness. "I have both a sword and a dagger."

"Give them to me," she commanded.

"But—"

"If you want my help, you'll hand them over." She wasn't heartless, but she wasn't stupid either.

After a pause, the sound of rustling could be heard as Luc removed his weapons belt and extended it to her.

"Throw it down." She heard it hit the ground between them. "Now turn around and walk ahead until you reach the incline." Stella waited until Luc's footfalls receded before she reached down to grab his belt. Once she had it in hand, she immediately recognized her challenge. Since she was already wearing her own belt, she would have to carry his. Not only that, but she still clutched her dagger in one hand and had no intention of sheathing it. She picked up the belt. His sword—long, heavy and cumbersome—dragged along the ground. This wasn't going to work. "Wait, come back!"

Luc returned as instructed. She threw the belt back at his feet. "You carry it. In your hands."

She thought she saw a gleam of teeth in the darkness. "As you wish," Luc said, as she heard him retrieve the belt. Then she heard a hiss of pain, reminding her of his injured arm. A twinge of guilt shot through her, which she quickly suppressed.

"Go on," she urged, waving ahead with her dagger. "I'll be right behind you."

Guarding Luc proved just as problematic. Unwilling to turn her back on him, he had climbed up the steep slope of the ravine ahead of her. Now that he was at the top, she was left in a vulnerable position. Especially when it came time for her to climb, which she would need to do with both hands. Which meant sheathing her dagger. She looked up at him in frustration.

"You can trust me, you know," Luc said, guessing her dilemma. "Why would I hurt you when I obviously need your help?"

His reasoning made sense enough. Setting aside her unease, Stella sheathed her dagger and began to climb. When she neared the top, she was startled when Luc grabbed her hand to help her up. She yanked it away, dismayed by the tingling heat from his skin. "Don't touch me!"

Luc held his hands up in a conciliatory gesture, though he could only raise his injured arm halfway. "I'm sorry. I was only trying to help."

"Well don't," she snapped, annoyed that she could still feel the warmth of his hand. "Besides, you stink!" This close to him, she could smell the stench of his body, proving he'd been wandering the woods for quite some time.

"Is it much further?" he asked, suddenly sounding weary.

"We have another two hours at least," she replied, subduing her guilt once more. "And I suggest you no longer speak from this point on."

"Why not?"

"Because it's dangerous, and we don't want to draw attention." In truth, she didn't want to alert anyone to her secret trail and hidden spot. "Follow me," she instructed, resigned to the necessity of being his guide.

The trek through the forest was silent and tense. Luc made no sound, his feet moving with impressive stealth. It was impossible to forget his presence, but several times Stella found herself checking over her shoulder to make sure he was still there. He was that silent.

When it became apparent that he would not attack, she finally allowed herself to relax. All the while, questions swirled in her head. Where had he come from really? And what was he doing in Darkwood? She was also curious about his appearance. Was he young or older? Plain or handsome? Dark-headed or fair-haired?

The hours passed. The trek was longer than usual with no moon to guide the way. But eventually, Stella stopped. Behind her, she could feel Luc's warm breath on the top of her head. Ignoring the sensation, she focused on the familiar woods before her. They had reached the Hollow, the most populated part of the forest. Cottages were spread out within a square league of the area, which meant a high probability of running into another person. Stella wondered why that should matter. After all, what reason did she have for keeping Luc hidden? None that she could think of.

Still, something urged her to maintain secrecy and stealth.

"Stay quiet and follow me," she whispered to him, choosing a circuitous path to minimize the likelihood of being seen.

After a time, they reached the edge of the clearing where her cottage stood. She had kept a lantern lit and its light seeped through the curtains Marta had made. It was always a risk to leave a flame burning, but it was one of the few things that acted as a deterrent for those who might otherwise break into an empty home. Unfortunately, it could also act as a beacon for a Shade.

"Is this where you live?" Luc whispered.

"Yes."

"Does anyone else live with you? Your husband might not be happy with you bringing home a stranger."

"You don't have to worry about that." Though husband or not, bringing a strange man home was not something most would approve of.

Without warning, Stella stole across the clearing like a thief—ironic since she was stealing into her own home. She unlocked the cottage door, and waving Luc over, kept a lookout as he slipped through behind her. It wasn't until she had entered and locked the door that she turned to face her unusual houseguest.

To her surprise, Luc had already made himself at home. He was sitting in one of the upholstered armchairs, revealing just the back of his blonde head. So he was fair-haired, she noted. Curious to see the rest of him, Stella rounded the armchair to take a look. She hadn't known what to expect, had given little thought beyond simply wondering. But when she finally saw Luc by the light of her lantern, her mouth promptly fell open.

8

The Northern Lights

E very wintertide, the Northern Lights swept in without fanfare to grace the black skies of Noctum. For a land steeped in darkness, the sudden appearance of those vibrant celestial lights brought joy so euphoric it inspired a response akin to worship. While they lasted, which was all too briefly, it was not unusual for forest dwellers to spend much of their time gazing upward until the lights faded from sight. Stella still remembered the first time she saw the colorful lights as a young girl, and could clearly recall the wonder that had filled her at its beauty. The moment was forever burned into her memory.

Likewise, she would never forget the first time she laid eyes on Luc.

With wild golden hair, brilliant green eyes and skin the color of honey, he was like no other man she had ever seen before. Stella took in his thick, wavy hair, admiring the rakish way it fell over his forehead. She noted his emerald eyes that, despite being weary, were vibrant and arresting. But it was his skin she couldn't get over. Never before had she seen skin so rich and warm in color. Its unusual hue made his eyes seem greener, his hair lighter. She was tempted to reach out and stroke it.

Alarmed by the thought, Stella forced herself to observe the rest of him. She already knew he was tall, judging by his silhouette in the dark. But by lantern light, she saw that he was taller than she thought, perhaps six and a quarter feet. His build was slim yet well-proportioned, and she found herself admiring his wide shoulders, broad chest and trim waist. His long limbs were toned and she saw that his arms ended with large hands possessing elegantly tapered fingers. Simply put, he was utterly stunning.

"Like what you see?"

Stella's gaze snapped upward, and she realized she had been gaping. Mortification stole through her at the amusement in his green eyes. "Your skin...I've never seen anyone with your color before," she said, trying to salvage some shred of dignity.

Luc tilted his head quizzically. "Is everyone here as pale as you?"

Pale? Stella lifted her hand and glanced at it in bewilderment. It was smooth and milky white. "Yes, everyone has skin like mine. How did you get yours to look the way it does?"

He seemed to sway even as he sat. "Do you mind if I saw to my wound while we have this conversation?"

At once, Stella was reminded that he was tired, hungry and hurt. "Yes, yes, of course," she stammered, leaving him to light a few more lanterns and gather the necessary supplies.

When the cottage was sufficiently illuminated, she went to her sideboard and pulled out some bandages and a tincture. Then she poured some water into a bowl and grabbed two clean washcloths. Placing them on a tray, she carried the items over to Luc.

Earlier, she'd been so focused on his face and physique that she'd barely noticed his odd clothing...or his injury. Ashamed, she took the time to study both more carefully. Now that she paid closer attention, she saw that his clothes were dirty and disheveled, and that his left sleeve was torn and bloody, though the blood was old and dried.

Before she could offer him the privacy of a bedroom, Luc began to remove his shirt. When he sat before her bare-chested, she swallowed discreetly and forced her gaze to his injured arm. His golden, muscled arm. Why were attractive men suddenly baring themselves before her? Though there was something especially intriguing about Luc's tanned chest. "Well, it doesn't look to be infected," she said with forced nonchalance.

"Thank goodness for that, though it still hurts like hell."

"It is rather deep," she acknowledged, laying the tray down on a nearby table.

"You know, you've yet to tell me your name," Luc said, as she began to turn away.

"It's Stella," she said, glancing at him side-eye.

Luc smiled, which did something alarming to her heart. "Stella, do you think you could help me tend my wounds?"

Her first instinct was to decline. After all, he was sitting there shirtless and she could hardly keep her composure as it was. But at the sight of his weary, shadowed eyes, she found herself reconsidering. "It would be highly inappropriate."

"I promise to behave. And I honestly don't have the strength to cause trouble anyway."

"Alright then," she relented, after some hesitation.

"Thank you," he said, softly.

Stella wrinkled her nose as she drew near to kneel at his side. His odor was all sweat and salt and filth. But underneath it rose another scent, a base note she couldn't quite place her finger on, one that reminded her of warm summer nights. Puzzling over this, she picked up the rag, dipped it in the bowl of water and began to wash his wound. Determined not to be distracted by the man himself, she concentrated on his arm, cleaning his wound with careful deliberation.

"Do you always approach everything you do with this much focus?" Luc asked, after long moments had passed in silence.

Stella started. "Would you rather I was less attentive?"

"No, but by the way your brow was furrowed, one would think my wounds hid the answers to the universe."

Stella couldn't help but laugh at the absurdity of his remark. "Maybe my brow is furrowed because of your stench."

Luc grimaced at that. "I could do with a bath."

"I thought that was why you were at the grotto," she said with an arched brow.

"Not to bathe, but to quench my thirst. Besides, what use is bathing if you have no soap to cleanse with? I would just be wet *and* smelly."

"True enough," she agreed. "When I'm done here, I'll give you soap so you can wash up."

"I would appreciate that," he said, his gaze straying to where Garrett's armor sat on display in the corner of the room. It was draped on a wooden stand fashioned in the general shape of a body.

Trying to see the cottage through his eyes, Stella took in the various tools that hung on the wall next to it. Beneath her tools sat a long, narrow table covered with segments of tanned leather. The perpendicular wall held her skins, which were displayed above the stuffed couch. There was no hiding the evidence of her trade.

"Did you make that?" Luc asked, still staring at the unfinished armor.

"Yes."

"That's impressive. I don't know of any woman who works with leather, not in Aurelia at least. It tends to be a man's trade. Is it common here in Cal—I mean Noctum?"

Stella shook her head. "No. My ma was the only woman I knew who worked with leather besides myself. And she learned it from her da who had no sons to pass his skill along to."

"Was he a master craftsman?"

"How did you guess?"

Luc nodded at the armor. "It's obvious you inherited his talent. I know superior quality when I see it."

Stella couldn't help the pleasure that flooded through her at the compliment. She took pride in her work, even though initially it had only been a means to make ends meet. It still was, of course. But she had since grown to enjoy it, finding satisfaction in being excellent at what she did. "Thank you," she murmured, not meeting his gaze as she continued to clean his wound. By the time she was done, the bowl was bright red with blood. Grabbing the tincture, she poured some onto the second cloth. "This will sting," she warned, before dabbing it onto his arm.

Luc hissed in pain. For the first time since kneeling at his side, she looked him fully in the face. A mistake. This close, she was in danger of drowning in the green depths of his eyes. "Don't be such a baby," she said, trying to hide her attraction. Then she dabbed at his wound again. Though he tried not to flinch, the muscle in his arm twitched reflexively.

"It's only because I'm so weak," he said, using his pitiful voice. "I haven't eaten in so long and I haven't slept much either."

"You poor baby," she mocked.

Luc laughed, shaking his head. "You're so unfeeling!"

"Surely not. After all, here I am tending to your wound in my home, and you a perfect stranger."

"Will you feed me and let me sleep in your bed, too?"

Stella lifted her brow, though inwardly her heart was thumping wildly. "Are you always so bold and shameless?"

The mischievous gleam dimmed in his tired eyes. "Bold, definitely. Shameless, not usually. It must be the combination of exhaustion and mild delirium. In truth, I'd settle for sleeping on the floor. It's sure to be more comfortable than most of the places I've laid my head recently."

"I'll feed you if I must," she said, completing her application of the tincture. "And while I won't make you sleep on the floor, you can forget about sleeping in my bed. Besides, I have another bed you can sleep on."

His mouth curled up in a lion's smile. "Thank you, Stella."

"You're welcome." She reached for the bandage and wrapped up his arm. When she was done, she went to her sideboard and grabbed a small yellow bar.

"Here you go," she said, handing it to him.

THE NORTHERN LIGHTS

He sniffed it. "Verbena?"

"I also have lavender if you prefer," she said, offering him a clean rag as well.

"Verbena is fine."

"Alright then." She went to retrieve the tray. "The pump is outside, to the right." She had a perfectly good washroom, but he was too filthy to use her soaking tub. Besides, she hadn't offered it to Damian either. Nor would she ever.

Luc was gone long enough for Stella to get a fire roaring in the hearth. When he still hadn't returned, she walked to the door of the bedroom opposite her own. She hesitated before entering. Belonging most recently to Erik and Marta, it had once been her ma and da's room. And before them, her grandma and grandda's. Everyone who'd ever used the room was now gone.

Shaking off the somber thought, she pushed the door open and headed straight for the large trunk at the foot of the bed. Most of the clothes inside had belonged to Erik, but a few of the items had been her da's. Sighing, she pulled out one of Erik's shirts and trousers. Her da had been a big man, thick and burly. Erik's slimmer clothes would fit Luc much better. Laying them on the bed, she turned to see that Luc had returned, his silhouette filling the bedroom doorway. As he stood there, the light from the living room gave her a glimpse of his golden skin. In that moment, her situation fully sunk in. Here she was, alone in her cottage with a beautiful and mysterious young man, a stranger she had met only hours ago. "You can change into these," she said, once she'd found her voice. "And this is where you'll sleep as well."

"Whose room is this?"

"It used to be my brother's."

Luc hesitated before stepping into the room, as if reluctant to intrude. Stella brushed past him to exit and caught the faint scent of verbena from his skin. No more salt and sweat and dirt, though that warm summer scent was still there. Intoxicating. Shaking her head

71

as if to clear it, she continued out the door.

While Luc dressed, Stella fought to collect herself. It was unnerving how Luc affected her. She feared making a fool of herself if she wasn't careful. He was a stranger, she reminded herself sternly, a man she knew next to nothing about. So what if he was attractive and intriguing? He could be a liar, a thief or worse. And with looks and charm like his, he was certain to be the dangerous sort—much like another man she knew. It would behoove her to proceed with caution, especially since she had no idea why he was even in Darkwood.

When Luc emerged, amusement flashed in Stella's eyes as she took in his loose attire. Though the length of the clothing was fine, both the shirt and pants were too wide. He looked like a scarecrow, if scarecrows could be handsome.

"Your brother must have been quite brawny."

"It's a good thing I didn't give you my father's clothes. He was even brawnier."

"They must have been an intimidating pair."

"They were, but in a good way," she replied, going to the cupboard and laying out dried fruit, meat, and a crusty loaf of bread. "I'm sorry this is all I have."

"It's a veritable feast," Luc said, practically lunging for the table. "It's certainly more than I've eaten in days." He promptly tore into the food with astonishing speed. Sympathy coursed through when she saw just how famished he really was. Since Erik's death, there'd been times when she feared going hungry herself. Were it not for Garrett and now Damian, her fears might have been realized. Suddenly, Luc stopped, gazing at her in apology. "I'm sorry. I nearly ate everything."

"It's alright. If you'll just save me a bite or two, I should be fine."

Red-faced, Luc pushed the rest of the bread and the last two slices of dried meat toward her. "I'm sorry," he apologized again.

Stella sat down across from him. "Had it been my brother, everything would have already been gone and in half the time," she said, to ease his guilt. "I'm sorry I can't offer you anything else, but

I should have fresh meat by tomorrow." When Damian came by to deliver it.

"You've been more than generous, Stella," Luc said, his gaze blazing with intensity. "Were it not for you, I might still be lost in the forest. I might be dead."

Stella pondered that sobering possibility, which led her back to the questions that had been hovering in her mind. "Perhaps it's time you tell me exactly who you are and why you came to Noctum."

9

An Impossible Truth

Luc's face clouded. Then he rose to his feet and began to pace, clearly agitated by her query. "I'm afraid you won't believe me."

With his tawny skin and odd accent, Stella thought that she was willing to believe quite a bit where he was concerned. "So long as you tell me the truth, I'll do my best to."

Luc nodded, his golden hair falling into his green eyes. He pushed the lock back without breaking his stride. "You asked me about my skin color. You wanted to know how it got to be this way." When Stella nodded in confirmation, he continued. "The reason is because where I come from, the sun always shines."

"What is a sun?" she asked, furrowing her brow.

Luc halted in his tracks. "You've never heard of the sun?"

"No."

He appeared stupefied, as if she'd claimed not to know what a sword or a bird was. "How is that even possible?"

"Are you going to tell me what it is or not?" she asked, a touch impatiently.

"The sun is…it's like the moon, only bigger and a thousand times brighter." At her look of disbelief, he added, "The reason it's so bright is because it's a giant ball of fire."

Stella straightened in her seat. "I saw a ball of fire just the other night. It came from the mountains and shot over the forest like a falling star."

"You did?" he asked, startled.

Stella nodded. "The strange thing was no one else seemed to notice it."

Luc exhaled in relief. "Good."

"Why is that good?"

"Because...that ball of fire was me."

Stella stared at Luc, wondering if he was jesting. But his serious expression never wavered. "How is that even possible?"

"Through magic," he stated simply.

Noctum, too, possessed magic, but not like the kind Luc spoke of. In Noctum, magic was reserved to the royals. It was what made Draven and the other rulers so much more powerful than everyone else, giving them superior strength, speed, and beauty. And in the king's case, invincibility. The magic from Luc's land was clearly of a different quality altogether. "So you traveled here via a blazing ball of fire?" she asked dubiously.

"Yes. We have powerful sorcerers in Aurelia."

"Is that what you are? A sorcerer?"

"No, I was sent here by a sorcerer, but I'm not a sorcerer myself."

"Then what are you?"

Something fleeting passed through Luc's eyes. It almost looked like sadness. "I'm a warrior."

Stella gazed at him in assessment. Having had a brother in the Shadow Guard, she knew her fair share of warriors, Garrett and Damian included. They all exuded a confidence that stemmed from being assured of their physical prowess. She hadn't sensed this in Luc, despite the weapons he bore. But then again he'd been suffering from exhaustion, injury and hunger. Still, there were ways to find out if he spoke the truth.

With lightning speed, Stella hurled her chunk of bread at Luc's head.

His arm was a blur as he caught it mid-flight before it could strike him in the face. "Why did you throw your bread at me?" he asked, flabbergasted.

"I was checking your reflexes."

"You were testing me?" He looked amused now.

"Of course," she said, rising from her seat. In five strides, she was picking up his sword, which he had propped up against the wall. The scabbard and belt from which it hung were plain and nondescript, as was the hilt. But when she pulled out the blade itself, she was stunned to find it a thing of beauty, all deadly lines and gleaming steel. And from the looks of it, wicked sharp.

Stella heard a gasp. Turning, she saw that Luc's eyes were wide, his hands up in warning. "Be careful," he urged, as if terrified she might cut herself.

Half amused, half insulted—*Did he think she carried her own sword for pretense?*—she whipped the sword around in series of swift moves Erik had taught her, one that displayed her ease and skill with the weapon. She was nowhere near as good as her brother had been, but she was competent enough. She finished with a flourish before returning the blade to its scabbard and hanging the belt by a hook on the wall. "That's a fine weapon, fit for a warrior."

"Who taught you that?" Luc asked, crossing his arms against his chest...and wincing.

"My brother." Stella dropped onto one of the upholstered chairs and Luc joined her, sitting in the chair directly across. She saw that his feet were bare and just as tanned as the rest of him. "So where exactly is Aurelia, and why did you leave it to come to Darkwood?"

"I thought you said this was Noctum?" he asked, confused.

"Darkwood is just one part of Noctum," she clarified.

"Oh, like a city?"

"No, the cities are all walled. Darkwood is a part of the forest surrounding the cities."

Stella watched as Luc considered this. "Well, Aurelia is on the other side of the Altous Mountains."

"But those mountains are impassable!"

"They are unless you use magic, powerful magic," Luc replied. "Hence, the ball of fire."

Stella shook her head, but she had promised to try her best to believe him. "But *why* did you come?"

"Remember what I said about the sun?"

"You said it was like the moon, only bigger and a thousand times brighter." She tried to imagine such a thing hanging in the sky, but couldn't. "What is that like?"

"Well, it's like…" Luc glanced around the cottage, searching. "Imagine you had enough lanterns or candles in here to drive away every shadow, so that not a single shred of darkness remained. That's what the sun is like. It sheds light over the entire land, allowing you to see everything clearly and vividly."

Stella furrowed her brow as she tried to picture such an image. Again, she failed.

"Here in Callipia, I mean Noctum, the sky is always black, isn't it?" Luc continued.

Stella nodded.

"Well, in Aurelia, and everywhere else south of the Altous Mountains, the skies can be blue or gray or even white at times."

"Blue skies?" she marveled.

"As blue as your eyes."

Combined with his unusual accent, his words sent a ripple of pleasure through her. "It sounds…impossible," she said, embarrassed by how breathless she sounded.

"Only because darkness is all you've ever known," Luc replied sadly.

He was right. Darkness was the way of life in Noctum. It was the first thing to greet her when she awoke, and the last thing she saw before she closed her eyes each night. It cloaked everything, crouching in every corner and pressing in on every side. Heavy and pervasive, she feared the darkness would slither beneath her skin and threaten to suffocate her soul. "Tell me more about Aurelia."

A wistful look passed over Luc's face as he obliged her. "In Aurelia, verdant green fields are dotted by lakes of deepest azure. Celenia, its capital, gleams white atop a tall hill, its golden roofs radiant beneath the blazing sun. To the west, lies the turquoise waters of the Aladean Sea. To the east, towers the mighty forest of Erudea, which is dressed in various shades of green during the spring and summer, but in the fall is a riot of red, orange and gold. The spring rains often bring rainbows to the sky and flowers that carpet the ground in similar shades. But in the winter, the entire land is cloaked in pristine white. Or they used to anyway." Luc fell silent, the longing on his face indicating he hadn't left his land willingly.

There was much about what he said that confused Stella, especially one thing in particular. "What is a rainbow?"

Luc smiled and she couldn't help but stare. "Imagine a giant arc that stretches across the sky, one that is striped in ribbons of purple, blue, green, yellow, orange and red."

Stella furrowed her brow, trying very hard to do as he asked. "It sounds beautiful," she said, though she wondered if the picture in her head was anything close to what he'd described.

"It is," Luc agreed, gazing at her. "It's the kind of beauty you never grow tired of."

Stella willed herself not to look away. Instead, she studied Luc intently, and saw no deceit in his eyes. The things he spoke of were beyond what she could fathom, and yet she was inclined to believe what he said. How else to explain his unusual skin tone? His accent? His odd clothing? And perhaps a part of her *wanted* to believe, if only to feed the hope that there was more to the world than what she'd always known. "If Aurelia is as wonderful as it sounds, why would you ever leave it to come to Noctum?"

Luc's eyes clouded, but he continued to hold her gaze. "Because of the curse."

"What curse?" she asked, frowning.

"The one that brought unnatural darkness to Noctum."

If Draven himself suddenly walked through the door, Stella couldn't have been more stunned. The notion that Noctum's darkness was unnatural shook her. It rattled the very foundation upon which her whole world view was built. Never would it have occurred to her that the way she lived was not how it was supposed to be. "What are you talking about?" she asked, half in hope and half in dread.

"At one time, Noctum was known as Callipia, and it was a land that observed both night and day, both dark and light. Until the curse."

"Who cursed it?"

"A mage named Stavan Arthanos."

The name was unknown to her. "Why would he do such a thing?"

Luc went to stand behind the chair across from her, his hands gripping the headrest. "He did it to stop a madman from destroying the world."

"What madman?"

"The same one who rules Noctum."

Stella stilled, her shocked gaze fixed on Luc. "You mean Draven? The king?"

"He was a bloodthirsty warlord before he was ever a king," Luc said grimly.

Feeling sapped of strength, she sunk into her chair, pondering Luc's revelation, wondering if she should believe any of it.

"Do you want to hear the story?" he asked tentatively.

Stella weakly nodded her head.

Luc sat and was silent for a time as he gathered his thoughts. When he spoke, his speech was slow and deliberate. "Over three thousand years ago, Draven was a general in a warlord's army. Under his banner, attacks were made on neighboring lands, leaving behind a trail of destruction and bloodshed. With each kingdom that fell under his assault, his hunger for power grew. So when the warlord he served ceased all further attacks, content with the territory he had amassed, Draven overthrew him. Intent on ruling a vast and mighty empire, he then set out to conquer every kingdom under the sun. He was brilliant and bold, using swift and vicious methods that none could prevail against. Kingdom after kingdom fell to his cruel might until he reached the Altous Mountains. By then he had conquered every land north of the mountains. Fortunately, the Altous's nearly impregnable heights and jagged peaks provided a natural barricade, one that proved impossible to breach when defended by the combined forces of the southern kingdoms. For a time, Draven was thwarted." Luc paused and Stella waited impatiently for him to continue. "Frustrated, Draven turned his energies to a different pursuit altogether, though one that was just as nefarious. Somehow, and it's still not known how, he managed to unearth an ancient scroll containing secrets to the forbidden. It was believed to be one of the original Anathema Scrolls, banned long ago to protect the world from its evils. It was in that scroll that he discovered the means to obtain immortality and invincibility. Once he achieved both, he became unstoppable."

Stella sat in silence, pondering Luc's tale, which painted a picture of Draven that was all too easy to believe.

Luc got up to pace once more. "The years that followed were bleak and brutal. Draven became known as the Dark Lord after he crossed the Altous Mountains and mowed down the southern armies like a scythe through wheat. Hope was all but lost. And then a mage named Stavan Arthanos rose up to challenge him. It was Stavan who discovered Draven's aversion to sunlight, a counterpoint to his immortality and invincibility. Stavan, with the help of several other mages, sought every spell they could find to stop Draven. None succeeded. Until, finally…one did." Luc stopped, staring blankly at the wall. "The spell was powerful but it came at a great cost. Stavan, along with every mage who aided him, were killed after it was cast."

Luc became lost in thought, leaving Stella to contemplate his words. "So the spell that was cast…it covered Noctum in darkness, effectively banishing Draven here while leaving every other land free of his tyranny?"

80

Luc turned to focus his gaze on her. "That wasn't the intent. Stavan sought to destroy Draven, so the spell he conceived was meant to keep the sun in the sky, eliminating darkness altogether. Without darkness, there would have been nowhere for Draven to hide. But it seems that when the laws of nature are twisted, it seeks to find balance somehow. Stavan succeeded in keeping the lands south of the Altous Mountains in perpetual light. But as a result, the northern lands were doomed to perpetual night."

"Where Draven rules unchallenged forever," Stella supplied, unable to hide her bitterness.

"Nothing lasts forever," Luc said, his eyes sliding away.

And then she remembered something. "You said you came because of the curse? Do you think to break it?"

"I have every intention of breaking it."

He made it sound like a done deed. Would the curse really be so easy to defeat? "But why you?"

"Because of this." Luc pulled up his left pant leg, exposing a crescent-shaped mark upon his shin. "Every male member of my family bears this birthmark, identifying us as those belonging to the Arthanos bloodline."

"So only someone of his bloodline is able to lift the curse?" When Luc nodded, she continued. "Then why has no one attempted to before?"

"Because no one knew. Not until a scroll was unearthed where Stavan's home once stood."

"I see," she replied, mulling over this. "But why would you *want* to lift the curse? It seems to me you have nothing to gain from doing so, since Aurelia has been free from Draven's tyranny all these centuries."

"Because it's the right thing to do," he replied, perplexed. "Because no one should be cursed to live in perpetual darkness."

Stella looked at him dubiously. "In my experience, no one does anything for nothing."

"Have you always been so cynical?" Luc asked, with a look akin to pity.

Her hackles rose, but Stella bit back a cutting retort. *Was* she cynical? Life in Noctum had taught her to be cautious, wary. She never thought herself to be cynical, but perhaps she was wrong. Suddenly she was envious of Luc, envious that he'd never been touched by darkness. "Maybe. I don't know," she answered tersely, trying to reconsider her point of view. The task Luc had set out to do was sure to be challenging, if not impossible. And he was a better man than most to leave his land for a cursed one. If anything he deserved her respect, not her cynicism. "What is it you need to do to break the curse?" she asked.

Luc took a deep breath before turning to her with a grimace. "I need to kill Draven."

10

The Questionable Quest

S tella paled as she stared at Luc in horror. So she was right after all. He *had* set out to do the impossible! Opening her mouth to protest, she was interrupted by the sudden sound of loud knocking. She whirled, staring at the front door as if hoping to see through it to the other side.

"Hide in the bedroom," she whispered, her gaze never leaving the door. Once she heard the bedroom door click shut behind her, she grabbed her sword and strode over to the heavier oak one. "Who is it?"

"It's Damian."

A gasp slipped past her lips. What was *he* doing here? He wasn't scheduled to come until tomorrow night. "You're a bit early, aren't you?"

"Something has happened. Open the door so we can talk."

Annoyed by his commanding tone, Stella failed to note the strain in his voice. "What is it? What's happened?"

"Open the door, Stella," he insisted. "Please," he added as an afterthought. "It's a matter of great urgency and I'd rather not discuss it through a damned door."

Stella pressed her forehead to the smooth wood, loath to let him enter. What would Damian do if he found Luc in her home? But if he had come to warn her of something, it would be unwise to dismiss him. Keenly conscious of the seconds that ticked by, she stalled as she deliberated.

"Stella," he urged impatiently. "Open the door, now."

With a heavy sigh, she did so reluctantly, but only wide enough to show her face. "There, the door is no longer between us. Now what is it you needed to say that was so urgent?"

Instead of answering, Damian gently but firmly pushed the door—and herself—back. When he walked in uninvited, Stella gaped at him. "I did not give you leave to enter."

Damian's eyes dragged over her from head to toe. "It's not as if you're indecent," he said, sounding almost disappointed.

Stella crossed her arms and glared at him. "Again I ask, what is it you needed to tell me? Say it and leave."

His eyes flashed. "Several people were killed not far from here."

Stella took in a sharp breath. "A Shade?"

Damian nodded stiffly.

"Then what are you doing here?" she admonished. "Shouldn't you be out hunting them with the other guards?"

"I came to warn you." His tone was sharp with irritation. "Lock your door, put out the lanterns and arm yourself. And under no circumstances are you to leave the cottage until I or another guard tells you it is safe to."

Stella nodded, feeling somewhat badly for being so uncooperative. Damian sighed as he turned toward the door, deepening her guilt. She could thank him for the warning, but it was too late now. So she said nothing at all as she watched him walk back out into the night.

Shutting the door, Stella stared at it blankly as grim thoughts assailed her. How many more would be killed before the night was through? How many mothers? Fathers? Children? The attacks were so unpredictable, so arbitrary. Her brother had been killed in the last one. Before that, twelve had been slain in one night. Sometimes weeks or months passed between attacks, sometimes mere days.

For this reason, the people of Darkwood lived in constant dread, never knowing if they would survive to see the next moonrise, and wondering which friend, neighbor, or loved one might never be seen again.

It was a bleak way of living. But it was what she and the rest of the forest dwellers were accustomed to. Life in Darkwood had always been brutal and brief. Which made it easy to believe that Noctum was indeed cursed—not only because of the darkness that smothered the land, but because of the evils it spawned.

"Stella? I heard what that man said." She turned to see Luc emerge from the bedroom, his handsome face etched with worry. "What is a Shade?"

Moving with purpose, Stella hurried to put out the fire in the fireplace and blew out each lantern, throwing them into complete darkness. Relying on memory alone, she lowered herself onto a chair before answering. "Noctum is a dangerous place, Luc. The darkness hides many sins, among the worst of them are the Shade."

"And what are the Shade exactly?" he asked, his voice drawing near.

"Vile creatures that strike from the shadows and leave corpses in their wake." She glanced around her, waiting for her eyes to adjust. "No one knows where they come from, or when they will attack. It's only when the body of a victim is found that we are alerted to their arrival."

"And that man who warned you, he's a soldier of some sort?" There was a note of keen interest in Luc's quiet voice.

"He's a member of the Shadow Guard, as my brother once was. They are tasked to protect and defend all forest dwellers from any danger, including the Shade."

"You seem to dislike him," Luc remarked, his statement sounding more like a query.

Stella was glad for the darkness that hid anything her face might reveal. "It's not that," she replied uneasily. "I could hardly welcome him in while you were hiding in the bedroom."

"I see," Luc replied, sounding as if he saw far more than she wanted.

"Anyway," she said, eager to move on. "You should know that the Shade are very difficult to kill, as they are far stronger and swifter than most men." She paused before saying the next part. "It was a Shade that killed my brother, Erik, nearly two months ago."

"I'm very sorry, Stella," Luc said, his voice soft with sympathy.

Stella nodded sadly. "He was a great warrior, one of the best. That should tell you how dangerous the Shade are."

"How does one kill a Shade?"

Her eyes had adjusted, so she could now make out the shapes in the room, including Luc's form seated in the chair across from her. "The head must be removed, its heart destroyed. If not, they can rise again."

"At least they're not invincible," he muttered under his breath.

"Unlike a certain king you wish to kill," she pointed out. "You can't possibly expect to succeed in such a mission."

"I must and I will."

Again, Stella was taken aback by the fire in his words, which was out of line with the calm demeanor he exuded. "But he's invincible! You yourself said so. How can he be killed?"

"There is a way," Luc said, rising to his feet. She watched as he walked over to the window, carefully pushing aside the curtain to look outside.

"How?" she asked.

"I can't share that with you."

Can't or won't? Stella wondered somberly. "I've seen Draven rip the heart out of a man's chest with his bare hand. Others have witnessed him knock a man's head off with just a swipe of his arm. The man is ruthless and terrifying. And worse, he's not alone. There are thirteen cities in Noctum, each one ruled by an immortal royal. None are as powerful as Draven, but if they were to band together, there would be no stopping them. Those thirteen have crushed countless rebellions and uprisings, brutally eliminated every opposition. All it's accomplished were harsher restrictions. No one has made an attempt in the last century."

"I know my task sounds like a fool's mission, but know this Stella...I am no fool."

Stella stared at him, his back still to her. From the faint moonlight that slipped through the curtain's thin opening, she could make out his tall, rigid silhouette. Luc looked resolved, a man intent on accomplishing what must be done.

"I don't think you a fool at all," she said softly.

Luc turned, and though she couldn't see the green of his eyes, she could feel them boring into her. "I'm glad because there's something I want to ask you."

"What's that?" she asked cautiously.

"I want to know if you'll help me."

"That isn't a question," Stella stated as her heart sank. *Help him?* It would essentially be helping him to his death. She didn't know if she could do that. She knew she didn't *want* to do it. It didn't matter that he'd been but a stranger only hours ago. She'd lost too much already. The thought of losing someone like Luc filled her with a profound sense of sorrow.

She heard him sigh. "Never mind. I ask for too much. You've done enough as it—"

"What sort of help?" she asked reluctantly.

Luc held his breath a moment, as if fearful she might withdraw her offer. "It will take some time to prepare and plan. I will need a place to stay while I do both."

"You wish to stay here?" she asked, her pulse skipping at the thought.

"You know this place better than I. You know the lay of the land, the way of its people, its customs. I will need your help to fit in, so I can draw near enough to Draven to kill him."

At once, her thrill of excitement fled as she was reminded of his purpose for staying. But if she were to turn him away, where would he go?

Luc came forward until he was standing right before her, swamping her with his summer scent and heat. "You want to free Noctum from the darkness, don't you?" he asked.

Before she could answer, the window behind him exploded in a shower of wood and glass.

11

The Shade Attack

Stella froze for half a heartbeat before lunging for her sword. But Luc had already seized it. Aided by the moonlight that now flooded in, she watched as he whirled—the blade spinning with him in a wide arc—to face the Shade that had crashed into the cottage. An inhuman shriek rent the night as the blade found purchase, slicing across the Shade's chest to leave a gaping wound that spilled black blood. The creature lurched backwards, rage shining in its reddened eyes. Luc charged, her blade a furious blur of motion in his deft hands. The Shade dodged and darted, its movements too quick to be natural. Suddenly aware that she was just standing there, she ran to Luc's sword, still hanging on the hook by the door.

"Watch out, Stella!"

She swung. The blade just missed the Shade, who twisted out of the way with uncanny agility. Fortunately, Luc was immediately upon it. With a mighty swing, he cleaved the creature's head from its neck, releasing a violent spray of black blood. Wasting no time, Stella then plunged Luc's sword straight through its heart. When she yanked it back out, it pulled away with a sickening sucking sound. Disgusted, she watched the headless body collapse to the floor.

"Was that a Shade?"

Stella looked up to meet Luc's gaze. He appeared perfectly at ease, while her heart was beating wildly within her. "Yes."

"I thought you said they were hard to kill."

"They are," she replied, looking at him in awe before returning her gaze to the creature. "Though this was my first time ever seeing one."

"They're hideous creatures."

They really were. Stella studied the Shade's pale, withered skin, its red eyes and sharp yellow teeth. When she recalled how it had moved and the way it had shrieked, she shuddered involuntarily. "We should bar the window somehow. There could me more of them."

At once, Luc headed for the large, heavy cupboard, which, despite his injured arm, he moved as if it weighed no more than a stone or two. How had he fought with his injury? Other questions swirled through her head, but now was not the time to ask them. First they had to make it through the night, for who knew how many more Shades were out there?

They switched swords and Luc posted himself by the barricaded window. Stella stayed by his side, keeping a nervous eye on the bedroom doors while doing her best to ignore the decapitated Shade lying nearby. Both bedrooms had windows, but there was nothing with which to barricade them. She could only hope that nothing would draw the foul creatures to the cottage.

For the next few hours, Stella barely dared to breathe. With their keen hearing, they had likely lured the Shade with their careless conversing. In the ponderous silence, she found herself becoming attuned to the man beside her—his soft breathing, his masculine scent, the mere inches that separated them. Considering the ease with which he'd dispatched the Shade, he really was a skilled warrior. Her estimation of him increased, as did her attraction.

"I hear something," Luc whispered, his sword poised for action.

Stella tensed at his pronouncement. They had survived one encounter with a Shade, but could they survive another? Maybe Luc could, but she doubted her chances.

Loud pounding sounded at the door, causing her heart to leap to her throat. "Open up, Stella. It's Garrett and Damian," Garrett shouted.

It was no Shade, but her panic remained. "Quick!" she frantically whispered to Luc. "Hide!"

Luc shot her a bewildered look before darting into Erik's room. Stella quickly glanced around to ensure no signs of Luc were visible before she opened the front door. As soon as the two men on the other side saw her, they shoved their way in.

"Are you alright, Stella?" Garrett asked, eyeing her anxiously while Damian immediately honed in on the beheaded corpse behind her. "There's blood all over you."

"I'm alright, Garrett. My blood runs red, remember?" She looked down with distaste at the black splatter that covered her.

"You did this?" Damian asked in astonishment, gesturing to the Shade. Garrett's eyes flew wide at the sight.

"I told you I could take care of myself," she replied, avoiding the question along with his gaze.

"You killed this Shade, all on your own?" Damian clarified, his eyes boring into her.

Stella refused to flinch, knowing Luc's safety was on the line. "Do you see anyone else here?" she challenged, evading his question yet again. She knew her irritation was uncalled for—he had every reason to doubt her—but the man had a way of inciting her.

Damian's gaze narrowed before leaving her face. When he headed for the bedrooms, it took everything in her not to hinder him. Fortunately, he went into her bedroom first. Finding nothing there, he then headed for the other. Stella didn't realize she'd been holding her breath until Garrett asked, "Are you certain you're alright, Stella?"

Tearing her gaze from the bedroom, she said, "I will be once this body is removed."

Garrett surveyed the damage with a grimace as Damian rejoined them. Stella avoided facing him, for fear he would see her anxiety. Only when he stooped to grab the Shade's clawed feet, did she allow herself to breathe a silent sigh of relief. Luc hadn't been spotted!

"I assume the danger is past then?" she asked, as Garrett opened the door for his partner.

"There's been no attack in the last few hours, so this and the one Damian killed must have been the only Shades responsible," Garrett replied, moving to pick up the Shade's head with a look of disgust.

So Damian had killed a Shade that night as well.

While Garrett helped him dispose of the body and head, Stella began to sweep up the debris that littered her cottage. The damage was extensive. She picked up broken items and righted upturned furniture, then inspected the gouged floors with dismay. But it was the black blood covering them that bothered her most. She feared the stains were permanent. And there was still the broken window to worry about. How would she afford to fix it? The smell of smoke reached her nostrils. Hurrying to the door, she flung it wide open to find a fire burning at the edge of the clearing, its flickering flames throwing orange-yellow light on the two men watching over it.

She was reminded of Erik's funeral pyre.

When Garrett and Damian returned, Stella was scrubbing furiously at the stained floors. Her back ached and the skin of her fingertips were raw, but she was determined to leave no evidence of the Shade behind.

"Stella, stop," Damian ordered, snatching the worn rag from her hands. "It will never come out."

It was the wrong thing to say. A deep sense of bleakness suddenly filled her, bringing with it an oppressive weight that seemed to crush both her spirit and her soul. The blood stains would remain, ever reminding her of danger and death. In Darkwood, the two were constant and inescapable. No place was safe, not even her own home.

More than ever, Luc's description of Aurelia—a land full of light and color—filled Stella with profound longing. In Aurelia, there were no such things as Shades or immortal royals. It possessed none of the dangers that plagued Noctum. What if Luc was right about the curse? More importantly, what if he really could lift it? With his golden skin, vibrant green eyes, and brilliant smile, he was the very picture of bright promise.

Faint hope flickered, a stubborn spark amid her deep-seated doubts. The question was, would she help Luc or not? Fear for him had her wanting to refuse, but it was clear he would try to lift the curse whether she aided him or not.

"But I can paint over it, so you'll never have to see it again," Garrett offered, snapping her out of her thoughts.

"Thank you." Fully aware of the dark eyes watching her, she bestowed Garrett with her most gracious smile. "I would appreciate that."

"You should probably stay elsewhere until your window is fixed," Damian said, his tone oddly cool.

"I see no need to," she replied, her tone matching his. "It's secure enough with the cupboard there."

Upon her mention of it, Garrett turned to study the heavy solid furniture blocking the window. "However did you move that across the room on your own?"

Stella shrugged, the careless gesture belying the sudden racing of her heart. "Perhaps the same way Bianca managed to lift that massive boulder off of her son's legs during that accident?"

Garrett placed both hands on the side of the cupboard and gave it a slight shove. It didn't move. He pushed harder. It still didn't budge. The third time, he pressed against it with his shoulder and finally succeeded in moving it a few inches. "That's impressive, Stella."

Damian shoved the cupboard back to cover the small gap that had been exposed, exerting considerably less effort.

"Show off," Garrett muttered, before turning back to her. "But Damian is right. I don't like the idea of you staying out here alone. I never did. I think it's time you moved to the Hollow."

"I'm no safer there than I am here," Stella argued. "When a Shade is on a rampage, no one is safe, whether they live alone or are surrounded by others."

Garrett shook his head in disagreement. "There's safety in numbers, Stella. Besides, Jenna would feel better knowing you were nearby."

"I can't," she replied, apologetic yet unwilling to yield.

"Why? Because you're so attached to this cottage?" Garrett asked gruffly. "If you stay, I fear you may die here." Then he added something that felt like a blow to the gut. "Erik asked me to watch out for you. After tonight's attack, I feel like I've failed him."

Again. Stella heard the word, though he didn't say it aloud.

"Of course you haven't," she assured him. "It's not your fault I'm so difficult and stubborn."

"Ah, she finally admits it," Damian said, without the slightest hint of humor.

Stella shot him a glare before addressing Garrett. "I'm a grown woman. If something happens to me, it will be through no fault of your own. I take full responsibility for my actions."

Her declaration was met with silent disapproval. Both men stared at her, and Stella fought the urge to shift uncomfortably. Garrett's dismay was hard to bear, but it was Damian's disappointment bordering on contempt that made her blood heat.

"Let her be, Garrett," he said, heading for the door. "There's no reasoning with the unreasonable."

Damian was gone before she could attempt a reply. Suppressing the urge to run after him and shout something rude at his back, Stella turned to Garrett instead, her anger dissipating.

"If you change your mind, let me know," Garrett said, gazing at her solemnly. "And I do hope you change your mind."

Stella watched as the door shut behind him, feelings of guilt and uncertainty threatening her resolve.

"They worry for you."

Turning, she saw that Luc had emerged from the bedroom. For a moment, she drank in the stunning sight of him, wishing she knew nothing of his impossible mission. For the first time in her life, she had found someone who thrilled her, who made her heart race and her breath quicken. For the first time in a while, life seemed worth living again. It was unfortunate Luc planned to throw away his own.

"Garrett was my brother's best friend and partner. Damian is his new partner. Both feel obligated to watch over me," she explained.

"Why *do* you choose to live alone, Stella?" Luc asked, studying her thoughtfully.

That was a difficult question to answer. There were several reasons, including the one Garrett had accused her of. She *was* attached to the cottage, and to the memories of those she had loved and lived with here. She was also a solitary creature by nature, content with her small circle of family and friends when not preferring her own company. There were too many people in the Hollow, too many eyes and ears. She preferred the solace of the empty woods, where she could hear the whisper of the trees or the call of the elusive snow leopard. But there was another reason, one she was loath to confess. For doing so would expose just how low she had reached. By living alone, she knew she courted danger. Perhaps, she even welcomed it.

Until now.

"You're fortunate that I do," she answered. "Otherwise, it would be very difficult for me to harbor you."

Luc's eyes widened slightly as her words sunk in. "You'll let me stay?"

"So long as you behave," she replied, as sternly as she could manage.

But Luc wasn't the least bit daunted. He responded with a broad grin, which lit up his entire face and caused a familiar tug at her heart. "For you, Stella, I'll do my best."

12

The Unlikely Accomplice

S tella held the shirt up to the fire, studying it intently. The dark green material was smooth and fine, the stitching seamless. Though odd in style and unusual in appearance, the shirt was clearly of high quality. She marveled at the feel of it between her fingers, the way it slid between her skin, so soft and thick. It was a shame the garment had been damaged.

"It's beyond salvaging," Luc remarked.

Stella turned to him in surprise. "You're awake," she replied, feeling sheepish for stating the obvious. "Did you sleep well?"

"Like the dead."

She didn't much like how he'd worded his answer, but was glad at least one of them had slept deeply. Stella herself had tossed and turned for hours, expecting another Shade to come bursting through her bedroom window at any moment.

"The wildcat never would've gotten me if I'd seen it," Luc said, still staring at his shirt.

"I've not seen material so fine, nor so well made," she remarked, suddenly self-conscious of her simple linen dress and the humble cottage they sat in. "Except possibly among the city dwellers."

"It's just clothing," he said, speaking as one who'd never had to worry about such things.

"If you plan to stay here long, we should probably alter the ones you're wearing." She set down the shredded shirt and studied the clothes Luc wore, shoving aside a sense of guilt. Her brother no longer needed his clothes. Would, in fact, never be able to wear them again. Besides, it would be challenging to try to procure men's clothing unnoticed. With her luck, it would be Damian who caught her making the attempt.

"You think no one will notice my *differences* if my clothes fit me properly?"

"Not if you powder your face and pretend to be mute."

Luc chuckled heartily at that until he realized she was in earnest. "You're serious?"

"Completely." She'd given the matter much thought during her restless night and decided it was the only thing that could possibly work. "Unless, of course, you intend to remain hidden in my cottage the entire time?"

"Well…no," he replied uncertainly.

"Then how did you plan to make your way about?" she asked with genuine curiosity.

"I thought if I stuck to the shadows…"

"Like a creeper? That will only make you more conspicuous," Stella said, with a shake of her head.

Luc laughed again. She'd never heard someone laugh so readily and freely before. It was a beautiful sound, one that made her heavy heart soar. "Not like a creeper, more like a mysterious figure."

Stella considered this. Luc *was* mysterious and intriguing and attractive. If she found him to be all these things and more, others certainly would as well. Jealousy reared its ugly head at the thought of some other girl sniffing around Luc. The emotion both startled and embarrassed her. She had no claim on the man, and certainly no right to feel jealous. Still, part of her wished she could keep Luc hidden after all. Though it was too late for that now. "I still think my idea is better."

"Powder my face and pretend to be mute?" Luc gave the suggestion some serious thought. "Yes, I suppose it will have to do," he conceded reluctantly.

Stella wondered if she should also suggest he shave his head and wear a scar on his face. She tried to picture both on him, but determined it would do little to detract from his overall appearance. "In the meantime, I might as well start on your clothes." She went to retrieve her sewing basket. "If you wouldn't mind standing by the fire."

"As you wish," Luc replied, moving to position himself directly before her.

Ignoring the way her pulse sped up, Stella took a cursory glance at his shirt before grabbing a pin. Then starting at the shoulders, she began to mark where she would take it in. It was impossible to avoid touching him, and therefore impossible not to notice the firmness of his body beneath the fabric. Perhaps now was as good a time as any to bring up the idea she'd come up with.

* * *

"So your friend is a historian? And he works at a secret library?" Luc clarified.

Stella focused on his face to keep from dropping her gaze to his chest. Then she turned her attention back to the shirt she held in her hands, still warm from his body. "That's right. He just started there, but he might have access to information that could help you."

"What sort of information?"

Stella shifted in her seat. "I don't know exactly."

Luc furrowed his brow in confusion.

"I'm not even supposed to know the library exists," she explained. "So I certainly have no idea what information is stored there."

"Exactly who is allowed to know about this library then?" he asked, perplexed.

"The master librarian, the historian and a number of the Shadow Guard."

"That's it?"

"As far as I know."

"But why?"

"According to Elias, the library before this one was discovered and destroyed because someone revealed its existence. That was nearly three-hundred years ago. To keep that from happening again, only a select few are privy to knowledge of the Repository—which is what they call the current library."

"Then how did you come to find out about it?" Luc asked. "Did your friend tell you?"

"No, I overheard my brother and his partner talking about it. Elias was quite upset that I knew about the Repository actually. Especially that I'd known of its existence before he did."

Luc pondered that for a moment before asking, "Am I right in guessing that Draven was responsible for destroying the last library?"

"None other," Stella confirmed, laying the garment down on her lap in defeat. She had managed only three stitches, too nervous and antsy to focus on the task at hand.

"Are you certain this friend of yours can be trusted?" Luc asked.

She met his wary gaze from across the room. "I'm certain. Along with his sister, Jenna, Elias has been my friend since we were children. I'd trust him with my life." This much was true. She was utterly confident that Elias would never betray them. What she doubted was whether he would actually agree to help them.

"But can I trust him with mine?" Luc asked.

Before she could answer, there was a knock on the door, followed by a pause then three raps in quick succession.

"It's him."

Luc jumped to his feet. "You didn't tell me he was coming now!"

"He's coming now," she said, tossing his shirt aside as she rose to get the door. Behind her, Luc hovered near Erik's bedroom, ready to flee if necessary.

She pulled the door open and was greeted by the sight of Elias's familiar, pleasant face. "You weren't followed, were you?" she asked, scanning the trees behind him.

"Of course not," her friend replied, slipping inside without waiting to be asked. "Now why all the secre—" The rest of his sentence died as soon as he caught sight of Luc.

Stella immediately shut the door. "This is why."

"Who is *he*?" Elias asked, gaping at the stranger before him.

"My name is Luc," the other man answered, leaning against the wall casually. To her dismay, she suddenly remembered that he was shirtless. This didn't seem to faze Luc, however, who watched Elias with wary eyes.

Elias startled upon hearing Luc's unusual accent. "Why does he sound like that? How does he *look* like that?" He was staring at the blatant display of Luc's tanned torso.

"Because I'm from a place called Aurelia, which is south of the Altous Mountains."

This time, Luc's reply rendered Elias speechless.

"Remember that fireball I told you about?" Stella prodded him.

"What about it?" Elias asked, his gaze never leaving Luc.

"It's how I arrived here," Luc said in reply, a corner of his mouth turned up in a bemused grin.

"I need to sit down," Elias declared, making his way to the couch. He plopped down onto the cushioned seat, looking bewildered as he turned from Luc to Stella and back again.

Stella sat down in the stuffed chair across from him. "Do you believe us?" she asked tentatively.

"Believe you? Look at him!" Elias waved a hand in Luc's direction. "His skin...his accent. He's most definitely *not* from Noctum. Where did you find him?"

"Actually, I found her," Luc piped.

Elias merely stared at him before turning back to Stella, waiting. "Several leagues from here," she answered, not bothering to elaborate. She had no desire to reveal the grotto nor the circumstances of her meeting with Luc. She hoped *no one* ever found out she had been naked at the time. "But what's more important is why he came."

Elias stilled. Then he squared his shoulders, as if preparing himself for what was about to be revealed. "Why *did* you come?" he asked, addressing Luc directly for the first time.

Luc glanced at Stella. There was nervousness there, but it was quickly replaced by determined resolution. Launching into his account, Stella sat at the edge of her seat, carefully gauging Elias's reaction. Everything hinged on whether he believed what Luc said about Noctum being cursed. If he thought it could be broken, then she was almost certain he would lend his aid. But while his face revealed a whole gamut of emotions—from astonishment to doubt to bewilderment and even a hint of excitement—in the end, she couldn't tell if Elias was dubious or if he had been convinced.

It didn't help that he remained mute once Luc concluded, having retreated deep into his thoughts. Luc appeared concerned as well, but was content to let Elias muse.

"Well?" Stella prodded, when she could stand the suspense no longer.

Elias blinked, then frowned as he stared at the floor. "What is *that?*"

Confused, Stella glanced down to see that he had noticed the black blood splattered on her floorboards. "Garrett didn't tell you?"

"Garrett doesn't tell me a lot of things," Elias said, his gaze finding the cupboard that blocked her shattered window. "What happened here, Stella?"

"A Shade broke into the cottage," she admitted with a grimace. "But we can talk about that later. Right now, we need to know if you'll be able to help Luc."

Elias stared at her as if she'd lost her mind. "A Shade?" he exclaimed in disbelief. "You're saying a *Shade* broke in?"

"Elias," she pleaded, begging him with her eyes.

He shook his head in exasperation. "I don't know if I can help him." She felt her heart sink. "But I'm certainly willing to try." And like that, it lifted again. "But tell me…are you saying that is Shade blood on your floor?!"

"Luc beheaded it," Stella said with candor. "That's why there's so much of it."

"Also because you stabbed it in the heart, remember?" Luc added.

Stella shuddered. How could she forget?

Elias gaped at them. "You killed a Shade? Right here?"

"As far as Garrett and Damian know, I alone killed it," Stella said, recalling Damian's skepticism. "They don't know about Luc. Only you do, and for now, I think it best it stay that way."

Elias frowned at that. "How do you plan to keep him hidden? Between the two of them, Garrett and Damian are here nearly every night."

"He can easily hide in Erik's old room."

Elias appeared doubtful.

"So," Stella began, knowing no other way to bring up the matter but to just dive right in. "What convinced you?"

"What convinced me of what?"

"To help Luc."

Elias studied the man in question. "No one is supposed to know about Aurelia. Yet not only does he know about it, he comes from there."

"You know about Aurelia?" Stella asked in amazement. "Then did you already know about the curse?"

Elias shook his head. "Nor did I know about Stavan Arthanos. The only reason I'm familiar with Aurelia is because there is a copy of the Midland map at both Nyxus and the Repository."

Stella frowned. "What is Midland?"

"It's the name of the continent to which both Aurelia and Noctum belong to," Luc answered, before turning to Elias. "Do you have

102

information on Draven?"

"There are several journals worth of observations and reports on him," Elias revealed. "But I've yet to read them…or even see them."

"But you can get to them?" Stella asked, just as eager as Luc to find out everything she could about the king—particularly his weaknesses and vulnerabilities. If he had any.

Elias nodded, but he looked worried. "I can. But that particular information is restricted, which means I would need to obtain permission from the master librarian to access it."

"Surely he'll grant it?" Stella remarked.

"She," Elias said.

"What?" Stella replied, confused.

"The master librarian is a woman."

Stella stared at him, confusion turning to indignation. "What?"

Elias quickly turned to Luc. "Is there any particular information you seek?"

Luc shrugged, but his countenance was grim. "I just need to know how to get close enough to Draven to kill him."

Elias's expression turned troubled. Did he also think Luc attempted the impossible? "I'll see what I can do to get the information you need," he replied. "Stella, if I could have a word with you in private."

Standing at the edge of the clearing, Stella studied her cottage in the near distance. With its warm lantern light spilling from the windows, it promised warmth and welcome, a safe haven in the dark wood. She knew better. "You have concerns, don't you?"

"Yes, I'm concerned!" Elias exclaimed, shaking his head as he crossed his arms. "You're a lone woman with a strange man. A strange, shirtless man. Why is Luc shirtless?"

Stella's face burned hot with embarrassment. "You saw his injured arm, didn't you? His shirt was torn, so I was altering one of Erik's when you arrived. Also, the clothes he had on were too unusual."

"Oh," Elias replied, looking slightly sheepish yet relieved. "Though he'll hardly blend in even wearing your brother's clothes."

"I'm working on that. What I was waiting for you to bring up is the fact that Draven cannot be killed."

"That was my next concern."

"He claims he knows of a way to kill him, but he won't reveal how."

"That's annoying," he replied, scratching his chin. "But there must be a reason why he won't say. In which case, I suppose all we *can* do is help him find a way to get close enough to do the deed."

"Why are you willing to help?" Stella asked, genuinely curious.

"Isn't it obvious?" Elias returned, flabbergasted.

She shook her head. "I wasn't sure you would even believe him. Not without proof."

"Stella, Luc himself is the proof! No one like him has ever been seen before. And I may not have known about the curse, but I've always felt deep down in my bones that Noctum is not normal. That life here isn't as it should be."

Stella looked at him in surprise. "I never knew you felt that way."

Elias quirked his lip, but there was no humor in it. "You should know, because you've always felt it, too."

"But you never said anything." Her tone was accusing.

"Who was I to complain, Stella?" Elias said softly. "Despite what I felt, I didn't dare. Not when you had lost so much and I...haven't. I've seen how it weighs on you, the darkness and the loss. My complaining would have been..."

Insensitive. And Elias was anything but that. "It would have been wrong," he finished. "So I did my best to be content instead."

Not just content, Stella thought, but cheerful. It wasn't just his flaming red hair that made Elias stand out, he was a light wherever he went. It was why so many people were drawn to him, because his light also carried warmth.

"And now?" Stella asked.

"Things have changed."

Because of Luc. With Luc, things had changed because change itself was now a possibility.

"You risk your position as historian, you know," she gently reminded him.

Elias's hazel eyes gleamed, and in them she saw what she, too, felt for the first time in a long while. Hope. "To bring light back to Noctum, it would be a small sacrifice."

13

The Secret Passage

"What now?" Luc asked, after Elias had left.

"I should probably finishing altering your shirt," Stella replied, still keenly aware of his bare chest.

"But?"

She met his gaze in surprise. How had he known she was hemming? That was Jenna's gift. "But there's something I should show you first."

A moment later, Stella was kneeling before the thick, heavy rug that lay between the couch and the stuffed chairs. She lifted the edge and rolled it back.

"A hiding place," Luc marveled, staring at the faint outline of a door. It was well concealed, its seams hidden within the wooden planks of the floor.

"No one outside of my family knew about it. But you should in case you need to use it."

"How does it open?" he asked, furrowing his brow. There was no visible knob or handle.

Stella pressed down on one of the planks. There was a small click and a three foot by three foot section popped up slightly at one end, revealing a gap wide enough to slip her fingers beneath. "Come on, follow me," she said, pulling it up.

Directly beneath the door was an earthen cavern Stella's grandda

106

had dug out when the cottage was first built. She jumped in and Luc jumped in after her. At only six feet high, the ceiling was too low for Luc, forcing him to crouch.

"It's not just a hiding place," Stella said, turning to her left. "Do you feel that draft?" Cool air whispered against her face, gently ruffling her hair. "There's a passageway here as well. It leads to the center of a small copse of elms just beyond the clearing to the west."

"I don't understand," Luc said. "Why didn't we use this during the Shade attack?"

Stella hesitated before answering. "I wasn't ready to reveal it at the time," she admitted.

"Then thank you for trusting me now."

Stella shifted uncomfortably. It had been wrong not to use the hiding place when they needed it. If Damian knew, he would say she had been foolish, taking unnecessary risks with her life. The troubling thing was that he would be right. Worse, she had risked not only her own life, but Luc's as well.

Wallowing in a bout of self-recrimination, Stella was unaware at first of the silence that had fallen. But in time, she became conscious of the sounds of quiet breathing, both from her own mouth and from Luc's. The underground space was small, but somehow it felt smaller. Why was Luc standing so close?

Stella cleared her throat. "Why don't you try out the passageway while I return to your shirt?"

"Good idea," Luc replied, clearing his throat as well.

Several hours later, Stella had completed her alteration of both Luc's shirt and pants. She waited while he dressed in the bedroom, preparing a light meal that consisted of more dried meat, oatcakes and a handful of nuts. When he stepped back into the room, Stella held back a wistful sigh. Now that the clothes fit him perfectly, there was nothing to detract from his good looks.

"Well, do I look like a proper forest dweller now?" Luc asked, spreading his arms wide. "Do you think I blend in?"

Stella shook her head. He would stand out wherever he went, be it Aurelia or Noctum or anywhere else. "Not quite. Let's try and put some powder on your face."

Unfortunately, the powder didn't work. It was too thin to hide his tanned hue, and using a heavy hand only made it cake, especially in the lines of his face. "I'll have to think of something else," she sighed. "In the meantime, you can use Erik's cloak. It's in the trunk in his room."

"Did you want me to get it now?" Luc asked, noting her expectant look.

"If you want to see Caligo, then yes," she replied.

* * *

Stella first started watching over the walls of Caligo after her da died. Back then, as on many nights since, sleep had been hard to come by. Watching the city had been a means of distraction, a way to pass the time while she tried—but failed—to forget her woes. And then her ma had died a year later, hurling her down a path so dark she had nearly lost her way. Caligo's lights became her lifeline, one she clung to in desperation lest the darkness consume her. Like a moth to a flame, it had drawn her. And time and again, she'd had to remind herself of its danger.

Tonight, however, the city lights no longer seemed so alluring. Luc had given her hope that something brighter and better existed. Aurelia—the land of sun and color and warmth. His descriptions of it had put to words the desires of her heart, desires she hadn't known how to name. To discover that they actually existed evoked a deep, almost painful, yearning within her. What were Caligo's tarnished silver torches and gaudy brass lanterns compared to rainbows and brilliant skies? How she longed to see them! To walk upon grass as green as Luc's eyes, and sink into warm cerulean seas with him.

Stella felt a rush of heat climb up her cheeks at the unbidden thought. She stole a glance at Luc sitting on a branch slightly below her, his gaze fixed on the city beyond. Sighing, both in relief and disappointment, she turned to study the city as well.

"You say that all of the cities are walled?" he asked.

"Yes."

"Do you know why?"

"To keep us out."

"Do you mean to say you're not allowed to enter the city...ever?"

"Not unless you're unfortunate enough to catch Draven's eye," Stella replied.

Luc glanced at her sharply. "What do you mean?"

"Our king has a penchant for pretty faces," she replied grimly. "He collects women like trophies. No, that's not right. Trophies at least are valued. He uses them until he grows tired of them, then he moves on."

Stella saw Luc's jaw clench at that. "Are the people inside able to leave?"

"A few have been seen traveling to the other cities, but this is rare."

"Why is that?"

"As much as they may fear Draven or the other royals, I suspect they fear the forest more. Not only are there Shades to worry about, there are wild animals and murderous brigands hidden here as well. Aside from the soldiers, the city dwellers are a soft, pampered lot. I think the royals purposefully keep them that way. To make them more...pliable."

"Sheep for the slaughter," Luc murmured.

Stella nodded in agreement. "For all their wealth and privilege, I never envied those from the city. Not that it's so great living in the forest, but at least here we're not under Draven's ever watchful eye."

"Does he leave you alone?"

If only. "Not entirely. At least two times a year, he sends his soldiers to do a census of those who live in the forest. The ones who comply are compensated by coin for their cooperation."

"And those who do not?"

"If they're caught, they can be thrown into the king's dungeon or, worse, brought before the king himself."

"You never comply, do you?" Luc asked.

"How do you know?" Stella asked, glancing at him.

"Because with a face like yours, Draven would certainly want you."

She turned away from his admiring gaze, feeling conflicted. She was pleased he thought her attractive, but the very thing he admired was a hazardous liability, as his own remark attested.

"Three nights a month, when the moon is at its brightest, a market is set up right here in the Killing Fields," Stella intoned, staring at the spot where Draven had taken the poor, young girl. "It's the only time forest and city dwellers ever mingle with one another. At the last market I attended, Draven was there."

"The Killing Fields? That's an ominous name for a marketplace," Luc remarked.

"The market itself is known as the Luna Market, but this field where it's held has been the site of numerous battles over the centuries. Though it would be more appropriate to call them slaughters rather than battles. No one stands a chance against Draven and his royals. This field has been drenched with the blood of thousands of forest dwellers, while they continue to live their long unnatural lives."

A cloud passed over Luc's face, but it was gone swiftly. "When does the next market take place?"

"Nine nights from now."

"Then I hope you find a way of disguising me by then," he said. "Because I plan to attend that market."

* * *

Stella was just about to step into the clearing when Luc stopped her short. With one hand on her arm and a finger to his lips, he silently pointed in the direction of the cottage. Perplexed but curious, she followed his lead as he peered at her home from behind a tree, wondering what he had heard that she hadn't.

When she saw Damian standing at her front door, she wanted to kick herself. How could she have forgotten? Tonight was a hunting night! On the heels of that thought, another one quickly followed. Anxiety rose in her chest as she began to search the immediate area.

And then she heard a low growl behind her.

Stella whirled to find Dartan fixing his intimidating gaze on Luc, while from her rear she could hear Damian making his approach. "When I distract the dog, run," she urged Luc. "Then when it's safe, use the passage to get inside the cottage." She waited for him to nod, then she removed her cloak and promptly tossed it over the hound's head. Wasting no time, Luc took off, disappearing just as Damian came on the scene.

Seeing his hound struggle to untangle himself, Damian turned to her in exasperation. "Why do you keep molesting my dog?"

"He keeps molesting me! He's lucky I didn't stick him through with my sword instead," Stella retorted, grabbing her cloak and shaking it out. Disgusted by the slobber smearing it, she draped it over her arm and strode to her cottage.

Damian and Dartan followed, though the latter scanned his surroundings, no doubt wondering where its lost prey had vanished to.

"Where were you?" Damian asked, not bothering to hide his impatience. "I nearly left. I'd been waiting for nigh on an hour."

"I'm sorry. I forgot you were coming."

"You've never forgotten before. What could have possibly distracted you?"

Another man, she thought snidely.

"Stella?" Damian prodded, when she failed to reply. "What is it you find so amusing?"

"Nothing," she said, wiping the smirk that had crept onto her face. When she was several feet from the cottage, Stella noticed a horse and cart half-hidden in the shadows of the trees. Not one of the tall, swift steeds reserved for the king and his men, but a squat beast of burden. "What is that?"

"Materials to fix your window."

She looked at him in surprise, her coolness thawing. But just as quickly wariness settled in. "I won't be able to pay you back anytime soon."

"Did I ask for repayment?" Damian replied.

Stella considered protesting further, but decided against it. Damian would fix her window whether she wanted him to or not, so it was no use arguing. And the sooner he did, the sooner Luc could return. With this thought in mind, she hurried inside.

The last time Damian stepped foot in her cottage was the night he had caught her off guard in the garden. Since then, she had taken to limiting their interactions to the front door. There, he would hand her some meat, leaving the skin or skins outside to dry, and she would pass him a rag and bar of soap. Occasionally she would offer him a beverage as well. Tonight, however, he followed her in without hesitation, first to bring in his catch of the night, then to bring in the materials for the window.

Stella worried her lower lip. What would Luc do while he waited? Out loud, she asked, "How long will it take to repair the window?"

Damian pinned her with an unsettling look. "Why, is there some place else you need to be?"

"I'm just curious."

"However long it takes," he said, his gaze never wavering from her face. "It depends on the extent of the damage."

"Alright," she replied, compliant for once—even if she wasn't alright at all. She only hoped Damian wouldn't see through her lie. Though from the careful way he was watching her, he was already suspicious.

14

The Wrong Invitation

There was nothing more uncomfortable than having someone in your home who wasn't welcome. Especially if that unwelcomed someone was doing you a favor.

In danger of being driven to distraction—by either worrying about Luc or watching Damian with growing impatience—Stella sought some means to keep herself busy. Glancing at the bucket he had brought in, she reached for a cutting board and laid it on the table. Then grabbing her salt cellar, she sprinkled coarse gray salt on top of it. She might as well prepare the new batch of meat. Thanks to Damian, she nearly had enough cured and stocked to last through the approaching winter. Taking a leg of venison from the bucket, she began to roll it onto the salt, slow and methodical. After making sure every bit of surface was covered, she speared it onto the metal hook that hung inside the large cupboard, now pushed back to its original position. Then she grabbed another leg, ready to repeat the process. She was on her fourth cut of meat when Damian finally broke the silence between them.

"The Winter Solstice is five nights away."

"It is," Stella agreed, glancing at his back, which was strained with the effort of pushing the window casing into place. She swiftly glanced away. Why was he mentioning the Winter Solstice?

"Umbria usually has a party to celebrate it."

"We celebrate it in Darkwood, too." Though she wasn't one for parties, Jenna had convinced her to go the previous year. It had been a lovely event—magical and mysterious—but she knew she would not be attending again.

"I was hoping you would accompany me."

Stella nearly dropped the flank she held in her hands. She stared at Damian's back in surprise. "Why?" she asked, when he continued to hammer away at the window casing.

Damian stopped to look at her, the hammer in his hand. "Because I'd like you to be at my side."

Because he wanted a new conquest. "I can't," she said, shaking her head as she continued her task.

"Can't or won't."

"Both," she answered tersely.

"Why not?" he asked, with unusual calm. "At least give me a reason."

"Because I don't like you, alright?" she admitted with candor. "There, does that suffice?"

Damian laid the hammer down then stalked toward her, making Stella's eyes go wide. Her breath caught as he stopped only inches away, but she refused to retreat in fear. Holding her ground, she gazed up at him in defiance, trying not to be intimidated by how he towered over her. "You don't like me," he said, his tone dangerous, seductive. "And yet your breath hitches whenever I draw near." She glared, slowly releasing her breath. "You don't like me," he continued, his voice pitched lower. "Yet your cheeks redden whenever you catch me staring at you. You don't like me and yet"—he reached out to stroke her face—"my touch makes you shiver." Stella was mortified when her body did just that, betraying her. "You may not like me, Stella, but you can't deny that you're attracted to me."

Furious, she recoiled from him, overcome with mortification. "I can and I will," she retorted. "You may have looks, but you're also arrogant, annoying and aggravating. Others may be willing to overlook these fatal flaws, but not me. Now please go. You're no longer welcome in my home."

Damian backed away, allowing her room to breathe. "I'll go, Stella." His voice stiff yet resigned. "But I will be back."

She watched him leave, wondering if he meant it as a promise or a threat.

* * *

Stella was still standing by the table, troubled by what had just transpired when she heard the sound of soft knocking. It was coming from the floor, however, rather than the front door.

Luc!

Running and falling to her knees, she lifted the edge of the rug to open the door. Luc's golden head promptly popped into view, followed by the rest of his long, lean body.

"Were you down there long?" she asked, watching as he brushed leaves and debris from his clothes.

"Long enough to overhear a very interesting exchange between you and a certain Shadow Guard," he admitted.

Stella groaned, embarrassed all over again. "Well, never mind that. I'm sorry about what happened. I had no idea he would stay so long."

"The man is smitten with you," Luc remarked. "Arrogant though he is."

"What makes you say that?" she asked uneasily.

"Isn't it obvious? He goes out of his way to look out for you. He came to warn you about the Shade then returned to make sure you were alright. And just now he was working to repair your window. There's also the meat and skins he brought you."

"The hunting is part of our arrangement."

"What arrangement?" Luc asked.

"He hunts for me, and in return, I'm to make him a set of armor."

Luc glanced at the nearly finished armor in the corner. "Is that his then?"

"No, that one is Garrett's. Once I finish it, I begin work on Damian's."

"That explains the hunting," he said. "But what about everything else?"

Stella shrugged uncomfortably. "Damian is a known philanderer. I suspect he just wants to ravish me." She could feel the weight of Luc's gaze, but she refused to meet his eyes. Instead she grabbed the bucket of fresh meat and carried it to the hearth. "Are you hungry?"

"Famished," Luc declared.

Relieved, she threw herself into cooking him the tastiest stew she could make.

* * *

"That was amazing!" Luc declared, leaning back in his chair. "I swear I've never tasted venison so good."

"That's your recently famished stomach talking," she replied, secretly delighted.

"It's the truth," he insisted, gazing at her in bewilderment. "How is someone like you not already married?"

Stella flinched, dismayed by the unwelcome reminder. "You're not married either."

"How do you know I'm not?"

Stella felt as if the air had been punched from her lungs. She hadn't seen a ring on his finger, but perhaps they did things differently in Aurelia. "Are you?" she asked, wondering why she hadn't considered the possibility.

"No, I'm not married," he said, solemnly. Then he smiled, chasing away whatever sadness she thought she'd seen. "But I'm not nearly as much of a prize as you. I don't possess your many skills for one.

The only thing I'm good with is a sword."

Stella couldn't help wondering if he was being modest or if he truly underestimated his appeal. "Here in Darkwood, being good with a sword is the most valued skill a man can possess. Shadow Guards are highly esteemed and they earn more coin than any other trade." Though their life-expectancy was also the shortest.

"That's very interesting," Luc remarked. "But you never answered my question."

"What question?" she asked, feigning ignorance.

"How are you still unmarried?"

"I've had offers for my hand," she replied with a shrug.

"How many?"

"Several."

"Come now," Luc urged. "Give me a number."

Stella grimaced as she sighed. "There were five that I recall."

"Five!" Luc appeared both bemused and horrified. "What was wrong with all of them?"

None of them were you. The thought slipped out before she could stop it. It was foolish and reckless, she had no business thinking such a thing. And yet there it was. "I just couldn't find myself loving any of them," she confessed.

Luc pondered that, his eyes going distant for a moment. "Just remember that love isn't always a lightning strike. Sometimes it's a gentle rain that washes your doubts and fears away."

"Who told you that?" Stella asked, looking at him in surprise.

Luc eyes dimmed, his tone wistful. "Someone I once knew."

15

The Historian's Request

I*t was done, finally!*

Stella studied the armor with deep satisfaction. It had taken her longer than usual to finish, but only because she had added and changed certain details to improve on the design. Among them were a higher collar to better cover the neck, an extra layer of leather to pad the back and chest, and the inclusion of built-in sheaths to tuck daggers in, eliminating the need for a cumbersome belt or harness. Compared to the last armor she had made Garrett, this one was more protective yet still streamlined. She couldn't wait to reveal it to him.

Stella inclined her head at a sound outside her door. Laying the armor on her bed, she went out to the main room of the cottage, shutting the bedroom door behind her. To her surprise, she saw Elias standing there with Luc.

"I knew it was him because of the secret knock," Luc said, looking apologetic. "And you were in your room so I wasn't sure if I should bother you."

"What if someone had seen you?"

"No one could have seen," Elias answered for him. "He barely opened the door a crack, and when he was certain it was me, he stepped back as I slipped in."

Stella still thought Luc had taken an unnecessary risk, undoubtedly because he was eager to find out what Elias had gathered. "Have a seat," she said to her friend, gesturing to one of the chairs near the rug that hid the secret passageway. "I honestly didn't expect you back so soon." It had only been two nights since he was last at her cottage. What information had he gathered since then?

Elias sat down, running a hand through his red locks, leaving them unkempt. Then she noticed the dark circles beneath his eyes. He must've exhausted himself in his search for information. Stella sat at one end of the couch while Luc took the other. "What did you find out?" he asked Elias.

"That nothing is ever as it seems." Elias said solemnly.

"What are you talking about Elias?" she asked, a frisson of dread running through her.

"Remember how we used to wonder why every city was walled?" Stella nodded, remembering the answer she had given Luc. *To keep us out.* "We suspected it was to protect the citizens of the city," Elias said. "But it seems that in reality it's to keep the citizens corralled."

"But what about the Luna Market?" she pointed out.

"It gives the illusion of freedom," Elias replied. "But I'm certain you've noticed how many Nighthawks guard the market. And other than the market, they are never allowed to go anywhere else."

"But Stella says that on occasion some travel between the cities," Luc remarked.

"Rarely and always escorted by guards. They—and by they I mean librarians current and past—suspect the city dwellers don't travel by choice. Rather they think it's a transaction or agreement of sorts between the royals."

Anger rose within Stella at the thought of people being offered or traded as commodities. "How were the city dwellers chosen? I know it happened long ago, but do you know the reason?"

Elias shook his head. "I don't know the how, but I do know the why." Suddenly, his hazel eyes looked haunted. "Once I tell you, you'll be glad to live outside the city walls instead of within them. You see…" He cringed. "Draven and his royals, they're just like the Shade. They drink blood to live."

Stella gave an involuntary shudder as his revelation sunk in. "Are you certain? There's never been any evidence of such a thing."

"It's not something they willingly reveal. In fact, they take great pains to keep it hidden."

"Then how do you know?" she insisted.

"There have been witnesses."

Stella's eyes widened. "Do you mean to say there are spies inside the city?"

"Yes, and you can't breathe a word of it to anyone," Elias said grimly. "By telling you, I don't just risk punishment, I risk execution. You can imagine how dangerous it is to be a spy in Caligo. Protecting them is paramount."

It was sobering to think how much Elias himself was risking. She looked at him with both worry and gratitude. "I swear on my life I will never speak of it," she assured him.

"Nor will I," Luc vowed.

"So the city dwellers," Stella ventured. "The royals use them as a…food source?"

"Yes," Elias confirmed. "And we believe they're responsible for the Shade somehow."

"They are," Luc said, with startling certainty.

Both Stella and Elias turned to him in surprise. "How do you know?" Elias asked.

"Because Draven and his royals are vampyres."

* * *

Stella and Elias listened in morbid fascination as Luc explained what a vampyre was, weaving a tale so horrifying Stella wished she could unhear it. It was terrible enough knowing that Draven and the royals were immortal, but to realize they were demons made her want to run from the house screaming. Then Luc shared what he suspected about the Shade, and Stella truly felt sick. Her gaze sought Elias's, hoping to find comfort and strength. What she found was the same stark fear that twisted in her own gut.

Noctum wasn't just cursed. Noctum was a nightmare of Draven's making.

"You're saying the Shade were once human?" Elias asked, shaking his head as if unable or unwilling to believe it.

"Our records tell of certain people whose blood did not react well to vampyre venom. These victims took on the worst of the vampyre traits, exhibiting extreme violence and bloodthirst without the control or restraint."

"Why are you only telling us all this now?" Stella asked, too overwhelmed to be upset. "When I first told you about the Shade, you said nothing. You knew about Draven and the royals and yet you made no mention of them being vampyres until now. Why?"

"You must understand, everything I've told you was gleaned from texts that are three thousand years old. Vampyres were nothing more than a myth. Draven and his royals were only ever legends. Having never seen either before, I wanted to reserve judgment on whether the accounts were true or not. As for the Shade, you made no mention of them drinking blood, so I thought they might be another manifestation of the curse. But after hearing what Elias shared..."

"You're now certain," Stella supplied.

Luc nodded somberly. "It would answer your question, Stella, about how city dwellers were chosen. If I'm right, then the ones who live in the city are those whose blood has no adverse reaction to vampyre venom."

"If that's true then why are the Shade still created?" Elias asked.

"Because," Stella piped, her words seething in anger. "Draven doesn't care enough to restrain himself, not when it comes to indulging himself. And if a Shade happens to be created, he just unleashes it in the forest where he doesn't have to worry about it attacking his precious blood supply."

"Hellfire, I think you're right, Stella," Elias said in a horrified tone. "The Shade, Garrett says they're usually female."

Silence fell as they each retreated into their own troubled thoughts. Stella thought about the Shade she and Luc had just killed, whose blood still stained her floors. Could that have been the innocent young girl Draven had snatched from the market?

Her stomach turned.

"Do you still believe you can kill Draven and lift the curse?" Elias's question pulled her back. Her friend looked dubious, and she couldn't blame him. The hope she had allowed to flare was barely a sputter now.

But Luc was as determined and resolute as ever. She could see it in the gleam of his emerald eyes. "Yes," he answered. "But you've yet to tell me how I can get near him."

Elias's shoulders fell. "About that...I have a bit of bad news."

Stella sighed. Why should she be surprised? When was the news ever good?

"What is it?" Luc asked, his face pinched.

"It seems I don't have permission to access the restricted section for at least another year."

An exclamation of frustration bubbled to Stella's lips.

"But," Elias continued, before she could erupt. "I have an idea of how to access it anyway."

"How?" Luc asked, leaning forward eagerly.

"Moira almost never leaves the Repository, but she will five nights from now."

"What is happening five nights from now?" Luc asked.

Stella was still mulling over the master librarian's name, trying to picture a face to go with it, when she absently answered, "The Winter Solstice."

Elias nodded. "Moira plans to attend the celebration and expects me to be there, too. I thought to make an appearance then slip back to the Repository."

"Is it really that easy?" Luc asked, frowning. "Won't the restricted area be under lock and key or something?"

"Yes, but I know where the key is kept. It never leaves the Repository. The hardest part will be getting past the guards, but I have an idea for that."

"Do you need our help?" Luc asked eagerly, itching for action.

"I do. I need you to keep an eye on Moira, to make sure she stays at the celebration for as long as possible."

"We can probably keep an eye on her, but how are we supposed to keep her from leaving?" Stella asked.

"I don't know, but I'll need as much time as I can get to search for and gather information. It may be my only opportunity."

"We'll figure something out," Luc said with a confidence she didn't possess.

Elias filled them in on all the details they needed to plan for the Winter Solstice and Stella listened dutifully. But it wasn't until he was gone that she fully comprehended what she'd agreed to. Damian had asked her to the Winter Solstice and she had turned him down. But now she would be attending it with Luc.

16

The Hidden Agenda

Stella was well and truly panicked. The Winter Solstice was in exactly five nights, leaving her that much time to make suitable outfits for her and Luc, along with the masks to go with them. And there was still the small matter of finding a solution to hide Luc's tanned skin.

"I need to go to the market," she announced.

Luc frowned. "But last night you said it wasn't for another nine nights."

"Not the Luna Market, Darkwood's Market. It's held twice a week and"—she glanced at the carved wooden clock on the mantel—"tonight it opens in two hours." She began to gather what goods she hadn't yet sold and stuffed them into a sack. She would need more coin to purchase fabric and other materials.

"I'd like to come."

Stella's head snapped up. "But you have no disguise yet."

"I'll don the cloak and keep my distance. I need to learn the lay of the land if I'm to navigate my way through these woods. I can't always rely on you to guide me."

"I suppose you're right," she agreed. "But don't you think you should wait until I find a way to conceal your skin?"

"I can't wait, Stella. I'm not used to being cooped up indoors. I'm not used to inaction. If you leave, I won't know what to do with myself."

Stella nodded, but she still felt uneasy. Luc was taking a risk, but she could hardly prevent him from leaving if he wanted to. He was a grown man, a warrior. And he wasn't so much asking her permission as he was informing her of his intentions. "Well, it *is* nearly winter, so you shouldn't stand out too much with a hood on. But you'll need to hide your hands somehow."

"Do you have a pair of gloves I can borrow?" Luc asked.

"Fortunately, I do."

Not long afterward, Stella was exiting the cottage to make her way to the market. The night was crisp and clear. Up above, the stars bore down like needles piercing the black sky. She grasped at the neck of her cloak, pulling it close. Soon she would have to start wearing furs and gloves as well. The forest had grown quieter, the summer song of frogs and crickets silenced and stored away for another year. She glanced around slowly. It was Luc's idea to use the secret passageway, so as not to be seen leaving the cottage with her. He would be returning later on in the same manner. Stella couldn't see him, but the sensation of being watched told her he was somewhere nearby.

The thought comforted her. And she needed comfort after what Luc had told her and Elias. *Vampyres!* Stella didn't think the situation could get any worse, but she was wrong. So very wrong. And yet nothing had truly changed. The state of Noctum had always been dire. She just hadn't realize the extent until now.

She yearned for the curse to be broken, to be freed from the horrors of this life. But she feared kindling any kind of hope in that regard. Breaking the curse seemed even more impossible now. And her fears for Luc felt like a dead weight pressing on her heart. The stakes were too high. If Luc failed to kill Draven, any chance of lifting the darkness would be lost. And very likely Luc would be, too.

Stella arrived at the market without incident. But when Luc failed to appear, worry gnawed at her as she waited at the arched entrance. She glanced around, searching for him, but all she saw were strangers coming and going from the marketplace. Perhaps he had gotten lost? Perhaps he was already in the market? Or had he run into trouble? Dread curdled in her gut at the last possibility. He was armed and a skilled warrior, she reminded herself. But he was also a stranger to the forest and had no experience navigating the dark.

Stella might have continued to stand there had Anson not suddenly appeared. He was talking with another man as he approached, but when he caught sight of her his eyes hardened. Not wanting a confrontation, she finally entered the market and headed straight for her stall.

It was while haggling with a customer over a leather belt that Stella spotted him. Luc, weaving through the stalls to her far right. He passed through the crowd smoothly and no one seemed to pay him any mind. The worry that had weighed on her slipped from her shoulders. Once Luc disappeared behind a stand, she sighed in relief as she dealt with the stingy man before her.

The night proved to be a successful one. Stella sold every item she had managed to produce while still working on Garrett's armor, which admittedly wasn't many. The coins lay heavy in her purse as she doused her lanterns, locked up her stall and went to buy the things she needed.

The Winter Solstice was one of Darkwood's most elegant events, requiring attendees to be masked and dressed all in white. Last year, she had worn a simple gown of white linen paired with an unadorned mask. As a result, she had paled beside the creativity and splendor of the other gowns and suits. "You're still one of the loveliest women here," Jenna had said, upon observing her discomfort. "You can dress up a duck, but a swan needs no adornment." While she had appreciated her friend's sentiment, she was determined to put a little more effort into her attire this time around, especially since Luc would be at her side.

Stella visited several stalls before finding all the materials she needed, then she headed back home, unaware of the watchful eyes that followed her.

* * *

"Stella, this is…there are no words." Garrett studied his new armor with unabashed awe and admiration.

"I remember when he used to stare at me like that," Jenna teased, her hazel eyes glinting.

"I still catch him staring at you like that," Stella assured her, before turning back to Garrett. "You should try it on."

"Stella's right," Jenna agreed. "It will look even better once you don it."

Garrett shot his wife a broad grin. It made Stella glad to see it. His smile had been missing since Erik died. It made all her hard work worth it. More importantly, she hoped the armor would do its job to protect him.

Jenna helped him put on the armor while Stella glanced at the paint supplies Garrett had brought. "Thank you for bringing the paint, but there's no need for you to do the labor. I can manage myself."

Garrett turned and Stella studied his armor with a critical eye—checking the seams, the rivets, the overall fit. "I insist, Stella. It's the least I can do."

"How does it feel?" she asked him. "Move your arms, reach for your sword. I want to make sure nothing catches or pinches."

Garrett did as he was told, while she and Jenna watched.

"It fits even better than the first armor you made me," he said, moving his sword arm, first slow then fast. He did the same with the other arm.

"Good," she said, with a satisfied nod. "Now if you don't mind, I have things I need to attend to."

They looked at her in surprise, unused to such brusque treatment. "Are you kicking us out?" Jenna asked.

"Yes, I'm very busy, and as much as I enjoy your company, I need to get back to work."

"But the floor—" Garrett began.

"I told you I would take care of it."

"But—"

"Out!" Stella insisted, pointing at the door.

Stunned, the couple gathered their belongings and exited the cottage. Stella watched them from the door. When Jenna glanced over her shoulder, still perplexed, Stella gave her a friendly wave before shutting the door.

The Winter Solstice was just two nights away and she still had so much to do. Heading into her bedroom, Stella grabbed the unfinished dress that lay on her bed and continued her work. The night before, she had finally succeeded in creating a tint to lighten Luc's skin and he had gone out to test it.

"Don't forget, you're supposed to be mute," she'd reminded him.

That had been hours ago, and she hadn't seen him since. She tried not to worry, but it was like asking a flame not to flicker. Despite her busyness, her thoughts often turned to him.

Hours later, Stella finished her dress. She laid it on the bed beside Luc's suit, which she'd completed two nights ago. Her lips turned up in a smile when she saw them side by side, imagining how they would look worn. She had made sure they coordinated, his outfit complementing her own attire—he a white hawk and she an elegant swan. All she had to do now was create their feathered masks.

As she began picturing different designs in her head, a light noise from outside her bedroom reached her ears. Grabbing her dagger, she stepped out to inspect it. What she found was Luc, kneeling on the floor with a paintbrush in his hand. He must have returned some time ago. For while she had been engrossed in her sewing, he had painted the entire floor, leaving no trace of the Shade blood that had previously stained it.

"I was going to do that," she said.

Luc rose to his feet, the motion fluid. "Now you don't have to," he said with a smile. "I borrowed some nails and a hammer and finished repairing the window as well."

"Borrowed?" she asked, wondering if he actually meant stolen. Luc had no coin and was supposed to be mute, so she didn't see how he could manage such an arrangement.

"I found Elias," he said. "He leant me his tools."

Oh.

"Did you go to the tavern?" she asked, furrowing her brow.

"Yes, but that's not where I found him, or rather where he found me. It was at the Hollow where he took me to his nest. It's amazing," Luc marveled. "People living like birds, all those houses so high up in the trees."

"I take it the tint worked? No one stopped you or took notice?"

"No one carted me off to the stocks," Luc replied. "So yes, I'd say it worked."

"And you remembered to act mute?"

He nodded. "I didn't speak until we were safely in Elias's nest. By the way, Elias came up with a story to explain my presence."

"What is it?"

"He says that if anyone asks, he and I met in Nyxus and that I'm here to visit him. He plans to tell Jenna and Garrett so that they'll already know about me."

"Good idea," Stella said, grateful for Elias's smart thinking. "And what were you doing at the tavern?"

"Elias brought me. He introduced me to his parents and a few of his friends. He says the more people who know about me the better, so that I don't seem so mysterious."

"Did anyone ask where you were staying?"

"I'm supposedly living in a wagon in the woods, not staying in any one location."

"Well," Stella said, impressed. "It seems Elias has thought it all out."

17

The Winter Solstice

On the night of the Winter Solstice, the forest decided to take part in the festivities, clothing itself in gauzy white. Stella stared out of the window—the one both Damian and Luc had repaired—to study the carpet of mist that covered the ground and wound its way up the towering trees. Hanging high above the treetops, the gibbous moon was just visible, its lazy eye gleaming softly through the thick white wisps. She smoothed her hands over her satin skirt, glancing down at her dress nervously. The neckline was scooped and her sleeves were fitted from shoulder to elbow before flaring to her wrist. But what made the dress stand out were the seed pearls that decorated both the neckline and the sleeves' edges. Her fair hair was up in an elaborate twist that had taken far too long to assemble, and tucked into it were the same white feathers that decorated both hers and Luc's masks. Never before had she taken such pains with her appearance. It was both exciting and nerve-wracking.

"I'm having trouble buttoning these cuffs," Luc said, finally emerging from his bedroom. "Do you—" He stopped cold at the sight of her.

But Stella was just as riveted. The brushed wool jacket and cotton pants fit Luc perfectly, highlighting his broad shoulders and slim waist. "You look good in white," she said, an understatement. Contrasted with his tawny skin and golden hair, he looked utterly stunning. It was a shame she would have to cover up all that lovely color with the lightening tint. "Here, let me help you," she offered, reaching for his sleeves. Once she was done buttoning them, she then began to apply the tint. It was an intimate act, rubbing the tint onto the warm skin of his face, neck and hands. "There," she said, after she'd finished, hoping he didn't notice the slight shake in her voice. "Now we're ready."

"Not quite," Luc said, staring at her intently as he drew closer. Stella's heart began to crash against her chest when he reached for her face. *Was he...? Would he...?* But all he did was put on her mask before donning his own. "Now we're ready."

* * *

They glided through the trees like phantoms in the mist—silent, ephemeral—as if they might vanish with a mere gust of wind. Or so they appeared to the dark eyes that followed them through the fog-shrouded forest. She with her moonbeam tresses gleaming silver-white, his slightly darker like a flash of gold in the moonlight. The watcher studied the man with a critical eye, noting his easy, loping gait that spoke of confidence and quiet strength. Like himself, a sword was strapped to the man's side, and even from a distance he could tell that the hilt was well-worn. Not just for show then. His eyes slid back to the beauty beside the man, fierce possession in his gaze. Who was he, and what was he to her?

The watcher intended to find out.

"Isn't this where the market was?" Luc asked, gazing in wonder at the transformed ruin. Gone were most of the stalls that usually occupied the space, leaving only those that hugged the stone walls where they bore the burden of food and beverages. Overhead, strings of twinkling white lights criss-crossed the open air, their warm glow casting the white-clad crowd to advantage.

"Yes," Stella replied, pulling her sheer white shawl tighter around her shoulders. It did little to protect her from the sudden nip in the air. "It's also where most of Darkwood's events are held. Lovely, isn't it?" she asked, gazing appreciatively at the variety of finery on display.

"Almost as lovely as you."

Stella turned to Luc in surprised delight. Earlier, she had been so certain he would kiss her and her heart had crashed in disappointment when he hadn't. Now it soared at his compliment. Luc was no longer looking at her, but a small smile played at the corner of his lips. The sight sent warmth curling through her. She quickly turned away, lest he should see how much he and his words affected her. "You are too kind."

"I only speak the truth," he said, staring at the scene before them once more as if to savor the sight. "There is a certain beauty to darkness that light can never possess."

Stella thought about that. "I suppose there is," she reluctantly agreed. "But it's the light that makes the darkness shine, not the other way around. Even on the darkest nights, so long as you can still see the stars, the darkness is bearable. Without them, it would be desolate."

Luc looked at her thoughtfully. "And so wise, too." He offered her his arm. "Shall we?"

She took it eagerly. Linked together, they stepped through the arched lintel that had somehow remained intact. As soon as they were inside the ruin, a dozen sets of eyes swung in their direction. Stella fought the urge to flee, reminding herself that their identities were concealed. Her feathered mask hid more than half her face, while Luc was unknown, a stranger. If the others stared, it was only to admire their coordinating attire.

Taking a deep breath to calm her nerves, she inhaled the heady bouquet of rose, jasmine and gardenia. The air was heavy with their fragrance, but it also carried the soft sound of instruments—violins, flutes, guitars and cymbals. The atmosphere was romantic and alluring, pulling her in. It must have pulled at Luc, too, for he began to lead them in further. Remembering why they were there, Stella began to scan the crowd, searching for Elias.

"There he is," she remarked, when she spotted his flaming red hair. Elias was wearing the same outfit he'd worn last year. Not that it mattered since he wasn't planning on staying long.

Noticing them a few seconds later, Elias's eyes widened before he began to approach. "How did you do it?" he marveled, once he reached them. "How did you lighten his skin?"

Stella glanced around to make sure no one was nearby to hear. "It's a mixture of pearl blossoms, snowpea roots and willow worms."

Elias cringed. "Willow worms?"

Beside her, Luc made a sound of distress but otherwise remained mute, dutifully playing his role. There was a reason she hadn't volunteered the ingredients to him.

"It worked, didn't it?" Avoiding Luc's gaze, she asked, "So have you spotted her?"

Elias nodded. "Yes, she's currently indulging in some spirits at one of the beverage stands. Come, follow me."

They skirted the edges of the ruin to avoid the crowds. The gentle strain of music grew louder, its lively melody mimicking the song of the chill arctic wind, carrying the whirling dancers along like the flurry of snowflakes that would soon sweep over the land.

They had just passed the band and two food stands when Elias suddenly halted. "There she is, the one with the ash brown hair and thin, almost gaunt, figure, wearing an owl mask."

"The snow owl," Stella noted, discreetly studying the master librarian. Based on the strands of gray in her hair, she guessed the woman to be in her forties. "Has she already seen you?"

Elias nodded. "I made certain of it as soon as I arrived. And now that you've seen her, I'll take my leave." His glance darted to Luc. "If

I'm lucky, I hope to have at least two or three hours to try and find something useful."

Luc nodded, unable to speak a word, though his eyes displayed his gratitude.

"Wish me luck," Elias said before, making his departure. But after two steps, he quickly doubled back. "You look beautiful, by the way," he told Stella. "And you don't look so bad either," he offered to Luc.

They watched as he slipped through the crowd, a fond smile on Stella's lips. The feel of a hand upon her arm had her turning. With the other hand, Luc gestured to the dancers nearby.

"You want to dance?" she asked, warmth unfurling in her belly.

When he nodded, she asked, "Do you know the steps to this one?"

Luc shrugged but tugged her toward the dance floor anyway. His large warm hand engulfed hers in a firm grip, while the other clasped her at the waist. When she looked up, the drum beneath her chest began to beat faster. Lost in a sea of emerald green, she didn't realize they were swaying—a calm, steady motion against the lively movements around them. Not that she noticed the other dancers. This close to Luc, Stella could see the golden flecks in his irises. She could smell the scent of his skin and feel the heat of his body. Her entire world narrowed to the small space between them, and it was as if nothing else existed—just her and Luc and this wondrous thing between them.

But the illusion was soon shattered. "May I cut in?"

Stella froze at the sound of the familiar but unwelcomed voice. She hadn't seen Damian since spurning him several nights ago, and she had hoped to avoid him that evening. Turning reluctantly, her gaze fell upon the face of a white wolf. Fitting. Above the mask, Damian's raven hair fell in thick waves, while below it she recognized his square jaw and full lips. At first glance, he looked relaxed, almost bored, but his ebony eyes were ablaze. She tensed at the sight. He was angry and who could blame him? She had turned down his invitation only to show up with another man.

How had he found her anyway? There were easily a thousand people in the crowd. Yet here he stood before her looking both terrifying and impressive in a pristine fur cape draped over his broad shoulders like some warrior king.

Stella glanced over at Luc and saw him carefully assessing Damian. It occurred to her that while Luc had overheard Damian's voice on at least two occasions, this was his first time actually seeing him in the flesh. She was shocked to find that, side-by-side, the two were surprisingly similar as far as height and build were concerned. But in everything else, they were polar opposites. Light versus dark. Saint versus sinner. Hero versus hedon. Even their masks were at complete odds—Luc, a sleek bird of prey and Damian, a vicious canine.

"He can't speak," Stella said, turning back to Damian.

Damian tilted his head as he studied Luc. "But you can understand, can't you?"

Luc nodded stiffly.

"And my request?"

Stella gritted her teeth, wanting to answer. But custom dictated that Luc reply, since the request had been made to him by Damian, man to man. Finally, grudgingly, Luc nodded in assent, much to her dismay. Why did he have to be such a gentleman?

Having no choice but to oblige, Stella allowed Damian to take her by the hand. But her eyes remained on Luc, who stood to the side watching her.

"Stella." Damian's voice was stern, and there was a note of warning in it.

"Damian," she returned, her own voice clipped.

The fire in his eyes flickered as he stared into her face. He stared for so long she was tempted to pull away. "What?" she finally snapped.

"You look beautiful," he said gruffly, as if it pained him to admit so.

Stella said nothing at first, unsure how to respond. "How did you recognize me?" she asked, deciding to dismiss his compliment.

A hint of a smile ghosted his lips. "I would recognize you anywhere."

"How?" she demanded, perplexed.

"By the way you walk, the way you stand, the manner in which you move your hands. I notice everything about you, Stella."

Stella gulped, both alarmed and strangely flattered by the admission.

"Why did you interrupt me and Luc?" she asked, determined to hold onto her anger.

"Luc?" His gaze shot over her shoulder. "Is that his name? And how do you know this mysterious Luc?"

"What's so mysterious about him?"

"Aside from the fact that he appeared out of nowhere and you've never mentioned him before until now?" he asked archly.

"When have I ever mentioned *anyone* to you?" Stella returned. "You're no confidante of mine."

"Who is he, Stella?" he asked in a way that demanded compliance.

She narrowed her eyes in irritation. "He's a friend of Elias's from Nyxus."

"What is he doing here?"

"I don't know," she retorted. "Why don't you ask him?"

"I thought the man couldn't speak?" he said with a suspicious look.

"He can't. It was a jest," she replied, her heart thumping unsteadily. If she wasn't careful her attempts at sarcasm might be taken for a careless slip.

"Why is Elias's friend with you and not Elias?"

"Maybe because he finds me prettier."

The scowl on his face told her Damian didn't much care for that answer. He suddenly spun her around to face him. Then he grabbed her by the waist, pulling her close. Too close. A thrill ran through her, though she couldn't tell if it was from dread or excitement. She hated that the man could unbalance her so easily. What was he doing anyway? Why did he insist on dancing with her when she had already confessed to him how she felt about him? Was it some petty form of punishment or revenge? He had to know he was making her uncomfortable. "Why did you cut in?" she asked, remembering that he had never answered her question.

"Because you obviously needed a better partner to lead you," he said, as he guided her effortlessly through a series of moves. Somehow, Stella didn't think he was talking about dancing.

"Luc was leading just fine," she said, glaring at him.

Damian made no reply as he turned then dipped her. When he pulled her back up, her face was only inches from his own. His dark gaze bore into hers for what felt like an eternity, allowing her to see the naked desire in his eyes. And then he was turning and swinging her again, his moves smooth and elegant yet completely masculine.

Stella was under Damian's complete control, like an instrument in the hands of a virtuoso. Or a marionette being manipulated by a master puppeteer. She couldn't decide which. All she knew was that she felt both helpless and exhilarated. She was being carried away, and she wondered if she shouldn't be pulling away instead.

"Why aren't you dancing with the woman you came with?"

"What woman?" Damian asked, never breaking his stride.

"Surely you didn't come here alone?"

"The one woman I asked turned me down."

"Yes, but you yourself said you had many to choose from. One is as good as another, isn't that right?"

Damian was quiet, and she wondered if he would refuse to answer. "Maybe when one doesn't know what one seeks, one turns to variety to satisfy, partly in the hopes of eventually finding what one truly desires."

Stella pondered this. "I see. So it seems I've been doing this wrong all along. Instead of waiting and saving myself for the right man, I should follow *one's* example and allow myself to enjoy all the men available to me until I do," she said with mock thoughtfulness. "Thank you for helping me to see the error of my ways."

Damian smirked, though a muscle in his jaw twitched. "It was an explanation, not a suggestion. And I think I know you well enough to know you would never cheapen yourself that way."

Stella quirked her brow. "The way you do?"

"Careful, Stella," he warned. "You know as well as I that men have much more leeway than women do."

"It doesn't make it right," she snapped.

"No, it doesn't," he agreed, surprising her.

Silence fell as they continued to dance. Stella tried to search for Luc through the crowd, but all she could see were a myriad of masked faces whirling and twirling around her. She began to grow dizzy, lightheaded, as if she were floating through a hazy dream. So she turned back to Damian, hoping to center herself, but the intensity of his gaze only unbalanced her further. She could do this no longer. His presence was too overwhelming, she had to get away. But when she pulled at her hands, his grip on her tightened, refusing to let go.

"You won't wear me down," she blurted.

"Won't I?" he asked, his expression unreadable.

"Never," she insisted. "You will never conquer me."

There was a gleam in his eyes, one that sent a shiver through her. "Who says I'm trying to conquer you, Stella?"

"Aren't you?"

He didn't answer.

"Speak plainly already," she cried in frustration. "What is it you want?"

Damian stilled, and Stella stumbled as they came to an abrupt halt. Around them, everyone else kept dancing, their pace increasing as the music rose to a deafening crescendo. Damian's eyes were hard and probing, seeming to pierce through her outer shield to access her innermost thoughts. "Since I've met you you've been waylaid by brigands, threatened by one of your suitors and attacked by a Shade in your own home. Right now, all I want is to keep you alive," he growled, before letting her go.

Damian glanced over her shoulder, and when she turned to see what he was looking at, she was relieved to find Luc. His expression was one of protective concern and there was a question in his eyes.

"I'm alright," she answered, giving him a reassuring smile. Turning back to Damian, she said, "Thank you for—" But her effort at civility was in vain, for Damian was already gone.

18

The Unwelcomed Guests

When they went to find Moira, the master librarian was no longer at the beverage stand. Together, she and Luc wove through the party looking for her. Stella spotted a few familiar figures she took pains to avoid, but when she recognized Jenna and Garrett she nearly forgot herself and began to approach. Only the reminder that she wasn't there to socialize spurred her past them without stopping.

Stella suddenly halted and looked around. The fog was creeping in. She saw it billowing over the low eastern wall, seeping through the various cracks and chunks in the stone, and rolling over the ground like a carpet being unfurled. By the time they located the master librarian, it completely cloaked the ruin, lending it an air of mystery.

"The revelers look almost like ghosts," she murmured, as two women in flowing dresses floated past them, their features and forms obscured by the mist. Were in not for the loud music and chatter, the sounds of raucous laughter, she could imagine they had stumbled upon some haunted scene.

Luc made a discreet motion with his hand and she turned to see that he had found the librarian. This time she was talking to a tall man, older but well-built. No, not talking. From the expressions on their faces it was something more heated than that. *Why was she arguing with the commandant?* For she knew Everard Gaven, the man her brother had served under, and who still led Garrett, Damian and the rest of the Shadow Guards.

Eventually, Moira stormed away and after glaring at her, Everard melted into the misty crowd. Once he was gone, Stella and Luc hurried after the master librarian. From one end of the ruin to the other they followed, her path as random as a leaf blown in the wind. The woman knew many people, most unfamiliar to Stella. Though at one time she stopped to talk to Joss, which surprised her. But what surprised her even more was when she approached Damian, pulling him away from another woman to engage in a brief but intense discussion. As soon as she was on the move again, so were her and Luc.

"The woman is exhausting," Stella complained, straining her eyes to see through the mist. She glanced at Luc, thinking how inconvenient it was that he couldn't speak. She missed his voice, missed hearing his distinctive lilt. And there was something lonely about talking to someone who couldn't—or in his case, wouldn't—reply. Still, she had to admire how well he played his role. It had to take great effort to hold one's tongue when speaking was so natural, so instinctive.

Suddenly, Luc grabbed her arm forcing her to a standstill. When she looked at him quizzically, she saw that his entire body had gone rigid, his other hand on the hilt of his sword. His head was tilted to the side, listening. To what she couldn't say. All she heard were the sounds of revelry. But a moment later, the music stopped and so did the laughter and chatter. It was replaced by a faint murmur that grew louder and louder. Like a ripple that finally reached them, the alarm soon rang in their ears.

"It's the Nighthawks!"

"They're here!!"

At the panicked cries, blood drained from Stella's face. *Nighthawks at the Winter Solstice?* But why? Such a thing had never happened before.

"Who are they?" Luc asked, his voice a strained whisper. "Who are the Nighthawks?"

"They're Draven's soldiers," she replied, glancing about desperately. Chances were the soldiers already had the perimeter surrounded. Even if they were to push their way through the frantic crowd, it was doubtful they would find a way out of the ruin.

"We have to get you out of here," Luc said.

"It may be too late." But he was pulling her behind him, using his body to plow a path through the crowd.

There were mixed reactions among those they passed. Some, like them, were attempting to escape. But most were either frozen in fear or resigned to their fate. Stella had never felt so terrified in her life, not even when the Shade had burst into her home. This was what she and everyone who had ever cared for her had worked so hard to avoid. Being taken by Draven was a fate worse than death by a Shade.

When they neared the west side of the ruin, Stella saw that several dozen Nighthawks lined the wall. More could be seen on the north side as well. She didn't need to check the south or east sides to know that they, too, were blocked.

"What's happening?" one of the forest dwellers dared to ask, his question directed to a group of Nighthawks standing near an entrance.

Another soldier appeared, this one mounted on a massive black horse. The crimson plume on his black helmet and the gold epaulets on his shoulders declared him to be an officer. With gauntlet-covered hands, he removed his helmet to reveal cold eyes in a lean, stern face. "The king demands a tribute," he declared.

"A tribute?" The question was repeated on the tongue of every man and woman who heard him, including Stella's. Why would the king want a tribute when he took whatever he wanted anyway?

"What is the tribute?" someone else asked.

The officer's face tightened. "All you need remember is that resistance to the king's decree is an act punishable by death. Those who refuse to cooperate will be dealt with accordingly." A cruel smile tilted his lips. "Now...all of you are ordered to remove your masks."

Most began to comply. From his horse, the officer nodded to a group of soldiers who made their way into the crowd to encourage those who were slower to submit.

Stella turned to Luc, her eyes wide with dread. But he shook his head, his own eyes blazing with determination. "I'm getting you out of here."

He tugged her after him, this time heading east to where the fog was thickest. When they neared the eastern wall, she saw that the forest-dwellers there still donned their masks, too far from the officer to have heard his command. As for the Nighthawks, they stood sentinel along the wall, their swords drawn and ready. Despite the heavy fog, there were too many to sneak past.

Beside her, she saw that Luc had his dagger in his hand. She had one as well, hidden beneath her skirt, but felt naked without her sword. She should have known better than to leave the cottage without it. Never again. "We'll wait until the soldiers disperse into the crowd," Luc whispered.

"And then what?"

He turned to look at her. "Do you trust me, Stella?"

"I do," she said, without doubt or hesitation.

"Then just stay near and do as I ask."

She nodded, though there was no hiding her worry.

Stella's thoughts turned to Jenna. She knew that Garrett would do everything in his power to protect her, but there was little he could do against so many. She was glad Marta was safe at her ma and da's house. Or was she? Who was to say that Draven hadn't ordered the Nighthawks to inspect every home as well?

"Remove your masks!" a harsh voice ordered, as soldiers began to make their way over to ensure the command was obeyed.

"Here we go," Luc said, under his breath. "Follow me." He darted through the crowd, easily dodging the soldiers whose black armor stood out against the masses of white.

Maybe a dozen Nighthawks had stuck to the wall, but they were now spread twenty or so feet apart. Despite the wider space, Stella didn't see how they could slip past unnoticed. The soldiers were on high alert, their eyes constantly moving to and fro. And the mist couldn't hide them completely.

But to her alarm, Luc was leading them directly toward one of the Nighthawks. The soldier merely looked at them at first, as if they were confused or daft. Then he narrowed his eyes and raised his sword. Still, they drew nearer. Only when the soldier opened his mouth to shout did Luc act—though Stella didn't realize it until she saw the dagger stuck in the man's throat. And even then it took her several seconds to understand what had happened. Too swiftly for her to track, Luc had managed to hurl his dagger.

"Quick, climb over," he urged, as they reached the wall.

Stella scrambled upward. But at the top of the wall, she paused to glance over her shoulder. Several forest dwellers stared back, wide-eyed. Below her, Luc had reclaimed his dagger only to fling it at another Nighthawk. When he began to scale the wall, she hurried down the other side, landing on the ground a second or two before him.

To the right, Stella could hear the sound of horses. She could smell them as well. They crept along the wall, away from the horses and whoever might be guarding them. Then Luc grabbed her hand and they ran. There was a shout. Stella's heart stopped, certain they had been spotted. But the sound of pounding feet receded rather than neared. Though perplexed, she didn't have time to think on it as she fled for safety, her mind a jumble of heightened emotions—fear and panic, confusion and curiosity, relief and guilt.

They used the secret passage to access the cottage, but they didn't enter right away. Instead, they waited in the space hidden beneath the floor, Luc silent and Stella shaking. She didn't know how long they waited, not speaking and barely breathing. It felt like hours. The next thing she knew Luc was rousing her from sleep.

"I think it's safe to go in," Luc said.

Slowly, her limbs feeling weighted, Stella followed Luc up into the cottage. She didn't bother to light any lanterns. The last thing she wanted to do was invite more trouble. Instead she wearily sunk onto the couch, gazing at Luc's silhouette in the dark. "What do you think happened?"

"I don't know," he replied grimly.

"I hope Jenna and Garrett are alright." And Joss and even Damian. She had recognized several familiar faces at the celebration, none she wanted to see harmed.

Luc made no reply, unwilling to offer false assurances.

"Thank you for getting us out. I didn't think it was possible, and I still don't quite know how you did it, but thank you."

"You're welcome, Stella." He moved and a short blade glinted in the darkness.

"Where did you get a second dagger?"

"I didn't."

Stella frowned in bewilderment. "But you threw your dagger. I saw you. How did you get it back?"

"Remember how I told you we have powerful sorcerers in Aurelia?"

"Yes."

"One of them charmed my dagger so it can always be retrieved. At least by me."

Stella let out a sound of amazement. "Truly? That's…useful."

"Very." She heard rather than saw his grin. "You should go to bed, Stella. It's been a long night."

She nodded and rose, wondering if she'd be able to return to sleep. What she wanted to do was check on her friends and make sure they were alright. But when she went to her room and laid down, exhaustion soon stole over her. Her eyes slid shut and didn't open again for some time.

19

An Awful Confession

Stella was blinking up at the ceiling, having just been awoken—by what, she didn't know—when the door to her bedroom flew open with a crash.

Pure adrenaline shot through her and she jumped from the bed, scrambling backward until she thudded against the wall. A man stood in the doorway, but she couldn't make out his features. Remembering her dagger, she grabbed it from beneath the gown she still wore.

"Stella."

She didn't lower her weapon. "What are you doing here, Damian?" And then she recalled the events of the evening. Or was it the evening past? "The Nighthawks, are they gone? Are Jenna and Garrett alright?"

Damian entered her bedroom, a place no man—other than her da and Erik—had ever stepped foot in before. "They're gone...for now. Jenna and Garrett are fine."

Stella's shoulders sagged in relief. "Thank you."

"What are you thanking me for?"

"For telling me. Isn't that why you're here?" She frowned. "Though there was no need for you to break into my house."

He now stood before her, his face hidden in shadows. She could smell him, though, that familiar scent of leather and spice. But something else mingled with it, something with a metallic tang. "I came to see *you*, Stella. To make sure *you* were alright."

Her eyes flew to the doorway to where the other bedroom could be seen across the hall. Was Luc there, hiding and listening? "You shouldn't be here," she said to Damian, pushing past him. "How did you get in anyway?"

In the main room, she lit the lantern that sat on the dining table. When she heard Damian behind her, she turned around and gasped.

Like her, he was still wearing his outfit from the Winter Solstice celebration. But his was no longer all white. Blood covered him. His white fur cape was splattered with it. Red blood. Human blood.

"What happened?" she asked, her other question completely forgotten.

"Some Nighthawks were killed. When it was discovered, their captain ordered the women be separated from the men. Our weapons were taken then they sought to find out who was responsible for killing their men. When no one stepped forward, ten of our own men were killed. I helped carry the bodies to be burned afterwards."

Stella's legs folded under her as she collapsed onto a nearby chair. Guilt, like bitter acid, ate away at her. Ten men were dead. Because of her. Because Luc had killed those Nighthawks to help her escape. "Who?" she asked, embracing the pain that was hers to own.

"I only knew one of the men," Damian said. "Everard Gaven, the commandant."

Stella sucked in a breath. "He's dead?" The man had led the Shadow Guard for decades. Erik had looked up to him, despite complaining about his demanding, exacting methods. His death was a tremendous loss to the Guard. "Who-who will take his place?"

"I will."

Stella fell silent, stunned by the admission.

"That's not all," Damian added gravely. "Several women were taken."

Stella shivered, her blood ran cold. *That* was the tribute? But why would Draven demand tribute when he had no need to? The pretense was an insult, a mockery.

"Where were you, Stella? How do you not know what happened?"

"I-I left early," she stammered, refusing to look at him. And though her gaze was drawn to Erik's bedroom, she fixed it firmly on the floor.

Damian lifted her chin with his fingers. His dark eyes were stormy. "With him?"

"If you mean Luc, then yes," she answered, jerking her face away. "He wanted to make certain I got home safely."

Damian's eyes narrowed. "Then how did you know about the Nighthawks?"

Stella's heart gave a violent lurch. "We heard them as we were leaving."

Damian exhaled loudly. "It's fortunate you weren't there. For a time, I thought...I thought you'd been taken as well."

That's why he had come. That's why he had arrived in such a state, barrelling into her bedroom without regard for propriety.

"I'm still here," she said weakly, wishing she could escape the guilt and pain of the fact.

But Damian had other plans. He descended on her without warning, a storm suddenly breaking. There was only the vaguest sense of inevitability before his lips were upon her, warm and insistent. It stunned her, alarmed her, but she didn't move. She froze, a captive to the soft lips that caressed hers, not a tempest but a gentle rain. The sensation was soothing, drugging, pulling her under. Then his tongue touched hers and Stella felt as if she had been struck by lightning, jolting her body and sizzling her soul. Only then did she yank away, her heart thundering with the violence of passion, desire and shame.

"You never should have done that!"

"I should have done it sooner," Damian countered, his gaze upon her intense and fevered. "I want to do it again."

Stella rose and retreated so quickly, the chair she'd been sitting on toppled backward with a loud clatter. "No, it will never happen again.

I won't allow it."

"Why not?" he asked, stalking her. She backed away until there was no place else to go. He leaned down over her, caging her in. "Because you fear what you feel for me? You fear what could happen between us?" He reached up to stroke the side of her face. "You make me feel things, too, things I've never felt before. You make me yearn. You make me hunger. I need you, Stella."

"I'm not available to appease your *hunger*," she sneered, shoving him. "Go to Ana or Nettie or whoever you usually go to for that. How many times must I tell you I won't be used by you?" The pain that flashed on Damian's face stilled her, causing her to choke back the rest of what she'd intended to say.

"I can't change my past, Stella," he said, his voice strained. "I've used women, it's true. They've used me, too. But do you remember what I told you earlier? I didn't know what I wanted then. I didn't know what I needed...until you. I don't want to use you, I want to cherish you. I want to be the one to protect you and care for you. If you'll let me."

For a moment, Stella could only stare and marvel. Damian's confession was like sparkling ice on a frozen lake—beautiful and alluring, but she didn't know if she could trust it. She would be wise not to. After all, he made no mention of devotion or faithfulness. He offered no promises of commitment. All he'd spoken of was desire and need, easily spent once satisfied.

"You're no good for me, Damian," Stella replied. "My heart has been broken too many times and I've lost too much already. My da, my ma and my brother. I barely hold on as it is most nights. A man like you would devastate me, you know you would. So I'm asking you to please stay away."

Damian stared at her mutely. But his eyes! The bleakness she glimpsed in their dark depths wrenched her, but she adamantly stood her ground. For all she knew it was an act. Though a niggling thought told her Damian had no need to rely on such ploys, nor was he the sort to do so.

"And what of our arrangement?" he asked stiffly.

Stella frowned. "I thought it was over."

"Why would you think that?" he asked, his dark eyes glinting.

"Because you haven't shown up to deliver any skins."

"Only because you asked me to leave, but I told you I would return."

Stella sighed in frustration. The truth was she still needed the skins and the meat, but had been too proud to ask for them. She couldn't afford to be proud, however. Not if she wanted to eat. "If you're still willing to continue the arrangement, so am I."

"Then I can't stay away from you, can I?" Damian returned.

"No, I suppose not," she agreed, with another sigh. At least not for another few weeks.

"Good." Damian was suddenly a blank slate, a wooden figure, with no trace of the turbulent emotions she had seen on his face only moments earlier. As if they had never been there at all. If he could turn it on and off so easily, perhaps it *was* all an act. "I saw Garrett's new armor," he continued. "It's a work of art."

Stella couldn't hide her surprise, amazed that he could still praise her after she'd thoroughly rejected him. More proof that he hadn't felt for her as deeply as he claimed. He strode to the front door, his hand grabbing the knob. Before he exited, however, he glanced at her over his shoulder. "I expect mine to be better."

20

A Dangerous Resolution

When Luc didn't exit his bedroom, Stella went to his door and knocked. There was no reply. She knocked again, and when silence alone answered, she pushed the door open.

Luc wasn't inside.

An hour later, he still hadn't returned. By then she had washed and changed out of her white gown, which was fortunate since her friends decided to stop by. The moment she opened the door, Jenna threw her arms around her and held her tight. The looks on their faces told her Garrett and Elias were greatly relieved to see her as well.

"Oh, Stella, it's a good thing you didn't attend the celebration this year," Jenna said, once they were seated around the table. "I still can't believe what happened."

"The commandant is dead," Garrett announced, his voice wooden. "Along with nine other men."

Stella swallowed down her guilt with great difficulty. "That's...terrible. I'm so sorry."

"It seems Damian is the new commandant now," Elias said, his gaze on his brother-in-law. "How did that happen?"

Garrett laughed, though without humor. "No one else would step

152

in, and no one else is more qualified. So Damian is our commandant whether he wants to be or not. And I am now a captain."

Stella didn't have to pretend to be surprised at that last bit. "That's...I mean, congratulations."

"It's now how I'd hoped to be promoted, Garrett said grimly.

"It's still an honor," Elias said, throwing in his support.

Stella hesitated before asking the question that weighed on her mind. "Who else was killed?"

Garrett began to name the men and she was relieved to find that she knew none of them.

"Ana Septiva was taken," Jenna suddenly volunteered. "And Nettie Loula." She went on to name three other women, two of whom Stella was also familiar with.

She recalled the flash of pain on Damian's face after telling him to appease himself with Ana or Nettie. Perhaps it wasn't just pain she'd seen, but guilt, too. Yet he had kissed her knowing these women had just been taken! Her distrust of him turned into disgust. She had been wise to doubt his honeyed words. The man would use any means to obtain what he wanted.

"Some wonder if the king is looking for a wife."

Stella pulled herself from her thoughts to gaze at Elias. "That doesn't make sense. Why would he suddenly want a wife?" And a human one at that, she thought privately. One didn't marry one's food.

"He doesn't," Garrett said angrily. "More than likely, he's just grown bored and is looking for new ways to torment us."

The idea was disturbing. Stella hoped Garrett was wrong, that there *was* a reason for what happened last night. That it wasn't just a careless whim, one that cost ten men their lives and five women their freedom.

"It's fortunate you escaped notice, Stella," Jenna remarked. "Elias told us how you two evaded the Nighthawks."

Stella glanced at Elias, a hint of panic in her eyes.

"It's a good thing you suggested gathering willowtips for the winter," Elias said smoothly. "It brought us far out of the Nighthawks' path."

Garrett rubbed his face wearily, and she wondered how much sleep he had gotten. "It seems they searched every home they could find."

"They didn't search mine," Stella said, voicing her realization aloud. "The lock was still intact when I returned"—though Damian had somehow managed to pick it—"and nothing was taken." She looked at Garrett. "They didn't find your armor, did they?"

"No, thank goodness!"

Stella knew that all guards were instructed to hide their armor and weapons when not in use, but mistakes happened. In Garrett's case, it would have meant his death. It would have meant hers as well had they gone to her cottage just a week prior. The armor had been lying right out in the open! She couldn't afford to be so careless next time.

"So what happens now?" Stella wondered.

Everyone looked at each other uncertainly. Nobody knew what to expect. And that was just as terrifying as anything else.

* * *

Luc returned shortly after her friends departed, entering through the door in the floor though she knew he hadn't departed that way.

"Where have you been?" Stella asked, eyeing his white suit, which had become wrinkled and dingy.

His face was drawn, his eyes somber. "Nowhere. Everywhere. I wandered, got lost for a bit then found my way back."

"You should have changed first." He would have glowed like a beacon in the moonlit forest.

He glanced down at his attire as if noticing it for the first time and shook his head. "I didn't even think about it." He looked up to meet her gaze. "I heard what Damian said...about the men who were killed. I'm sorry."

"It's not your fault. You couldn't have known."

"The thing is I would have done it again to spare you."

"So you heard about the women who were taken?" What else had he heard between her and Damian? She cringed at the thought.

Luc nodded. "I could never let you fall into the hands of such a monster."

"Thanks to you I didn't," she said softly. Silence fell, heavy and awkward with the things left unsaid, the questions she dared not ask.

"I wanted to pummel him."

"What?"

"Damian. I wanted to lay him out for kissing you," Luc confessed. "I had to leave before I was tempted to."

Stella shut her eyes tight for a moment. "It's a good thing you didn't."

Luc sighed, his shoulders still tense. "I would have, if I didn't think you could handle him."

"You think I can handle him?" She wasn't so certain of that herself.

"I don't know much about the man, but I know he would never hurt you."

"How do you know that?"

"Because he wouldn't go through so much trouble to protect you otherwise."

Stella stilled, recalling Damian's words. *I don't want to hurt you, Stella. I want to cherish and protect you.* They were pretty words, she reminded herself, nothing more.

"I passed through the Hollow," Luc volunteered, moving on. "The people are scared. It seems Nighthawks were sent to search every home as well."

Stella nodded absently, recalling that Garrett had mentioned the same thing. But then her heart dropped when she realized what she had overlooked the first time. Suddenly frantic, she grabbed her cloak and weapons then headed for the door

"Where are you going?" Luc asked in bewilderment.

"I'm going to check on my sister-in-law."

The Rodevs lived in a cottage much like her own, only theirs was located at the edge of the Hollow. It was dimly lit, with pale yellow light seeping through a single window. Stella glanced over to where Luc waited for her, unseen in the shadow of a large alder, then she knocked on the pinewood door. A man's voice called out. "Who is it?"

"It's me, Stella."

The door opened to reveal a balding man of average height and weight. "Mister Rodev," she greeted solemnly.

"Stella," he returned with equal solemnity. "It's been an eventful night. I'm surprised to see you out so soon." There was no missing the note of censure in his voice.

"I came to check on you all. When I heard that the Nighthawks had searched through homes..." she trailed off and his eyes softened.

"We're fine. Marta is fine. They left us alone as soon as they saw she was pregnant." He scanned the woods before stepping back. "Come in."

The cottage smelled of tallow and wax. On a long table, candle molds along with candles of various sizes sat on the wax-mottled surface. Marta's ma was busy pouring wax into one of the molds while Jess, Marta's younger brother, stood at a large cauldron stirring.

"She's in her room," Mistress Rodev said, giving her permission to enter.

Marta's room was dark and stuffy. As soon as she entered, the form in the bed stirred but didn't awaken. Stella left the door open to allow some air and light then she pulled up a stool. Marta faced her and she could see the soft curves of her profile, made plumper by pregnancy. At first glance, one might think her unremarkable. Until you became aware of the intelligence in her doe-like eyes, the gentleness and compassion they radiated. It was her inner light that made her lovely, a light that Erik had immediately noticed.

Stella reached out to sweep back an errant black curl and a pair of brown eyes blinked at her. "Stella?" Marta sat up until her back was propped up against the pillows. Dark circles lined her eyes. Despite all the sleeping she did, she looked exhausted. "You don't know how relieved I am to see you! I was so worried!"

"I worried the same for you. That's why I came."

"You needn't have. I possess neither the looks nor the allure that draws a man like Draven."

"He's a monster, not a man," Stella said grimly. "Which is why he can't recognize what true beauty is. Which is a good thing for you."

Marta looked at her with tenderness before her face fell. "We heard what happened at the celebration. Ten men killed and five women taken!"

Stella could only nod sorrowfully.

"It's a good thing you didn't attend, but I fear the Nighthawks may return. I know you've always been very careful, Stella, but what if they finally catch you off guard?"

Stella made no reply, unable to admit to Marta that she had attended the celebration. To do so would require explaining why she'd gone and how she'd escaped, neither of which she was willing to do. Not to mention the fact that she *had* been caught off guard, and might even now be in Draven's clutches were it not for Luc.

"Marta, I know you worry for me, but I'd rather you think of yourself and the baby. He's due any day now, isn't he?"

She nodded, her expression clouding. "I'm so scared, Stella, now that it's so close and after what just happened. I'm afraid to bring a baby into this world, especially without Erik by my side to protect us."

Stella grabbed her hand and squeezed it. "You're not alone, Marta." It was the best she could offer, wishing she could do better.

"I've been thinking..." Marta paused, her expression making Stella uneasy. "That if something were to happen to the baby, it might be a mercy."

At the look of horror on Stella's face, Marta's crumpled as she began to sob. "Oh, god! I know how it sounds! I would never h-harm m-my baby. All I mean is that should he or sh-she not m-make it—"

"I know what you meant, Marta. But I also know this. Once you see your baby and hold him or her in your arms, you'll never want to let go."

"That's not what I fear." Marta looked at her with dread and deep despair. "What I fear is having my baby being ripped from them."

Stella left the Rodevs shaken. She had stayed long enough to ply Marta with words of comfort and encouragement, an effort that left her emotionally drained. She understood the mother-to-be's fears all too well. She understood the temptation to give up, to stop fighting, stop trying. Not because life was pointless, but because it was so terrifying.

She shivered, surprised by how steeply the temperature had fallen in such a short space of time. The wind had picked up as well, howling through the trees and rattling its naked limbs like bare bones.

When she reached the alder tree where Luc waited, he detached himself from its shadow to meet her. "Is all well?"

Stella shook her head, too weary to share the burdens of her heart. There was just one thing she wanted to know. "Do you really believe you can break Noctum's curse?"

Luc paused to stare, as if recognizing that something significant had shifted within her. "Yes, Stella, I really believe I can."

She nodded, satisfied. "Then I promise to do everything I can to help you," she vowed.

21

A History Lesson

Back at the cottage, Stella saw that Elias had returned alone. He now wore a thick leather coat and was pacing back and forth as she approached, the sword at his side repeatedly bumping against his left thigh.

"There you are!" he exclaimed, upon seeing her.

"Come inside," she urged, leading him into the cottage to where Luc was already waiting.

Elias looked at him in surprise. "Have you been here all along?"

"I just got here," Luc replied.

A knowing look came over Elias's face. "I see."

"What do you see?" Stella asked worriedly.

"I deal in secrecy now, Stella. It's part of the profession. And it's a good thing Luc has a secret passageway to come and go undetected."

Stella sighed. "No one is supposed to know about that."

"You can trust me, Stella," Elias replied in mild exasperation. "I've been keeping your secrets since we were children. Not to mention the fact that I'm about to trust *you* with something that could cost me, well…everything."

At his words, she and Luc eagerly drew near. "So you found something then?"

Elias nodded, looking at Luc. "As terrible as last night's events were,

159

it allowed me to gather information I think you'll find useful." He reached into his right boot and carefully pulled out a folded piece of parchment, which he opened and laid flat on the table.

Stella's eyes widened as her eyes followed the vaguely familiar curves and lines. "Is this a map of Caligo?"

"A partial map," Elias replied, before reaching into his left boot. "And this is a map of the castle's layout. Also partial."

Luc leaned in, his gaze darting back and forth between both maps, while Stella's mind began to spin. Someone, or more likely several *someones,* had been brave enough to not only spy from within the king's city, but from inside his castle, too! And there could only be one way the information was transferred—during the Luna Market. Questions burned on her tongue, but she bit back her curiosity, knowing it was secondary to the information itself.

"How accurate are these?" Luc asked.

"I can't say with any certainty," Elias answered. "But there were several versions of both the city and castle maps, so I copied the most recent ones."

"How recent are they?" Luc asked, tracing a route through the city with his finger.

"The city is dated from last year. The castle is from six years ago."

"Six years ago?" Stella queried. "Why? Has no one dared enter the castle again since that time?"

Elias nodded, a look of uneasiness coming over him. "That was when our spy was discovered. And the reason no one has dared is because of how he was tortured and killed. It was said his screams were heard for weeks before he was quartered and beheaded, his parts displayed on the city walls."

"An effective deterrent," Luc murmured as Stella shuddered, grieving for a man long dead. "Do you know if they discovered what he was doing?"

Elias shook his head. "I suppose that might make the map unreliable. Much can change in six years, especially if Draven knew the castle was being mapped."

"It's a possibility," Luc said, shrugging. "But it's just as possible no changes were made if security was heightened after the last breach. Who knows? But the map is still helpful. It's easier to change the purpose and use of the rooms than it is to move castle walls."

"These will have to be burned as soon as you memorize them," Elias said.

"Burned?" Luc said in surprise. "But these must have taken you hours to copy."

"I can draw another copy if necessary."

Luc stared at Elias dubiously.

"Elias is gifted with an astounding memory," Stella supplied, knowing her friend was uncomfortable singing his own praises. "Which is why he was chosen for the role of historian."

"Does that mean the librarian—"

"No," Elias replied. "She was chosen for her ability to collect information. Moira knows many people and her connections have proven to be a valuable asset to the Repository."

Speaking of knowing many people... "We saw her arguing with the commandant," Stella remarked.

"They were arguing?" The idea seemed to perplex Elias.

"Did they not get along?" she asked.

"Some brothers and sisters don't," Elias replied. "Though I imagine she must be devastated by his death."

Stella said nothing, feeling sorrow for the librarian. How terrible to lose someone in such a way, to know that reparations could never be made.

"Are you ready to hear what else I learned?" Elias asked.

"There's more?" Luc asked, snapping his head up from the maps.

"If you're at all interested in some family drama," Elias said with a grim smile.

"Not usually, but if it has to do with Draven's family, I'm willing to make an exception," Luc replied.

Stella rose to heat some water in the kettle. A good mug of tea was in order, if only to offer some comfort on that cold night. She had a feeling she would also need something to hold onto as Elias recounted what he'd learned.

"We had always wondered about the relationships between the royals," Elias began. "We suspect a few to be related to Draven somehow. Vladimir, Nikolai and Mishka, for example, look like they could be Draven's brothers. Or they could be his sons. Likewise, Olga and Natalya could be his sisters, or they could be his daughters. The other females are thought to be his mistresses and perhaps one was even his wife. As for the other males, it is speculated that they are Draven's former generals. Of course, none of this is confirmed. The relationships between the royals are complex, to say the least. Most of the time they barely tolerate one another, and they certainly don't trust one another. There are factions and sub-factions among them as well, but alliances are always shifting. Can you even fathom the histories they share with one another? Thousands of years of bitterness and betrayals. It would explain why each rules his or her own city and seldom come into contact with another."

"Are there no true loyalties between any of them?" Stella asked, disturbed by the idea of living for so long, but essentially doing so alone and with enmity.

"It's hard to say," Elias answered. "The closest would be Natalya and Nikolai. Their cities are not far from one another and they visit each other more often than any other royal. On the other hand, the two who despise each other the most are Zara and Tatiana."

Stella raised a brow. "The wife and one of his mistresses perhaps?"

"Possibly," Elias said. "Tatiana seems to despise Draven almost as much as she does Zara, while Zara keeps as far away from the king as possible."

"Interesting," Luc murmured. "But how exactly does this help me?"

"You wanted to know how to get near Draven," Elias remarked. "Every three months, the king travels to visit one of the other royals—alone. No walls and no Nighthawks surrounding him. If you want to strike Draven, that would be the time to do it." Elias leaned forward. "And it seems he's scheduled to visit Vladimir after the last night of the Luna Market." Something tightened in Stella's chest. *That was only four nights from now!* "Is the market still happening?" she asked instead. "After what happened at the Winter Solstice…"

"I don't know," Elias said, with an uncertain frown. "I suppose we'll find out tomorrow night."

* * *

When Elias left, Stella turned to Luc questioningly.

He looked up, feeling the weight of her gaze. "You want to know what I plan to do, don't you?"

"Of course," she said with emphasis.

"I don't think I should let this opportunity pass," he answered. "Otherwise I'll have to wait three months for another one."

"No, you shouldn't let it pass," she agreed. "You should use it to observe, and if possible see what you're up against. You can't afford to be hasty. Should you make your attempt and fail, you may not get another chance." You might not live to make another attempt, was what she didn't say.

"I understand, but are you willing to harbor me for that much longer? I'm well aware of how my presence complicates your life."

If he only knew *how* he complicated it! It wasn't so much the challenge of keeping him hidden, it was the challenge of guarding her affections. Though it seemed a lost cause already. How could she resist him when he anticipated and met her every need? When he fixed her window and painted her floors? When he fought like a warrior yet could charm her with a sweet smile? When every little thing he did won her over without much effort on his part? So, yes, she was willing to harbor him for longer, but she feared what it would do to her heart.

But it wasn't about her, she had to remind herself. It wasn't even about Luc. It was about something much bigger than the both of them. It was about freedom from darkness and tyranny. It was about hope and light and life. It was about her brother's child having a chance at all of these things and more.

"If it means greater success in killing Draven and breaking the curse, then yes, I'm willing despite the complications," she said.

Luc stared at her for a time. Then he nodded and smiled, though it failed to reach his eyes. "Alright then. No rush."

Despite a sense of unease, Stella exhaled in relief.

Luc then turned to study the maps Elias had left on the table, so she reached for a piece of raw boar hide. If she had known that urgency would come to define the pace of their nights, she would have taken more time to savor the moments of calm. The dance at the Winter Solstice had been a rare moment of bliss—before Damian had interrupted them. She wondered if they would ever have another chance to just be, without fear of discovery or disruption. Sighing, she studied the boar hide in her hands before taking the first steps to fashioning Damian's armor.

22

The Birth of Hope

Luc had stepped out for fresh air as he sometimes did when Jess arrived at her door, red-faced and puffing. There was no need to ask what he was doing at her cottage. Before he could catch his breath to speak, Stella was already grabbing her weapons and cloak, wishing there were some way to let Luc know where she was going.

"Is the midwife already there?" she asked Marta's younger brother.

"Yes," Jess croaked through his dry throat. "She got there right before I left to fetch you."

After offering the boy some water, they hurried out into the woods. Conifers eventually gave way to bare trees, and Stella looked up to see the pale moon watching them. Unbidden, thoughts of Marta's last labor filled her head. She shook away the distressing memories. This time, her niece or nephew *would* survive!

When they reached the Rodev's cottage, Stella flew through the front door without bothering to knock. The first thing her eyes fell upon was Marta's da staring blankly into the fire. His head snapped toward her in surprise. "You got here quick."

"How is she?" she asked, her words delivered in a pant. In the other room, she could hear groaning and muffled voices.

"I don't know," Mister Rodev said, his voice full of anxiety. "I haven't been allowed in there."

He was afraid. And she couldn't blame him. Like her, he had watched as his daughter nearly bled to death the last time she delivered.

"May I?" she asked, nodding to the chair beside his. The bedroom would be full with Marta's ma and the midwife already assisting. And there was little she could do anyway, except pray. Which is what she did, while Mister Rodev continued to stare into the fire.

The clock on the mantel ticked. One hour passed and then two. The fire was nearly dead, its orange embers fading to gray. Sometime after the second hour, a small shrill cry replaced the low moans that had filled the air. Stella's gaze clashed with that of Marta's da. His remained wary. She could guess what he was thinking. The baby was alive, but what of his daughter? When the door swung open, they both jumped to their feet.

It was Mistress Rodev who emerged with a small bundle in her arms. Stella's heart immediately soared. "Would you like to meet your grandson?" she asked her husband.

His eyes darted to the bedroom, relief sagging his shoulders when he saw that Marta was awake and alert. Finally, he nodded and went to inspect the baby.

A boy! Stella didn't even try to hold back the tears that spilled from her eyes. She couldn't recall the last time she'd felt so relieved, so thankful, so…overjoyed. She briefly closed her eyes, savoring the feeling.

Since Mistress Rodev was disinclined to give up her grandson, Stella sat at Marta's bedside. Marta looked tired but hale, her cheeks flushed and strands of damp hair clinging to her forehead. "Thank you for being here, Stella," she managed weakly.

"You don't have to thank me. I wanted to be here. And not just for the baby." She glanced to the door, beyond which she could see Marta's ma cooing at the new infant she cradled, while her husband and son looked on contentedly. "Though he is one of the most beautiful things I've ever laid eyes on. You did well, Marta."

"Erik and I both did," Marta replied, tears filling her eyes. "How I wish he could've met his son."

Stella spoke past the lump in her throat, knowing she had to be strong for the both of them. "Even if he didn't, you know how eagerly he looked forward to this night. And you know how proud he would have been of your strength and courage."

"Yes. You're right, of course, Stella." Marta sniffed, trying hard to collect herself. "And I am grateful for little Aron. I'm thankful to have a piece of Erik to hold close, something the two of us created together."

"You're naming him after our da?" Stella said in wonder, glancing over her shoulder at the baby.

Marta nodded. "It was what Erik wanted. If it was a girl, we would have named her after your ma."

Stella didn't know whether to beam or weep. It was both perfect and heart-breaking. Just then, Mistress Rodev came in to place the baby in Marta's eager arms. Stella watched the squirming bundle, thinking of all the hopes placed on its tiny head.

She stayed long enough to watch the baby feed then held him while his tired ma rested. After determining that little Aron had his da's mouth and nose and his ma's eyes and chin, she reluctantly passed him on to his grandma. By the time Stella left the Rodev's cottage it was late in the evening.

Her own cottage was dark and silent when she finally came upon it. Had Luc not yet returned? It wasn't until she was inside lighting a lantern that she recalled it was the first night of the Luna Market. Stella had no idea if it was still being held, but where else would he have gone?

The Killing Fields were bright with lights, but the crowds were thinner than usual. Sparse even. Most of those in attendance were citizens of Caligo, with very few vendors from Darkwood.

Stella strained her eyes, searching for a head of golden hair upon a tall, trim figure or a hooded one donning her brother's old cloak. So far, she'd seen neither. She stayed for a while longer, safely nestled in the tree. After the events of the Winter Solstice she wasn't so foolish as to risk venturing into the market itself. When it became clear that Luc was nowhere to be seen, she decided to return home, a feeling of anxiety coursing through her.

She was heading past the Hollow when she took a sudden detour, making her way through instead of around the cluster of homes. At one of the giant pines near the center of the Hollow, she began to climb the steps—dozens of small planks—that had been nailed into the trunk.

"Elias!" she called out, as she knocked on the door of the nest perched in the branches. She knocked for a time, even though the silence and stillness indicated no one was home. Finally giving up, she climbed back down.

As a last resort, she headed for the Tangleroot Tavern. It was packed, filled with the people who would have usually been at the Luna Market. Squeezing her way through the crowd, whose mood was morose rather than rowdy, she managed to reach the bar without being groped or harassed, for which she was thankful.

Both Mister and Mistress Parnassa were hard at work, the latter looking frazzled as they struggled to meet the drink orders that were being thrown at them. Everyone was drinking to drown their sorrows in forgetfulness. Where was Elias? He could usually be counted on to lend a helping hand whenever the tavern got busy. Even Jenna offered her services on occasion, though that happened less and less now that she was married.

Stella looked on hesitantly, anxious to ask his parents if they'd seen Elias but reluctant to interrupt them when they were so harried. But then his ma glanced in her direction and hustled over. "Have you seen Elias? We could use his help as you can see."

"I was just about to ask you if you'd seen him," Stella admitted, disappointed to find out that she hadn't.

Beside Stella, an older man spoke up. "I saw Elias. He were with two tall men, one dark haired, the other light."

"Where?" both Stella and Elias's ma asked.

"Just outside the Guard barracks. Can't say for certain, but things seemed a bit heated between the lot of 'em."

Stella immediately headed for the door. "Tell that boy of mine we need his help!" she heard Mistress Parnassa call out as she fought her way through the crowd.

The Shadow Guard barracks were a collection of cottages to the west of the Hollow, located much further from the Hollow than her own cottage which lay east of it. Most everyone from Darkwood knew it was where the guards trained and met. But to outsiders, it was meant to appear as nothing more than a bunch of homes clustered together. Behind the barracks, hidden in the trees, was a sizeable field where maneuvers were practiced. The entire area, however, was well guarded.

Stella was just about to cross the invisible perimeter when a voice called out from above. "Stop where you are! You have reached a restricted area. Unless you have business being here, remove yourself at once."

Stella stopped immediately, aware that at least two unseen arrows were trained on her. "Please inform the commandant that Stella Varden is here to see him."

Two figures promptly dropped from the trees above, one in front of her and one behind. These men were new and young, which explained why they didn't recognize her. "Erik Varden's sister?" one of the men queried, his surprise quickly turning to admiration as he studied her.

The other man came around to face her. "Go give word," he said to the first guard. "I'll keep an eye on her until we get approval."

Though the first guard looked disgruntled, he left to do as told. The second guard watched her with cool detachment and she had to admire his devotion to duty. She knew that most men were taken in by her beauty, but either this man wasn't or he hid it well.

"What's your name, guard?" she asked, after the silence stretched uncomfortably between them.

"Teren," he replied tersely.

"You're new here, aren't you?" He looked affronted, and she wondered if he thought she was questioning his experience. "I only ask because I've never seen you or the other guard before."

"Why, do you know all the guards?" he asked skeptically.

"Most of them," a familiar voice replied from behind.

Teren turned to see the man Stella had already observed approaching, along with the other guard.

"Garrett," she greeted, noting the strained look on his face. The sight immediately raised her guard. Something was wrong.

"Captain Lucan," Teren said, standing at attention.

Garrett acknowledged the guard with a nod before turning to her. "Stella, how did you know to come here?"

"A man at the tavern said he saw Elias with Luc and Damian near the barracks. What is going on, Garrett?"

"We'll discuss it inside. Guards, resume your duties," he instructed the two younger men.

As she left, she saw the guards watching her curiously. When she was certain they were out of earshot, she repeated her question. "What's happened?"

"Please, Stella, I'm still not quite sure what is going on myself so I think it best you talk to Damian and Elias directly."

"What about Luc?" she asked, wondering why he'd been left out.

Garrett heaved a heavy sigh. "I'll leave it to Damian to explain."

Frustrated, Stella was about to demand an explanation *now* when they reached the command post. She had never stepped foot inside, but she knew it housed Everard's office. No, Damian's office now, she reminded herself. She still hadn't quite wrapped her head around the fact that he was the new commandant.

"After you," Garrett said, opening the door.

Outside, the barracks had been quiet, almost abandoned in feeling. Inside, the building buzzed with voices as men huddled in several groups conversed. The nearest group seemed to be discussing weapon supplies, but they ceased as soon as they noticed her. One by one, all conversation stopped as she and Garrett crossed the room to the other side, picking up again in hushed whispers.

Garrett stopped before a door and reached for the knob. He paused before turning it. "A word of warning, Stella," he said quietly, so no one else could hear. "Tread carefully. Damian is in a volatile mood."

Without giving her any time to prepare, Garrett opened the door and she had little choice but to enter. To her relief, he followed after her. Already ensconced within were Damian and Elias, staring at each other warily.

Intimidated by the hardened gaze Damian fixed on her, she turned to see the look of helpless frustration on Elias's face. "What is going on?" she asked, hoping her question would finally be answered.

"Luc has been imprisoned," Elias replied.

She whipped back around to face Damian. "On what grounds?" she demanded.

Instead of answering her, he looked to Garrett. "Take Elias, but hold him here for the time being. I need to question Stella."

Garrett hesitated, but nodded his head and gestured to Elias. "Let's go. The sooner he questions her, the sooner this can all be sorted out."

Elias gave her another helpless look as he passed, and then he and Garrett were gone, leaving her alone with Damian. She pulled herself together, determined not to be intimidated. When she faced him, she wore a look of confusion. "Well?" she asked. "What is this all about?"

Damian was leaning against a table, dressed neck to toe in dark brown leather, his arms crossed against his broad chest and his long legs crossed at his ankles. Though relaxed, he looked formidable. "What brought you here to the barracks, Stella?"

It annoyed her that he kept evading her questions, but she answered his anyway. "I was looking for Elias."

"Just Elias?" he asked, studying her with his knowing eyes.

Two could play at his game. "The tavern was busy. His parents were looking for him and asked me if I knew where he was. A patron mentioned seeing you and another man with Elias here at the barracks, so I came. Now why is Luc imprisoned?"

"Because I suspect he's responsible for the deaths of ten men," Damian replied, his tone hard and unyielding.

Stella willed her face not to betray her fear. "Why would you suspect that?"

"Because witnesses at the Winter Solstice celebration say they saw a man matching his description attack two Nighthawks before escaping...with a woman," he said, his dark eyes never leaving her face.

"Everyone was masked," she countered, her heart beating wildly. "There's no way to identify the man responsible with any certainty."

"Well, they did say that the man and woman were both fair-haired, and that they were both wearing feathered masks."

"That could be anyone," she insisted. "There were hundreds of people at the celebration. Any number of couples there could have had fair hair and feathered masks."

Damian nodded in agreement. "So then let me just ask you directly, Stella. *Was* it you and Luc who escaped that night?"

"Of course not!" The lie slipped from her tongue easily. "I already told you we left early."

Damian uncrossed his arms and ankles and rose to his feet. Panic began to bloom in Stella's chest as he stalked toward her. "You're lying, Stella. You're lying to cover up for him. And you know how I know?" He stopped a mere breath away, his face hovering over hers.

Stella shook her head, rendered speechless by the intensity of his dark gaze.

"Because one of the witnesses was Anson and the other was a man named Isaac. Both swore it was you they saw. They even described the way your hair was styled down to details of your dress. That's the hazard of being unforgettable, Stella. You tend to leave an impression."

She tore her gaze away, unable to bear the anger and accusation in his eyes. Shame filled her, not because she had lied, but because she had been exposed. When she tried to move away, Damian grabbed her by the arms. "Where do you think you're going?" Too late, she remembered Garrett's earlier warning.

"He didn't realize what would happen," she said in Luc's defense. "He was just trying to protect me."

"But *you* knew, Stella. And yet you let him kill the king's men anyway."

"I didn't realize he would…but I should've known it was a possibility," she conceded guiltily. "That makes me just as responsible as Luc. I should be imprisoned as well."

Damian released her arms. "How could he not have known what would happen when he killed those Nighthawks?" Doubt mingled with suspicion in his eyes. "The soldiers in Nyxus are no different than the ones here in Darkwood."

Stella floundered, realizing she had been caught in a trap of her own making.

"And how would you know anyway, since according to you the man can't speak?" Damian continued.

Stella suppressed an audible groan. Having no other choice, she decided to take a gamble. "It was Elias who told me that because of his muteness, Luc has managed to avoid run-ins with any soldiers. For his own protection."

"Is that so? Then how did he learn to fight with enough skill to slay two Nighthawks?"

"I don't know," she replied, her voice weak and thready. "You'd have to ask Elias."

A muscle twitched near Damian's clenched jaw. "Then that's what I'll do, but first I have another question. Who is Luc to you?"

"Someone I care about," she admitted, after a brief hesitation.

His eyes hardened before he headed for the door. "You're free to go," he declared, opening it.

"And Luc?" she asked.

"He and I aren't finished yet."

Before she could protest, Damian had shut the door on her and two guards had appeared to escort her out. A quick glance showed her that neither Garrett nor Elias were about. She wanted to flee from her guards and search for Luc, but she hadn't the slightest inkling where to find him. Besides, she'd seen the look in Damian's eyes when he'd answered her last question. Defying him would not bode well for either her or Luc.

23

The Winning Sport

The hours that passed brought Stella closer and closer to the brink of insanity. Restlessness assailed her, triggered by anxiety she could do nothing to contain. Too many worries tormented her. How long would Damian imprison Luc? Would he release him? How long before Luc's lightening tint faded? Would Damian question Elias to corroborate her claims regarding Luc? Around and around the questions whirled, wearing a path through her head as surely as she would wear out the floor.

Needing something to distract her—something more productive than pacing back and forth—she picked up the beginnings of Damian's armor. Scoffing, she threw it back down, only to take it up once more. There was nothing else with which to occupy herself. Laughing darkly at the irony, she set to work on the boar hide, losing herself as she always did when it came to her leathercraft.

Stella was nearly finished with the breastplate when the door on the floor was thrown open. She rushed over to see two faces peering up at her. Luc clambered up first, followed by Elias. Both looked worn and disheveled as they sat there on the floor, but only Luc sported a bloody bandage on the same arm that had only recently healed.

"What happened?" she asked in dismay.

Luc smirked, his eyes glinting with what she could only describe as

175

haughty delight. "Damian challenged me to a fight."

"What?"

Luc slowly rose, while Elias remained mildly out of breath on the floor. "He said he would free me if I could beat him."

Which meant that Luc had won, since he was here. *He had succeeded in beating Damian!*

"You should have seen it," Elias piped in, forcing himself to his feet. "It was quite thrilling."

"I wish I *had* seen it," Stella replied, gawking at Luc. "But since I didn't, I wouldn't mind hearing the details."

"Could we have some water first?" Luc asked with a slight grimace, as he began to remove his weapons.

Stella shot Elias a quizzical look before grabbing her jug of water. The barracks were a good distance from her cottage, but they looked as if they'd suffered more than a simple trek.

"We were followed after being released," Elias supplied. "So we couldn't head directly back to your cottage. It took some time, and many, many leagues to finally lose our tracker."

That explained their worn appearance. Stella handed them each a mug of water, which they downed greedily. Then realizing they must be hungry as well, she began to prepare a simple repast. After offering it to them, she sat down while they ate and drank.

"That Damian is a force to be reckoned with," Luc remarked. "And I don't just mean physically. He nearly succeeded in getting me to speak…twice."

"How?" she asked.

Luc dropped his eyes, frowning down at the plate of cheese, nuts and dried meat on the table. "By getting me so angry it was everything I could do not to curse and insult him."

Stella couldn't help but smile at that. "It's a skill of his."

"Yes, well, it wasn't until he had me riled up that he challenged me to fight. I was seeing red at the time, so it's a good thing Elias was there to keep my head on straight. If he hadn't calmed me down, I might not have won. It was close, though. Damian is good, one of the best I've ever fought against."

"He was spitting mad when he lost," Elias remarked, cringing at the memory before biting into his cheese.

"He also suspects I was here the night we killed that Shade," Luc said.

"Which is why he had you followed," she realized with dismay. She recalled the times she had felt like she was being watched. What if it had been Damian and not Luc following her then? "We'll have to assume he'll be keeping an eye on all three of us from now on."

"It's a good thing you have that secret passageway to get in and out," Elias said. "Even so, you'll have to be even more careful using it."

"When Damian questioned me, I had to tell him that Luc had somehow managed to avoid the soldiers in Nyxus. Did he ask you anything about that?" she queried.

"No," Elias replied. "But it explains why he wanted to know where in Nyxus Luc lived. I told him you were practically a hermit," he said, looking at Luc. "But he did ask how you had learned to fight."

Luc's green eyes widened. "What did you say?"

"I claimed I didn't know, that I never realized you were skilled in that way," Elias said.

A veritable man of mystery, that was what Luc was to Damian. But Stella suspected it would only make Damian more driven to uncover the truth about him.

"How *did* you learn to fight anyway?" Elias wondered. "Are you a soldier of some sort in Aurelia?"

"Yes, I am."

"A captain?" Elias guessed. "Or a commandant?"

"No, I was one of the king's personal guards."

Elias's eyes widened at that. "Was? Meaning you no longer are?"

The question seemed to perturb Luc. "Well, I suppose I still am. But since I'm no longer there..." he trailed off.

"What is your king like?" Stella asked, unable to imagine a king other than Draven.

"He's wise and fair for the most part. He's not perfect, but he does what he believes is best for his people."

"He sounds nothing like Draven," she remarked darkly.

"Was it he who sent you here?" Elias asked.

Luc chewed on a piece of meat before answering. "Yes, when my ancestry was discovered, he asked me to break the curse."

"And you agreed, just like that?" Elias asked.

Luc shook his head, avoiding their gazes. "No, not at first. But I was eventually persuaded."

This time it was Stella who questioned him. "What persuaded you?"

He didn't answer right away, as if wrestling with his choice of words. "The fact that Aurelia is dying."

"What?" she exclaimed, staring at Luc in surprise and dismay. "Why is it dying?"

He fixed her with a long, appraising look. "The land is drying up. With no respite from the sun, its light and heat beat down on the land relentlessly. Much of the region south of the Altous Mountains have dried out. Many parts have turned into deserts and wastelands. Aurelia itself is on the verge of complete desiccation when it was once a lush oasis. Forests like the one you live in are few and rapidly dwindling. People kill for water. Times are desperate, and have been for a long time. We need darkness, just as much as Noctum needs light. Light and dark, day and night, they were never meant to be separated."

Stella finally understood. Luc hadn't come just to save Noctum. If Aurelia hadn't been cursed as well, he never would have come at all. Something twisted in her stomach, a sense of betrayal. Luc had deceived her by withholding the truth. "Why did you not say so from the very beginning?"

"Remember how you didn't tell me about your secret hiding place?" he reminded her. "Not at first."

"I remember," she reluctantly admitted. She hadn't trusted him at the time, which meant she could hardly fault him for not trusting her.

"I didn't mean to deceive you. I just didn't want to reveal more than was necessary."

So he'd told her enough to gain her aid and support. "Is Noctum dying, too, then?"

"I think so, yes," Luc mused. "I've noticed that everything here seems frailer. Your vegetation, your animals, the people. The citizens of Caligo appear especially anemic and weak. I suspect it has to do with all of their inbreeding, to keep their blood pure."

Stella shuddered, feeling sorry for the people she had known better than to envy. They were no more than domesticated livestock, rendered too weak to even defend themselves.

"It's true," Elias said, looking perturbed. "We used to have more animals in Noctum, but bears have since died out, as have raccoons and badgers, elk and moose. And according to texts I've read, the Wastelands were once verdant forests a millennia ago."

Stella had never heard of any of these creatures before. As for what Elias said about the Wastelands, it was a stunning yet depressing revelation. "Did you ever make it to the Luna Market?" she asked, ready to change the subject to something less grim.

Elias shook his head. "Damian detained us on our way there."

Stella suddenly wondered what he would think of Luc's mission. Damian would be a powerful ally if convinced. Unfortunately, she didn't think that his suspicion of Luc, nor the fact that Luc had defeated him, helped with their cause. "There's still two more nights left," she said. "Though there were few vendors from Darkwood in attendance tonight."

"You went?" Elias asked, looking upset.

"Only to look for Luc." She turned to him. "You'd been gone for so long and I was worried. I wasn't so foolish as to actually attend, however. I merely searched for you from the trees." She went on to explain the detour she'd taken that had finally led her to them both.

179

"And by the way, Marta had her baby. It's a boy, and she's named him Aron."

"After your da?" Elias asked.

Stella nodded, longing to hold the tiny infant once more.

"So that's where you went," Luc said. "When I came back before leaving with Elias to the market, you were gone."

"I'm sorry. Jess came to get me so I couldn't wait for you to return."

"A note would have sufficed."

Elias and Stella exchanged a look. "We can't afford to leave anything written lying around," she replied.

"Why not?" Luc asked, confused.

She left it to Elias to explain, who did so in thorough detail. By the time he was done, she felt certain Luc had a better understanding of Draven's tyranny and the importance of the Repository.

"No wonder there are no books or scrolls anywhere," Luc marveled. "Nor any written signs. They're all inscribed with images."

"Now you know why," Stella replied, picking up the leather she'd been working on. "What did Garrett think of the whole affair?"

"He doesn't know what to think," Elias said. "It was his first time meeting Luc after I'd told him and Jenna about him. He was there when the witnesses were questioned, but he doesn't believe there's enough evidence to prove Luc is the man responsible for killing those two Nighthawks. He cornered me afterwards to ask my opinion."

"What did you tell him?" Stella asked, while Luc listened intently.

"That I thought Damian's suspicions of Luc likely stemmed from jealousy."

Stella felt her face heat. "You couldn't have given him another reason?"

"I couldn't think of one on the spot," Elias said with an unapologetic shrug. "Besides, Garrett didn't disagree with me, which means he believes it to be possible."

"We're going to have to watch out for Garrett as well," Stella said, sighing.

"Which is why we decided it best not to involve you from now on," Luc said. "Elias and I will reconnoiter together, since it's you that Damian and Garrett are so protective of. And rightly so."

Stella frowned, not liking the idea of being left out. But when she considered the importance of what Luc was doing, she knew she needed to aid him, not hinder him. And if the best way was to distract Damian and Garrett so Luc and Elias could move about freely, then so be it.

"Damian is supposed to hunt for me tomorrow night," she said, holding up the finished breastplate. "I'll find a way to keep him occupied for as long as possible when he comes by."

Too busy scrutinizing the work of her hands, she missed the worried look that passed between the two men.

24

A Dismal Distraction

Stella was beginning to worry that Damian wouldn't show. Nearly two hours had passed since Luc had left to meet Elias, and the thought crossed her mind that perhaps Damian had turned his eye to a different sort of quarry. Part of her was relieved, not that her friends might be hunted, but that she might avoid the discomfort of Damian's presence. Still, the longer she waited, the more frazzled her nerves became. She nearly yelped when a loud knock sounded at her door.

"Who is it?" she called through the thick oak.

"Damian."

Relief mingled with dread. She slowly pulled the door open, bracing herself as she always did when confronted by the sheer force that was Damian. A gasp escaped her. Marring his handsome face was a black bruise that encircled his entire left eye. She nearly asked what had happened, but stopped herself just in time. This was Luc's handiwork, she remembered. How could she have forgotten that he had challenged Luc and lost?

"Come in," she said, trying not to stare.

"Come in?" The look of suspicion on his face nearly had her laughing out loud.

"Or don't," she said carelessly. "I can see if the breastplate fits you just as easily outside."

"And Dartan?"

Stella eyed the black hound sitting beside him with a frown. "He stays outside as usual."

Damian gave his hound a look of apology. "Sorry, old boy," he said before entering, his sable-lined cloak brushing against her skirt. He carried a brace of rabbits in one hand and a bucket of fresh meat in the other. "The boar skin is hanging out to dry."

She noted his slight limp before shutting the door behind him.

"Thank you," she said, grabbing a knife and cutting board. Reaching into the bucket he had placed on the dining table, she began cutting the meat into smaller cubes, while Damian walked over to the breastplate lying on her work table. He removed his thick cloak and she paused to watch him lift it to his chest. It fit perfectly.

"You haven't even taken my measurements."

Stella furrowed her brow, confused by the note of satisfaction in his voice. Her face flushed when understanding dawned on her. *I notice everything about you, Stella.* Did he think she did the same for him? She noticed *some* things—more than she cared to admit—but certainly not everything. She frowned down at the meat she was cutting.

"You added an extra detail with this trim," he said, sliding a finger over the metal rivets that lined the overlapping layers running down the sternum.

"I aim to please," she said archly.

Damian grinned, and even with a black eye it was a dangerous thing. "If only that were always true."

Stella bit her lip, refusing to rise to the bait. She salted the cubes of boar meat and slid them onto wooden skewers.

"What are you doing?" he asked.

"I'm cooking," she replied, placing the skewers on the metal grate that hung over the fire. "What does it look like I'm doing?"

"That's plenty of boar," he said, his tone suddenly wary. "Are you expecting company?"

"None except your own. I planned to take your measurements tonight."

"Apparently you don't need to," he said, with an arrogant smirk.

Stella longed to wipe it off his face. "You have a similar build to someone else I know. I used him as a model."

It worked. Stony-faced, Damian stalked toward her. But all he did was reach for the rabbits on the table. Placing them on her cutting board, he grabbed one of his daggers and began to skin them.

"I can do that," she protested.

His answer was short and clipped. "I know."

With a sigh, she turned the skewers over the fire. It sizzled as the juices from the meat spilled, releasing a delicious aroma. From the corner of her eye, she saw Damian inhale deeply. She thought of how eagerly he had devoured her food the night Garrett had brought him to dinner, and wondered how often someone cooked for him.

"Aren't you going to ask what happened to my eye? Or do you already know?"

Stella hesitated, caught off guard by the question. "Was it a scorned lover?" she taunted. "Or perhaps an angry husband?"

"Not in this case, no." Damian's voice had gone back to being flinty. "Why do you insist on thinking the worst of me, Stella?"

That gave her pause. Was that true? Granted, he hadn't given her a favorable first impression. Or second. Or third. But he did have his good qualities—courage, intelligence, strength, and leadership, to name a few. "You must understand why I'm so leery of you."

Done skinning the rabbits, he rinsed his dagger with water from a pitcher, catching the bloody wash in a waste bucket. "I haven't been with a woman since the night you saw me at the tavern."

Stella was stunned by the unexpected and rather discomfiting admission. *Could it be true?* And then she remembered... "But you were with Ana and you said—"

"I know what I said, and I only said it because you frustrated me as you always do," he growled, drying his blade with a rag—the movements rushed and agitated. "Ouch!" A string of curses followed, spilling from his tongue unchecked.

Stella winced and drew near to survey the injury. She saw that Damian had sliced his thumb before he quickly wrapped it in the rag.

"You were being careless," she chided, as she went to the cupboard to grab her tincture. "And there's no need for such foul language."

Damian scowled at her then shook his head, frustrated with her yet again. When she reached for his hand, he yielded it to her warily. Ignoring his gaze, she unwound the rag and tended to his wound, first washing it gently then dabbing it with the tincture. His whole body began to vibrate from the pain.

She knew how much it stung and glanced up at him in sympathy. She never should have. Standing that close to him, his heated gaze and lips were only inches away. When they descended on hers she realized he had been shaking not from pain, but from want. She felt it in the crush of his lips and the sweep of his tongue. His kiss was not gentle, but sought to dominate, even claim. And, heaven help her, she felt powerless to resist.

Only when Luc's face flashed in her mind did she remember herself. When she managed to pull away, slightly dazed and panting heavily, she saw Damian gazing at her with both hunger and awe.

"Stop kissing me!" she exclaimed, though it was more of a plea.

Damian shut his eyes, looking pained. But when he opened them again he wore an expression of resolution. "It won't happen again," he said gruffly. "Not until you want it to."

Stella wanted to assure him that she would never desire such a thing, but it would've been a lie. His kisses were devastating. They were the sort of kisses that threatened to ruin her if she let them, a terrifying realization.

Damian was right. She did insist on thinking the worst of him, because it was the only defense she had against him.

"What I want is far more than you could ever give me." The words were designed to discourage and hurt him, but they rang with truth.

Smelling the roasted meat, Stella pulled the skewers from the fire and laid them on a platter. Then she went to bandage Damian's thumb, but saw he'd already taken care of it. Her heart ached at the hardened look on his face. Pushing the platter of boar meat toward him, she said in a light tone, "Have some. You know you want to."

Damian looked surprised, and she couldn't blame him. Normally, she would have kicked him out by now. She feared he would refuse, but hunger won out. Grudgingly, and looking angry about it, he took a skewer and began to tear into the meat with his teeth.

Hiding her satisfaction, Stella left him to eat in peace. At her work table, she found her measuring strip then looked over some sketches of various designs she had come up with. Compared to Garrett's armor, Damian's was sleeker and more elegant. She told herself it was because he was the commandant and needed to stand apart. In truth, much of it had to do with Damian's slim build, which allowed her to consider sharper lines and angles. Of course, design and execution were two different things. Not everything she imagined was possible, or even advisable. The spiked collar for instance. Or the horned pauldrons. Both added in a fit of pique the first time Damian had kissed her.

"Those are interesting details," Damian said, from over her shoulder.

Stella whirled, unaware that he had snuck up behind her.

"But I prefer my armor be free of spikes or horns if you please."

"Are you certain? If anyone can carry it off, it's you."

"I'm certain," he said drily.

Stella shrugged. "As you wish." Taking the measuring strip, she took a step back and looked him up and down, willing her expression to remain carefully neutral. "Are you ready to have your measurements taken?"

Damian nodded.

"We'll start with your arms," she said. "Hold your right one out first."

186

Stepping behind him, she stretched the measuring strip alongside the length of his arm. Then did the same with his left.

"Most tailors and seamstresses measure me from the front," Damian remarked.

Stella bit her lip. It was what she usually did as well, but measuring him from behind allowed her to avoid his gaze. If that made her a coward then so be it. "I'm not most tailors or seamstresses," was all she could say. "Next, I'll measure your chest and waist," she said, wrapping the strip around his upper torso.

The woolen shirt he wore was thin, allowing her to see the hard planes and ridges of his muscled back. Pulling her gaze away, she dropped the strip lower to measure his trim waist.

"Now for your legs. Just stand straight for me." When he did, she got to her knees and measured him from waist to ankle. She cleared her throat. "Now spread your legs apart."

She ran the strip from his inner ankle to as high as she dared, trying hard not to stare at his backside. A difficult feat since it was right in her face. "There, all done," she declared with obvious relief.

Damian took his time to turn around. When he did, he went straight to the cloak and weapons he had discarded earlier. Stella glanced at the clock and grimaced. It was still early in the evening. She would have to find some other way to delay him.

"I-I was hoping I could ask you for a favor."

Damian froze. "What sort of favor?"

"If you're heading to the Hollow, I was wondering if I could accompany you partway."

"Partway to where?"

"Erik's widow had her baby recently. I was hoping to see him."

Damian nodded, giving no indication whether her request pleased or annoyed him. "Wear a thick cloak," was all he said. "It's a cold night."

25

The Hollow Ambush

It wasn't just cold, it was frigid. Stella tightened the scarf around her neck as she and Damian crossed the clearing side by side. The moonlight soon faded as they entered the pinewoods, the gloom settling over them as heavily as the silence. Up ahead, Dartan was like a lithe shadow, dark and noiseless. Damian said not a word though she could feel his gaze upon her.

"What is it?" she asked, when she could stand it no more.

"I'm trying to understand something."

"Understand what?"

"You've done two things tonight you've never done before," he stated. "Feed me and seek my company."

"Wrong. I've fed you before."

"Feed me willingly then," he amended. "What I'm wondering is why. And I can only think of one reason."

"Oh?" she replied, feigning ignorance.

"You're trying to distract and delay me."

"And why would I do that?" she asked, her pulse skipping.

"To aid a certain someone you care about," he said stiffly. "What you forget, Stella, is that I'm a commandant now, which means I have an entire garrison of Shadow Guards at my disposal."

Stella felt her heart stutter. He didn't have to spy on Luc or Elias himself because he could order any number of guards to do it for him. He could even have guards stationed at key locations throughout Darkwood just waiting for them. She turned to glare at Damian. "Or maybe I was merely making an attempt to be friends, since you and I are so often thrown together."

"Friends?" Damian looked at her as if she were absurd. "I don't want to be your friend."

"You're right. Friendship with you is impossible anyway," she snapped. "I don't know what I was thinking."

Silence reigned once more, allowing her anxious thoughts to run freely. She was so caught up in her head, wondering and worrying about Luc and Elias that she didn't immediately notice the cold wetness tickling her face, landing on her brows and lashes. Perplexed, Stella blinked and looked around.

Snow!

It was falling softly, dusting the bare branches and pine needles alike, before landing on the leaf-littered ground. She took the time to appreciate the sight. It looked pretty now, under the moonlight. But in a few weeks time, when the ground was buried under several feet of snow, it would be nothing more than a burden and a pain.

"We should hurry," Damian urged. And she agreed. A harmless flurry could swiftly turn into a storm.

The snow began to fall faster and then harder. Stella ducked her head but refused to pull up her hood, not wanting to obstruct her peripheral view. She kept a lookout for landmarks, grateful for the full moon that lightened their path once more. It wasn't until she reached the Rodev's cottage that she realized Damian was still with her.

"Weren't we supposed to part at the Hollow?"

Damian lifted a snow-dusted brow. "Now you want to get rid of me?"

"Why not? We're not friends after all," she couldn't resist retorting.

He smiled darkly. "Since I'm here, I might as well see you safely inside."

Stella shrugged. She knocked on the door and waited. Mistress Rodev answered, her gaze going from Stella to Damian to the large dog between them. There was no missing the mild alarm that passed over her face at the sight of the hound.

"Stella?" She could hear the question in the woman's greeting.

"Hello, I hope you don't mind that I've come to see Marta and the baby. This is Dartan and his master, Damian Dagnatari." Then remembering his black eye and wanting to put Mistress Rodev at ease, she added. "The new commandant."

"The commandant?" Marta's ma immediately stepped back. "Please, come in." She squinted as she gazed behind him. "Snowing, eh?"

Stella stepped through and turned in surprise to find Mistress Rodev ushering Damian inside, while keeping Dartan out.

"My husband once served in the Shadow Guard," she was telling him, guiding him to a chair. "He should be out shortly. I'm sure he would like the opportunity to meet you."

"Damian only meant to escort me, Mistress Rodev. He must have duties he needs to attend to."

"I can stay for a little while," he countered, taking a look around.

Bewildered by the turn of events, Stella studied him, wondering why he had chosen to remain. Especially if he was aware she was trying to distract him. But then the door to Marta's room swung open, and the new mother and baby came out. At the sight of her little nephew, she forgot about everything else.

"You can hold him, if you want," Marta offered.

Stella didn't hesitate to take the infant in her arms. The warmth of his little body penetrated right to her heart. "He looks plumper already," she murmured.

"He's a lusty feeder," Marta said with a smile, the first Stella had seen in a long time. Marta turned her gaze to the stranger in the room. "Hello."

"This is the new commandant, Marta," her ma said. "Damian

Dagnatari. This is my daughter, Marta Rodev."

"Varden," Marta said firmly. "It's still Varden."

Dismay passed over Mistress Rodev's face, but she let Marta's comment pass. "Can I offer you anything to drink, Commandant Dagnatari?"

"No, but thank you for your offer," he replied, just as Mister Rodev emerged from his room.

The two men studied one another, Damian fit and trim and in the prime of his life. Marta's da older and grizzled, but still a man to be reckoned with if pushed.

Marta's ma introduced them to each other, while Marta and Stella sat down to coo over the baby. When the men began to converse, Mistress Rodev busied herself at the hearth. It was a normal, domestic scene, but it was odd for Stella to see Damian taking part in it. She gave half an ear to the men's conversation, but soon lost interest when the bulk of their discussion centered around military planning and organization. At any other time, it might have interested her, but not when her nephew was so alluring.

Stella stayed long enough for little Aron to wake up, feed, have his diaper changed then fall back asleep before she decided she should go. When a glance at the clock showed that two hours had gone by, she was shocked. Partly because the time had flown, but mostly because Damian had stayed for the duration.

"We should go," she said, rising reluctantly. "The snow was coming down hard when we arrived."

Damian nodded. "And Dartan is probably half frozen by now."

They said their goodbyes and stepped out to find the forest completely transformed. The winterscape that greeted them was at once stark and seductive. Stella studied the blanket of white that covered the ground and dusted the trees, recalling a time when such a scene might've delighted her. Watching Dartan gallop toward them—the snow flying up behind his paws—reminded her of when she used to frolic through the snow, laughing as the snowflakes kissed her skin. Now the snow reminded her of her ma's frozen body.

"It's still snowing," she remarked, trying to banish thoughts of the past.

"It's not so deep yet," Damian replied, venturing forward.

Stella fell in step beside him, questions whirling in her head. Why had he stayed? And why was he still with her? But she didn't ask because she wasn't certain she wanted to know the answers.

"Do you have family?" she asked instead.

"Everyone has family, Stella."

"But you never mention yours."

"For good reason."

The answer both troubled and intrigued her. "Are they so bad?"

"You couldn't even begin to imagine."

Immediately, she began to do just that. "Are your parents still alive?"

"No."

"Do you have brothers or sisters?"

"I hope not," he replied grimly.

At that point, Stella desisted her line of questioning, perturbed by his curt responses. It was just as well, for Damian had his own questions for her.

"Were your family good people?" he asked.

"Yes," she replied, without hesitation.

"Did they care for you?"

"Yes."

"Then be glad, even if they're gone. You may miss them, but at least you can think of them fondly."

Stella opened her mouth only to close it again. Damian was just like her, she realized. Alone in the world. But while she missed her family terribly, he seemed relieved to be rid of his. As much as she wanted to find out why, she feared intruding where she was doubtless unwelcome. But how sad to think that Damian had never known the warmth and security of a loving home.

They had just reached the outskirts of the Hollow when Dartan began to growl. Damian immediately drew his sword. Stella did likewise, standing still and listening. It wasn't long before she detected the sound of distant screaming.

"Run back to the Rodev's cottage," Damian instructed.

"Wait!" Stella exclaimed, grabbing his arm before he could rush off. "What is happening?"

"I don't know, Stella. But I intend to find out."

"Then I'm going with you," she said, heading for the Hollow.

This time, Damian grabbed her. "No, you're not."

"Yes, I am. I—" The blood swiftly drained from Stella's face. Damian spun around to see what she was staring at.

A Shade, standing roughly ten feet away.

Dartan shot past them to barrel into its chest. The creature grabbed it by the scruff and flung it more than fifty feet away.

Stella turned, catching something from the corner of her eye. A second Shade stepped out from behind a tree. "There's two of them," she told Damian, her voice surprisingly even as she lifted her blade.

Damian began to curse under his breath as he shoved her behind him. Did he think to take on both Shades himself? He could barely see out of one eye and his leg was injured! Stella wanted to check on Dartan, to see if the hound was alright, but she refused to tear her gaze away from the creature before her. Under the light of a full moon, she could see it clearly. Emaciated body. Pale, withered skin. Blood red eyes in a skull-like head. Only the small, sagging breasts gave any hint it was female. There were two here. Did that mean the other three were at the Hollow? What else would account for the screams?

Damian suddenly charged. When he did, so did the Shade before her. Stella thought her heart would jump from her chest as she swung her sword left then right, forcing the creature back. They circled one another, Stella catching a glimpse of Damian wielding his sword with skill. The snow continued to fall, but the cold didn't seem to bother the creature. It watched her with deadly intent, its eyes unwavering.

193

Could this be Nettie or Ana? Suddenly, it leapt, giving her less than a second to brace for the impact. Her sword pierced it through its gut, but the force of its charge threw her back, ramming the hilt of her sword against her ribcage. She groaned, but it was lost beneath the Shade's shriek of rage. Stella stumbled backward, but not in time to avoid the slash of razor sharp claws that shredded her cloak and upper right arm. Reaching for her dagger with her left, she took careful aim and threw. But the creature lurched and it sunk into its shoulder rather than its heart.

She was now out of weapons.

Stella watched in dread as the Shade yanked at her dagger, tossing it to the ground as if useless. With greater trouble, it pulled at her sword, cutting its own hands as it slowly slid the blade from its body. Black blood gushed from both its wounds, but it wouldn't die. Not until its heart was pierced and its head removed. Unfortunately, she was in no position to do either.

Stella unclasped her cloak.

The Shade charged, its claws extended. Stella threw the cloak as she darted to her right then dove for her sword. She grasped it in time to deflect the creature's next attack. Its arm flew, severed below its elbow, spraying black blood on her face and neck as she scrambled to her feet. To the right, she saw Damian behead the other Shade before thrusting his blade through its heart. Dartan's jaws were clamped around its leg, refusing to let go even as its body fell limply to the ground.

The Shade before her howled in pain and fury, fixing her with a look of such hatred Stella shuddered involuntarily. Faster than she thought possible the creature pounced, swiping her sword away as if it were nothing more than a stick. But before it could slash at her, the Shade spasmed, arching backward as it sought to dislodge the dagger Damian had hurled into the center of its back. The next thing Stella knew its head was flying from its body, which fell forward as Dartan jumped on it from behind.

"Move, Dartan!" Damian ordered. The moment the hound leapt off, he plunged his sword through the Shade's heart.

With shaking hands, Stella retrieved her sword and dagger, her eyes scanning the surrounding woods. Two Shades lay dead on the ground, their black blood staining the once pristine snow. That was twice now she had faced a Shade and survived, though she knew she could not have done so alone. In the direction of the Hollow, silence had replaced the screaming, but it did little to reassure her.

Stella noted that the snow had stopped falling when the sound of tearing cloth turned her head. She watched as Damian wrapped her arm with a strip taken from the bottom of his shirt. Her blood quickly soaked through it.

"We need to check on the Hollow," he said, draping her cloak, now shredded, over her shoulders.

We, he said. Not *I*. Either because he knew he couldn't stop her from joining him, or he decided it was better to keep her close by. Taking her sword and dagger, Damian cleaned both in the snow. He did the same with his own weapons before they trudged to the Hollow.

26

The Friendly Enemy

W hen they reached the large clearing where most of Darkwood's citizens chose to dwell, they saw that much blood had been shed there. Bodies lay scattered in the snow. Humans, no Shades. Soft weeping had replaced the usual chatter, and stunned, terror-filled faces mingled with those bearing sorrow and outrage. As they walked through the Hollow, surveying the damage, Stella saw the wounded being tended to and grieved with those mourning the dead.

Two men approached them, and Stella saw from their weapons and armor that they were Shadow Guards.

"Commandant," one of them greeted Damian, even though he was dressed in hunting gear rather than uniform. "Captain Lucan just sent for you. We didn't expect you so—"

"What happened here?" Damian demanded.

"A Shade attack. There were three of them."

"Casualties?" Damian asked.

"Eleven dead. Six injured."

"And the Shade?"

"All killed, sir!" the second guard crowed eagerly.

Stella saw the look of surprise on Damian's face. "Show me," he said.

The guards nodded, glancing at Stella curiously, before leading them both to the east end of the Hollow. She soon saw a crowd of people standing in a large circle, many of them Shadow Guards. When Damian maneuvered his way through to the center, she followed curiously.

She wasn't too surprised to see the bodies of three dead Shade lying in the middle of the crowd. What she was surprised to see was Luc standing there with both Elias and Garrett. The narrowing of his eyes told her Damian had noticed them as well.

With seemingly great effort, Damian tore his gaze from Luc to study the dead creatures lying at their feet. All three were properly beheaded and stabbed through the heart. "Well done," he conceded. "Who is responsible for this?"

Oddly, no one eagerly claimed credit or seemed willing to volunteer the information. But a number of sly glances were directed Luc's way.

It was Garrett who spoke. "We have Luc here to thank for slaying the creatures."

"Alone?" Damian asked, his hardened voice laced with disbelief.

"Mostly," Garrett said. "He killed two on his own and we killed the third together."

Damian nodded stiffly. "Burn the bodies if you can. You three"—he looked at Garrett, Luc and Elias—"come with me."

The guards proceeded to do his bidding, and when the ones he'd singled out made their way over, Stella noticed the looks of awe and respect that followed Luc.

"Not you, Stella," Damian said, when she made to join them.

Incensed, she watched as the four men stood off to talk in private. Irritation turned to worry, however, when she wondered what Damian intended to do. Surely he didn't think to find fault with Luc? Though that was exactly what she feared he would do.

Though their expressions were tense, the men spoke calmly. Well, except for Luc who tirelessly maintained his charade. She gazed at him in admiration, thinking of what he had done. As if feeling her gaze, his eyes met hers. Even from distance, she saw the way they brightened. *For her.* A small smile played on his lips, turning her own up as well. Until she noticed the cold, dark eyes watching her. She swiftly turned away, not wanting to make things worse for Luc, hoping it wasn't too late. But standing there in the cold snow, Stella felt an undeniable warmth in her chest.

Across the way, she saw a young woman watching as the guards gathered wood and kindling, laying them in a pile. "When did the attack happen?" Stella asked her.

The woman looked at her with haunted eyes. "Less than an hour ago. It happened so quickly. Fortunately, someone had time to raise the alarm."

Elias broke away from the group and Stella went over to meet him. "Are you alright? You weren't injured, were you?"

"I'm perfectly fine," he replied, somewhat guiltily. "Not a scratch on me."

"Good," she replied. Elias was no warrior and the thought of losing him was not something she wanted to consider.

"I was nowhere near the fighting," he continued. "Because on our way back from the Luna Market, Luc took off like an arrow and left me behind. He must have heard something I didn't. By the time I arrived at the Hollow, he and Garrett were battling the final Shade."

"Did the visit to the market prove useful?" she asked, though it seemed almost trivial to inquire after what had just taken place.

"Luc seems to think so. He was studying everything from the Nighthawks' movements to the height of the walls to the size of the Killing Fields."

"The king made no appearance?"

"No, not this time."

Stella was relieved, her gaze turning back to the group of men Elias had left. "So what was discussed?"

"It was less a discussion than an interrogation," Elias replied with a frown. "The commandant wanted to know where we had come from, what we'd been doing, and how we'd stumbled onto the scene."

"And you told him...?"

"The truth. Except I left out the part where Luc took off without me. I don't think we want Damian to know Luc possesses sorcery-enhanced hearing."

Stella looked at him in surprise. What else did Elias know about Luc that she didn't?

"Why is Luc still there when Damain knows, or believes rather, that he can't speak?" she asked.

"In case you didn't realize it by now, Damian doesn't much like or trust Luc. I suspect he's either being threatened or browbeaten."

Stella immediately marched toward the group. When she neared, Damian ceased his tirade, but not before she heard him saying, "Something is not right about you. Whatever it is you're hiding, I will find—"

"Are you done harassing him yet?" Stella asked coldly. "In case you've forgotten, he just fought and killed three Shade. You should be thanking him, not threatening him."

"This is a private discussion, Stella. One you were not invited to. You should know better than to intrude on Shadow Guard matters," Damian returned stonily, while Garrett looked on in silence, clearly uncomfortable.

"It's not a discussion if the man can't speak," she pointed out.

Damian's eyes glinted in anger, but he nodded his head to Garrett. "I'm done with him."

Garrett, at least, had the grace not to treat Luc like a lowly criminal. "You may go." He followed after Luc, leaving her to face Damian's wrath alone.

"You will not question or defy me like that again," he commanded, the coldness in his voice chilling her.

"I never would have if I thought you were being fair," she returned, careful to keep her tone reasonable.

"I don't care what you think, Stella," he bit out. "I am the commandant. To question me is to undermine my authority. *Do not* do it again."

Or what? she wanted to retort. But wisely, she kept her mouth shut. She knew she had committed a grave error. Erik would have been mortified at her disrespect, especially to one of Damian's rank. "I'll try my best not to," she allowed, turning away.

An iron grip stayed her. "You won't try, you'll do."

Stella wanted to yank her arm away, but he was gripping the one that was injured. "I'm not one of your soldiers," she seethed. "You can't command me to do anything."

"Perhaps not," Damian allowed, releasing her. "But I can make you regret defying me."

Stella's eyes flashed, more shaken by his threat than she cared to admit. How Damian could go from being protective to brutish was unnerving. But she shouldn't have been surprised. After all, he could go from thoughtful to insensitive, amorous to odious, gentle to rough just as easily. She stayed her tongue, not for herself but for Luc. For she had a feeling that Damian was not above using him to get to her. Shooting him a look of contempt, she hurried away.

27

The Result of Revenge

The night Draven was to leave for Blackbriar coincided with the fulfillment of Stella and Damian's agreement.

Luc had left to spy on the king alone, refusing to take Elias with him. Elias had told her this *after* Luc had already left. He had been gone for hours now and there was no knowing when he would return, which of course, swamped Stella with fear and anxiety. Who was to say Draven hadn't already killed him? He could be lying dead in the woods, his body frozen in the snow. That was the hazard of doing anything alone. There was no one to watch your back. No one to know if you succeeded or failed, until it was too late. Worse, he hadn't bothered to tell her where he would be. So even if she wanted to search for him, she had no idea where to look.

Stella tried to keep busy, but was too agitated to follow through on any task. Even now, Damian's armor sat neglected on her lap, needle and thread forgotten between her fingers. Tossing the armor aside, she grabbed her weapons and cloak and braved the wintry night.

Last night's storm had brought knee-deep snow to the forest, causing the trek to the Rodevs' cottage to take twice as long. To make the effort worth it, Stella spent hours with Marta and the baby. Then she decided to pay a visit to Jenna as well. Struggling through the snow was still better than being stuck waiting at home. And perhaps it was petty, but it would serve a certain menacing commandant right if he came by the cottage to find her absent. The way he had threatened her two nights ago still heated her blood.

"Stella!" Standing at her doorway, Jenna looked at her in surprise, her hazel eyes moving over Stella's shabby cloak to the piles of snow she had waded through. "What are you doing here?" Then realizing her friend was standing in the freezing cold, she said, "Come in, come in."

Stella entered gratefully, relishing the warmth emitted from the roaring fireplace.

"Why are you wearing this old thing?" Jenna asked, taking her cloak. "It's not even thick enough for the season." Then she noticed Stella's bandaged arm. "What's this? When did this happen?"

"I injured it two nights ago," Stella replied, as she went to warm herself by the fire. "The same time my cloak was destroyed."

"Two nights ago? The night of the Shade attack? Garrett didn't tell me you were injured," Jenna said, sounding incensed. "He said that you and Damian arrived *after* the attack."

Stella thought back to that night. When she and Damian had reached the Hollow, her tattered cloak had hidden her wounded arm. "Much was happening that night. I don't think he even noticed. Besides, Damian and I were attacked outside of the Hollow, by two other Shades."

"What?" Jenna exclaimed.

So Stella told her what happened. When she was done, Jenna stared at her in dismay. "It's a good thing Damian was with you. But what were you doing together anyway?"

Stella could hear the clear reproof in her voice. "He had escorted me to Marta's and insisted on escorting me back home," she answered, deliberately concealing the fact that she had initially asked him to do so.

"Stella, you're aware that Damian is infatuated with you, aren't you?"

Stella averted her gaze. She had never confided to Jenna any of the things that had transpired between her and the Shadow Guard. There hadn't been opportunity. But even if there had, she wouldn't have willingly volunteered the information. It was too delicate, too complicated, too...awkward.

"I'm aware," she finally admitted. "But it will pass. After tonight, our agreement ends, so we'll have no cause to see much of each other in the future."

Jenna looked dubious. "Do you know that he's not been seen with another woman in months? Ana was all but throwing herself at him in desperation. Well, that is, before..."

Before Draven took her from the Winter Solstice celebration.

Stella shuddered, but her thoughts soon turned to Damian's admission. *I haven't been with a woman since the night you saw me at the tavern.* She had dismissed his claim at the time, too unnerved by the kiss that followed. But now here Jenna was confirming it.

"Anyway," Jenna said, shifting uncomfortably. "It seems that's highly unusual behavior for Damian. He's known for having a healthy, uh...appetite."

"Can we please talk about something else?" Stella pleaded. Damian was the one person she was trying her best not to think about, especially in that way.

"Yes, of course," Jenna said, rueful. Her eyes lit up as she quickly seized on another topic. "Everyone's been talking about Elias's friend, Luc! Have you met him yet?"

"I saw him at the Hollow," Stella admitted with caution.

"Is he as handsome as everyone claims?" Jenna asked eagerly.

"He is."

"Elias failed to mention that when he told us about him. So did ma and da," she said with a frown. "Did you hear about how he killed those three Shades?"

"Garrett helped him with one of them," Stella remarked.

Jenna nodded, smiling proudly, but prattled on in her excitement.

"I told Elias to bring him over for dinner so we could meet him. Of course, all of a sudden he's too busy." Stella knew her brother had been spending his time at the Repository. That is, when he wasn't with Luc. "It's a shame, though, that he's mute."

"A shame," Stella murmured in agreement.

Jenna suddenly got to her feet. "You might as well stay for dinner. I was just about to prepare some food."

Stella glanced at the clock and noted that Damian would have already arrived at her cottage. She swiftly pushed the thought from her mind.

They cooked together and then ate, all the while chattering about everything and anything. Jenna filled her in on the latest gossip, while she discussed her recent visit to Marta's, gushing about her nephew. When she was ready to leave, however, they opened the door to find that it had been snowing in earnest.

"You can't go out in that," Jenna declared, staring at the thickly falling snow. It was so heavy the trees standing only fifteen feet away were invisible.

So Stella spent the night, though she couldn't sleep. Thoughts of Luc kept her up most of the evening, along with a small amount of guilt concerning Damian. It wasn't until Garrett returned in the late hours that she finally drifted off, comforted by the sounds of his and Jenna's hushed voices.

The following night found the land covered in several more feet of snow.

"I'll take you home," Garrett offered, after they'd broken their fast.

Borrowing Jenna's cloak, she said goodbye to her friend and followed Garrett through the waist-high drifts. The gibbous moon hung in a clear sky, and the forest gleamed a silver-white. It was beautiful and deadly. One wrong step could twist an ankle, leaving one vulnerable to the cold or to predators. One wrong turn could cause confusion, leading one in the wrong direction, away from home. It was easy to lose your bearings when familiar landmarks lay hidden beneath deep snow.

Stella's breath came out in a vapor.

In the distance, a wolf howled and then another. They instinctively picked up their pace.

By the time they reached her clearing, Stella's legs were numb and she could barely feel her toes.

"Wait here," Garrett said, when they plowed their way to the front door. These were the first words he'd spoken in hours and the warning in them immediately put her on alert.

When Garrett pushed the door open, she realized the reason for his concern. The door had been locked and she alone possessed the key. With sword raised, he entered the dark cottage. Seconds later, he was yelling her name.

Inside, she was able to discern Garrett bent over a body sprawled out on her floor. He was blocking the head and face, revealing only a bloody torso, arms and legs. Stella's heart lodged in her throat. *Luc!*

Then Garrett moved, and in the moonlight, she saw that it wasn't Luc but Damian.

"Stella!" Garrett's tone indicated that he'd been calling her name. "We need light and rags to staunch his bleeding. And any healing herbs you may have."

Snapping out of her daze, Stella began to move with purpose. First, she lit several lanterns. Then she grabbed everything Garrett asked for, including her tincture and the comfrey she'd recently purchased.

"What happened to him?" she asked. Though it became evident once she began to treat his wounds.

Damian had been mauled.

"Looks like a wolf attack," Garrett said grimly. "There are dozens of bite marks all over his body."

Stella winced as she washed the worst of them, a large chunk that had been bitten out of Damian's left thigh.

She and Garrett worked together in tense silence—cleaning then bandaging his wounds one by one. They would have to be stitched, but for now the priority was to stop the bleeding and avoid infection. It was slow work. By the time Stella was tending the last bite, silent tears were streaming from her eyes.

"It's a wonder he had the strength to break down your door," Garrett said, as they gazed down at the unconscious man.

"Let's carry him to my bed," Stella suggested, wiping her tears away.

"I hate to move him, but I suppose we can't leave him on the floor. Though…perhaps we should put him in Erik's room?"

"Yes…yes, of course," she stammered, moving to lift his legs.

"I have it, Stella. You're injured," Garrett said, lifting Damian with ease.

Garrett carried him to the bedroom and gently laid him on the bed, being mindful not to exacerbate his injuries

"He hasn't stirred," Stella said worriedly.

"But his pulse is still steady," Garrett assured her, his finger at Damian's neck. "I'll go find a healer. Will you be alright staying here with him? I may be a while."

"Oh no!" Stella cried out, as a sudden realization hit her.

"What is it?" Garrett asked, gazing at her in alarm.

"Dartan! He always has the hound with him when he hunts."

Garrett sighed. "That dog would die for him. I suspect that's what happened when he tried to protect his master."

Stella wanted to cry harder.

After Garrett left, she attempted to scrub Damian's blood from her floor. She only succeeded in scrubbing off the paint that covered the Shade's black blood. She stared at the stains in dismay. Heavy in both body and spirit, she went to the room to check on Damian, but it only made her feel worse. He looked so broken, when he had never been anything but strong and fierce.

"I'm sorry," she whispered, her voice raw with emotion. While tending his wounds, all she could picture was him waiting outside her cottage, unaware of the pack of wolves ready to descend on him. Her guilt was great, especially when she considered that the creatures were likely drawn by the scent of the fresh meat he'd brought for her. "I should have been there. If I'd known—" her voice cracked. "If I'd known what would happen, I swear I never would have left."

Tentatively, she reached over to lightly trace one of the four grooves slashed across his right cheek, so perilously close to his bruised eye. He twitched and mumbled something so softly she couldn't be certain what he'd said. It had sounded very much like her name, though she couldn't be certain.

She poured water into a cup and tried to tip some into Damian's mouth, holding him upright so he didn't choke. Afterwards, she laid him back down and began to carefully undress him. Even with all his bandaged wounds, it was easy to see how well-built he was—lean and muscular, without an ounce of fat on him. Leaving on his undergarment, she covered him with a thin sheet. His wounds would be easier to tend if he wore no clothes. When she was done, she brought a chair into the room and sat at his bedside. Moments later, she was fast asleep.

28

A Light in the Dark

"Stella! Stella!"

Stella parted her eyes, disoriented. The first thing she registered was Damian lying on her bed. But he was still unconscious, so he couldn't have been the one calling her. She turned, and that was when she saw Luc gazing down at her, concern in his vivid green eyes.

She leapt from her chair, hugging him tightly. "You're back!" she cried, tearing in relief.

Luc held her for a long moment, before gently pulling back. "You're crying," he said in wonder, wiping her cheeks with his thumbs. "You don't have to cry anymore." His expression turned solemn as he glanced at the bed. "What happened to him?"

"Garrett and I found him. We think he was attacked by wolves."

Luc nodded, an odd knowing look on his face. "There's something I need to show you."

Curious, she followed him out of the bedroom, stopping at the sight of a bloody, matted pile of black fur on the floor. "Dartan!" She dropped to her knees beside the hound. "Is he still alive?"

"Barely."

"How—where did you find him?"

"In the copse of elms near the secret entrance."

He's an excellent tracker, Damian had said. She looked at the dog and shook her head in amazement.

Together, she and Luc cared for the hound. It was a miracle the dog was still breathing, for he was in worse shape than his master. Among his many injuries, his right ear was torn off, his left jaw flayed open, and the tip of his tail was missing. Stella found herself having to choke down bile more than once.

When they did all they could, Luc lifted the dog and laid him at the foot of Damian's bed, formerly his bed.

"Is that the best place for him?" Stella asked, dubious.

"I've had several dogs of my own," Luc replied. "I think it will be good for them to be near each other."

In the main room, Stella turned to give Luc a thorough look. "I'm so glad you're alright. You were gone for so long, I thought—"

"I'm sorry I worried you, Stella. It wasn't my intent."

"But what delayed you?"

"I did more than just observe Draven. I snuck into Caligo after he left."

Stella went stiff. "You did what?"

"I knew that the city would be safest with Draven gone. I couldn't pass up the opportunity."

"But…how?"

"I avoided the guards, climbed over the walls and stole some clothes so I could blend in with the citizens," he said, making it sound like a breezy jaunt through the woods. Ruefully, she doubted he could have accomplished any of this had she accompanied him.

"And then?"

"I learned quite a bit while I was there. Elias will be pleased with the information I've gathered, particularly the missing areas of the castle layout."

Just when Stella thought she couldn't be more shocked. "You went into the castle?"

Luc nodded, grinning.

"What is it like?"

"The castle or the city?"

"The castle, the city…everything."

Luc's head suddenly snapped to the door. "Are you expecting someone?"

"Garrett went for a healer," she remembered, hurrying to the door. "Quick, hide in my room!"

Knocking sounded on the door. "Stella, it's me!" Garrett called out.

She pulled the door open to find Garrett…alone. "No healer?" she asked, dread like a heavy lump in her belly.

"She was killed in the Shade attack," Garrett said, rubbing his forehead. "It will be up to us to help Damian until another can be located."

Stella swallowed. This meant they would have to sew Damian up themselves.

"How is he?" Garrett asked, glancing in the direction of the bedroom.

"Come see for yourself," she said, leading him there. "He stirred…just a little. Otherwise, nothing has changed." She opened the door to let him in.

Garrett froze at the sight of Dartan at the foot of the bed. "Where did you find him?"

"Oh…" Stella racked her brain for a likely explanation. "I heard a scratching at my door, and he was just there."

Garrett chuckled darkly. "He's as hard to kill as his master."

"Or just as stubborn, but he's in much worse shape."

"Damian will be grateful nonetheless." He continued to stare at the hound in disbelief, before turning to look at her. "Are you ready to sew him up?" he asked, hesitantly. "I'll help, of course. There are far too many wounds for just one person."

Stella nodded with reluctance. This would be very different from sewing leather.

Procuring two needles, she passed both over a flame before

threading them with her thinnest but strongest twine. Sewing Damian's wounds proved far more difficult than treating them. His skin was tender but slippery with blood. And it was a test of Stella's will not to gag at the messy work.

Hours later, she and Garrett sat back wearily, their backs aching and their eyes strained.

"Your stitches are much cleaner and neater than mine," he said, grimacing at his handiwork.

"Which is why I sewed up his face, not you."

"Damian will thank you for that," Garrett replied, standing to stretch.

"You should get home. Does Jenna even know what happened tonight? You were supposed to just escort me to my cottage," she said, as they exited the bedroom.

When she glanced at the clock, she was stunned to discover the lateness of the hour. An entire evening had passed.

"She knows. I returned home briefly. I also stopped by the barracks to inform the other captains about what happened." He strapped on his weapons and reached for his cloak. "I'm on duty tomorrow, so I may not be able to return until late. I'll send another guard to check on you, though." He pulled the door open, frowning at it. "And to fix your lock. Barricade it until then."

"I will." As soon as he left, she jammed a wooden chair beneath the knob. A noise had her turning.

"You look ready to collapse," Luc said, gazing at her in dismay.

"I am feeling faint," she admitted. "I haven't eaten in ten hours or so."

"Sit down," Luc instructed. "I'll get you something to eat."

Grateful, Stella dropped onto the couch, listening absently as Luc rummaged through the pantry. She glanced down at her hands and realized they were still stained with blood. She sighed, too weary to get up and wash them.

When Luc brought over a plate of meat, cheese and carrots, he saw her hands and returned with a bowl of soapy water and a damp rag. He had her dip both hands in the bowl before taking one and rubbing each finger with the rag. Stella leaned her head back and closed her eyes, lulled by the soothing sensation. It felt good to be taken care of, especially by Luc.

"There you go," he said, when he was finished. "Now you can eat."

Stella opened her eyes and gave him a tired smile. "This is a lot of food," she said, gazing at the plate.

"I thought we could share. I'm famished myself. My last meal was a stolen tart from a market stand in Caligo."

As they ate, Luc finally told her all that he'd seen and learned in the city. Stella listened, fascinated, though she was mostly just glad to have him alive and well, and at her side.

"How's your arm?" he asked, when the food was all gone. "Do you need me to change your bandage?"

Stella shook her head but smiled, warmed by his thoughtfulness. "I took care of it earlier."

They talked a while longer, allowing their food to digest. But when Stella stifled a yawn, Luc urged her to go to bed. She nodded and rose tiredly. Halfway to her bedroom, she paused and turned around. "You have nowhere to sleep," she realized with a frown.

"The couch will do."

The couch barely fit her and Luc was at least nine inches taller. Stella shook her head. "*I* will sleep on the couch. You take the bed."

"I won't take your bed, Stella."

Too late. She had already stretched herself out on the couch.

"Stella!" Luc's tone was reproving, but she merely shut her eyes.

She heard a deep sigh. The next thing Stella knew she was being lifted, strong hands supporting her back and knees. Her eyes flew open to land on Luc's handsome tanned face. "What are you doing?" she asked, the question sounding breathless.

"Carrying you to your bed, you stubborn woman."

"You're the stubborn one," she grumbled.

Too soon, she was being laid down gently. Though her bed was welcoming, she missed the feel of Luc's arms. "Good night, Stella," he whispered. For a moment, he gazed down at her, his smile warm and his eyes soft. Then he was shutting the door behind him, leaving her feeling bereft.

29

The Unwilling Patient

T he following night, Stella found Luc twisted on the couch, his neck bent at an awkward angle, one foot on the floor and the other hanging over the arm of the couch. The night after that, she discovered him stretched out on the rug.

It was on that same night that Damian opened his eyes.

"You're awake," she breathed, relief breaking over her. Moments earlier, she had been tending to his wounds and had just returned with fresh supplies to do the same for his hound. "How do you feel?"

"Like picked over carrion," he rasped, trying to rise.

Laying the supplies on a small table, she hurried to his aid, arranging the pillows so that he could sit upright. She pointedly ignored the bare chest that was now on display, a chest that hadn't bothered her nearly so much when he was unconscious.

"Where am I?" he asked, wincing as he surveyed the room.

"In Erik's old bedroom," she replied, noting his look of surprise. "We carried you in here after we found you."

"We?" he asked suspiciously.

"Garrett and I."

"I was attacked by wolves," Damian said, his brow furrowed and his eyes clouded. "Dartan had gone after a squirrel, leaving me alone. I was distracted, and they pounced on me before I could draw a weapon."

Distracted by what? But Stella was afraid to ask.

Damian's eyes suddenly cleared. "Dartan! Where is he? Did he—?" Pain twisted his features as he shook his head. Stella could only imagine what he was remembering.

"He's in bad shape," she supplied. "But still clinging to life. He's actually here at the foot of the bed."

"I want to see him."

Stella cringed. The hound was not fit to be seen. "You need to stay in bed and he's in no state to be moved. Hopefully soon, though," she added, to appease him.

"He's alive," Damian breathed with relief. Then he shut his eyes, as if their brief exchange had exhausted him.

"Are you hungry, or thirsty perhaps?"

"I could use some food and water."

When Stella returned with both, she found that Damian was unable to lift his arms without a great amount of pain, so she resigned herself to feeding him. As awkward as it was for her, it was far more humiliating for Damian, if his scowl was anything to go by.

"Come now," she said. "This may be the only time you have the privilege of me serving you."

Damian considered that before grudgingly opening his mouth. She tipped the mug against his lips, letting the water slowly trickle in, and congratulated herself when none spilled out.

"There," she said, satisfied. "Now what would you like to eat first?"

Damian glanced at the plate she had prepared. "The cheese."

Nodding, she picked up a small cube and placed it near his mouth. When he bit into it, his lips brushed against her fingertips, letting loose a flock of frenzied butterflies in her stomach. Pretending not to be affected, she dropped her eyes to the plate and picked up another cube of cheese. Though she held it in such a way as to avoid contact, Damian still managed to touch her fingers with his mouth. Five minutes into feeding him, Stella was feeling so flustered and overly warm, she wanted to bolt from the room though the plate was still half full.

"Have you had enough?" she asked, hopeful.

Amusement seemed to dance in his eyes as Damian studied her face, but it was soon replaced by something more serious. "Where were you, Stella?"

And just like that her discomfort gave way to guilt. "I went to visit Marta and the baby," she admitted, averting her gaze. "Then I went to visit Jenna."

"You went even though you knew I was coming." It wasn't a question, and the accusation tore at her already battered conscience.

"Yes," she answered, forcing herself to meet his gaze. "And I'm sorry. So sorry."

Stella had braced herself for anger and condemnation, but what she saw was far worse. In his dark eyes, she saw disappointment and hurt.

"You have every right to be upset with me," she continued. "What I did was petty and inconsiderate. If I could do it all over again…" She trailed off, realizing how lame her apology sounded.

"I'm tired, Stella," Damian said in reply. "If you could just leave me alone now, it shouldn't be any trouble for you, since it's what you prefer to do anyway."

Feeling as if he had struck her, Stella left, shame souring her belly.

Out in the main room, she found Luc waiting for her. But even his handsome face wasn't enough to dispel her guilt and shame.

"He's awake?" Luc whispered.

Stella nodded. "Which means we'll have to be more careful from now on," she whispered back. "He could be up on his feet at any moment and we don't want to be caught off guard."

"Elias knows the situation," he replied, staring at the closed bedroom door. "And he's offered to have me stay with him while Damian remains."

Stella gazed at him in dismay. "You don't have to go."

"But—"

She quickly cut him off, unwilling to hear any of his arguments. "Please. Don't leave." The last time she had begged for anything, she was a child entreating her ma for a treat.

Conflict played over his face as Luc studied her. "Alright," he conceded. "I think it's risky, but I'll stay."

Stella rewarded him with a grateful smile.

"But I do have to leave right now to meet with Elias."

As much as she disliked it, she had to admit that it was good Luc was gone for most of the night. Between Damian, Garrett or one of the guards, there was no knowing who would be in the cottage at any given hour. But so far, Luc had managed to avoid any encounters in the last two nights.

"Be safe," she urged.

Luc dropped down into the secret passage, the rug rolling back on its own to hide the door. Then Stella went to her work table to tackle her latest projects. After finishing three belts and two pairs of gloves, she sat back in her chair and stretched, careful not to pull the wounds on her arm open. Her gaze drifted to the bedroom opposite hers. She suddenly realized that when Damian had asked her to leave, she had failed to treat Dartan. Rising, she walked to the bedroom door. She didn't want to go in, but she had to. After a pause, she swung the door open, hoping Damian was asleep. Instead, she found him staring up at the ceiling.

"How long have I been here?" he asked, not bothering to look at her.

"Three nights."

Damian tried to rise but promptly fell back, wincing in pain. "Three nights! You mean to tell me I've been lying in this bed for that long?"

"Yes," she replied, grabbing the supplies she'd left on the table. She then knelt at the foot of the bed and began to tend to the motionless creature lying there. With the rag, she dabbed at any seeping wounds, reapplied the tincture, and repacked the gaping wounds with comfrey before wrapping them in fresh bandages.

"How is he?" Damian asked, his voice much softer now that he was discussing his beloved pet.

"Still breathing." In her opinion, it would be a miracle if the dog survived. His injuries were beyond severe, they were extreme.

"Who has been running the regiment while I recover?" Damian asked.

"As I understand it, Garrett along with the other captains."

Damian nodded, looking satisfied by that. "Who stitched me up? Whoever the healer was, they clearly grew weary by the time they reached my left side."

"Actually, Garrett was unable to locate a healer. The local one was killed in the recent Shade attack, so it was Garrett and I who stitched you."

Damian's eyes widened at that. "I don't have to guess who did which side."

Stella smiled. "Garrett is still looking for a healer and he's been sending a guard each night to check on you and to assist me as needed. One should be arriving sometime soon."

"What is it?" he asked when she rose to stand at his bedside.

"I-I wanted to ask for your forgiveness," she said, heat crawling up her face.

"My forgiveness?" He spoke the word as if it were foreign to him, and she wondered if perhaps it was. "I've never forgiven anyone in my life."

His admission was disheartening, and Stella wondered if she'd made a terrible mistake. But having already humbled herself, she decided it couldn't hurt to humble herself further. "Will you forgive *me*?"

"That depends…on if you can forgive me."

Stella looked at him in surprise. "Forgive you for what?" she asked, bewildered by the unexpected turn the discussion had taken.

"For my past."

Stella fell silent as she pondered what it was he was asking. He wanted her forgiveness. He wanted to be free from her condemnation, knowing that she held his past against him. "What does your past have to do with me?" she asked.

"If I hope to have a future with you, I need you to forgive me for it," he said with utter earnestness.

Stella stared at him, feeling a flutter of panic. *Future? What future?* They had no future. Not in the way he hoped. The most she could offer him was friendship. With that he would have to be content. Still, she wanted—no needed—his forgiveness, so she nodded her assent. She could afford to forgive him his past, since she was certain it had no direct bearing on her whatsoever. "Then I do forgive you," she conceded.

Nodding solemnly, Damian said, "And I forgive you."

30

The Peace Offer

T he night after his master awoke, Stella found Dartan sleeping at Damian's feet. Literally. Flabbergasted, she wondered how the mutilated dog had managed to leap upon the bed. Moved by the creature's devotion and loyalty, she shut the door, not wanting to disturb the two. Somehow she thought it important that they reunite in private.

"How is our patient doing?" Garrett asked, when he came by later on.

"You'll never believe it, but Dartan woke up."

"Did he?" he asked, pausing in the midst of removing his cloak.

Stella nodded. "I found him on the bed."

"This I have to see," Garrett said. The moment he opened the bedroom door, however, a low growl could be heard. It was followed by Damian rebuking Dartan.

"There you are," Damian said, addressing the other man. "I was beginning to think you were avoiding me."

Stella remained outside the door, listening.

"Every time I've come by, you were sleeping like a baby. It is good to see you alert, though," Garrett replied.

"How are things with the Guard?"

"The weapons arrived and training of the new recruits has begun.

Otherwise, things have been quiet with Draven gone."

"He should be returning soon, though."

"We're prepared. Or as prepared as we can be," Garrett amended with a sigh. "On a different note, I've yet to find a healer. But even if I did, I fear few would be willing to travel in this weather."

"Shut the door," Damian commanded.

Stella frowned as Garrett complied. Hearing only muffled voices and unwilling to stoop to putting her ear at the door, she went to find something to do, settling on Damian's armor. Shadow Guard matters were usually confidential so it shouldn't bother her to be left out, even if it was in her own cottage.

She thought about what Garrett had said about the healer. It seemed she would be on her own caring for Damian, a prospect that distressed her. She only hoped he was spared an infection, for she felt ill-equipped to deal with one should it occur. As it was, his injuries were so severe it would take weeks for him to recover. Weeks in which she would have to continue to treat him and feed him. But he wouldn't always be so helpless, she reminded herself.

His prolonged stay presented another challenge, however. Now that he and Dartan were both awake, it would make things that much more difficult for Luc.

Upon leaving, Garrett informed her that Damian had requested her presence. So after locking her door with her new lock, Stella returned to the bedroom. She found Damian sitting up, the sheet at his waist, while Dartan remained curled at his feet, watching her.

"You called for me?" she asked, with a lift of her brow.

"I need a bath," he declared, without preamble.

"I noticed," she returned, wrinkling her nose for effect.

"I can't bathe myself."

"Obviously."

"Which means you'll need to bathe me."

Stella choked. "Excuse me? I will not be bathing you. Besides, your wounds need to be kept dry."

"Then you will need to wash me at the very least."

"Tomorrow night," she promised. "I'll have one of the guards assist you."

Damian scowled darkly. "I'll not let another man touch me. You must do it."

Stella glared at him, but even she had to admit that a good wash was in order. Damian's hair had gone lank and his stench was bordering on offensive. "Fine," she relented grudgingly.

Washing Damian proved to be as harrowing an experience as she had expected. Stella tried her best to separate the man from his body, pretending it could belong to anyone. It didn't work. She was far too aware of him. And now, she was aware of him in ways she could have done without.

"Satisfied?" she snapped, as soon as she was done.

A lazy grin spread across his face. "For now."

* * *

Over the course of the next two weeks, Damian and Dartan continued to improve steadily, while Stella neared the completion of Damian's armor. Visitors were a nightly occurrence. With people coming and going at various hours, there had been several close calls where Luc was concerned. Once, he arrived through the floor just as Garrett exited the front door, missing him by a split second. Another time, he was sneaking out right before Damian shuffled out of the bedroom. But it was when Dartan barked wildly upon hearing or scenting Luc that he decided it was time to stay with Elias. Though Stella was unhappy about it, she had to agree.

Three nights had passed and she was still feeling the loss of Luc's presence. In contrast, she was becoming all too familiar with Damian. It was impossible not to when she spent hours feeding him and tending nearly every inch of his body. It was an intimacy she had shared with no one else. Even his hound had become inordinately attached to her.

"I do believe you've stolen my dog's affections," Damian remarked, when Dartan whined as she made to leave the room.

"It was easily done. He's a faithless creature, offering his devotion to whoever indulges his appetite," she replied, gazing at the horribly disfigured hound with grudging fondness. She had learned to hand feed the dog on the right side of his mouth to keep the food from falling out. The poor creature was stuck with a crooked leer that displayed his fangs on the left side. "Besides, I think he's just tired of being confined to such a small space."

"I know the feeling," Damian replied, his gaze drifting to the window.

Later that night, Stella accompanied Damian as he ventured outside for the first time. He was dressed in the clothes Garrett had brought for him. He even wore his sword at his side, though she knew he could barely wield it. Standing in the middle of the snowy clearing with Dartan at his side, he gazed up at the Northern Lights that had appeared several nights after his attack.

"It's sad, isn't it? That something so beautiful lasts so briefly," she mused, staring at the ephemeral lights.

"But isn't it its brevity that makes its beauty so profound?" he returned.

Damian had been doing this more and more. Surprising her by revealing a side of himself she never expected or even imagined existed. It was intriguing but disconcerting, challenging the view of him she clung to. How was she supposed to reconcile this sensitive philosopher with the callous womanizer she knew him to be? He even looked different, his face soft with wonder as the purple and green lights glowed upon his skin.

"I suppose you're right," Stella replied uneasily, turning away from him.

"I'm almost fully recovered," he remarked.

"Do you think so?" she asked, skeptical. Scabs had replaced his open wounds, but they could be opened again if he wasn't careful. He certainly wasn't ready to swing a sword anytime soon. "Another week to recover would do you good."

"I would think you'd be eager to get rid of me." She heard the hidden query in his words.

"Not necessarily," she replied, choosing her own with care. "I won't miss washing you." She ignored his smirk. "But your health and recovery matter to me. And I will miss this hideous creature," she added, rubbing the mangled fur on Dartan's head.

"He'll miss you, too," Damian said, his tone wistful. "I can recover well enough in my own home, but if you wish to enjoy another week in Dartan's company, we can stay."

"You may as well." Stella was surprised when the words slipped out, but there was no taking them back.

Beside her, Damian smiled, his gaze never leaving the colorful sky.

31

The Truth Revealed

The Northern Lights vanished three nights later. Unfortunately, so did their luck. Stella had already felt a nervous anxiety at the thought of leaving Damian and Dartan to attend the market. So when she returned to the cottage and heard commotion from within, her mind immediately leapt to the wildest and worst of possibilities. But when she flung the door open, she was still caught off guard by the scene that greeted her—Luc, Elias, Damian and Garrett in the midst of a standoff.

Eyes wide, she glanced at Dartan, barking furiously while his master restrained him. "What is going on here?" she asked, when she finally found her voice. Though it was thin and shaky with dread.

"Perhaps *you* could tell us," Damian replied, turning stormy eyes her way.

"Dartan, hush!" she chided, trying to take control of the situation. Her nerves were jumpy and the noise didn't help.

To everyone's surprise, the hound ceased its barking.

Stella turned to the men, all of them tensed and distrustful. They were armed, but fortunately no weapons had been drawn. Good, there was hope for some civility. "Why don't we all have a seat first?"

"Stella," Damian said in warning.

But Garrett wordlessly complied, making himself comfortable in one of the two armchairs. Elias followed suit, settling himself into the second chair, leaving Luc to take one end of the couch. Stella waited, but when it became clear Damian had no intention of sitting next to Luc, she readily occupied the couch with him. Left to stand, Damian crossed his arms and leaned against a nearby wall with Dartan at his feet.

"Will someone please explain what happened?" she asked, looking to Garrett and Elias hopefully.

But it was Damian who chose to reply. "*What happened* is that I found your friend Elias and Luc entering the cottage through a hidden door I had no idea existed," he bit out.

Stella looked to Elias, who was sitting directly across from her. There was an apology in his hazel eyes. Why had they risked coming, knowing both Damian and Dartan were both up and about? She then turned a questioning gaze to Garrett.

"I arrived afterward," he supplied. "Through the front door."

Reluctantly, Stella directed her gaze in Damian's direction. "I imagine that must have startled you."

Damian's jaw tightened, not in the least bit amused by her light approach. "Dartan nearly attacked them, and I was right behind him. It would have behooved you to inform me that you had a hidden entrance, one you make available to other men." There was no missing the condemnation—or insinuation—in his tone.

Beside her, she felt Luc stiffen as Elias rose to her defense. "It's not what you think."

"What am I to think?" Damian asked, his gaze going from Elias to Luc to her.

Stella glanced at Garrett helplessly, but it was foolish to hope for aid in that corner. She may be his wife's best friend and Elias might be his brother-in-law, but he was as eager for answers as Damian was. Still, Stella looked to him as she answered. "You know that Elias and I have always been the closest of friends since we were children. We share many secrets, this hidden entrance being just one of them."

"So I assume Jenna knows about this hidden entrance as well?" Garrett replied, with a raised brow.

Stella hesitated, and that was a mistake.

Damian was quick to pounce on it. "She doesn't, does she?" Without need for confirmation, he asked, "So why does Luc know about your hidden entrance, too?"

"It was my fault!" Elias piped. "I was careless and Luc saw me use the passage."

"Explain," Damian commanded haughtily.

Elias's eyes briefly flared in panic. "Well…as you know, Luc can't speak and, well, I had left something behind with him. I didn't realize he had been following me to return it. That was when he saw me use the passage that leads to the cottage."

As far as impromptu explanations came, Stella thought it was a pretty good one.

"I don't understand. Why not just use the front door?" Garrett asked, unhelpfully. Stella glared at him in irritation.

"I, uh, only use it when Stella is not home to let me in," Elias replied, cringing slightly. It was a good thing his back was to Damian, but it was clearly visible to everyone else.

"And why would you need to enter when Stella is not home?" Damian asked.

Stella could foresee the direction his line of questioning was leading. Whatever answer was given, it would have to line up with why Elias and Luc were in her cottage now. Her gaze landed on the work table beside Damian.

"Because I gave them leave to access my tools," she blurted. "Elias knows he's welcome to use them and when he mentioned Luc was interested in my trade—"

"Enough, Stella!"

She turned to Garrett in surprise, taken aback by the sternness of his tone. More so by the impatience on his face. "I know you two are lying," he said, looking from her to Elias. "And I know you two are

227

up to something." His gaze went from Elias to Luc. "And I know that you,"—he leaned forward to point at Luc, his eyes narrowed—"can speak."

The pronouncement was met with stunned silence.

Garrett leaned back in his chair and added one more. "And I know that the three of you are are going to tell us what is going on."

It was as if everyone else had forgotten how to talk…or breathe. Even Dartan was oddly quiet. Stella knew that they were beyond denial now. Their stricken expressions had all but given them away.

"I suppose there's no point in maintaining the charade," Luc piped, his accent sounding more distinct than usual after the heavy silence.

Both Damian and Garrett's heads snapped in his direction. Were she not so horrified, Stella might have laughed at the way they gaped at Luc.

"I thought you heard him speak," she said, gazing at Garrett. "Why do you look so surprised?"

"We only ever saw his mouth moving from a distance. We never actually heard his voice."

"We?" Elias asked.

"Myself and the others Damian had watching you two," Garrett admitted candidly, still staring at Luc. "Why does he sound like that?"

Stella looked to Elias and Luc, the three of them reaching a silent agreement. There was little point in holding back now, not when Luc had already revealed himself. "Perhaps you'd like to answer?" she suggested to him, somewhat tersely.

Luc nodded. "It's because I'm from Aurelia."

"Where is that?" Garrett asked with a frown.

"It's the land south of the Altous Mountains," Damian answered, before Elias could. Elias looked at him in surprise. That was knowledge reserved to the Repository.

"We're supposed to believe Luc crossed those impregnable mountains?" Garrett asked. "The one no man has ever succeeded in crossing?"

Luc suddenly rose, causing Damian to reach for his sword. Everyone watched as he headed for the bowl and pitcher at the sideboard. "What is he doing?" Damian asked warily.

"You'll see," Elias replied.

Luc turned from where he'd been washing his face, hands and neck. At the sight of his golden skin, Damian and Garrett once again imitated caught trout. Stella and Elias, however, glanced at each other worriedly.

"What is this?" Garrett asked, rising to his feet.

"Proof," Stella answered. "Unlike Noctum, Aurelia is a land of light. Luc's skin color is a result of their sun."

"What is a sun?" Garrett asked, while Damian maintained his unnerving silence.

Stella gave him the same answer Luc had given her. "It's like the moon, only a thousand times brighter."

Garrett dropped back into his seat. "What is going on?" he asked, utterly bewildered.

Luc turned to look at her. Stella sensed he was asking for permission or approval. With a sigh, Stella nodded, reluctantly giving her assent. Though she was still upset that he had given himself away so quickly.

As she listened to Luc recount his tale for a third time, her gaze wandered between Damian and Garrett, attempting to gauge their reactions as she had once tried to gauge Elias's. Unlike then, however, her nerves were wound so tight, she felt in danger of snapping from the stress. Damian was a commandant. He had the power to impede Luc at nearly every turn. He also didn't like Luc...because of her.

When Luc finished his astounding account, Damian promptly turned to Stella. "How did you get involved in all this?"

Luc had focused on explaining his purpose for coming, leaving out that particular detail. Considering how they had met, she was glad.

"It was purely by chance," she admitted. "I found Luc several leagues from here, in the direction of Nero. Though I actually saw him weeks before that. I just hadn't realized it at the time."

"What do you mean?" Garrett asked, furrowing his brow in confusion.

"Remember that ball of fire I asked you and Jenna about?" she prompted. "The one I told you I saw traveling from the direction of the Altous Mountains? That was Luc arriving in Noctum."

From the corner of her eye, she saw Damian stiffen, for she had told him about the fireball as well. Like everyone else, he had dismissed her claim. "So what?" Damian asked. "You found him and then you brought him home?"

"He was injured," she replied, annoyed by his disapproving tone. "He'd been wandering the woods for weeks, unaccustomed to the darkness, so he was hungry and exhausted as well."

"Yet here he is still after all these weeks, looking hearty and hale," Damian stated, scowling at Luc.

"I see what's going on here," Garrett piped, drawing away Damian's ire. "You two intend to help Luc break the curse."

32

A Fateful Blow

S tella was tired and cranky and getting rather hungry.
Hours had passed since she first found the four men glaring
at each other. Now they wouldn't stop talking. Garrett
and Damian, especially, peppered Luc with endless questions about
everything and anything to do with Aurelia. They also demanded to
know the details of his plans to kill Draven. He patiently answered
their questions on the first topic. On the second, all he would admit
was that he was still in the planning phase.

"No wonder you and Elias have been skulking around Darkwood,"
Garrett remarked.

"We haven't been skulking," Elias replied. "We've been doing
reconnaissance."

"Reconna-what?" Garrett asked, staring at his brother-in-law with
a frown.

"It's an Aurelian term," Elias informed him proudly. "It means to
survey, explore, examine, observe—"

Stella rose impatiently, feeling irrelevant. Nearly an hour had
passed without any acknowledgement in her direction, so she decided
to fix herself a plate. Dartan trotted after her eagerly, knowing that
the hearth and pantry promised something to eat.

Her action had the effect of reminding the men of the lateness of the hour. Garrett glanced at the clock and made a sound of displeasure. "Your sister is going to kill me!" he said, hurrying to his feet. "I need to go. Jenna was expecting me hours ago."

"You won't say anything to her, will you?" Elias asked worriedly.

"Of course not," Garrett replied. "She doesn't know about your other secret either, and this one is possibly more important."

Damian nodded somberly. "Whatever was said here does not go beyond us five."

Stella breathed a sigh of relief. For now at least, the commandant was willing to believe Luc.

"It *is* rather late," Elias said, rising as well. "I suppose we ought to leave, too." He said this hopefully, as if afraid Damian might refuse to let them go.

But Damian nodded in agreement. "We've exhausted the matter for now. Though no doubt more questions will arise. In the meantime, you are to do nothing without first informing me, do you understand?" He glanced at Elias before fixing his unwavering gaze on Luc.

"Nothing?" Elias asked. "Not even take a piss?"

Damian turned to glower at him, the look so menacing Elias gulped.

"We understand what you mean," Luc replied. Though he didn't necessarily agree to it, Stella noted.

Garrett left first. When Elias and Luc followed, Stella gazed at them wistfully. Sighing, she sat down to nibble on the repast she had prepared, though her appetite had diminished. It was hard to eat knowing she would have to face Damian alone. When he sat down across the table from her, she braced herself before looking at him.

It was a good thing she did. Damian's anger was a frightening thing, and she flinched when she saw it directed at her.

"You lied to me." The accusation was delivered in that deceptively soft voice that made her want to shiver.

"About?" Her calm was false, her courage feeble.

"Killing the Shade that broke into the cottage."

She dropped her gaze to the plate before her, unable to bear his accusing gaze. "Oh, that."

"What else did you lie to me about?"

Stella didn't answer. The truth was, she couldn't remember.

The chair screeched as Damian shoved it back to rise. "Don't ever lie to me again, Stella." Then he went into the room that should have belonged to Luc and slammed the door shut with a violent crack.

That night, Stella slept fitfully and for the first time in months, she dreamed. In her dream, she was running through the forest after Luc. League after league, she pursued him—but he was always too far ahead or just out of reach. Until finally, when she was a hair's breadth from touching him, a cry of triumph fell from her lips, only to turn into a cry of dismay when arms encircled around her from behind, trapping her in the darkness as Luc pressed forward into a bright, white light.

Unbeknownst to her, the tears in her dream crossed over to reality. All Stella knew was that the arms that entrapped her morphed into a comforting embrace as a low voice whispered soothing words in her ear. But by the following night, she had no memory of any of it.

* * *

Stella waited for Damian to enter the washroom before she slipped out of the cottage. Outside, it was a clear, bitterly cold night and she was nearly tempted to head back inside. Instead, she readjusted the sack on her shoulder and began to trudge through the crusty snow. There was no reason for her to sneak out; heading to the market was hardly a crime. But she had no desire to deal with Damian's suspicious queries. He would be irritated, no doubt, when he discovered her gone without a word. But hopefully the surprise she left him would help to assuage his anger.

For the last week and a half, she had been working on the finishing details of his armor—in her bedroom. This would be his first time seeing the completed product. It was her finest work so far, and she almost regretted not seeing his reaction.

The cold was beginning to numb her face and glove-covered fingers, but at least the snowfalls had temporarily ceased. Warmer temperatures had melted much of the snow, encasing the skeletal branches in ice. They glittered—sharp and clear—reminding her to avoid the dagger-like icicles overhead.

When she reached the marketplace, she paused outside of the ruins. After what had happened during the Winter Solstice, it had taken a while for people to feel comfortable returning to the site where ten of their men had been executed and five of their women abducted. Tonight, it was as full and busy as it had ever been—a sign of the forest dwellers' resilience.

Lured by the tantalizing scent of roasted chestnuts and spice cakes, she made her way inside. She breathed deep, revelling in the winter scent. If she sold enough of her goods perhaps she could afford to indulge in a treat or two. Smiling at the prospect, she yelped at the feel of a hand suddenly grasping her arm. Ready to deliver a sharp retort, she turned to face her molester. But the words on her tongue quickly died.

"Luc!" Her heart thumped in her chest. Glancing around to find curious eyes watching them, she tugged on his arm. "Come, there's more privacy at my stall."

He nodded, grabbing her sack and placing it on his own shoulders before following her through the crowd. At the stall, she lit her lanterns while Luc laid out her goods for display.

"Thank you," she said, looking up into his handsome face—a face she missed seeing every night. "I'm glad you're here."

Luc quickly scanned their surroundings before leaning in to whisper, "I've missed you, too, Stella."

A wide smile split her face. No more words were spoken between them, but Luc's presence continued to buoy her spirits the rest of the night. Those accustomed to her usual solemnity were surprised to observe her quiet happiness, the hint of a smile teasing her lips. Not that everyone was pleased by the sight, certainly not her rejected suitors who knew the reason had to do with the distinctively handsome man at her side.

Stella was having a good night. Her goods were selling quickly, earning her much coin. But even if she hadn't sold a thing, she would have been happy. She looked at her last three items, and decided to pack them up. She wanted to buy herself and Luc some hot apple cider and a spice cake before the market ended. As she began to place the items in her sack, the buzz of delight she was feeling became a persistent note of alarm.

Instinct honed by years of detecting danger had her head snapping up.

"What is it?" Luc asked, somehow noting her alarm.

"Something..." Stella carefully scanned the crowd until her gaze landed on a tall, hooded figure roughly fifty feet away. There was nothing distinct about him, nothing to make him stand out. But he had snagged her attention because of the way he was just standing, staring at her. The hairs on her flesh began to rise as an ominous feeling twisted low in her belly. "Do you see that man over there? The hooded one by the woodwork stands?"

Suddenly, the man rose, as if he had been crouching, revealing his unusual height. He began to move toward her, his face completely hidden but his stride disturbingly familiar in its power and smoothness.

"We need to go, Stella!" Luc exclaimed, grabbing her hand.

The panic in his voice spurred her into action. They tore through the crowd, leaving everything behind—her goods, her coins, and her weapons.

Screams of pain and shrieks of terror followed in their wake. Swearing under his breath, Luc threw her over his shoulder and put on a burst of speed that had her vision blurring, impossibly fast.

One moment, they were in the middle of the marketplace. The next, they were outside of the ruin.

"Take this," Luc said, shoving his dagger into her hand. "And run back to the cottage as fast as you can. I'll meet you there as soon as I'm able."

"Wait!"

But he was already gone, charging back into the mayhem that had erupted. With adrenaline coursing through her, Stella choked on a sob, hesitating. But when terrified men and women began to pour out of the ruin, nearly trampling her in their panic, she turned and fled, leaving Luc to confront Draven alone.

33

A Frantic Flight

Stella threw herself against the door, banging on it frantically. When it swung open, she stumbled and nearly collapsed, only to fall into Damian's arms.

"What is it? What's happened?" he demanded, tilting her face upward to study her wide, frightened eyes and tear-stained cheeks.

Her stammering tongue refused to cooperate. Her heart was beating too furiously and her breath squeezed from her lungs in short, painful gasps. Absently, she registered Dartan licking her icy hand to comfort her.

"D-D-Draven at m-m-mark-k-ket. Luc s-s-stayed. T-t-told m-m-me t-to run."

Damian began to move. He sat her in front of the fire and handed her a mug of water. Then he went to strap on his new armor, unable to hide his wincing. After securing his belt to his side, he grabbed a sack and began to pack it with various items he scoured from around the cottage: food, tinder, candles, and a skin full of water. Beside the sack, he laid down rope and a rolled up blanket.

"Tell me exactly what happened," he urged, kneeling before her.

At once, the sounds and scenes from market returned to her, replaying with startling clarity what she had experienced in a fearful haze. Stella took a deep breath, her heart still racing but feeling a

237

strange outer calm. "I had gone to the market to sell my goods. I was packing what few were left when I felt it…this sinister feeling. I looked up to find a hooded man watching me from a distance. I never saw his face, but somehow I knew. It was the king." Terrified faces flashed in her mind, the horrible screams. "People were hurt, possibly killed. The ones who were in the way as he came for me."

"How did you escape?"

"Luc grabbed me and we ran. He carried me out of the marketplace, but then he went back in." Her heart clenched in fear. "He said he would meet me here at the cottage…after."

If he made it. The unbidden thought taunted her cruelly.

"He'd better not!" Damian growled. "Lest he lead the monster here."

"He wouldn't do that!" she replied, outraged.

"You need to hide." Grabbing the travel pack, he went to pull open the door beneath the rug. "Take this and wait down there, Stella."

Too overwrought to argue, Stella climbed down as instructed, seeking solace in the darkness. Already, the worst played out in her mind. Luc lying dead in the middle of the marketplace, his heart ripped from his chest or his head torn from his body. Draven threatening death and destruction unless someone gave her up. Damian doing his best to save her but dying as well. These weren't just possible scenarios, they were almost certain events. It was only a matter of time before they came to pass, and time was something Draven had a limitless supply of.

Stella had no idea how long she waited. It could have been half an hour. It could have been two. But suddenly, the air changed and she became aware of a presence. Tensing, she slowly turned.

"It's me, Stella."

"Luc! Oh, thank goodness! You made it! How did you—"

The door above flew open, shedding light into the once black void. Stella blinked to see Damian scowling down at Luc. "Is he dead?"

"If he were, you and everyone in Noctum would know," Luc replied.

In the light, she saw that Luc was hurt. There was a gaping wound on his forehead and his left arm was bleeding beneath the shoulder.

"Then you shouldn't have come here," Damian snapped. "You endanger Stella. He could be here in moments."

"It will take his heart sometime to repair itself," Luc replied wearily. "I only came to make certain Stella was safe. I'll leave now to ensure I don't endanger her."

"No, wait!" Stella cried, clinging to him. "We need to treat your wounds."

She glared at Damian, daring him to defy her. He merely looked disturbed, so she clambered up and offered Luc her hand. He took it, but not for assistance. Despite his injured arm, he was still able to climb up on his own strength.

"You were able to strike him in the heart?" Damian asked dubiously, as Stella proceeded to wash Luc's forehead.

"Only because I caught him off guard."

"I've only heard of that happening once before," Damian said. "And it was a long time ago. They say it took a little more than three hours for his heart to mend. That doesn't give you much time."

"Time for what?" Luc asked.

"Time to take Stella someplace safe."

Stella faltered in her task of applying tincture to Luc's wound. "Someplace safe? Draven doubtless knows every corner of Noctum. He's lived long enough to explore every inch of it. There's nowhere you can take me that he can't find me." She shook her head sadly, accepting the inevitable. "My fate is sealed. It was sealed the moment he laid eyes on me."

"What are you talking about Stella?" Luc asked, his green eyes troubled.

"She knows that Draven will stop at nothing to find her," Damian replied grimly. "A man like that, a man who has lived too long in absolute power, is used to getting what he wants. And a challenge will only entice him more, especially when he is so rarely challenged."

Fear flashed in Luc's eyes, fully understanding the ramifications of the chance encounter. "I'll do everything in my power to protect Stella, but I'm a foreigner to your land. How will I take her someplace safe when I don't know where such a place is?"

"I'll show you," Damian said. "But it will have to be quick."

"No!" Stella protested. "I won't run. There's no point."

Damian rounded on her. "Will you risk Marta and Aron? Will you risk everyone you care about? Because that's what you'll do if you stay."

Stella shook her head. "No, that's not true. They'll be in more danger if I run away. When Draven can't find me, he'll look for the people I care about. He'll question them, threaten them or torture them. To get to me."

"Not if I make sure to hide them," Damian said.

Stella hesitated.

"If I promise to take care of them, will you go?"

Stella could hardly think. Everything was happening too fast.

"Quick, pack what you need," Damian told Luc, not waiting for her answer.

She watched as they began to scramble, preparing a second pack of supplies for Luc. Snapping out of her daze, she pulled clothes from Erik's trunk to outfit Luc in additional layers. Then she added a few layers of her own beneath her borrowed cloak. Once they were bundled, their packs on their backs, Stella looked around her small cottage, wondering if she would ever see it again.

"It's time, Stella."

Choking back a sob, she turned to Damian. "You promise you'll take care of them? Marta and my nephew? Elias and Jenna?"

Damian nodded silently, his eyes dark with some hidden emotion. "I'll do what I can."

Then she and Luc were dropping back down through the hidden door. Before Damian shut it after them, Stella glanced up. That's when she saw it, the emotion Damian had been concealing from her. The memory of it stayed with her long after Luc pulled her away.

34

The Smallest Spark

Stella didn't notice when the snow began to fall. She was lost in the thoughts swirling through her head. Over the hours, she had fallen into a rhythm, trailing behind Luc's tall form which blocked the northern wind, and following him step for step, her footsteps hidden within his larger ones.

She was content to let Luc be their guide, even though she was the one from Noctum. She knew all she needed to know. The place Damian wanted them to go to—the Barren Keep—was across a desolate wasteland no one bothered to travel, because it ended at a great chasm no one dared to cross. When Damian first suggested it, she couldn't believe he would jest at such a dire hour. When she realized he was serious, she wanted to laugh until she cried.

But it wasn't thoughts of survival that plagued her. No, all she could think about were the people she had left behind, the people in Draven's destructive path. Her fear for them was a great and terrible burden. Any concern she had for herself was miniscule in comparison. She prayed Damian made good on his promise. She was entrusting those she loved into his hands. While he had entrusted her to Luc, a man she knew he considered a rival.

"This is where we stop."

Stella looked around to find that they were at the face of a small cliff. Looking up, she could see scraggly pines sitting atop it. The wall of rock would provide a shield against the bite of the northerly, but there was no overhang to protect them from above.

"Perhaps we'd be better off beneath the firs over there?" she suggested.

"Damian says there's a cave here," Luc said, staring at the cliff face.

"A cave?" If so, it wasn't easily seen. Moreover, she couldn't recall any mention of a cave. Though admittedly, she had found it difficult to latch onto every piece of information Damian had hurriedly thrown their way. Luc had obviously done a better job.

"Come, it's probably easier to find it up close."

Luc was right. Within minutes, they were able to make out a jagged section of rock that protruded slightly, concealing a narrow fissure behind it. It couldn't be seen straight on, and only at a certain angle. Luc lit a candle and slipped in first, with Stella following. The scent of damp earth and minerals saturated the close air. The flame revealed a tight passage that made Stella feel suffocated. Avoiding thoughts of being buried alive, she squeezed through after Luc. When the passage opened up onto a large dry space, she was able to breathe easy again. Stella was so tired, she immediately unrolled her woollen blanket and stretched out on top of it. Within seconds, she was sound asleep.

* * *

Stella awoke feeling disoriented. It was dark, darker than a storm on a new moon night. It was also cold, but a large, warm body was pressed up behind her. That was when she remembered that she was inside of a cave...with Luc. So many things had gone wrong that night, but at least she had Luc. Grateful for his arms around her, she placed a hand over the one he had wrapped around her waist. Because of him, she had escaped Draven's clutches. But because of her, he was now on the run.

"You were shivering from the cold," Luc said softly, as if she needed an explanation for why he held her.

"Thank you for warming me."

"Can you not sleep?"

"I'm afraid."

"What is it you're afraid of?"

"That none of us is safe. Not you, not me...not anyone I care about." She choked down a hysterical sob. "I'm afraid for Erik's son."

"You have every reason to be afraid. Noctum is a frightening place and Draven is evil, which makes your strength and courage so remarkable."

"What are you talking about?" she asked, perplexed. "How can you call fear courage?"

"Everyone has fears. The courage comes from how those fears are faced. You're no coward, Stella. A coward wouldn't do the things you've done. They wouldn't wander the forest alone or draw a sword against a Shade. They wouldn't bring an injured stranger home."

"Some would call that foolishness," she said, thinking of Damian.

"They would be wrong. It takes incredible courage just to live in your world. None of the women in Aurelia have half your courage because they've never faced your dangers, endured your hardships or suffered your heartbreaks."

All of which she would have happily done without. "I just don't see any of this ending well," she admitted fearfully. "And I'm afraid I've ruined your chance to kill Draven."

"Ruined how?"

"Because of me, you were forced to face Draven before you intended to. And now you've lost a valuable advantage—the element of surprise."

"Don't blame yourself, Stella. You couldn't have known he would appear at the market, under the cover of a disguise no less. No, the fault lies with Draven, not you. He has always been the one to blame, which is why he needs to die."

And Luc was the only one willing to kill him.

"How did you become a guard for the king?" she asked, wondering how he had been led to this path.

"My father encouraged me to take the position."

"Is he a guard for the king as well?"

"Yes, he was captain of the guard."

"Was?"

"He died two years ago, an arrow to the heart."

"I'm sorry."

Luc sighed. "We weren't close."

"Oh." What else was there to say to that?

Stella didn't think he would add anything more, so she was surprised when he continued. "My da was a tough bastard, even cruel at times. Growing up, he belittled me for being soft and weak. He started training me in combat as young as four, always pushing me hard. Too hard. There were never any words of praise, no encouragement. And I tried so hard to please him, to make him proud. It wasn't until I became a guard that he ever showed any approval, but by that point I no longer cared. And when he died, I couldn't even bring myself to shed a tear."

Stella was at a loss as to what to say. How could a father not be proud of someone like Luc? How could he not admire his son's courage, intelligence and strength? And how had Luc managed to avoid becoming hard and embittered himself with a father like that?

"I feel sorry for your da," she said. "Sorry that he never recognized how fine a son he had. I'm not certain what it was that blinded him—past hurt or bitterness or disappointment—but it kept him from seeing what was right before his eyes. You are an amazing man, Luc, the finest I've ever known. It takes someone of great character to rise above your kind of upbringing, to not let it break him but instead shape him into a better man."

Luc was quiet for a time. All she could hear was his soft breathing, until… "Thank you, Stella. I've mostly made peace with that part of my past, but it still hurts sometimes. My ma died when I was young, so he was the only family I had."

Stella's heart was heavy, knowing Luc had lost just as much if not more than she had. At least she had known the love of her ma, da and brother before losing them. But Luc never had, and he was a man that deserved to be loved. A man who was worthy of it.

Stella's heart began to beat wildly at the thought of what she was about to do. Never before had she felt so bold or desperate. But never before had she felt such a powerful pull. She turned so that she was facing him and reached up to gently caress his bearded face. His breath grew shallow and she could feel his heart beating as quickly as her own.

"Stella?" His voice shook.

In reply, she leaned forward to gently press her lips against his. "You're not alone, Luc," she whispered, her mouth moving against his.

Luc was so still, it seemed he was holding his breath. She was afraid to move, afraid to speak, fearing she'd said too much—revealed what she should have kept hidden. But then, something within him seemed to snap, a restraint she hadn't known he needed. With a groan, Luc crushed her lips to his, devouring her hungrily. Without hesitation, she opened herself up to him, willing to be consumed. The kiss went on, passionate, demanding and fierce. She was lost to sensation, she drowned in desire. This...this was bliss.

He pulled away first, his breath coming in harsh gasps as he pressed his forehead against hers. "I tried so hard."

"Tried so hard to do what?"

"To resist you." He kissed her again, just a soft brush of his lips.

"There's no need to resist me," she said, stroking his face once more, memorizing its angles and planes.

"You make it very difficult to," he said with a heavy sigh.

"Good," she declared. "Because I'm tired of resisting you, too."

Luc groaned again and seized another kiss, this one tender and languorous. Outside, the temperature dropped as a piercing wind sliced through the air, violently tossing the snowflakes that fell. But all Stella felt inside their little cocoon was fire and heat.

35

A Chance Discovery

They crossed a roaring river, scaled a steep cliff, passed through a primordial forest and picked their way across a frozen lake before they reached the fringes of a windswept Wasteland three weeks later. It was the farthest Stella had ever traveled.

She stared out at the bleak landscape that stretched on uninterrupted as far as the eye could see. How many nights would it take to reach the Chasm? Their trek through the forest had been treacherous—navigating unfamiliar terrain while avoiding the usual dangers. Luc had narrowly missed being bitten by a snake, and Stella had nearly stumbled onto a brigand camp while seeking to relieve her bladder. The Wasteland, however, presented its own problems. *What would they eat? Where would they find shelter?* She looked over her shoulder, wondering if they weren't better off staying in the forest.

"I don't know about this, Luc."

"It is daunting," he admitted, dropping to his knees to begin gathering the snow at their feet. He was building the domed huts they had been using for shelter when none could be found. "But let's not worry about it until tomorrow night."

"Alright." Glad to put off the trek for several more hours, she got down to help him.

When they were done, they pulled out their blankets and crawled inside. This was by far the best part of her nights, being in the shelter of Luc's strong arms. It still struck her that she had finally gotten the very thing she'd wanted while fleeing for her life. It was strange finding happiness when she struggled through some of the hardest nights she'd ever known. And the nights had been hard! The times of painful hunger and bone-deep exhaustion. The moments of paralyzing doubt and debilitating fear. And the cold! The relentless cold would be forever seared in her memory. Were it not for Luc, she was certain she would have succumbed to defeat long ago. It was his strength and affection that carried her, his unspoken love that pushed her beyond her limits.

"Damian wouldn't have told us to cross the Wasteland if it wasn't possible," he remarked, once again assuring her.

At the mention of Damian, she found herself wondering how he was faring. Had he fully healed? Was he back in command of the Shadow Guard? "No, he wouldn't have," she agreed.

"Get some rest, Stella," Luc urged. "We'll need all of our strength for this next stretch." In moments, he was snoring softly behind her. Marveling at his ability to fall asleep so swiftly, she closed her eyes until she joined him in slumber.

When Stella awoke, it was to Luc's low voice accompanied by the sounds of soft snickering. Perplexed, she scrambled out of the snow dome to find an unexpected sight—Luc standing before two magnificent white horses, both saddled but bereft of their riders.

"Where did you find them?" she marveled.

"I didn't. They were already here when I awoke."

Stella turned her startled gaze from Luc back to the horses. "You mean someone left them here?" she asked, unable to conceal her nervous anxiety. "But that would mean…"

"That would mean what?"

"They were stolen somehow. Only the royals and their soldiers are allowed horses. They are banned to anyone else. Who would leave them here…and why?"

"Maybe the horses were lost?" Luc suggested. "But I'm not about to pass up a boon such as this one. It will shorten our trip across the Wasteland by a considerable amount. Let's go, before whoever left them or lost them comes for them."

Grabbing their belongings, they broke up the dome and hid all evidence of their camp. Then Luc helped her to mount, her heart thumping rapidly as she held onto the reins in a white-knuckled grip. The horse was so tall and she was sitting so high off the ground. Would she be able to control such a large, powerful beast?

"Don't be afraid, Stella. I'll tell you what to do." As Luc explained how to hold the reins, how to start and stop the horse, and how to change directions, it was clear he was accustomed to riding. She listened carefully, determined not to be tossed and trampled underfoot. "Ready?" he asked, when he finished with his instructions.

Stella nodded uncertainly and then they were off.

Though they rode at a light canter, the wind bit at her face like hundreds of tiny teeth, and the razor sharp air stung her lungs with each breath. Unable to stand the cold, she bent low over her horse's back and tucked in her chin, watching the leagues pass beneath its hooves. Snow eventually gave way to icy ground, slowing their progress. The last thing they wanted was to twist one of the horse's ankles.

"Let's stop here," Luc suggested, digging his heels into his horse. Stella's horse stopped as soon as his did.

"Your horse leads and mine follows," she noted.

"Perhaps they're mates," he remarked, pulling out some hare he had roasted the night before. Planning for their trip across the Wasteland, he had caught and cooked enough meat to last them for at least three nights.

Chewing on the cold, tough meat, Stella scanned their surroundings. The quarter moon was waxing, providing enough light to reveal occasional tufts of low-lying scrub and a smattering of boulders. From

249

the corner of her eye, she caught movement and was surprised to see a pair of white foxes sprinting in the distance before disappearing into a den below ground. So it was not completely barren after all.

Something dimmed the moonlight, drawing their gazes upward. Awed, Stella watched as a large flock of birds darkened the sky, the sound of their flapping wings drowning the sigh of the wind.

"We'll ride for most of the night before stopping again," Luc said, after the birds had passed.

Stella groaned inwardly. Her backside was sore and her thighs were chafed, making her wince at the thought of riding all night. Perhaps she could dismount and stretch? No, if she did, she might have to be dragged back on again.

"Are you ready?" Luc asked, when he saw she had finished her last bite of hare.

"Ready," she said, with little enthusiasm.

* * *

"Stella, we're here."

It took some time for the distant words to penetrate her sleep-shrouded mind. But when it did, Stella awoke with a start. Either Luc was on her horse or she was on his, for she was sitting in front of him with his arms around her. Not that she minded, but she couldn't help wondering why.

"What happened?"

"You fell asleep then nearly fell from your horse," Luc replied, his voice strained. "I'm sorry, Stella. I pushed you too hard."

"My horse..."

"She's fine. She's right here."

Stella turned to see the horse standing by idly. Only then did she realize they weren't moving as his earlier words suddenly registered. Sitting up, her gaze immediately landed on the giant crack that split the ground directly before them. It stretched from right to left as far as her eyes could see, and it looked to be about five hundred feet wide. Beyond the Chasm, a thick fog obscured the land on the other side. A most unusual phenomenon.

"Have you ever seen anything like it?" she asked.

"Never," Luc replied.

"How are we supposed to cross?"

"Damian said to look for a bridge." Luc scanned from side to side. "The question is, which way do we go?"

"Left?" Stella suggested.

"West it is," Luc said, spurring the horse in said direction.

"Should I return to my own mount?" she offered.

"There's no need. You'll be much warmer staying with me."

Stella agreed.

The Scorpius constellation was far to the north when she asked, "When should we try the other direction?"

"I don't know," Luc admitted. "I keep fearing that we'll turn back too soon, that the bridge is just a little further."

Stella knew the feeling, so she made the call to change directions. That way, she could take the blame should Luc turn out to be right and the bridge *was* further west. It took several hours just to return to their starting point, but they switched horses and continued on until one night turned into the next. Behind her, Luc had fallen silent. Stella sensed from the tension in his body that frustration was warring with his determination. He didn't want to stop until the bridge had been found, even though he had to be delirious with exhaustion and the horses were on the verge of collapse.

"We should stop," she suggested gently.

Luc immediately halted the horse. "I did it again, didn't I? Pushed too far?"

"Your tenacity is admirable," she answered carefully. "I'm certain it's what makes you such a formidable warrior, and why the king trusts you to break the curse."

"You're right about stopping, Stella," was all he said. Dismounting, he helped her to the ground.

Stella studied him worriedly before looking around. The wind had mercifully stopped, leaving no trace of snow on the hard, frozen ground. Just as she was contemplating the unpleasant thought of sleeping out in the open, completely exposed, the sky split and snow began to fall in earnest. Now she understood why Luc had been so determined to find the bridge. He wanted them out of the Wasteland as soon as possible.

She continued to scan her surroundings, for what she didn't know. But she spun in a full circle, feeling a rising sense of desperation. Suddenly, she stopped, her eye catching a glimpse of something out of place. She squinted, wondering if she was seeing correctly or if exhaustion was playing tricks on her mind. But the longer she stared, the more convinced she was that the sight before her was real.

"Luc! Luc!" she called excitedly.

"What is it?" Luc asked, turning to her with the reins of both horses in his hands.

"Look!"

Luc's eyes widened when he saw what she was pointing at. Over the Chasm, seeming to gradually unfurl before their very eyes, was a bridge. As the snow fell, it dusted the once invisible surface until a solid white carpet stretched from one side of the Chasm to the other.

"I can't believe it," Luc murmured.

When they drew near, they saw that the bridge was no more than three feet wide.

"We'll have to leave the horses," Luc's said, his voice heavy with regret.

Stella nodded, hating the idea but knowing they had no choice. It was too risky to try to bring the horses across. She walked up to the stately creatures and placed a hand on each head. "Thank you."

Luc then secured the reins around their pommels so they wouldn't drag, and they made their way to the foot of the bridge.

"I'll go first," Luc said. "Follow slowly and be careful."

He placed one foot on the bridge, while Stella held her breath. It wasn't until his fourth step that she finally released it. Somewhat confident that the bridge was more or less stable, she proceeded to make her way across, praying no strong wind began to blow. She willed herself not to look to the sides, where the drop-off was visible. But when her foot slid, she found herself staring straight down into the fathomless abyss, causing her heart to nearly jump out of her throat. In front of her, Luc continued on, oblivious.

Halfway across, the snow fell even heavier, concealing the dangerous depths that lay just inches away on either side. It was painfully slow-going. She followed Luc's lead of getting on her hands and knees when her vision became almost completely obscured. When she finally made it to the other side, she nearly wept with relief.

But there was no time for crying or rejoicing. They were still exposed and in need of shelter. So they pushed on wearily, having no idea where they were going. The dark world had turned white, but they were blinder than ever. It was Stella who broke first. Stella who couldn't find the strength to take another step. She sunk to the ground, defeated, numbed by the cold. And then Luc was there wrapping his arms around her, lending her his warmth. It was the last thing she remembered before slipping from consciousness.

36

The Prison & Inquisition

Stella woke up in a cell. Alone.

She blinked as she studied the dank, cramped quarters. There was a rock wall to her right, stone blocks behind and before her. And to her left, was a thick wooden door with a barred window near the top.

Panic assaulted her, thick and suffocating. Where was she? More importantly, where was Luc? Her weapons were gone. Her pack, too. Besides herself, there was nothing in the cell but the lumpy cot she sat upon and the waste bucket in the opposite corner.

She flew to the door. "Luc! Luc!"

"Stella!" Relief flooded her. His voice was only a short distance away. "Are you alright?"

"Yes, I'm fine. And you?"

"I'm alright, Stella. Did you just wake? I'd been calling you."

"I'm in a cell."

"I know," Luc replied, his voice strained.

"What happened? I-I don't remember."

"We—"

The sound of footsteps echoed outside her cell, halting Luc's words. "Release the girl," a man's voice said. "Then bring her to me."

At once, Luc began to protest. Stella stumbled backward until she hit the wall, her heart pounding painfully as she waited. Through the barred window she glimpsed a black-bearded chin before the cell door swung open with an ominous creak. In the doorway stood an enormous man who gazed at her without expression. "Come," he ordered, his deep voice rumbling through his chest.

Stella didn't move, too terrified to take a single step. With a menacing frown, the man reached her in two steps and yanked her by the arm. A scream built up in her lungs as she struggled in vain. Only the fear of upsetting Luc kept it from erupting. It didn't matter. As the giant dragged her out of the cell and through a dim hallway lined with several other cells, she caught sight of Luc's face. His shouts and bellows followed her up the steep stone steps.

The air grew warmer as they ascended. Stella considered grabbing one of the torches lining the stairs, but the passage was too tight for her to confront her captor, who was at an advantage being behind her. Resigned to the fact that she was at his mercy, new fears assailed her. Who were these people and what did they want? What would they do to her and Luc? How horribly unfair to endure so much to escape danger only to run into more danger.

"Who are you?" she asked, hating how her voice shook.

The giant refused to answer.

Before long, she was stepping into a long, windowless corridor. The large man came to her side to lead her through it, the flickering torches throwing their shadows against the arched walls. Was she in a castle? When they reached a door guarded by two men, the giant pushed it open before shoving her through.

Stella stumbled into a large room with a blazing fire in a massive fireplace at one end and a wide window at the other. The snowstorm must have stopped, because through it, she could just make out the faint outline of jagged peaks in the silver moonlight. In the center of the room stood a raised dais.

Three people sat upon it—two men and one woman. The man in the center was tall and lean, his features sharp and severe. He was dressed all in black except for the white fur cape that topped his attire. It reminded her of the one Damian had worn to the Winter Solstice celebration, though she had to admit it had looked better on him. To his right, the other man had a warrior's build, evident under the gray leathers he wore upon his broad, muscular body. The woman on the left was a stunning beauty, though her features appeared harsh—high cheekbones, slanted cat-like eyes and generous lips. The scarlet gown she wore all but demanded attention.

Unlike herself, all three were dark-haired. But that's not what seized her attention or made her stomach flutter with unease. Nor was it the way they studied her, their gazes practically unblinking. It was the aura of danger they emanated, much like another dark-haired man she knew.

The giant guard led Stella to within fifteen feet of the dais before retreating to one side, leaving her to face scrutiny alone. Looking around nervously, she realized that they were the only five people in the room.

Stella stood stiffly, conscious of her filthy, bedraggled state. Her hair was lank, her skin grimy with grit and dried sweat. She hadn't bathed in days and she knew she smelled rank, but she refused to be cowed by these strangers who studied her appraisingly.

"Where am I?" she asked, relieved that her voice came out steady.

"You are at Barren Keep," the man in the center replied. She recognized his voice as the one who had ordered her release.

"*This* is Barren Keep?" A thick woven rug of sapphire, emerald and crimson covered the dais and the three chairs upon it were of polished bronze. It was less barren than she had expected.

"Who are you?" the man asked, his heavy brows bunching together.

Stella licked her chapped lips, wishing they had offered her water for her parched throat. "My name is Stella Varden and I hail from Darkwood."

"You're a long way from Darkwood, Stella," the man replied. "How did you end up at my keep?"

His keep? "We were told to come here. We were told it would be safe."

The man narrowed his eyes, making him look like a hawk. "Who told you that?"

Stella hesitated. "Damian Dagnatari."

The woman in scarlet stiffened while the warrior to his right scowled. Stella felt her heart sink. Why would Damian send them to a place where he was looked upon with disfavor?

"Damian told you to come to me?" the man in the cape clarified.

"No, he told us to go to this place, Barren Keep. I didn't know—had no idea you would be here. Not any of you. I thought the place would be more...well, barren."

A hint of amusement passed over the warrior's face, but the one in charge looked perplexed. "The keep is named after me, not because it is barren."

"Oh." Barron Keep, Stella realized—irritated with Damian for not clarifying. "He didn't mention that."

"Who is Damian to you?" Barron asked, and she noticed the woman in scarlet seemed keenly interested in her answer.

It was an answer Stella had trouble forming. Damian was more than an acquaintance, but she would never call him a friend. Their relationship was too confusing, too tumultuous for that. "He considers himself my protector," she finally replied, an answer that seemed to surprise all three.

"Interesting," Barron murmured. "And the man we found you with?"

"A...friend."

"Tell us about him," Barron commanded.

"What do you want to know?"

"Where is he from?"

Stella stared in dismay, afraid to respond.

"Well?" Barron pressed.

"He's from Aurelia," she replied, seeing no reason to lie when it was obvious he wasn't from Noctum. "It's south of—"

"The Altous Mountains," Barron finished, earning her surprise.

"How did you know that? I was under the impression such knowledge is privy to only a select few." Damian knew, but she assumed that as commandant he had access to the Repository.

Barron smiled, but it lacked humor. "We are the inquisitors here, not you." He looked to the side. "Jorg, take Stella to the north tower room, but set a guard on her. "Then bring the other prisoner."

The next thing Stella knew, the huge guard, Jorg, had her by the arm and was guiding her from the room. She was a mix of emotions, though uncertainty was the feeling that prevailed. She wasn't being returned to the cell, for which she was grateful, and she hadn't been mistreated in any way. But she feared for Luc.

Outside the doors, Jorg spoke to one of the guards who promptly joined them. At the end of the corridor, they ascended a set of steps that led to a small landing with a single door. When Jorg opened it, she found herself in a large, well-appointed room. There was a comfortable-looking bed in the center, a table with two chairs, a tall wardrobe and a fireplace that was currently cold and dark.

Stella entered hesitantly, studying the space. It was the grandest room she had ever seen; most of her cottage could fit inside of it. At the sound of footsteps, she turned to see two other men enter—one carrying her pack and the other carrying a stack of logs. She watched, grateful, as he proceeded to start a fire in the hearth. The other man had left, leaving her pack, but he was replaced by two women. One brought in a bowl and a pitcher of water. The other carried in a plate of food, causing her hungry belly to clench at the sight.

Soon enough, she was all alone, the door shutting her in. After quickly washing her hands, she fell upon the food, stuffing bread, meat and cheese into her mouth. It was divine—the best thing she'd tasted in weeks. Afterwards, she stared at the bed longingly, wishing she could lie down, but refusing to do so in her dirty state. What she really needed was a hot bath. More than that, she was eager to find out what was happening with Luc.

Anxious and restless, she approached the one small window in the bedroom and unlatched it. The shutter immediately flew from her hand to bang against the wall as a frigid gust blasted in, chilling her instantly.

"Best keep that shut."

Stella whirled to find her new guard peering into the room, no doubt drawn by the noise. Nodding, she fought to put the shutter back in place before relatching it. The bedroom door was also closed once more.

Perhaps an hour later, the door flew open yet again. This time the woman in scarlet stood in the doorway. "Follow me," she said, and left without waiting to see if Stella heeded.

Stella rushed out the door. The guard was gone, but up ahead a flash of scarlet fabric disappeared around a corner. She quickened her pace. The nameless woman moved with surprising speed down the spiral staircase. Stella followed wordlessly, anxious to be reunited with Luc. When the woman pushed through a door, however, she found herself in a room where a steaming bath waited. In the corner hung a gown of pale blue.

"You will bathe, then I will return for you."

"But—"

The woman was already gone.

With a sigh, she turned to the inviting bath. Unable to deny herself the very thing she wanted, Stella swiftly undressed and sunk into the water. She groaned in bliss as she relished the soothing heat. Finding a bar of soap on a nearby stool, she proceeded to wash her hair and skin. Only when every speck of dirt was removed did she step out to dry, a towel wrapped around her clean body as she warmed herself by the brazier.

"I could tell you were beautiful even beneath the grime of travel."

Stella spun, dismayed to find the warrior man standing just inside the door.

"Go away!" she demanded, sounding incensed when what she really felt was fearful.

Instead, he drew near, causing Stella to retreat. Undressed and unarmed, she was utterly vulnerable and helpless. Her back hit the wall as he loomed over her, twice her weight and size.

"Hmmm," he hummed, lifting a lock of her damp hair. Stella went rigid as he leaned in to sniff her, moving from the top of her head down to her neck. She smelled like the lavender that scented her bath, while she detected sandalwood on his skin.

"Please." Her voice cracked.

"Please what?" he asked, smiling suggestively.

"Please leave."

"Are you certain that's what you want?" he asked, lightly skimming the skin of her arm with his fingers, leaving goosebumps in their wake.

Panicked, she put her hands up and shoved. He didn't move. "I said leave!"

To her relief, he took a step back, allowing her room to breathe. "I think I understand now."

"Understand what?" she asked, shaken.

"Why Damian was willing to risk so much."

"What do you mean?"

But the warrior just smiled a mysterious smile before exiting the room.

Stella stood staring at the door, trying to determine what had happened. But when she remembered her undressed state, she hurried to throw on the gown that had been left for her. It was slightly long and loose, she noted, as she did up the buttons. She had just reached the last one when the woman in scarlet returned.

"Follow me."

Once again, Stella was hurrying to follow. "Do you have a name?" she ventured to ask, as she trailed the woman through the stone-walled corridors.

"Of course I have a name," the woman said with a sneer. "You may call me Mara."

"Have you lived in the keep long?" Stella asked, willing to overlook the woman's scorn in order to gain information.

"Too long," Mara replied, with what seemed to be a combination of resentment and resignation.

Just then, the man who had recently intruded on her reappeared. Stella glared at him before fixing her gaze ahead.

"Markus," Mara said in acknowledgement. "I thought you'd be in the dining hall by now."

"I made a brief detour," Markus replied. "But you know I wouldn't miss this for anything."

They rounded a corner that revealed a set of large double doors, already propped open. Passing the two guards on either side, Stella walked into a room with three long tables. Only the middle one was set and she immediately spotted Luc and Barron standing at its far end. He was already striding toward her as she called out, "Luc!"

He grasped her hands as soon as they met. "Are you alright, Stella?"

"I am now," she replied, looking him over eagerly. Like herself, he was washed and dressed in clean clothes, and he no longer sported the shaggy beard that had grown during their travels. With the fine attire he wore, he looked like a dashing nobleman. A sight that made her heart sigh.

"Shall we sit?" Barron interrupted, a command that was made to sound like a suggestion.

Stella tore her eyes from Luc to gaze upon the table. It was a heavy piece of furniture, surrounded by ten intricately carved chairs of dark wood. It felt surreal, to be dressed in elegant clothes about to sit down at a splendid table when the last thing she recalled was being in a snowstorm before waking up in a cell. Barron sat at the head with Luc to his left and Markus to his right. Stella sat on Luc's other side, while Mara sat directly across from her.

At some unknown signal, a door across from Stella opened and servants began to carry out platters of food. She was surprised to see fowl and hare and various root vegetables. She lamented having already eaten, for this food looked superior to what she had been offered.

"Eat," Barron encouraged before helping himself to some fowl.

Stella watched as Luc filled his plate. "Are you not hungry?" he asked her.

"I was given a plate in my room."

"I trust you find it an improvement to the cell?" Barron asked.

Stella nodded. "I take it you no longer view us as a threat?"

Barron's gaze flicked to Luc. "That remains to be seen."

Stella looked between the two men uncertainly. She wished she could have spoken to Luc in private, to find out what had been discussed in their meeting. She never had a chance to tell him what she had revealed—that he wasn't from Noctum. Though he had to know that his appearance and speech gave him away.

"I told them why I came," Luc said.

Anxiety curled in her chest. "What exactly did you tell them?"

"That he plans to kill Draven," Barron supplied, his eyes gleaming with an emotion she couldn't identify.

Stella glanced at Luc. Had he mentioned the curse as well? But she said nothing about it, in case he hadn't. "Do you also know why we came to your keep?" she asked Barron.

"Because you had the misfortune of catching Draven's eye," Barron replied. Across the table, Mara visibly paled while Marcus's face darkened.

"I'm assuming Damian sent us here because Draven has no idea it exists?" she ventured.

"No, though he took a great risk in sending you," Barron said, his gaze darkening. "Should Draven manage to track you here—"

"Luc struck him in the heart. Damian said it would take hours for the organ to be repaired, which is when we made our escape," Stella quickly explained.

"So I hear," Barron replied, taking his first bite of food.

"How does Damian even know you?" Stella asked, curious. "How does he know about this place?"

Barron chewed thoughtfully. "Damian is a...kindred of sorts."

"That's lucid," Luc muttered beneath his breath, causing Markus to quirk his brow.

"What exactly does that mean?" Stella pressed.

"It means..." Markus shot a challenging look at Barron. "That he shares a similar history with us."

Stella frowned at the unsatisfactory reply, but knew she wouldn't be getting a clearer answer. "Damian was protecting you. That's why he never mentioned you by name," she ventured.

Mara scoffed. "Protecting us or protecting you? The fool must imagine himself in love with you if he sent you here."

Stella said nothing at first, unprepared for the accusation. "If you knew anything about him, you would know he is incapable of the feeling."

"I know him well enough, which is why I said he *imagines* it," Mara returned haughtily.

Stella's jaw clenched in annoyance.

"Even from afar, Damian manages to ruffle the women," Barron said, amused. It earned him twin scowls from the only women present.

"What happens now?" Luc asked, diffusing the tension.

"That *is* the question, isn't it?" Barron replied, swirling his goblet of wine. "On the one hand, we have the woman Draven wants. On the other, we have the man intent on killing him." Barron took a sip of wine, prolonging the suspense. "Fortunately for you, not only am I inclined to deny Draven what he wants, I also wish to see him dead."

"So you're willing to give us safe haven?" Stella asked, with cautious hope.

"For the time being, yes," Barron replied. "It *has* been a while since we've entertained guests."

"How long?" Luc asked.

Barron gave him a wry yet wary look. "Oh, about a hundred years."

263

37

The Forsaken Found

"What are you doing?" Mara hissed, staring at Barron in indignant disbelief.

"Sharing in the spirit of disclosure," Barron replied calmly. "After all, our guests have been forthcoming with us."

"Maybe *he* has, but she has told us nothing, while we risk everything! Consider that before you choose to expose us."

"Her very life is at risk and we are offering her protection. Why would she betray us?" Barron asked Mara, though his sharp gaze was locked on Stella.

"I wouldn't," Stella replied, with full conviction—though she was still reeling from Barron's stunning admission. "What gain would I have by doing such a thing?"

"Perhaps you would bargain with Draven to turn us in, in order to spare your life?" Mara challenged.

Stella shook her head, gazing at Mara as if she were daft. "Draven spares no one."

"She's right," Markus piped, casually leaning back in his seat. "We have nothing to fear from the girl."

Stella looked at him with mixed feelings, grateful he had supported Barron in defending her, but annoyed at being dismissively referred to as the girl.

Mara rose from her chair with a jerk. "Fine, go ahead and say what you will, but I will have no part of it, even though you risk my life as much as you risk your own!" She swept away in a trail of scarlet and red hot anger.

Barron's dark gaze followed her, but when he turned back to Stella and Luc, there was resolution in his eyes. "How much do you know about Draven and his royals?"

Luc glanced at Stella briefly before answering. "We know that they are all vampyres, demons possessing incredible speed and strength. We know that they need blood to live. That so long as they feed on it, they can survive for years without end."

"Then you know more than most," Barron replied, nodding his head. "Though knowing your enemy is a must if you intend to kill him. Did you also know that they are capable of having offspring?"

Stella recoiled while Luc shook his head, looking surprised. "I'd not heard of that," he admitted. "Do you mean that a vampyre male and female—"

"No, a vampyre male with a human female," Barron corrected.

Stella felt her stomach roil with disgust.

"It happens rarely. Very rarely," Barron continued. "The royals don't want offspring. In fact, Draven himself forbids it on pain of death. There were once fourteen royals. Alexei was killed for failing to abide by Draven's edict. Then his offspring was tracked down and killed as well."

"How was Alexei killed?" Stella asked. Luc had refused to tell her how he planned to kill Draven, so perhaps now she would find out.

"He was starved of blood," Markus replied. "A slow and excruciating way for them to die, or so I hear."

Stella turned to Luc. Was that what he meant to do? Capture Draven somehow and starve him? Seizing him would be hard enough, how would he restrain him? Especially when it was known that the king was more powerful than any of the other royals. A knowing look came into Luc's eyes as he spoke. "Are you saying that you three are those forbidden offspring?"

Stella gasped, realizing that Luc had arrived at the heart of the matter while she had been solely focused on how to kill Draven.

"We are," Barron readily replied. "As is your friend Damian. The royals refer to us as the Forsaken."

It was a good thing Stella was sitting because she couldn't have been more floored. But then Barron's earlier words came back to her. *He is a kindred of sorts. We share a similar history.* And she thought about his ability to contend with the Shade, his skill better than most men though nowhere near as superior as a royal's.

"I can see the sincerity of your shock," Barron remarked, eyeing her. "Which means Damian has made good on his promise not to draw notice."

"He wouldn't still be alive if he wasn't discreet," Markus remarked.

"How are *any* of you still alive?" Stella asked. "How does Draven not know about you?"

"Because we've been very careful," Barron replied. "Which is why Mara is furious with me for being open with you, and rightly so. The only reason I am telling you any of this is because I want to see Draven dead as much as you do," Barron said, turning cool eyes to Luc.

"How did you elude Draven's discovery?" Luc asked.

"The story is slightly different for each of us, but essentially the same," Markus answered. "In mine and Mara's case, we are the grandchildren of Vladimir. Vladimir was smart enough to kill our mother when he found out about her, but he didn't realize she had children of her own."

"Are you and Mara brother and sister?" Stella asked, searching for similarities but finding few. Both had dark hair, and now that she thought about it, their noses were similar in shape.

"Half," Markus replied. "Same mother, different fathers."

"And you?" Luc asked, addressing Barron.

"I am grandson to Nikolai the Cruel. Like Markus and Mara, my grandfather killed my father not realizing he had had a son."

"And Damian?" Stella wondered.

"That is his story to tell," Barron replied, to her disappointment.

"Am I to understand that due to your...ancestry, you have inherited longevity of life?" Luc asked, bringing them back to the reason for their discussion.

Barron nodded. "Among other things. Longer life, greater speed and strength than the average man, but significantly inferior to the royals. Which is why we hide when I would prefer to fight them."

"It would be a slaughter," Markus remarked grimly.

At their words, Stella couldn't help but glance at Luc in dismay. If Barron and Markus—who had demon blood in their veins—feared facing Draven, how could Luc find the courage to do so? As if reading her thoughts, he said, "Sometimes it's not about greater strength or ability, but greater conviction. Draven *needs* to die, so that he can no longer use his power to oppress the people of Noctum."

"An admirable conviction. Noble even," Barron remarked, somewhat archly. "If Mara could understand such a trait, she would see there is nothing for her to fear."

* * *

After dinner, Stella stood with Luc before the huge fireplace, glancing to where Barron and Markus were conversing near the window. She couldn't hear their voices, so she hoped her conversation with Luc would be private as well. She stretched her arms to the flames eagerly. Despite the large blaze in the hearth, the cavernous room was still chilly. It was only here by the fire that she felt any warmth at all.

"It's hard to believe, isn't it?"

"What is?" Luc asked. "That we made it through the Wasteland? That we managed to cross the Chasm? Or that our hosts are descendants of vampyres?"

"All three, but mostly the last." She glanced warily in the men's direction. "I'm just glad they don't lust for blood."

"I'm glad for that as well."

Stella looked up at Luc. "How did we get here? The last thing I recall before waking up in a cell is being caught in a snowstorm."

"Jorg and three other men came upon us. You must have passed out because you never awoke, not even when Jorg carried you to the keep." Luc's green eyes briefly clouded. "It was fortunate, too. We wouldn't have survived the night. The temperature had begun to plummet."

Fortune or fate?

Stella thought of the saddled horses that had appeared to carry them across the Wasteland, and of the bridge that had taken shape before their very eyes the moment they stopped searching for one. She thought further back to when she had awoken to see a fireball shooting across the sky and then running into Luc at her secret grotto. She had never been one to believe in either fortune *or* fate, but these events were too timely to chalk up to mere chance. There was something at work here, as if something or *someone* were orchestrating their steps.

Stella lowered her voice to a whisper. "I know they're aware you plan to kill Draven, but do they know about the curse?"

"No, and I'm glad you were wise enough to make no mention of it."

"Why didn't you tell them?"

"Something cautioned me not to. They're aiding us, it's true, but that doesn't mean I fully trust them, and neither should you. Has it ever occured to you that some people might not want the curse to be lifted?"

"Who wouldn't want that?" she asked, bewildered.

"Those who love the darkness."

Stella pondered that somberly. Though she couldn't fathom it herself, she had to consider that there just might be those who not only accepted the darkness, but delighted in it. After all, didn't those with evil intent rely on the shadows to aid in their deeds? And what about the vampyres? Would the absence of darkness destroy them somehow? "You said that Draven couldn't bear the light, but I never thought to ask what would happen if he was exposed to it."

"He would be burned up, as would the royals."

"I see." Her gaze drifted to Barron and Markus, who were now staring back at them. She quickly averted her face before they could see her sudden dread. "And what of those with demon blood in them?"

Luc went still, the question catching him off guard. "I don't know," he replied, turning to face the fire with a troubled expression.

38

A Traitorous Heart

Stella saw Luc only briefly in the dining hall as they broke their fast. Then he was whisked off by Barron and Markus for reasons she wasn't privy to. She watched in dismay as the three men departed, leaving her alone with Mara.

The air had thickened with tension and bitterness. Stella avoided Mara's eyes, knowing she would find in them open contempt. Before she could make her escape, however, the woman volleyed a question in her direction.

"How long have you known Damian?" she asked without preamble, leading Stella to believe she had been waiting all along to spring the question.

"Not long," she replied, vaguely.

"How well do you know him?"

"Not well at all."

Mara narrowed her blue-green eyes. "Have you been intimate with him?"

"What?" Stella exclaimed, outraged. How dare she ask such a thing "Of course not!"

Mara lifted a manicured brow, her expression dubious.

"I haven't been intimate with *any* man," Stella said firmly.

At that, Mara's expression turned scornful, though Stella thought she caught a hint of envy as well. "I see. Well that would explain his interest in you."

Stella rose, tired of the woman's hostility. When she passed through the doorway to enter the corridor, her shoulders relaxed, relieved that she had been allowed to leave without challenge. She tensed again, however, when a shadow detached itself from a corner. It was Jorg, her personal guard.

"Where can I go to find amusement?" she asked, pretending his hulking form didn't intimidate her.

"Amusement?" His voice rumbled like a roaring avalanche. He stared at her long and hard—which made her want to squirm—before gruffly saying, "You'll need to put on something warmer."

Barron Keep was a stone fortress built against the north face of large, craggy hill. It was accessible by what looked to be a hundred steps carved into solid rock against the west side. A wide valley stretched away from the feet of the keep before crashing into more rugged hills across the way. Nestled in between was a lake, currently iced over. And by it, sat a large village. All this could be seen from the hilltop terrace Jorg had taken her to.

Stella stared, awed by the foreign landscape. She had seen many wonders since leaving Darkwood, but none compared to this severe and rugged vista. She gazed at the frozen lake, reflecting the moon and stars above it like a mirror—so clear it was as if an identical parallel world existed just beneath the surface.

"It's breathtaking," Stella marveled.

Beside her, Jorg said nothing, but his eyes held the reverence of one who was gazing upon the place he called home.

Clutching the neck of her fur-lined cloak, she walked to the edge of the terrace where the cutting wind blew more stiffly. Staring down at the flickering lights of the village, she thought of her own home, the one she had fled. It wasn't the place she missed, but the people she had left behind. Until now, she hadn't allowed herself to think of them. And in the difficult weeks when she and Luc had struggled just to survive, it had been easy enough to accomplish. Hunger and weariness had pushed every other thought aside. But now that she was warm, rested and well-fed, she couldn't seem to stop thinking of them. How was Marta and the baby? How were Jenna, Elias and Garrett? Even Damian frequented her thoughts, the last look he had given her still seared in her mind.

"How long have you lived here?" she asked Jorg, trying to dislodge the haunting memory.

"All my life."

"How long is that?"

Jorg furrowed his heavy brows. "Nigh on two and forty years now."

So fully human then, Stella thought, gazing at the grooves on his face along with the sprinkling of gray in his hair. She wondered if he had a wife and children down in the village, but refrained from asking.

Instead, she turned to eye the equipment she had spotted upon their arrival. Archery targets and wooden practice dummies were scattered along the perimeter. It seemed the terrace was used as a training ground. Was that what he had in mind as far as amusement? It would be one way to pass the time. That is, if Barron allowed her to have her weapons back.

"This is a large keep for just a handful of people," Stella remarked. Indeed, the number of guards and servants greatly outnumbered the three they served. Yet the dining hall held three long tables, and here on the terrace there was enough equipment to train dozens of men. She glanced at Jorg expectantly, but the large man merely shrugged his bulky shoulders. She sighed, trying a question he might be more forthcoming with. "Do you train here often?"

Jorg grunted and she glared at him in exasperation.

"Have you ever trained a girl before?" His look of indignant disbelief was almost comical. "You and I should practice together some time. I'm certain there is much you could teach me."

Jorg didn't answer, but the following night they were back at the terrace. Stella was surprised to find her weapons there waiting for her. She was even more surprised when Jorg engaged her in a test of skills.

Unfortunately, she was found woefully lacking.

Thus began her nightly training, which Stella fervently threw herself into. Not only as a way to pass the monotonous hours, but because she felt the need to be prepared. For what exactly she couldn't say.

The weeks passed, and before long, the dim corridors and drafty halls of the cold stone keep became as familiar as her cottage. In her explorations, she discovered the kitchens, the armory, and—to her surprise—a stable full of horses.

As for Luc, she saw him at every meal, but in between he spent much of his time with Barron and Markus. They would hole up in the great room, having discussions she was growing increasingly curious about. But she also knew they rode horses and practiced combat together as well. She came upon them on the terrace one night, and was stunned by the scene that greeted her. Swords sang in the air to clash against one another in a combination of incredible strength and extraordinary speed. She watched, riveted, as Luc fought both Markus and Barron. The two men had the advantage of centuries worth of experience, but Luc possessed impressive confidence and skill. That night, he lost to Barron, but beat Markus.

Their second night at Barron Keep, Luc snuck into her room in the north tower and had been staying with her ever since. Stella had been relieved, for she had grown accustomed to sleeping in his arms, and it seemed he had grown accustomed to having her there. Fortunately, the guards said nothing, nor did their hosts who witnessed the obvious affection between them.

Stella lowered her sword and wiped the sweat from her brow, her breath misting before her.

"Well done, Stella," Jorg said. "Your arm is getting stronger."

"Thanks to you."

Jorg had proven to be a surprisingly patient and adept instructor. Though she'd already possessed some skill, under his tutelage, she had become even better. It had been four weeks since he started training her, and not only was she stronger, but her stamina had increased. Because of both these things, her strikes were swifter and deadlier.

"One more time?" she queried.

Jorg lifted his thick brow. They had been practicing for hours already, but Stella found that the more she improved, the more driven she became.

"I'll take over from here, Jorg."

Stella turned around to find Luc approaching her. A smile broke over her face, her heart lifting as it always did whenever he was near. "Will you go easy on me?"

"Do you want me to?"

"No."

"I didn't think so."

Luc pulled his sword from his sheath and stood waiting. Stella came at him first, charging head on. Their blades met with a jarring clang. She stepped aside and swung again. He blocked her strike easily, along with the next. Though she used every move in her arsenal, there was no getting the upper hand. Within minutes, Luc had his sword at her neck, forcing her to yield.

Stella sighed, though in truth she was glad Luc was as good as he was. But he would need to be better if he ever hoped to defeat Draven.

She flinched inwardly. It was thoughts like these that tempered the happiness she'd been feeling. And she *had* been happy, happier than she'd ever been. Except that each hour with Luc felt like a precious gift that would soon be snatched from her hands.

"Stella, is something wrong?" Luc asked, detecting her distress.

Stella smiled and shook her head. "It's nothing."

Luc drew near and gazed down at her intently. "It's not nothing. Tell me."

She looked up into his emerald eyes, mesmerized by the tenderness she saw there. "Will you hold me first?"

Without hesitation, he enveloped her in his strong arms. She sighed contentedly, her ear pressed against his chest to hear the steady beating of his heart.

"Sometimes I feel like I'm living in a dream," she confessed.

"A dream?"

"This...what we have between us. I keep expecting to wake up and find out none of it is real."

She felt his hand stroke her hair. "It's not a dream, Stella. What I feel for you is very real."

"And what is it you feel?" she asked, wanting to hear the words.

"More than what I should."

Disappointment washed over her. She loved Luc. She was half in love with him the moment she first laid eyes on him. But did he love her? Lifting her head, she rose on her tiptoes to kiss him, needing to feel what he wouldn't say. They had shared many kisses in the past month—sweet kisses, passionate kisses. This one was not the sweet kind, but as always happened when their kiss grew too heated, he pulled away.

"More...please," she insisted breathlessly, dragging him back.

Luc looked at her in surprise. It was the first time she had ever begged. He kissed her on the forehead instead. "No, Stella. I shouldn't."

She sighed in disappointment.

"I wouldn't want you to do something you might regret."

"I wouldn't regret it, Luc." Stella took a deep breath, dredging up her courage. "I love you."

Luc's face displayed shock and dismay. The sight was a knife to her heart. Mortified, she dropped her gaze.

"Stella." Luc's voice was gentle, to soothe the blow.

She backed away, her eyes still fixed to the ground. "No...it's...I never should have said it."

"I wish you hadn't," he said sadly.

Tears sprang to her eyes as her shame burned hotter. "Please pretend I never did." She turned away from him, her heart completely battered. But it was her bruised pride that caused her to flee.

39

A Grave Mistake

S tella felt so fragile she was certain one wrong word or look would shatter her. Luc had apologized to her several times over the course of the week, but she was still too hurt to accept. Especially since he had stopped coming to her room after the ill-received confession. Actions spoke louder than words. So though he claimed to be sorry, it was clear that he was spurning her. Her confession had driven him away, because he didn't feel the same. Worse, he had become increasingly distant in the last few nights. Even when he was in the same room with her, it felt like he was leagues away.

It was stunning just how quickly one could go from heaven to hell.

"There's no need to be so glum. There's more than one handsome, strapping man in this keep," Markus drawled, as he came upon her gazing out the window of the great room.

Stella froze, debating whether or not to ignore him. She didn't want to face him, but neither did she trust having him at her back. He hadn't troubled her since walking in on her in the washroom, but the incident had done its damage. It didn't help that he was Mara's brother. The woman still scorned her at every opportunity. In the month that she'd been at the keep, she had done her best to evade the siblings, but of course, not all encounters could be avoided.

Bracing herself, she turned to face Markus. "Really? Where?"

Markus smirked as he leaned a shoulder against the wall opposite her. "You wound me."

"Doubtful," she replied, turning back to the window. The village twinkled from dozens of torches and lanterns. In the moonlight, smoke could be seen curling from nearly every chimney.

"Would you like to accompany me?"

Stella glanced at him in surprise. "Where?"

"To the village. I have business to attend to there."

Curiosity warred with wariness. A number of villagers had come to the keep for one reason or another, but she had yet to see the village itself. The thought interested her, but she had reservations about going with Markus. Why had he invited her?

"Jorg can join us if you wish," he offered.

"He wouldn't think of letting me out of his sight," she replied, glancing at the guard who rarely left her side.

"Meet me at the main entrance in half an hour," Markus said, before striding away.

"I never said I would go."

But he pretended not to hear her.

* * *

Stella was thankful for the lanterns Jorg and Markus carried to light their path for the steps were icy. Lanterns were rarely used for travel in Darkwood, since light tended to attract danger. What a luxury to live in a place where such worries didn't exist. If anything, the two men accompanying her were the most dangerous things around. Which begged her to wonder why she had agreed to go to the village with them.

Because she was bored.

And because Luc was still being distant. He had disappeared with

Barron hours ago and had yet to be seen since.

Despite her reservations, it felt good to finally leave the keep.

"What is your business in the village?" Stella asked, keeping her eyes on the slippery steps.

"I intend to pay a visit to a lady."

Stella paused mid-step, recalling his recent disappearance with one of the pretty village women who'd visited the keep. "Why did you ask me to accompany you then?"

"Why wouldn't I?" Markus asked. "I thought you might want to join me."

She shot him a quelling look. "I am not interested in your...activities. If you thought to involve me in them, you're sorely mistaken," she declared, turning on her heels to stomp back up to the keep.

She was immediately snagged around her waist by a band of steel. "I had no intention of involving you in anything you wouldn't be interested in," Markus growled in her ear. "But now I've changed my mind. Jorg, leave us. I have her from here."

"No, Jorg! Don't go!" she pleaded. But the guard she had so often resented turned his broad back on her and walked away.

When Stella began to struggle, Markus left his lantern on the step to carry her. She kicked and flailed the entire way, but he was much too strong to resist. By the time they reached the valley floor, she was worn out. Sensing she was done struggling, he put her on her own two feet. Shivering—he had been warm at least—she followed him woodenly toward the village. Just outside of it, she made another attempt to flee, only to find herself wrapped up in his arms once more.

"You are a feisty thing, aren't you?" Markus asked, half annoyed, half amused.

In reply, Stella screamed in frustration. He quickly clamped a hand over her mouth. "Stop that! You're disturbing the peace."

Her eyes bulged above his hand. He was intent on corrupting her and he was concerned about her making too much noise? She redoubled her efforts to free herself, but again met with failure. Tears threatened to spill from her eyes, but she refused to let Markus see them. She wouldn't give him the satisfaction.

They soon entered the village, which Stella saw was simple yet orderly. It hadn't snowed for days, so the muddy paths were visible between the banks of dirty snow pushed up against the small cottages that lined either side. Unlike the Hollow, where homes cropped up wherever they would, the cottages in the village were arranged in neat rows. Some were completely dark, but most glowed softly from within.

Few villagers dared to brave the bitter cold. Those who did watched curiously as they passed, nodding respectfully at Markus, but saying nothing of the captive at his side. Stella would get no aid from that quarter, she realized. She eyed each cottage they passed, her gut churning as she wondered which one Markus would force her into. When she saw an open space with a raised wooden dais at the center, she recognized it as the village square. Still, they continued on until the opposite end of the village came to view. Her heart began to slam against her chest. Where was he taking her?

And then she saw it. The statues and columns reaching up to the dark sky. Dozens upon dozens of them sat upon the frozen ground in various states of deterioration.

It was a graveyard.

Darkwood's practice was to burn the dead, so Stella had never seen one so large. The only reason she recognized it was because she had stumbled upon one years back, several leagues outside of Darkwood. It was so old, the forest had all but swallowed it up.

Markus released her and began to wind his way through the tilted tombstones. Stella followed behind, studying each one as she passed. There was something haunting and beautiful about the way the moonlight shone on the worn stone, highlighting the elegant script carved onto their surfaces. Forgotten epitaphs and faded memories.

Markus stopped, and she saw that he was gazing not at the large statue of the angel before him, but at the cold, hard ground at its feet. His head was bowed and his shoulders were slumped in sorrow. Stella felt a punch of guilt. The woman he had come to see was dead.

"Who was she?" she asked, after some time had passed.

He paused so long she began to think he wouldn't answer. "My wife."

"I'm sorry." The apology was meant for his loss, but also for her grossly erroneous assumption.

"Leave us. I'll find you when it's time to go."

Nodding dumbly, she turned and made her way out of the graveyard. She had misjudged yet again. People were so complicated. She was beginning to realize that they weren't always who she thought they were.

Back in the village, she wandered without direction, having no idea where to go or what to do. The villagers stared at her, but as before, none made any attempt to speak or approach her. Up ahead, she spotted a building larger than the rest. A sign above it simply read, "The Alehouse." Stella wasn't one for ale, but if it offered a warm spot to sit, she was all for it. Too cold to care for caution, she pushed the door open and stepped through. Immediately, all conversation ceased as everyone in the room turned to look at her.

Were it not for the blessed warmth of the roaring fire in the fireplace, she might have promptly left. Instead, she gathered her courage and sat at the first open table she spotted. Once seated, she stared at the fire, pretending not to notice the stares. At least the conversations had started up again, though in a more subdued manner.

After a time, a serving boy approached. "Can I get you something, miss?"

Stella looked at him in chagrin. "I wish, but I have no coin. If it's not too much trouble, I only hoped to rest a bit."

"Of course, miss. Stay as long as you like," he said, somewhat nervously. "And anything you want to order is on the house."

"On the house?" she asked, furrowing her brow.

"Yes, miss. Any friend of Barron's is welcome to anything they like."

"Well, then, a hot mug of tea would be nice."

"Coming right up." He hurried off to fulfill her order, leaving Stella to wonder at the extent of Barron's influence. Was it out of fear or mere respect for the man that she was being extended this kindness?

Warmed by the tea in her hands, Stella listened to the conversations around her. There was talk of ice fishing, seal hunting and keeping the wolves at bay, but no mention at all of the Shade or Draven or any of the other royals. This place was truly set apart, excluded from the dangers that threatened the rest of Noctum.

"Where did they find ya?"

It took Stella a moment to realize that the question had been directed her way. Turning to the table beside her, she saw three men gazing at her curiously. They were slightly older, perhaps in their early thirties. She pondered their question before answering.

"Do you mean Barron and the others?" she ventured cautiously.

The man in the middle nodded, and she assumed he was the one who had asked. "It's been a long time since they've found another of their kind."

Their kind. They thought she was one of the Forsaken, that she had vampyre blood running through her veins! She was about to correct them when she reconsidered. Perhaps it would be to her advantage to let them maintain the assumption.

"They found me in Nyxus," she lied, taking a sip from her mug. "What is the name of this place anyway? No one ever told me."

"This here is Icelake Valley, the coldest place in all of Noctum but also the safest."

"Safest?" the man to his right scoffed. "Gordy was killed by a pack of wolves three nights ago. Barely anything left to identify him. And last week, they found Arty frozen stiff not fifty feet from his cottage."

"Yeah, well you've never lived out of the valley, so you've never known a Shade attack or experienced the rage of a royal," the middle man replied, before turning to her. "It's been nine years since I left

Umbria. Is it still as bad as I remember?"

Stella nodded. "It is."

"Nothing ever changes," he said glumly. "And nothing ever will."

"Be glad Barron found you," the third man remarked. "Your blood might freeze while you're here, but at least no Shade will suck you dry."

"How did you end up here?" she asked, curious.

"I was hunting with a friend." His face briefly clouded. "We were attacked by a Shade. My friend was killed, sucked dry before my very eyes. I would have been next, but then a man came charging out of the trees. He moved so fast, I thought it was a royal. But it was Barron. He saved my life and brought me here."

Stella looked around the alehouse, wondering how many of the people here owed their lives and safety to Barron. Perhaps to even Markus and Mara?

"Were there more at one time? Of my kind, that is." Stella asked, thinking of the empty tables and chairs in the dining hall. "It's a big keep for only three."

"Five now from what I hear," the man in the middle said, gazing at her pointedly. "But yes, there used to be many more."

"What happened to them?"

"It's dangerous to be one of your kind. Those who leave tend not to return."

"Then why do they leave?" she wondered aloud.

The man shrugged. "Boredom? Restlessness? It can't be easy living so long and being stuck in one place."

"But most of them died during the rebellion," the second man said.

"What rebellion?" she asked, eagerly.

"There were over twenty of them that died trying to overthrow Draven."

"When?"

"A long time ago. Nearly four centuries past."

Stunned, Stella let that sink in. Did Elias know about this?

Somehow she didn't think so. She doubted he even knew about the Forsaken, unlike these villagers who possessed such valuable knowledge.

"How did Draven defeat more than twenty of the Forsaken?"

The men's eyes widened, seemingly surprised that she would use the unfavorable moniker.

"One of their own betrayed them. When Draven found out what was planned, he was able to gather all the royals. The, uh, Forsaken didn't have a chance against them."

"A man named Agmar Dagnatari. He was a direct offspring of Draven. It seemed he had hoped Draven would spare him, out of gratitude. He was wrong."

Stella's mind began to race. Was Agmar Damian's father or grandfather? Could that be why Damian had moved to Darkwood? Did his private matter have to do with Draven? She couldn't believe he was directly related to the king! Her skin crawled just thinking about it. Though it would also explain his grudging willingness to trust Luc despite everything. Perhaps like Barron, Damian wanted Draven dead more than anything. She opened her mouth to ask another question, but the door to the alehouse flew open, letting in a blast of icy air. Markus entered, heading straight for her. The three men she'd been talking to swiftly turned back to their drinks.

"Let's go," he ordered.

Rising reluctantly, she glanced at the three men with regret. There was so much more she wanted to learn. "How did you find me?" she asked, as she followed Markus out into the cold.

"It wasn't hard to guess. There aren't many places open to the public in a village this small, and I didn't think I'd find you in the brothel."

Stella flushed at that, quickly lifting her hood over her head.

"Did you enjoy your time in the alehouse?"

"It was informative."

"Oh?"

Too curious to stop herself, she asked, "Is Damian related to

Draven?"

"Ah, so the men have been talking. Yes, Draven is Damian's grandda, though he'll never call him that."

Because unlike his father, Agmar, Damian hated Draven.

"Are you and Damian friends?"

"Friends?" Markus sounded amused by the idea. "Hardly. We've competed with each other for too long to be friends. Then there's the matter of him trampling on my sister's heart."

That would explain Mara's animosity towards her. "How long ago was this?"

"About fifty years."

Fifty years! That was more than thirty years before she was even born! "Do you think you can inform your sister that I have never been involved with Damian in the way she thinks? Perhaps then she'll stop shooting daggers at me with her eyes."

Markus laughed. "I'm afraid Mara has always been a jealous, petty woman. It wouldn't matter what I said, but she would never harm you."

Stella had her doubts about that.

They traveled the rest of the way in silence, each lost in their own head. When Markus retrieved his lantern from the steps, it flickered faintly, having run low on wax and wick. Back inside of the keep, all was quiet and still. When they passed the great room, Jorg came out to meet them.

"Take Stella to her room and see that she is given a meal," Markus instructed.

Stella wanted to refuse. But it was past the dinner hour and these nights she never knew where to find Luc. Still, she was disappointed to have missed him, for she was eager to share with him all that she'd learned. The growing rift between them was beginning to terrify her, and she was anxious to bridge the gap. Now she a valid reason to do so. Tomorrow, she told herself, as she relented to Markus and followed Jorg to the north tower.

40

A Fool's Hope

Stella yawned as she walked down the corridor toward the dining hall to break her fast. Her sleep had been restless, troubled by dreams that left her feeling confused and shaken. She couldn't remember them now, though she tried hard to recall even the faintest detail. But like wisps of smoke, they dissipated as soon as she attempted to grasp one. No doubt it had something to do with her discoveries from the previous night. It still stunned her that Damian had Draven's blood in him. What would Luc think of that? She quickened her pace, anxious to see him.

Stella noted something amiss the moment she stepped into the dining hall. Mara was smiling, for one. Secondly, Luc was missing from his usual seat. A block of ice seemed to settle in her chest—cold and heavy.

"Where's Luc?" she asked, with a calm she didn't feel.

"He's gone," Barron replied, tonelessly.

The ice in her chest began to crack, seeping into her veins. "Where did he go?"

"Back to Darkwood, to complete his mission." His neutral facade wavered at whatever he saw on her face. But in the next moment, it was firmly back in place. "After all, it's the reason why he came to Noctum, is it not?"

Standing there, Stella shut her eyes as the tears streamed unchecked. Yes, she knew. Though, like a delusional fool, she'd done her best to deny it. She had known Luc's time at the keep was temporary, and that his mission hadn't been forgotten, only delayed. The mission was always first, even before her, though she had vainly hoped otherwise.

And now, he was gone.

She thought back to the night before. She hadn't seen Luc the entire time and then Markus had invited her to the village. When they returned, her dinner had been brought to her room. Luc had left yesternight without bothering to say goodbye.

Choking on a violent sob, Stella whirled and sprinted from the room. Though blinded by her tears, she somehow ended up on the terrace. There, her heaving breath formed tiny crystals that shattered once they hit the cold, hard ground. Her body followed, numb to everything but the piercing pain in her heart.

Luc had left her. She was all alone…again.

Stella had no idea how long she sat there, losing feeling everywhere but where it hurt most. But eventually, strong arms lifted her and she was held against a warm, broad chest. Not Jorg, but Markus. She recognized his familiar scent of sandalwood. She shut her eyes, not bothering to open them even when she was laid out on her own bed.

* * *

Time became lost in the fog of grief. If not for the candles that burned then sputtered out, the untouched meals that came and went, she would not have noticed its passing. She rose stiffly, not certain of the night or the hour, and walked by the latest meal that sat on her table. At the window, she unlatched the shutter, stepping back in time to avoid its swing. Bracing herself against the fierce northern wind, she gazed at the view outside. All she could see was the back of a hill that slid down to a flat plain before stretching on unbroken into the

287

distance. Her tower stood a good fifty feet above the hilltop, making escape impossible.

There was a knock on her door before it opened. Stella was surprised to see Barron standing in her doorway. "You're up."

She relatched the shutter before turning to face him again. "I'd like to leave."

"I'm afraid I can't allow that," he answered, entering the room to sit at the chair by the fire.

"Am I a prisoner then?"

"A prisoner, no. Under guard for your protection, yes."

"What if I don't want your protection?"

"Isn't that why you came to the keep in the first place?"

Stella sighed as she turned away. "Yes, but—"

"Do you really think Draven has stopped looking for you, after a mere month?"

She said nothing, unable to answer the way she would like.

"It was at Luc's request that we keep you here."

The admission was another painful blow. Not only had he left, he made it so that she couldn't follow. "How long am I expected to stay?"

"Until it is safe for you to leave."

So long as Draven was alive, there would never be any guarantee of safety. And worse than the thought of Luc going up against the king, was the thought of him failing. Failure would mean Luc's death. And then what? She would be stuck at Barron's Keep indefinitely. She began to understand how the other Forsaken could risk their lives by leaving. What was life without freedom? Dangerous as Darkwood might be, at least she had been free. But here at the keep, it would be Barron who determined when she could leave. The idea grated, but all she said in reply was, "I see."

The minutes felt like hours. The hours felt like weeks. Time passed like honey through a sieve.

A week after Luc left, Stella made her way into the washroom. There was little doubt that she was a captive, for though she was free to roam as she pleased, she was never without a guard. The only exceptions were when she slept, used the privy or bathed. Markus had invited her to the village yet again and Jorg continued to entice her to practice with him on the terrace, but none of their attempts to distract her succeeded. With Luc gone, her heart was no longer in the valley or at the keep.

She sat in the bath as the water cooled, absently watching the rings of lavender oil drifting lazily along the surface. No attempt had yet been made to escape, mainly because there had been no opportunity. The keep was a veritable fortress, her guards keen and watchful. But even if she made it out, she had no idea where to go. Nor did she think she could survive the harsh weather on her own.

Behind her, a whisper of sound alerted her to the fact that her sanctuary had just been breached. Throwing her hands over her chest, she looked over her shoulder to see Mara approaching.

"What are you doing here?" she asked, only mildly relieved that it wasn't Markus or any of the other men.

Mara wordlessly picked up the rag Stella had laid on the edge of the tub and began to scrub her back. Stella flinched, startled by the unexpected and unwelcome gesture.

"Relax," Mara crooned, continuing the soothing movement that made Stella so tense. "I'm here to talk."

"Talk about what?" she asked, suspicious.

"How unhappy you've been."

As if she cared. "I imagine it pleases you to see me so."

"Not as much as it would please me to see you go," she replied smoothly, still washing her back.

"I want that as well, but it doesn't seem either of us will be getting what we want."

Despite herself, Stella began to relax under Mara's ministrations. Her shoulders fell even as she wondered why the other woman had grown quiet.

"What if we could?" Mara countered. "Both get what we want, that is."

"What are you suggesting?" she asked warily.

"You want to leave and I want you gone. I believe I can make the necessary arrangements."

"You would defy Barron?"

"He needn't know."

Mara spoke with cool confidence, but Stella was loath to trust her. Still, she had no other options and decided to hear her out. "I'm listening," she replied, closing her eyes as Mara began to outline her plan.

41

The Promise of Pain

The silence seemed sinister, the shadows ominous as Stella stole through the darkened corridors of the keep. None of the torches were lit, forcing her to slow her steps though her racing heart urged speed. She could afford no misstep.

As promised, at the thirteenth hour, Stella had found her door unguarded. It seemed her guards were wont to wander off in the wee hours between deep sleep and wakefulness, something she wished she had known sooner.

According to Mara, the guards tended to concentrate on dangers from without rather than from within. Which meant there was little danger of being caught inside. Though tell that to her frantic heart. Outside, Mara assured her, was where things would get tricky. She shivered, anticipating the challenge, and pulled at the thick cloak she had donned.

Finally, the dining hall! Stealing through the open doorway, she passed the long tables and entered through the kitchen door at the back. There she moved with greater caution. She had seen the kitchen only once during her earlier explorations, but still recalled the array of accoutrements required for making the keep's meals. Now was not the time to test the sensitivity of Barron's or Markus's exceptional hearing, so she moved with stealth past the stacks of bowls and cauldrons as well as the other hanging cookware.

As she neared the servants' entrance a shadow slunk toward her. She might have screamed had she not been expecting it. Even in the gloom, Mara appeared stately and regal. It was hard to see her face, but Stella imagined the woman was looking at her with scornful amusement. "Are you certain you wish to proceed?"

For a moment, Stella hesitated, irritated that Mara would cause her to doubt. Why discourage her now? "Of course," she firmly replied.

Mara nodded then grabbed something from the ground. Stella saw that it was her travel pack. "Your blanket, rope, and waterskin are inside, along with several night's worth of food." She pointed to a nearby table. "And there are your weapons." Grateful, Stella strapped on her belt with its dagger and sword. Then she threw her pack onto her back. "Nyall will be right outside. Remember that after he leads you to the Chasm, you're on your own."

Stella nodded. Mara's gaze seemed to linger on her before she opened the door. Suppressing a sense of apprehension, Stella stepped out into the frigid night, refusing to let fear hinder her. The door closed behind her with a soft click just as a heavily-bundled man materialized out of the swirling snow. Like herself, he was dressed all in white, making it difficult to spot him in the wintry landscape. When he beckoned to her with a gloved hand, she followed wordlessly.

What came next proved to be a test in patience and trust. In order to reach the cleft of the hill where a winding path led down to the valley floor, they first had to cross the kitchen gardens then circle around the horse paddock. This they did. Though at Nyall's direction, they took over an hour to do what would've taken mere minutes were they not concerned with detection. There were times Stella thought she would freeze to death before they ever made it to the cleft. But when they did, all she could do was breathe a sigh of relief that they hadn't been spotted.

Once on the path, they moved with greater speed. Unlike the stairs on the west side, the path wasn't nearly as treacherous to traverse nor was it visible from the keep. However, it was a longer way to the valley, at times made longer still by the deep drifts that sometimes came up to their hips. Bogged down by her thick clothing, her pack and her weapons, Stella soon grew weary of the laborious trek. Determination alone pushed her to keep up with Nyall, who was pulling further and further ahead. She understood his rush; it was a race against the clock. He had to be back before Barron and the others awoke if he didn't want suspicion cast his way. No doubt Mara was safe and warm in her bed, and had been for hours.

Stella's thoughts began to drift, turning inward to avoid dwelling on the painful cold and the weakness of her limbs. It was her body's way of coping, protecting her from the misery of a situation she couldn't escape but had to push through. It was what kept her going when all she wanted to do was quit.

The thoughts that paraded through her mind were random and varied. Sometimes they were just flashes of memories. Sometimes they were entire scenes. Her ma's gentle hands. Her da's bellowing laughter. The first time she heard Luc's lilting voice. Little Aron's sweet face followed by that of her brother's. Damian staring at her from across Erik's funeral pyre.

Stella suddenly collided into Nyall. Shaken from her thoughts, she looked up in surprise to find that the snow had stopped.

"We're here," Nyall's raspy voice announced.

Stella stepped to the side to look around the broad man. He was right! They had finally reached the Chasm.

"The bridge is right there." Nyall pointed. "Do you see it?"

She squinted her eyes then nodded.

"Good luck," Nyall said, before turning to face the way they had come. She watched as he trudged away, gradually blending into the white backdrop.

* * *

Stella wasn't certain how she managed it, but somehow she made it across the Chasm and perhaps a league into the Wastelands before collapsing in exhaustion. Fighting the urge to sleep, lest she never awaken, she clumsily formed a crude snow shelter with numb fingers and shaking hands. Burrowing inside, she pulled out her blanket and wrapped it around herself with haste. Only then did she allow herself to succumb to the seduction of slumber.

She awoke to sharp pangs of hunger accompanied by a sense of urgency. She had to eat then keep moving. There was no knowing how many hours had passed, but the more leagues she put between her and the keep, the better. Grabbing her pack, she removed her glove before rummaging inside for something to eat. The rope and waterskin were easy to identify, but when her fingers brushed against something smooth yet hard, her brow wrinkled. She dug around further and found more of the same. She pulled one out to inspect it. A bread roll? But when she bit into it, she might as well have been biting into stone. In desperation, she dumped the entire pack, the rolls clattering against one another as they spilled. The sound sent sick dread slithering through her.

Mara had sent her out to die.

Stella slumped, cursing herself for her foolishness. She had no one to blame but herself. In her desperation to leave, she had rashly dismissed the very thing that had kept her alive all these years. Caution. Now she would die for her mistake, for she was too weak to hunt—too weak to even walk, much less track prey through the barren Wastelands. Her da had died in the snow, as had her ma. Perhaps it was fitting she died in the same way.

Whatever anger, frustration and disappointment she felt soon melted away. It was replaced by resignation and a calm sort of melancholy. She wasn't ready for the end, but it wouldn't be so bad, would it? Not if she got to be with her family again. She missed them all so much. Her only regrets were not seeing Luc again. And Damian. She owed him her thanks. And it saddened her to think she would never see little Aron grow up.

Weary in spirit and heavy of heart, Stella dug through the snow and crawled out. It was a perfectly still, clear night. Lying on her back, she stared up at the brilliant sky. She wanted it to be the very last thing she saw.

* * *

Stella awoke in hell. She gnashed her teeth in agony, moaning at the excruciating pain. Her limbs were on fire and razors sliced every inch of her skin. She writhed, searching for comfort, but there was no alleviating her torment.

"Shhh, Stella. It's alright."

Was that…Markus? With great effort, she parted her eyes to find that she was right. Markus's face swam blurrily in her vision. She blinked, trying to clear her eyes. After a time, she was able to make out the timber-beamed ceiling above his head. She was not in hell after all.

"Where am I?" she asked through gritted teeth.

"At the home of a friend," Markus replied.

"I thought I was dead."

"Had I not found you in time you would have been."

"How *did* you find me?"

A dark cloud passed over Markus's face. "My sister isn't as clever as she thinks she is. Jorg checked in on you as he always does when he returns to duty. When he discovered you were missing from your bed, he informed Barron. Barron then called for Mara and I, and I knew that she was somehow behind your absence. So I left to find you, while Barron stayed behind to deal with my treacherous sister."

Stella shut her eyes. "You should have just left me to die."

"What?" Markus growled.

"I don't want to go back to the keep."

"Who said I was taking you back?"

Her eyes flew open. "Aren't you?"

Markus shook his head. "If you were desperate enough to risk death by leaving, there is no point in returning you. As soon as you're recovered, I'll escort you back to Darkwood."

"You will?" Stella gazed at him in dubious disbelief. "But...why?"

He shrugged nonchalantly. "It would be interesting to see Damian again."

She whimpered, caught off guard by the sharp pain that suddenly shot through her.

Markus began to call to someone over his shoulder. Stella saw a door open, letting two men in. "She is still in pain. Is there nothing else we can do?" he asked them.

The older one shook his head. "We just have to let the tonic run its course. It will hurt for a time, but she should be fine in a night or two."

"Arya is making her a bone broth," the younger one added. "That will help warm her."

Markus nodded, and they left the room.

"Do they know about you?"

"They do. And it seems they know about you, too."

Stella frowned. "How? I've never seen either of them before in my life."

"Perhaps not, but you did use their horses to cross the Wastelands."

Her eyes flew to the door where the two men had left. "They were the ones who left the horses? But how? Why?"

"Apparently, Damian got word to them to keep an eye out for you and asked them to lend you their horses."

She felt a twinge in her chest. Damian had looked out for them, anticipating their need. "Did the horses return safely?"

"They did. Sinthian horses are the smartest, sturdiest and strongest horses there are. We keep as many as we can find, and Ornas and Erral help us to hide them."

"The horses at the keep are Sinthian horses as well, aren't they?"

"Yes, without one I would not have reached you in time. It will also shorten the journey to Darkwood."

A sudden thought crossed her mind. "Will you get in trouble for taking me back home?"

"Trouble? No. Barron knows we'll find enough of it in Darkwood," Markus said.

42

The Reluctant Reunion

S tella recovered in two nights. By the third, they were on their way. Had she considered the details of their travels, she might have been better prepared for the arrangements. But since she hadn't, she found herself in the uncomfortable position of being cradled in Markus's arms, her back against his broad chest as they rode upon his horse, Frullinger. And if that wasn't bad enough, winter's icy grip made it necessary to huddle close when they stopped for the evening. It was an intimacy she had enjoyed with Luc. With Markus, it was awkward and uneasy. At least on her part. It didn't seem to bother him too much.

Still, she knew she was fortunate to have his company. Like Luc, he took care of all the difficult tasks—the hunting, the fire-building and the erecting of shelter. She was now convinced she never would have made it on her own. Which became even more apparent when they reached Blackbriar.

"We're nearly there," she said, staring at the rushing waters of the Algus River.

"How much further?" Markus asked.

"Another night or so."

"It might be longer if we can't find a way across this river."

Because of Frullinger, they had taken a different route than the one she had used with Luc. Hence, they were at a part of the river that gushed and churned, spraying the icy boulders that lined its banks.

"I suppose we should head downstream," Stella suggested, hoping the waters would gentle when the land flattened out.

Beneath them, Frullinger threw his head back, his nostrils flaring as he suddenly whirled around. One moment, Stella was staring at the river. The next, she was facing the woods, her bewilderment turning to fear when she saw the figures that slunk out of the trees.

Wolves!

At least seven of the creatures surrounded them on all three sides, pinning them against the river. As she frantically searched for a way of escape, Markus dismounted in one smooth move. Faint moonlight caught the side of his blade as he pulled out his sword. The sight spurred her to action. Grabbing his bow, which he had secured to the saddle's pommel, she strung it and quickly nocked an arrow.

She heard a snarl, saw the alpha leap and the rest of the pack charged. Frullinger reared, causing Stella to release a shot that missed. As the horse went wild, its flailing hooves keeping the wolves at bay, Markus was left to fight on his own while she could do nothing but hold on for dear life. Thinking him the easier target, the wolves focused their attacks on the man rather than the creature. A mistake. In a matter of minutes, all seven wolves were dead, leaving him coated in their blood and gore.

"Are you alright?" he asked her.

"I'm fine," she answered in amazement. "And you?"

"I haven't had this much excitement in decades." He went to check on Frullinger. Satisfied that his horse was uninjured, he stooped over the river to rinse his sword then washed his hands before splashing his face. "Now, let's see about crossing over."

Eventually, they did find a way across. And the next night, they entered a part of the forest Stella was as familiar with as the moon in the sky. She knew each aspen, fir and spruce they passed, but gazed at the trees as if seeing them for the first time. The sight filled her heart—if not with warmth, then with a deep sense of belonging. No matter its shortcomings, Darkwood was home.

"It's been a long time since I've stepped foot in these parts," Markus remarked.

"How long?"

"Longer than you've been alive," he replied wryly.

It had only been two months for Stella, but it felt like so much longer. Emotions began to batter her chest, the most prominent being anxiety, anticipation and dread. She had no idea what she would find, or what it was she should expect.

"Shhh," Markus whispered, nudging Frullinger behind a large chestnut tree. Moments passed without incident. But just as she opened her mouth to question him, a line of figures wound through the trees up ahead. Dread bloomed in her breast. The shape of their helmets and the bulk of their armor made them easy to identify. Nighthawks. But what were they doing in the middle of the forest?

They waited for the soldiers to be well on their way before continuing. Speed competed with stealth as Stella led Markus closer to home. She longed for the shelter of her cottage, but knew haste could prove perilous. And then they were at the edge of the clearing, staring at the small stone building with its cedar shingled roof and thick oak door. She had never seen anything so lovely in her life.

"It looks empty," Markus remarked. And he was right.

No light emanated from within, and no smoke drifted up through the chimney. Had Luc returned to the cottage at all or had it been abandoned for some time? There was only one way to find out. Markus whispered a hidden command to Frullinger and the horse took off. Instead of heading for the front door, she led Markus to the copse of elms. Minutes later, she was climbing through the door in her floor, followed by Markus who entered with his dagger already drawn.

"We're not alone," he announced, causing the hairs on the back of her neck and arms to rise. He spun, quickly searching the dark corners, before stopping to stare at the short hallway separating the two bedrooms.

"Markus?"

The tentative sound of Luc's voice set Stella's heart racing even as overwhelming relief flooded her. Acting on pure emotion, she rushed forward and threw her arms around him, burying her face in his warm chest. She breathed him in, comforted by his familiar summer scent.

"Stella?" There was shock in his voice. Shock and consternation.

Another form emerged from behind him. "Stella, what are you doing here?" Garrett asked, coming to stand beside Luc. "You should have stayed away."

She pulled back from Luc, immediately feeling cold and alone. A deep ache formed in her chest. They weren't happy to see her.

"We intended to protect her at the keep as you and Damian wanted, but Mara helped her to escape," Markus explained. "She nearly died, but refuses to return."

"You should have forced her to return anyway," Luc said, in a tone so harsh it made her flinch.

But Stella hadn't endured all that she had to falter now. "It doesn't matter. I'm here and I'm not going back."

Her declaration was met with stony silence. The ache in her chest deepened, but pride refused to let her break down despite the burning in her eyes.

"Is there any reason we're all standing in the dark?" Markus asked, relieving some of the tension.

"Yes," Garrett replied. "Things have been bad. It isn't safe here for anyone connected to Stella. The cottage could be watched, but it was the only place Luc and I could meet."

Stella began to back away, guilt shredding her. "What do you mean? Has anything happened to Aron? To Marta and—"

"They're fine. Everyone is fine thanks to Damian," Garrett rushed to assure her. "After what happened with you and Draven, he made

301

sure to warn me, Jenna and Elias. Then he helped the Rodevs go into hiding."

Stella nearly collapsed with relief.

"It was just in time, too," Garrett added gravely. "The very next evening, Nighthawks were sent to search every house in Darkwood. The search was then extended to the rest of the forest."

"Is that why we saw Nighthawks at the border?" Markus asked.

"No, that's to prevent people from fleeing." Garrett hesitated before continuing. "You see, when Stella couldn't be found, Draven offered an award to whoever turned her in. Were it not for Damian's warning, I suspect fingers would have been pointed in our direction. Fortunately, Jenna, Elias and I left before anyone could inform Draven of our connection to you."

"But why would the other forest dwellers flee?" Markus asked, voicing the same question that had passed through her head.

It was Luc who answered. "Because, as of three weeks ago, Draven announced that a woman would be taken each week until Stella was turned in."

The blood drained from her face. Three weeks ago! "That means—"

"Three women have been taken, the third only last night," Luc supplied.

"That's not the worst of it," Garrett said.

Stella shut her eyes tight, wanting to cover her ears as well. She couldn't take anymore. It was too much! All of this...because of her. No wonder Luc and Garrett resented her return.

Garrett continued, heedless of her turmoil. "Damian was captured trying to help the third woman escape. In three nights, he is to be publicly executed by the king himself."

43

The End of Forever

A sudden roaring filled Stella's ears. She felt light-headed, ready to faint or possibly throw up. Collapsing onto the couch as her legs gave way, she swallowed thickly. "Can anything be done?" she asked, her voice a broken whisper.

"That's what Luc and I were discussing when you came," Garrett said.

"Do you have a plan?" Markus queried.

"Well…" Garrett hesitated. "We're still working on one."

"Tell us about the execution. Where is it to take place?" Stella was grateful to Markus for taking the lead, still too shaken by the terrifying knowledge that Damian was in Draven's hands to be able to think straight.

"The execution is to take place in the Killing Fields, and all of Darkwood's citizens are required to attend. It is likely many of Caligo's citizens will be in attendance as well," Garrett replied. "It's been some time since we've had a public execution, but from what I recall of the last one, a platform was erected a short distance from the city's main gates. Nighthawks were positioned along the back of the platform, ensuring a clear path for the king and Damian to travel to the platform. Nighthawks were also stationed all around the crowd, but I plan to place our Shadow Guards both within and without. When the time is right, we'll make an attempt to rescue Damian."

Stella noted what Garrett hadn't said. She turned to Luc, who was watching her with solemn intensity. "And what will you do?"

"What I came to do," he replied, all too calmly. "Kill Draven."

The last two words hung in the air, heavy and resolute. Stella closed her eyes, allowing the declaration to sink in. What she'd dreaded for months would finally come to pass, and there was nothing she could do to stop it. She sucked in a breath, trying to relieve the pressure building up in her chest, but to no avail. "Then I want to help," she declared, opening her eyes.

"No!" Both Luc and Garrett protested in unison.

Stella strengthened her resolve, securing it into place like protective pieces of armor. "You'll let me help or I'll turn myself in to Draven."

"Stella, please!" Luc pleaded. "Don't do this. Not after everything we've done to protect you."

"What makes you think my life is anymore valuable than yours or Damian's?" she retorted. "I've lost too many people I love already, I won't lose anymore. Nor will I stand by and do nothing while everyone else risks their lives."

"How do you propose to help, Stella?" Garrett asked, his voice strained.

"I thought I could serve as a distraction. Since Draven—"

"No!" Luc exclaimed, cutting her off. "We will not use you as bait!"

But Stella stubbornly continued. "Since Draven has been searching for me, he won't be able to resist coming after me when he sees me. I can draw him away so Damian can be rescued."

Luc's voice developed a hard edge. "We could be saving Damian just to lose *you*."

Stella let her gaze linger on him, her eyes soft. "I wouldn't be doing it just for Damian. You'll have a greater chance of killing Draven if he's distracted."

"No, Stella. I don't want you anywhere near him."

"She doesn't have to get near him at all," Markus interjected. "Draven just needs to catch a glimpse of her from afar. If you plan it right, you can whisk her away before he can ever reach her."

"It *would* provide the distraction we were looking for," Garrett reluctantly admitted. "And it's better than Stella turning herself in to him. At least this way we can make sure she escapes."

Luc looked away, a muscle twitching in his cheek. But when he turned back, his gaze on her was beseeching. "You won't reconsider?"

"I can*not* stand back and do nothing," Stella said with vehemence.

Luc seemed to deflate, his resistance crumbling. He gave no agreement, but he made no more protests either.

Markus heaved a heavy sigh. "I suppose I might as well help, too. You'll need all the help you can get if you hope to succeed."

Stella looked at him in both surprise and gratitude, while Garrett asked, "Who are you anyway?"

White teeth gleamed in the dark. "And old enemy of Damian's."

* * *

Everyone was seated, but no one was at ease. Stella's eyes had adjusted and she could now see the three other men in the darkness. Luc's long, lean frame perched rigidly on the chair across from her, while Markus reclined in the chair beside him. Garrett shared the other end of the couch with her, hunched over with his elbows on his knees.

They planned long into the night. Stella kept her armor firmly in place, not only to shield her from Luc's displeasure, but to strengthen her for the role she was determined—yet terrified—to play. But it wasn't just herself she feared for. Every single one of them would be putting their lives on the line for something that could go horribly wrong very quickly.

When they finished, drained and bleary-eyed, all Stella could think about were the numerous unknowns and the factors beyond their control. Since there was no predicting how Draven would respond, all they could do was consider the possible scenarios and try to plan accordingly, knowing it was impossible to fully prepare for every single one. In essence, their plan was far from foolproof, but it was the only one they had.

"We must go, Stella," Garrett said, rising. "The Shadow Guard needs to be apprised of our plan."

We? Stella gazed at Luc in disappointment. "Will I see you again? Before…everything."

"I will try, but there's much to do and very little time to do it," Luc said, apologetic.

Stella quickly tamped down a sense of desperation. "Then try your best," she said, when what she wanted to do was beg and demand and insist.

"I will."

Like their plan, Luc's assent held no promise and little by way of assurance. But there was nothing she could do to extract more. Each and every one of them were swept up in the tide of events they were powerless to control or escape. All of them were at the complete and unpredictable whim of chance or fate. With this sobering truth firmly in place, she watched as he and Garrett dropped down the hidden door to vanish from sight.

* * *

"I know of a way to keep you from moping," Markus remarked.

"What's that?" she asked, turning to him.

He drew out his sword with a flourish. "We could train."

It worked. For the next two nights, Stella threw herself into honing her combat skills, leaving little time for sulking. She was glad to direct her energies toward something that would prepare her to face what would come. Training with Jorg had helped improve her strength and stamina. Training with Markus helped improve her speed.

"Faster, Stella!"

"That's as fast as I can go," she said through gritted teeth.

"No, it's not. You can go faster."

Stella pinned Markus with a glare, and was awarded with a snowball to the face.

"Don't get distracted," he chided with an infuriating smirk.

Angered, she swung her sword in earnest, slicing at another snowball hurled at her head, but completely missing the one aimed at her chest. More came at her, flying so fast she could barely keep up.

"You're catching only half of them," Markus said in disapproval.

"I can never be as fast as you," she snapped. "I'm only human."

"That's no excuse. Luc is only human yet he manages to keep up."

"He also has magic on his side."

"That's no excuse either."

Stella bit back a retort and focused instead on the barrage of snowballs that converged on her. Try as she might, however, it was too difficult to track them all. Before long, she was cold, wet and miserable. She scowled at her tormentor who continued to gleefully hurl snowball after snowball at her. But as she watched, she began to focus on the motion of his arm, and the trajectory of the snowball as it left his hand. She swung her sword again, keeping her eyes on Markus while anticipating the location of each snowball. She missed most at first, but once she found a rhythm, she was making contact more often than not. And then came the moment when she missed none at all.

Markus finally stopped and grinned at her. "I knew you could do it."

"I suppose I should thank you for believing in me," she said, wiping at the snow that crusted her eyebrows before shaking some from her hair. "But I think I'll take a hot bath instead."

Back in the cottage, Stella soaked in the tub to reclaim some warmth while Markus went hunting. When she stepped out of the washroom, her damp hair hung over one shoulder as she tied the belt to her robe. It wasn't until she looked up that she sensed a presence in the darkness and realized she wasn't alone.

"It's me, Stella."

Relief coursed through her, followed closely by elation. Luc was here, when she had begun to fear he wouldn't come at all. He stepped into a pool of moonlight, the only light safe enough to allow. It took everything in her to refrain from drawing near. She remembered well how she'd been received the last time. So, from a safe distance, her hungry gaze took him in. Two nights had given her plenty of time to craft her accusations and rehearse an angry tirade. But now that he stood before her, all the things she'd been anxious to say faltered on her tongue.

When she spoke, what spilled out came from a heart so full of hurt it seemed to crack her chest open. "Why did you do it? Why did you leave without saying goodbye?"

Luc stood stone still, a statue, but his entire body vibrated with sorrow and regret. "Because I knew I wouldn't have been able to leave otherwise," he admitted. "I'm sorry if I hurt you, Stella. That was never my intention."

"Even when you distanced yourself after I told you that I loved you?"

He flinched, feeling the sharp sting of her bitter retort. His sigh was heavy, his expression pained. "That I did to protect myself."

The crack in her chest widened, dropping her heart and leaving it a pulpy mess. He had rejected her; he didn't want her love. Shame stole her breath, making it difficult to think, to breathe. His next words seemed to smother it altogether.

"I never should have kissed you, Stella. It was a temptation I was foolish to give in to, but like a fool I convinced myself I could pull away when the time came. And then you told me you loved me, and I realized how dangerous you had become to me—to my mission. A mission I had vowed with my life to fulfill."

Stella turned away, his explanation only adding guilt to her anguish.

"Don't think I distanced myself because I wanted to spurn your love, Stella," Luc continued, his voice now directly behind her. "Far from it. But I did it because knowing how you felt made me want things, things I shouldn't hope for. It tempted me to abandon my mission."

A tear slid from her eye. Wasn't that what she had secretly hoped he would do? Choose her over his duty? Had she not entertained the fantasy of them running away together? To find some distant corner of Noctum where no one could touch them? But such a place didn't exist, and such happiness could never be. Not while the taint of Draven's evil stained her dark world. It had never been her intention to hinder Luc, but that was exactly what she had done. She had shaken his resolve, made it harder to accomplish what he had set out to do from the very beginning.

Clarity put everything into focus, shining a light on the confusion and doubts that had shadowed her mind. Now she could see clearly for the first time. Luc had left—not because she loved him, but because he loved her back. The realization was a balm to her heart, soothing her soul. But she realized that he was hurting, perhaps as much as her. Love was not meant to harm, but heal.

"I'm sorry," she apologized, turning and lifting sorrowful eyes to him. "What I feel for you…I don't want it to drive you away."

"You didn't drive me away, Stella. My own weakness did that."

"You're not weak, Luc. You're the strongest man I know," she declared with conviction. "It takes strength to make difficult decisions, to do what is right no matter what. And I understand now that this is what you did when you left. You made the difficult choice. You did what was right."

Luc gazed at her in solemn wonder, profound gratitude gleaming in his eyes. "Thank you, Stella." His words were choked. "I wish—"

She quickly put a finger to his lips, stopping him. "No, no wishing or hoping." That way only promised more pain and sorrow. "Right here, right now, I want you to know that I stand by you, because your courage and strength inspires me. And tomorrow, when you face Draven, I want you to be assured of my love for you, so it can strengthen you even more."

At her declaration, Luc stilled—his face alone displaying the turbulence of his emotions. Then he crushed her to him, his heart beating a frantic rhythm against her chest. She held him tight, both comforted and broken by his desperation. The moment was powerful, sweeping. She sensed its significance in a way that made her frantic to hold on, fearful of letting go, knowing that once she did, something fragile but infinitely beautiful would be lost forever.

But Luc's own words echoed in her memory.

Nothing was meant to last forever.

44

A Fate Divided

S tella looked up at the starry sky. Antares had appeared, signalling a new night, and with its arrival Luc had gone. He had slipped away sometime in the wee hours, leaving her sleeping contentedly. Alone. Before the night was over, they would face Draven—which meant facing possible failure and death. She took a deep breath, embracing the sharp sting of the icy air. Life was both pleasure and pain. And right now, it was the latter that reminded her she was still very much alive.

"Are you ready?" Markus asked, coming to stand beside her at the doorway.

Stella took another breath then straightened her spine. "I'm ready."

* * *

The Killing Fields were crowded. Stella had never seen it so full, not even on the busiest nights of the Luna Market. All of Darkwood and Caligo had gathered to witness the execution of the Shadow Guard's commandant, mainly because they had no choice. King's orders. Only young children and those with nursing babes were exempt. In Darkwood at least, Nighthawks had been dispatched to round up everyone else. There was a clear delineation within the crowd—forest dwellers to one side, city dwellers on the other. She noted the advantage and disadvantage to that, as well as to the large numbers in general. On the one hand, it offered excellent concealment for Luc and the guards. On the other, it could impede their movements, making it difficult to get anywhere quickly. They had planned for all manners of obstacles and mishaps, of course. But no amount of preparation could guarantee flawless execution. Anything could go wrong, a fact that continued to gnaw at Stella.

Her gaze turned to the Nighthawks guarding the event. Like Garrett said, a good number loosely surrounded the crowd, though they were weighted more heavily on the side of the forest dwellers. And more stood guard at both the front and the rear of the raised platform. The trees had been scouted, assuring them no Nighthawks watched from above, so members of the Shadow Guard took advantage of the oversight and were perched in the branches with their bows ready.

Stella's eyes swept the crowd, wondering where Luc was waiting. He had refused to tell her, wanting her to concentrate on her own part, so she could make it out alive. Why couldn't he understand that she needed that assurance for him as well?

The brush of Markus's fingers on her arm signaled that it was time. Pulling up her hood, Stella followed him out of the woods. They were similarly attired with thick cloaks that concealed weapons underneath. It was a testament to Draven's utmost confidence or supreme arrogance that he failed to have his Nighthawks search each individual that attended the execution. No doubt he believed that all of his subjects cowered before him in fear. All but one, which was why he would be executing Damian himself. To show that he would personally deal with anyone who dared to defy him.

The press of bodies was thick as they pushed their way into the crowd. Most paid them no mind, other than to growl or mutter in complaint. Stella was glad for Markus, whose intimidating size discouraged anything more. She was also glad to see that many in attendance had donned their hoods as well, to combat the cold or perhaps to hide from Draven like herself. She stopped in the middle of the crowd, while Markus continued ahead. She watched his progress for a while, keeping her head low lest she be recognized too soon. Standing in the midst of the murmuring, stirring throng, she sensed the unease of her fellow forest dwellers. They didn't want to be here anymore than she did.

Stella knew when Damian appeared because the crowd suddenly quieted. Then a man began to speak, his nasally voice carrying through the thin, cold air. Not Draven, but his steward. As the man waxed on about the reason the people had been summoned, she lifted her gaze slightly to take in the scene. She saw the steward's long black robe brushing against high-polished boots. She saw a wooden block sitting in the middle of the platform. Then she saw Damian on his knees, his hands tied behind his back. Her stomach roiled and clenched when she saw his face. He had been beaten, almost beyond recognition. Nothing had been left untouched. Cuts and welts covered his arms, hands and bare feet. She choked on a sob, gutted to to see such a proud, strong man brought low.

The simmering hate she felt for Draven threatened to boil over. It was a furious, seething inferno that raged to be unleashed. She wanted to drive a stake through each of his limbs, pinning him to the ground. She wanted to make him watch as she used a dagger to slowly unman him. She wanted to carve out his heart and squeeze it in her fist until it was nothing but pulp. She wanted to starve him of the lifeblood he so desperately needed, leaving him to feel the excruciating agony of starvation. Then, and only then, would she sever his head from his body and give him up to the flames. Her hate was so great, she shook with the force of it.

Draven's sudden arrival only fed her desire to do him great violence.

Fighting to control her emotions, Stella turned her gaze from the king's large form and the wicked sword in his hand to Damian. His eyes, which earlier had seemed bleak and empty, suddenly blazed with fierce anger. The sight reassured her. The king hadn't broken him.

The steward began to lay out the charges against Damian. Markus, she saw, was nearly to the front of the crowd. It was time to make her presence known. Pulling her hood back just enough to reveal her face, she stared boldly at Draven, willing him to notice her despite the frenzied racing of her heart. She was a plump rabbit taunting a starving wolf. She watched as he scanned the crowd lazily, not at all deceived by his seemingly relaxed posture. There was a sharpness in his gaze that told her he missed nothing. A frisson of fear ran through her and she almost pulled her hood forward to hide her face, changing her mind. But that was the moment Draven's keen gaze landed on her.

Stella had no need to feign her terror. The moment she saw recognition register in his eyes, she turned to flee. She knew Draven had leapt into the crowd to come after her when shouts of panic erupted from the crowd to her left. The Shadow Guard had done what they were supposed to do, which was create a disturbance that sent the city dwellers bolting. The Nighthawks would quickly move to deal with the resulting chaos, or so she hoped.

Confused and terrified by the inexplicable reaction of the city dwellers, the forest dwellers grew agitated and began to make their escape as well. Those Nighthawks who attempted to cut them down were shot by the archers in the trees. Soon, complete pandemonium took over, orchestrated by the members of the Shadow Guard strategically placed around the Killing Fields.

Though shoved and jostled by the frightened mob surrounding her, Stella never once looked back. As soon as she made it to the relative safety of the forest, she began to climb the nearest tree. At the top, her gaze went straight to the platform. The torches surrounding it had been blown out, but she could still see that the platform was empty. She prayed that meant Damian was safe. When her eyes left the platform she was stunned by what she witnessed.

Men everywhere were fighting—forest dwellers and city dwellers alike. It seemed she, Markus and the Shadow Guard weren't the only unsanctioned citizens bearing arms. Numerous battles were being waged throughout the field. One in particular caught her eye, a Nighthawk engaged in a fight against Anson. Her gut clenched when the Nighthawk struck him a mortal blow, but in the next instant, she gasped when a city dweller lopped off the Nighthawk's head from behind.

Stunned, she tore her gaze away in search of the one she *wanted* to see dead. Her eyes roamed, moving from one battle to the next in the rapidly thinning crowd. And then she found what she was looking for, her heart lurching at the sight. There was Draven, locked in combat against Markus and Luc! Her breath caught as she honed in on the scene, immediately aware of the deadly intensity of the situation, the dangerous tension between all three men. It was like two wolves against a panther. All three were ferocious, but a panther was used to fighting alone. And in this case, Draven had been fighting alone for a very long time.

Stella was afraid to watch, but was utterly riveted, unable to pull her eyes away. For good or ill, she had no choice but to witness how the fight played out.

Markus charged, Luc immediately followed. Draven blocked Markus before swinging at Luc, successfully deflecting both. It happened again and again without pause, swift and unrelenting. Luc and Markus attacked, while Draven defended. The deadly dance seemed to go on without end, leaving Stella waiting in dread for a misstep. So locked was she on the three combatants, she didn't notice the loose circle that formed around them. Nor did she observe the Nighthawks being overwhelmed by the combined forces of both city and forest dwellers. But she did see when Luc hurled his dagger instead of swinging his sword, the blade lodging hilt-deep into the king's back. With a roar of rage, Draven whirled on him and Markus lunged, seizing his chance. He swung his sword, only for Draven to suddenly spin back around. With a flick of the king's blade, Markus's hand dropped to the ground, his sword still clutched in its grip. Draven might have finished him off, but Luc summoned his dagger, jerking it from the king's back.

Draven turned on Luc, Markus completely forgotten.

Fear, like a corrosive poison, ate away at her courage. She quickly climbed down and ran onto the field, her sword at the ready. She had promised to stay hidden, but nothing, not even her own vow could keep her from Luc. Bodies and blades peppered her path. Her sword swung, finding purchase again and again. Before long, it was dripping with the blood of those Nighthawks who had sought to stop her.

Fifty or so feet from where Luc and Draven fought, Garrett suddenly appeared before her. When she tried to veer around him, he snagged her by the arm. "Stella, stop," he warned. "You don't want to distract him, do you? You don't want to be the one who causes him to fail."

Stella yielded, knowing he was right. With her heart in her throat, she watched as man and demon continued to do battle. Then, from the corner of her eye, a movement drew her attention. It was Damian aiding Markus. What was he still doing on the field? Someone had given him a cloak, but he was still barefoot. Garrett's sharp inhale pulled her eyes back to Luc. She saw that his left arm was bleeding, dangling uselessly at his side. A cry tore from her lips.

Draven raised his sword. Behind him, Damian had Markus's weapon in his hand. *Strike him!* her thoughts screamed. But Damian merely stood there as if waiting. Draven swung his sword, cleaving the air so swiftly it was nothing but a blur. As blade struck blade, the unthinkable happened. Luc's hilt was ripped from his hand. Stella watched in horror as his sword was knocked to the ground. Stunned to see the weapon lying in the snow, she missed the dagger that reappeared in Luc's hand, never saw it slip beneath Draven's ribcage. Draven didn't realize it either—not until the blade pierced straight through his heart.

The Dark Lord stumbled, his eyes wide with shock. Stella yanked herself from Garrett's grip and began to run. Why was Luc just standing there? Why didn't he finish Draven off? Anguish fed the king's wrath. With a furious cry, Draven heaved his sword. Stella screamed as the blade flew through the air, sunk through Luc's stomach, and came out through his back. As he dropped to his knees, his eyes found hers. His mouth moved to form words she couldn't hear, but understood nonetheless. There was quick movement, the flash of a blade, then Draven's head rolled into view just as she reached Luc...too late.

The light was already fading from his green eyes when Stella gently cradled his head on her lap. She watched, helpless, as the last spark died, feeling like something inside of her had darkened and withered.

The sorrow was unspeakable, beyond words or tears. Stella felt as if she were drowning in it—a deep, dark ocean of misery and pain. As she sat there, bowed over Luc's body, those who witnessed her grief had to turn away, unable to bear the sight.

And then a strange thing began to happen, drawing their gazes upwards. It was subtle and gradual, but completely arrested those who witnessed the sight. Some stared in disbelief, some in wonder, but all watched as the sky began to change—fading from black to gray, then gray to violet. Violet soon softened to pale pink. And then suddenly, it was ablaze in brilliant oranges and vivid yellows. By the time Stella lifted her head, the sky was a clear, crystal blue, so light and bright she blinked at its radiance. She stared for a time, awed and mesmerized by the stunning spectacle. A tear tracked down her cheek as she closed her eyes and lifted her face to the warmth of the sun.

For you, Luc had said.

Epilogue

Ninety-three sunrises had graced the land once known as Noctum, but the marvel of witnessing its splendor had yet to cease for most of its citizens. Stella stood at her front door as she did every morning to watch the daily miracle unfold. She would never tire of seeing the golden sun vanquish the darkness, of observing the jubilant triumph of light over night. It was a gift without measure, unparalleled in beauty, and given at a great price.

It was the dawn of a new age.

The moment the curse was broken, every dark shadow had fled, taking with it the vile things it sheltered. The royals were dead, their foul flesh unable to withstand the radiance of pure light. Hence, the Shade were no longer a threat, and never would be again.

Luc was a hero, already a legend. In Aurelia, they were still celebrating his victory with fervent fanfare. Parades had been held in his honor, with people lining grand promenades to witness his fellow soldiers and the elite King's Guard to which he belonged marching in full regalia. A ceremony honoring his life and sacrifice had drawn hundreds of thousands of people from all over Midland. In several days, a fifty foot statue of his likeness was to be erected in the city square. Stella learned all of this from the letter Elias had sent her a week ago from Celenia, Aurelia's capital, where he and Moira had been working with the king's advisors to determine how best to rule Callipia, formerly Noctum.

While everyone else rejoiced, Stella had been quietly but steadily picking up the shattered pieces of her life. Marta often stopped by with little Aron, which helped. As did Garrett and Jenna's frequent visits. She kept herself busy with her leatherwork, and had begun to rediscover the place she called home.

More and more, she was stepping out to explore her new world, finding herself continually amazed by the multitudinous nuances of each day. Morning, noon, twilight—each reflected its own distinct beauty depending on the angle of the sun. Every time she caught herself marveling, she whispered her heartfelt thanks to Luc.

The fiery sunrise began to soften, giving way to a pale blue. As golden light began to touch the verdant green treetops, a familiar form astride a large, chestnut horse entered into the clearing. She straightened, a rare smile lifting the corners of her mouth.

"Elias!" She ran out of the house to meet him.

"Hello, Stella," he greeted, as he dismounted. Pulling her in for a tight hug, he then stepped back to study her, while she marveled at the vivid redness of his hair.

"You didn't tell me you were returning," she chided. "When did you get in?"

"Just last night. You're the first person I came to see after my family," he said with a smile.

Stella waited as Elias tied up his horse, thinking how strange it was to see him riding one, though so many others had quickly adopted the practice as well. Inside the cottage, she began to prepare their meals, while he recounted the things he had seen, learned and done during his month and a half stay in Aurelia. Stella listened intently, eager to hear of his experiences, though at times she felt a hollow ache whenever he happened to mention a place Luc had told her about.

They talked with the ease of old friends, and the hours quickly slipped away. When the conversation slowed, Elias pulled out an envelope from his cloak and extended it to her.

"What is it?" she asked, taking it warily. It was still difficult to accept that written correspondences were no longer unlawful.

"It's a letter," Elias replied, his tone carefully neutral.

Stella studied the envelope. There was nothing written on the outside, though it was secured with a simple black wax seal. "From who?"

Elias gazed at her with an odd mixture of sorrow and hope. "It's from Luc."

Within her breast, her heart twisted in opposing directions. How was it possible to feel both a surge of joy and a pang of agony at the same time? Stella was torn between wanting to rip the letter open and tossing it aside. Instead, she clung to it tightly and asked in a choked voice, "How...when?"

"He wrote it before you returned from Barron Keep. I've had it since then, but Luc asked me to wait a few months after..." Sadness flitted over his face. "Before I gave it to you."

Elias left shortly afterwards, with promises to see her again soon. She absently noted his departure, her entire being held captive by the yellow parchment she clutched in her hands.

* * *

Over nine months had passed since Stella had last seen the grotto. That was in autumn. It was now nearly summer. Birds sang in the trees, fragrant flowers bloomed, and iridescent dragonflies zipped through the temperate air. Her eyes hungrily savored the abundant display of riotous colors. The grotto looked so different in the daylight. Bright and airy, gone was the heavy gloom that had shrouded it in mystery. She sat at the pool's edge, noting the puffy white clouds that drifted across its surface in place of the star-filled sky she had once gazed upon. With a soft sigh, she pulled out Luc's letter. It had taken her three days to build up the courage to read it, and the grotto seemed the fitting place to do so. Before she could reconsider, Stella quickly broke the seal. Her hands trembled as she pulled out the parchment contained within the envelope.

My dearest Stella,

I hope that as you are reading this, you are basking in the warmth of the sun. I can imagine its light touching your lovely face, casting it in a radiant glow. But if not, starlight works just as well. For that is how I will always remember you—by the light of the stars and the moon. This is a hard letter for me to write, though perhaps it is harder for you to read it. I have no wish to cause you pain, but I know you will have questions. And when you are ready, I want to provide the answers you need.

As you already know, my path was set the moment I stepped foot in Noctum. My land was dying, thousands of people were suffering and I had vowed to my king that I would fulfill the task required of me. What you didn't know was that a sacrifice was required to break the curse. Not just Draven's death, but also my own. To restore the balance of nature, we both had to die. The Dark Lord and a Son of the Light.

You're probably wondering why I chose not to tell you this. And perhaps I should have told you from the very beginning. My only excuse is one I don't like to admit, since it is a cowardly one. I was afraid to die, and that is the simple truth. I had doubts that I would be able to do what was required of me. It was a fear that dogged me every hour of every day. So forgive me for not being forthcoming, for not wanting to admit my weakness to you.

You see, I never anticipated the complication that soon found me when I arrived in Noctum. That complication being you. You have been my greatest help and ally since coming here, but you've also become my greatest temptation—one that I thought I was safe from. Do you know why I was willing to die, Stella? I know you think me noble, sacrificing for king and country. But the main reason I was willing to was because I thought I had nothing left to live for. I was in love once—heart, body and soul. But Anna died, and I thought I had died with her. Then I met a woman with moonlight in her eyes and fire in her soul. A woman with a warrior's heart and a king's courage. Against all expectation, you awoke a passion in me I never thought I'd feel again.

Thank you for making me feel again.

Elias has just arrived and cannot remain long. Since I must give this letter to him before he leaves, it seems I will have to end it sooner than planned, and for that I apologize. Though perhaps it is better this way. There is so much I could say to you, but each word I write feels like a slash to my heart. It is already deeply scored by hundreds of tiny cuts, so instead let me offer the rest of my apologies here...

I'm sorry I left you at Barron Keep without saying goodbye. I'm sorry I never told you I love you. But if I succeed in breaking the curse—and I hope I do—then whenever you feel the sun on your face, may you have no doubt that I do. I'm sorry I have to leave you again. I'm sorry it will be for good. I'm sorry I won't be able to wake with you each morning and fall asleep with you each night. I'm sorry I won't see the awe on your face when you witness your first rainbow. I'm sorry we'll never watch a sunset together. I'm sorry if you'll miss me, as I already desperately miss you.

But don't mourn for me too long, Stella. Because this I know to be true, it is possible to love again. So promise me you'll eventually move on. Because you are brave and beautiful and fierce, and I want you to be as happy in life as you made me.

Yours til my dying breath,
  Luc

Stella looked up, her gaze sightless. She was sitting in a ray of sunlight, but her thoughts were in the past, steeped in shadows and starlit nights. She stayed until the sun moved on, leaving her chilled. Then she wiped her tears, tucked the letter away and made the long trek back home.

* * *

Twilight had stolen over the forest, weaving the trees in shades of indigo and deep blue. The peaceful hush that accompanied it was lost to Stella, whose head hung low with heavy thoughts. She never heard the rustle of movement up ahead, nor did she notice the dark form hurling towards her until too late. Not until Dartan collided into her in a writhing mass of frenzied excitement. Stunned, she stared down at the hideous hound who now circled her eagerly, sniffing at her hands and skirt, begging to be petted. Almost without thought, she began to run her fingers through his thick black fur, her mind a maelstrom of emotions. Somewhere nearby was his master, and the last time she had seen him, her rage and resentment had been an ugly, terrible thing.

"Hello, Stella." A soft thrill ran through her at the sound of Damian's voice, like hearing the beginning strains of a song she hadn't heard for too long. Inhaling deeply, she lifted her head to look at him—and immediately lost her breath. Seeing him standing there in the daylight, Stella realized that the sun loved Damian just as much as the moon. It gently caressed his raven hair revealing hints of gold, and brightened his dark eyes to a deep, warm brown. It toasted his skin, turning it several shades darker—no longer pale but the color of autumn wheat. Skin that bore not even a single scar, despite all that he had suffered.

"You're back," she said, showing her surprise, but concealing her relief. No one had seen him since the curse was lifted. But even as she'd cursed him herself for Luc's death, a part of her had feared never seeing him again.

"I was with Markus in Barron Keep," he said, offering the answer to a question she hadn't dared to ask.

She dropped her eyes, fixing them on Dartan. "I'm certain Mara was happy to see you."

"No, she was not," he replied, his voice as cold and hard as steel. "I heard what she did to you. Though Barron already punished her, I made certain she understood what would happen if she ever thought to harm you again."

Stella nodded noncommittally, not entirely certain what to make of that. "Have you returned for good or are you merely passing through?"

"Darkwood is my home, Stella," Damian replied, crossing his arms in that distinctly arrogant manner she was so accustomed to.

A corner of her mouth quirked. *He was staying.* "It's called Lightwood now."

His brows lifted. "Is that so?"

"Seems fitting," she said with a shrug. "And what will you do now that you're back? Join the Caligo Coldguards perhaps? Garrett says they have need of another captain."

Damian nodded. "I'll be training their Sinthian Cavalry."

"I see."

Stella brushed her hands against her skirts and turned to face the direction of her cottage. Silence fell, but the air between them was thick with uncertainty and things left unresolved.

"Can you ever forgive me, Stella?"

Her heart thumped hard against her chest as she glanced at him. She saw that he had dropped his arms, suddenly appearing nervous and vulnerable. It was an astonishing thing to see, cracking the shield she had instinctively thrown up to protect herself. He looked like a little boy or a lost child, not the intimidating warrior she had always known him to be. "Forgive you for what?"

"For allowing Luc to die."

She gazed at him steadily but he didn't flinch, allowing her to thoroughly search him. "You knew he was supposed to. That was why you waited, why you didn't strike Draven right away."

Damian's eyes dimmed. "He told me when he returned from the keep." He shook his head in a mournful move. "I've never known a man so noble and selfless. I understand why you chose him."

Luc's letter weighed heavy in her pocket, its contents pressing on her mind. *I know you think me noble, sacrificing for king and country.* And Luc *was* noble, though not as selfless as one might think—as she herself had believed. He was human, while Damian had demon blood running through his veins.

And yet…

Stella stared at Damian in shock and deep dismay, as if suddenly seeing him—and herself—for the first time. How quick she had been to judge him, how quick she had been to blame, when all he had ever done for her was sacrifice and give. How could she have been so blind?

"You have been noble and selfless as well," she told him, as he looked at her in surprise. "You protect people. You protected me and you've protected many others. Not only did you secure the safety of those I cared about, you were nearly executed for trying to save a woman. You've also fought the Shade for years to protect those who can't protect themselves. If that isn't noble and selfless, I don't know what is."

"What is going on, Stella?" Damian asked, bewildered. "Why are you saying these things?"

Stella blushed, wanting to turn away. Instead, she forced herself to meet his questioning gaze. "I just finally realized something."

He took a step closer, and Stella's heart began to pick up speed. "And what's that?"

"That you're a good man. I just refused to see it."

He gazed at her in amazement, but then quickly shook his head. "I wish that were true. I wish I could be good enough for you."

She noticed his balled fists held tightly at his sides, tempted to unclench them. "You are."

Disbelief and hope warred on Damian's face. "Do you know why I came back, Stella?"

"Because you missed me?" she teased.

"I missed you so much I thought I would go mad." Stella could only stare at him, sobered by the sudden agony she saw in his eyes. "I stayed away as long as I could, but I had to see you…even though I thought you might still hate me."

Her heart contracted then expanded, pain followed by pleasure. "I don't hate you, Damian, though I tried. I couldn't bring myself to hate you, even when I was furious with you."

"Because you loved him."

"Yes."

Damian grimaced and began to turn away, but she quickly grabbed his hand. "Can I ask something of you, Damian?"

He was staring at her hand on his. When he finally looked up, he nodded.

"Remember what you said the night you sliced your thumb? That thing you said you wouldn't do again unless I wanted it?"

Damian's dark eyes flared. "I remember."

"What if I told you that I *do* want it?"

He stared at her long and hard, as if daring her to flinch or retreat. She did neither. "Are you certain, Stella?"

"Do I need to beg?"

Damian shook his head and then his mouth was on hers, hungry, voracious, like a man starved who had finally found the only thing that could satisfy him. And she was more than willing to be consumed. When he broke the kiss, his arms continued to hold her possessively. "What changed?" he asked gruffly.

Stella stared into his eyes and saw his desire for her, but also his need for assurance. He wanted to know that he wasn't merely a convenient substitute, a replacement for her first choice. "Everything. First you. And then me. You, by learning what it is to be faithful and true. Me, by finally forgiving you and opening my eyes to see."

"See what?"

"That you love me."

Damian kissed her again, showing with his lips, his tongue, his soul that what she spoke was true. "Do you think you could ever love me, too, Stella?" he murmured, his deep yearning bringing a lump to her throat.

Stella put her hands on his chest, feeling the steady thrum of his heart, grateful that it still beat for her after everything she'd put him through. How many times had he laid his soul bare, only for her to spurn him? How many times had he asked for a chance, only for her to reject him? All because she had feared what she felt for him. She lifted her eyes to his, revealing the suspicion she'd kept hidden from everyone, including herself. "I think I already do."

Afterword

Thank you for choosing to read The Dark Wood. It is my first published work, the first I dared to put out there! I know taste is subjective and your time is precious, but if you enjoyed this book at all, please share it with others and write a review if possible. I have devoured hundreds of books on Amazon and reviews have certainly influenced my choices. Thank you again, and happy reading!

P.S. Be sure to check out my other book, **Shield of Shadows**, the first book in my Hidden Weapons Trilogy.

~ Sydney Mann

Made in the USA
San Bernardino, CA
22 December 2018